TRULY MADLY DEEPLY MINE

KATHERINE JAY

TRULY MADLY DEEPLY MINE

Copyright © 2023 by Katherine Jay

All rights reserved.

This is a work of fiction. Names, characters, places, brands, media, and incidents are either the product of the author's imaginations or are used fictitiously. Any resemblance to actual persons, living or dead, events, or locales is entirely coincidental.

Cover image by Madison Maltby Photography

Cover design by © Designed With Grace

Original concept by © Emily Wittig Designs

Editing by Happily Editing Anns

Contents

Author's Note

This book contains subject matter that some people may find triggering. A list of the main potential triggers can be found on Katherine's website:

http://www.katherinejayauthor.com

Please note, triggers are not listed here to avoid spoilers for the book.

A
Heartstrings
PLAYLIST

• truly madly deeply • kiss from a rose • perfect • invisible touch • let her go • dance with me • you can leave your hat on • hotel california • please forgive me • pump up the jam • maneater • black hole sun • shake it off • smells like teen spirit • I knew you were trouble • your song • you got it bad

PLAYLIST AVAILABLE ON SPOTIFY

To anyone who believes they're
not worthy of something better...
You absolutely are. Never settle.

Prologue

Wes

M y chest tightens as I push myself through the pain. My calves are aching, I'm struggling to get air into my lungs, and...what the fuck is with the wind?

Damn my best friend for being right. Beach running is fucking hard. And why didn't anyone warn me that San Francisco was going to have shitty weather even though it's California? I'm not saying it would have changed my decision to move here, but a little notice would have been great.

Scanning my watch as I sprint the last few yards, I slow to a walk the second I reach my goal, before doubling over to catch my breath. If my team trains on this shit, I'm fucked. Back in Chicago, I was one of the fittest, but I sure as hell don't feel very fit right now.

When my breathing evens out, I stand tall, pulling my soaked tee up over my head before dropping it to the sand. Hands locked behind my head, I stretch out my muscles while kicking off my sneakers, desperate to get into the water to cool down.

I've just removed my socks when a stunning woman appears in front of me, drawing my questioning eyes up to her hesitant ones. Dark golden-brown wisps of hair blow across her face, and her chest rises and falls like she was sprinting along with me. Beneath the windswept strands, she greets me with a tight smile plastered on her face, as her hand rises to her cheek, brushing the hair away.

"Can I—"

"Please hold your questions until the end," she says, cutting me off before reaching for my hand and intertwining our fingers, a determined expression in place. "Right now, I just need you to kiss me like your life depends on it." *Huh?*

"Uh, what?"

"No questions."

Without another word, she releases my hand, wraps her arms around my neck and slams her lips to mine. It takes all of two seconds for me to process her words before I'm gripping her waist and pulling her into me, instinctively matching her intensity. And fuck is she intense.

My hold tightens on her the longer we kiss, and a small gasp leaves her lips. It feels like the perfect moment to slip my tongue in her mouth, but... *what the fuck am I doing?* I don't even know this woman. I start to break away, but her hands come up to cup my face, keeping me in place as her tongue meets mine, drawing my attention back to the moment. And what an incredible moment. *Stranger aside, this is hot.* Although, it could be the stranger part that makes it hotter.

Bending her back slightly, our bodies align as I deepen the kiss, allowing myself to be a little crazy for once in my life. But when a cheer rings out behind me, I realize where I am and pull back, staring into a pair of unforgettable blue eyes. Our gazes lock for only a second before she blinks, cutting off our connection as she peers over her shoulder and yells, "Report that back, asshole," raising her middle finger in the air.

My eyes flash to the guy she's cursing out to see him scamper away to a nearby car, and an amused expression takes over my features.

"Want to tell me what that was all about?" I ask, eyebrows raised in question.

"Nope," she says, popping the *p*. "But thanks for the help."

So much for allowing questions after the fact.

Before I can say another word, she takes off in a skip-like run down the beach without even looking back, only stopping when she reaches another girl sunbathing on the sand.

Well, fuck me. That was weird, but not at all unwelcome. Maybe I even enjoyed it.

If only my ex-teammates could see me now. I'm not the stick-in-the-mud they thought I was—not only did I leave my team and move to another franchise, but I also made out with a stranger...on the beach...in broad daylight. *See, I can deal with change and spontaneity. Sometimes. God, why is my heart racing?*

My eyes stay on the woman for longer than they should, trying to make sense of what just happened, and when she looks back at me, I'm still staring. She gives me a wave and a shy smile before tucking her sun-kissed hair behind her ear and turning away. Moment over. *Right, okay.* I can take a hint.

Shaking out my crazy thoughts, I quickly revert to serious mode and try to pretend it never even happened. And with one last peek at my beautiful stranger, I dash into the ocean and dive headfirst into the crashing waves, letting the cool water soothe my joints.

It may not be the sunny California I was expecting, but I could definitely get used to a morning beach run and swim.

Especially if I get to see my mystery woman again.

By the time I get out, she's gone. Vanished without a trace. Like she was never even here. And yet, as our moment flashes across my mind, something tells me I'm going to have a hard time forgetting her.

Chapter One

Lucy – six weeks later

Letting out a slow sigh, I run my fingers through my thick hair, before pulling it up and securing it into a ponytail. After washing my face, I sink my head into my hands and press pause on my life for a second. I've been doing that a lot lately...taking a moment to reset before my mind spirals in the wrong direction. The past six months have been a roller coaster to say the least. I finished studying and officially became a certified physical therapist. I somehow secured my dream job working with a college football team, at my alma mater. And I'm finally single for the first time in two years, after a string of bad relationships. The latter being the main cause of my dark mood.

I made a vow to move ahead and find myself again, to get back to the fun girl I used to be. I just struggle with it all sometimes. Hence the need to reset.

Let's do this.

Patting my face dry, I look up into the mirror just in time to see my friend Summer enter the room. Her eyes find mine in the reflection and she smiles before arranging her long blonde hair into a messy bun on top of her head. "You ready to go?" she asks when she's done, grabbing the sunscreen I just pulled from my bag and squeezing it into her palm. It's strange to think that just over a year ago, she was a complete stranger to me, and now I couldn't imagine my life without her.

For both my sake and my brother, Dylan's.

Summer and Dylan started dating about ten months ago, and in such a short time it's easy to see he'd be miserable without her. To paraphrase Usher...he's got it bad.

"I'm ready," I say, answering Summer and reminding myself at the same time. *I'm ready.* For what? I'm not sure but I feel good about it. And what a place to make a start on whatever *it* is. We're currently sharing a room at a fancy beach resort just outside of San Francisco and about to take advantage of the services offered. I have to be here for a conference this week, and even though I live in San Francisco, my work offered to pay for my accommodation so I wasn't the odd one out, with everyone else coming in from across the country.

Summer's just here for the ride.

When I booked, they only had twin rooms available, and she called dibs on being my plus one. She's "keeping me company," apparently. It absolutely has nothing to do with my brother—a wide receiver for Denver—also being in San Francisco for a game this weekend. Not that he's a starter yet. But any time on the field is amazing to see.

"What time does your conference start in the morning?" Summer asks as we walk toward the pool.

My eyes briefly flash to hers before the beautiful gardens steal my focus. "It starts at ten because a few people are still flying in, but the days following will start at seven." I shiver. The thought of being ready by seven for an official breakfast each day doesn't thrill me.

"Seven!?" Summer exclaims, making me laugh. "You better not wake me. I'm on vacay. I'm sleeping in." She pouts, but a small smile shines through. She's not actually on vacay at all. She's supposed to be in class.

"I won't wake you, but your ass better be up by the time I get back."

Summer huffs out a laugh. "I don't need *that* much sleep. Just not seven a.m."

"I get it. Oh, how I miss being twenty-one and in college."

"Shut up, no you don't. You love the real world. Plus you're only twenty-four. Not that much older."

"I know. I do love it. But I wouldn't say no to sleeping in."

"That's one bonus to not living with your brother yet. I don't get woken up by his early alarms. When I visit Denver, they're awful." Her nose crinkles and I laugh. Deep down I know she'd take Dylan over sleeping in any day, but I'm glad she's here rather than there. While it was definitely Dylan that brought the two of us together, we've become fast friends in our own right, and she's been a rock for me over the past few months, along with her best friend, Cory, and our friend Delilah. Not to mention my work colleague, Dani. I'm still getting used to having so many female friends in my life. I've spent most of my time around guys—having grown up close with Dylan and his best friend, Joel, and then spending most of my time with various boyfriends and their friends. I always thought it suited me and never questioned it. But now that I know what I'm missing, I don't think I could go back.

When we reach the glass doors leading to the pools, Summer pauses and takes a deep breath. "Alright, let's see if Dylan was telling the truth about it being heated," she says as we step into the fresh San Francisco air.

It's chaotic outside, considering it's not a particularly warm day, but the sun is shining, and this is a resort, so it's not unexpected.

Summer and I weave our way through the lounge chairs as we move toward the adult pool, which thankfully, at least looks a little quieter than the others.

"Okay, are we both doing this?" Summer asks after laying her towel out on one of the chairs before kicking off her flip-flops.

"I think that's the best approach," I agree, wriggling out of my denim shorts and tossing them onto my pile of clothes.

When we're both ready to go, we stand by the edge, staring down at the glistening crystal water. "It doesn't look heated," I say with a furrowed brow.

Summer laughs beside me. "What were you expecting? Steam? It's not a hot tub."

"No, but I wasn't expecting people to look like they were freezing their tits off." I point to a woman who is literally holding herself as she shivers. "Case in point."

"Shit." Summer cringes. "Why did we think this was a good idea? And why do we believe Dylan?"

"I generally wouldn't trust him, but I didn't think he'd lie to you. Plus, we deserve a vacation, and *on* vacations, you're supposed to relax by the pool. I'll feel cheated if we don't at least dip a toe in."

We're both silent for a beat, processing what we're about to do, until Summer sighs. "Okay. It's going to be fine. Let's do this...on one?"

"Yep, three...two...one." I jump into the water and immediately regret my decision. "Shit! Shit!" I'm vaguely aware of Summer's laughter from above but can't bring myself to concentrate on anything other than the icy feeling seeping into my bones.

"Jesus Christ, that's cold." I turn quickly to swim to the edge. "Dammit, Dylan's a—"

Oomph. I crash straight into the hard body of someone trying to swim past, and the impact is strong. My feet come out from underneath me, and we both sink down in the water.

Limbs flail about everywhere, but I manage to make out a bare chest just as the man spins around under the surface and grabs my arms, lifting us both up for air. I flinch at his touch and kick my legs out, wriggling around until he releases his grip, allowing me to reach for the edge.

"Fuck! Are you okay?" he asks as I cough, brushing away the hair that's plastered to my face.

"I'm ssssooo ssssorrry," I respond through chattering teeth as my eyes meet his. *Oh God!* Of all the people in the world, I just swam into the gorgeous stranger I kissed on the beach. *Great.*

"You're shivering," he says, reaching for my arm, but I don't let him. Taking a step back, I watch as his hand falls to his side and a frown appears on his face. "Are you okay?"

"Yeeeppp. Jjjusst cccolldd," I say, wrapping my arms around myself before looking for an exit. With no steps in sight, I turn to face the edge and try to pull myself out of the pool. *No such luck.* My body has no interest in cooperating. I'm about to give it another go when large hands grip my waist and launch me up instead. I flinch again but allow the help, and as soon as my knees hit the hard surface, the hands disappear, and I hear a rushed, "Sorry," from behind me.

Shaking myself off as I stand, I close my eyes and take a deep breath. *I'm okay. I'm okay.* When I open my eyes to apologize, the guy is lifting himself out of the pool, and *my God, he's hot.* The first thing I notice are the veins in his arms pulsing as the muscles bulge with the movement. Next, my eyes flash to the water running down his body, pooling between the ridges of his sculpted abs, and that V—God, that V. I've never seen a more drool-worthy moment in my life. In fact, I subtly raise a finger to my mouth to double-check that's not happening.

Behind me, Summer whispers, "Holy shit," and I have no doubt she's watching the same thing I am. *This man is not only a pretty face, but holy hell, he's ripped.* I can't take my eyes off him. How I didn't notice this last time, I'll never know. But that's all I can focus on now.

I'm not even aware that I'm bouncing up and down shivering until a towel wraps around my shoulders, snapping me from my daze. I turn around to thank Summer and take in her amused expression. She's biting her lip to hold back a smile, but her eyes say it all. Raising an eyebrow, she tilts her head slightly as though signaling to something behind me, and when I turn back around I see the god of a man—the man I threw myself at not too long ago—patiently waiting for me to talk to him.

"Hi," I say awkwardly, making him laugh. I'd be offended by it if his laugh wasn't just as hot, if not hotter, than the rest of him. He runs a hand through his dark, wet hair and then blows out a breath as if he's equally embarrassed by our collision. But he shouldn't be. *That was all me.*

"I'm sorry about that. I wasn't really looking where I was going. I just needed to get out of that ice pit. My brother said it was heated, but that is definitely *not* heated, and—"

"They didn't tell you at check-in?" he says, interrupting my rant.

"Tell me what?"

"That the adult pool isn't heated. Just the others."

Fuck! My brows crease as Summer and the god before me burst out laughing.

"They did not," I say with a fake pout, while a little part of me wants to keep making a fool out of myself so he'll laugh some more. That is until I remember this guy was the best kiss I've ever had *and* my savior, even if he doesn't know it. My chest tightens, and my face drops as a memory tries to push itself to the forefront of my mind, but I refuse to let it. Putting on a smile, I wrap the towel around myself and clasp it with one hand, suddenly acutely aware of how close we are and how little I'm wearing, even though it's a bikini. "I'm sorry..."

"Wes," he injects, giving me his name. *And what a sexy name... It suits him.*

"I'm sorry, Wes. I hope I didn't mess up your swim, and..." I trail off as recognition hits me a second time. *Oh shit!* "I know you," I say, trying to hide my sudden panic over almost drowning an NFL star.

Wes's eyebrows rise as he smirks. "I was wondering how long it would take you to place me."

I frown in disappointment. I didn't think he was *that* kind of guy. "That's a little cocky, don't you think?"

"Is it? How many strangers have you kissed?" *Oooh.*

I bite my lip to stop myself from laughing but lose all control when Summer murmurs from behind me, "I am so glad I'm here for this."

I school my features so I can talk, but it's a real struggle when all I want to do is giggle. "I'm sorry. I recognized *that* version of you the second I saw you. It took me longer to recognize Wes the famous football player."

Wes laughs again and then grits his teeth. He's covered in goose bumps, so I'm going to guess he's just as cold as I am. *Shit!*

"I won't keep you any longer. Go and get warm. I'm sorry again. And good luck with San Fran. They're lucky to have you." I nod before turning back to Summer.

"While I agree it's fucking freezing, I don't particularly want to walk away without at least getting your name," Wes says, moving around to stand in front of me again. His hands clench slightly by his side before he hides them behind his back when he catches me staring. My eyebrows furrow, but I smile before looking up at him.

"My name is Lucy."

Wes smiles in return. "How long are you here for, Lucy? You know, so I can prepare myself for another run-in."

"A week, so best be on the lookout."

"Noted. Now, as much as I'd love to stay and chat, I'm pretty sure if I don't find my towel soon, I'm heading into frostbite territory. But maybe I'll see you again? Third time's a charm." He shrugs, suddenly coming across as adorably shy.

"Maybe you will." I shrug back but can't hide the happiness breaking through my nonchalant expression.

Wes grins as he walks away, shaking his head as he goes, and I can't take my eyes off his ass. His red shorts against his tan skin make it impossible to focus on anything else. I'm like a moth to a flame and—

Summer slaps me on the back as she steps up beside me, laughing as soon as he's out of earshot. I'll put every last dollar I have on her knowing exactly where I'm looking.

"Am I allowed to be happy?" she asks, suddenly serious. I only have to think about it for a second before giving her a giddy nod. Despite my reservations, there's a slight buzz of excitement coursing through me at the thought of seeing Wes again, and it's been a while since I've felt that.

"Oh, thank God," she says, releasing a breath. "So you've been keeping secrets?" She bumps her shoulder into mine as the hint of a smile returns.

I can't help but laugh again at her back and forth emotions, knowing how badly she wants to see me happy. "Yeah, so I kind of kissed Wes."

"Kind of?" she repeats as we collect our things, silently agreeing that we're done with the pool. When I look her way, the knowing smirk tells me she sees right through my bullshit.

"Okay, I did. I kissed Wes." I bite my lip and cringe as I remember back to that day on the beach. And how out of character I'd acted.

"But you didn't know who he was?" Summer asks, confusion flashing across her face.

"Not at the time. I ran up to him at the beach and begged him to kiss me a month or so ago." *God, it sounds so bad now that I'm explaining it.*

"You what? Why?" she says midlaugh.

"Stupidity," I say, and it's at least half true.

Summer stops midstep, forcing me to halt and look back at her as she shakes her head. "There is nothing stupid about kissing *that man.* I mean, I think the image of him getting out of the water will forever be ingrained in my mind. I love your brother, obviously, but damn."

"I, for one, am happy to hear you love me, even if you are fawning over another guy," Dylan says, his voice coming from behind us.

"Dylan!"

I turn to see him approaching as Summer drops her things and runs, leaping into his arms. "You're here!" she cries as he catches her easily and laughs.

"Hey you," he smiles, his eyes locked tight on hers.

I sense a moment coming—they don't get to see each other as often as they'd like—so I try to sneak away to give them some much-needed alone time. *And* maybe to avoid Dylan's interrogation. Picking up my pace as I near our door, I'm so close to freedom when he calls out, "Don't go too far. We have *that man* to discuss." *Dammit.*

Chapter Two

Wes

S he's here. The girl that's been fucking with my head for weeks is here. *Within reach.* And I walked away without a backward glance...because I was cold. I. Was. Cold. *What the fuck, Wes?*

I'm like a fish out of water when it comes to this stuff. For the past decade, football has been my only focus, as it should be, but one random kiss from a stranger and my focus drifts. Okay, that's not entirely true. Nothing will ever completely pull my focus, but the mystery brunette who I now know is *Lucy* has definitely been giving it a red-hot go. She's been on my mind since the second her lips touched mine, and she's completely shifted my thoughts. Why? It was just a kiss. I've kissed women before...plural. What's different about her? Nothing, right? Well, nothing should have been, and yet, seeing her again today had my heart sprinting as fast as it does during a workout. *Fuck!*

I'm almost to my room when I decide it's best if I'm not alone right now. Having time to think about Lucy's perfect ass, or the curve of her hips in her high-waisted bikini, or the way her crystal-blue eyes shine... *Jesus*...I'm trying *not* to think about any of this. Especially the way she flinched. I'm not even sure why I felt the need to touch her, but I wanted my hands on her so badly I had to clench my fists to keep them away. I'm not an idiot; she clearly didn't want to be touched by a stranger. And despite the fact that I can still remember the feel of her tongue in my mouth, I am just that...a stranger.

Bypassing my room, I lightly tap on the door adjacent to mine in the hotel, and wait patiently for a response. With the towel still wrapped around my waist, I grab a tee out of my bag and pull it over my head, knowing I'll get a smart-ass comment if I don't. It's another minute before the door handle rattles, and when it does, I knock again now that I know she's there, because it drives her crazy.

"Come on, open up. Jesus, woman," I joke, laughing at the visual of her shaking her head.

"Don't you 'Jesus' me, young man. For that you can stay outside," she says with a lightness to her tone.

"My sincere apologies; please open the door."

Gran pulls the door open and waves for me to enter. "Have at it then," she says as I walk inside. "Did you come straight from the pool? Could you not have at least stopped for pants?"

"I could have, but I was desperate to see you. Don't worry, I'm mostly dry."

She pinches my cheeks and raises an eyebrow. "If you didn't take such good care of me, you'd be off the Christmas card list."

"Nope, not even then. You love me."

"Huh. We'll see. What brings you over at this time of day?"

Good question. I'm not in the habit of lying to my gran, but we've also never spoken about women before, so I'm unsure how to approach this.

"Just saw your door and...thought I'd stop by," I hesitate, correcting it as smoothly as I can, running a hand through my still-wet hair.

"Nonsense. You're too busy for that," Gran calls me out, and *dammit, she's got me there.*

"Okay, I have an hour free, and I wanted to visit you rather than go home alone with my thoughts."

"I see...and are you going to fill me in on those thoughts?" she says, moving into the kitchen to make herself a tea. I stand and follow behind her, filling up a glass with water, knocking it back before I answer. Gran raises an eyebrow as she waits for my response.

"Okay." I sigh. "Sit down, and I'll tell you what's up."

Smiling brightly, she abandons her tea and moves toward the sofa, patting the spot beside her. "Thank you. I can't wait."

My gran raised me from the age of sixteen after my mom, her daughter, died of cancer. My dad comes and goes in my life, but he has another family, so it's mainly only birthdays or holidays that we talk to each other. Or if I'm in the news for something football related, which *was* rare until my recent trade. In fact, when news of my trade broke and the media discussed the money I'd be earning, a lot of family and friends came out of the woodwork. But the only one that got a cent was Gran. She's my world and one of the few people I really trust. I moved her here with me when I was traded, and I plan to set her up in a nice condo when I find the perfect one. But for now, we're hotel mates.

"So, come on, spill," she says, as impatient as ever. She turns eighty-two this year, but you wouldn't know it. She's a regular at yoga and will often join me for a swim, if I don't go at the "ass crack of dawn" as she calls it.

Sitting down beside her, I rest one leg on my knee and drop my head to the headrest behind me.

"I met a girl," I say with another sigh, rolling my head toward Gran. Her eyes light up right on cue.

"You met a girl? Gah! I never thought I'd live to see the day."

"Thanks," I say with all the sarcasm I can muster.

"Oh, shush. You know what I mean. You have a one-track mind, and right now, the train is destined for a football station, with no indication it will ever make another journey." *What?*

I stare at her with a furrowed brow, and she just shrugs. That's Gran for you. She loves to beat around the bush instead of getting straight to the point.

"Okay, would you like me to tell you more, or do you have something else to say?"

"I'm done...for now."

"Thank you." I roll my eyes, and she elbows me in the ribs.

"Anyway, a while back, I—"

"A while back? Why am I only hearing about this now?"

I shoot a glare her way, and she laughs. "Sorry, please go on."

"A while back, I was out running, and a beautiful stranger needed my help for something."

"Hmmm." Gran hums as she taps her cheek in thought. "Did she know you were famous? Sometimes you can't trust—"

"Gran!"

"Right, yes. I'll be quiet." She pretends to zip up her lips and throws away the key.

Resting my elbows on my knees, I grip the back of my neck and huff out a laugh. "God, I came here to avoid thinking about this. I have a strength training session in a couple of hours and a big game on the weekend. I need to keep my head straight."

"So, get it off your chest. I bet you'll feel lighter."

"Hopefully," I mumble.

"You met a girl who needed your help. What kind of help?"

"Just some help. It's not important... Anyway, I helped her, quite satisfactorily, and then she was on her way, never to be seen again. Or so I thought."

I can feel Gran's eyes boring into me, and when I look up, she's frowning. "Are you trying to tell me you had a one-night stand, and she ghosted you?"

"What?! No!" I choke back a cough and shake my head violently. This is not the direction I saw this conversation going. "No, Gran, we were on the beach. She needed help; I helped. There was no need for any further communication, so she left."

She rubs at her jaw and blinks a few times. It's what she does when she's trying to reconcile things in her mind. "Okay, I've got that part. What happened today?"

I bounce my legs as I answer. "She crashed into me in the pool. She's here. In the resort."

Gran cringes. "Yep, I was right. This has stalker vibes all over it."

I shake my head with a laugh and pull her into a hug, squeezing her tightly, a warm feeling taking over me.

"What was that for?" Gran asks when I finally release her, holding her at arm's length.

With a bright smile, I shrug. "Just for being you. Never change."

"Well, I'm a bit old for that now, aren't I?" She frowns, shaking me off as she eyes me curiously, no doubt confused about the weird version of me that she's getting. I'm not the guy that gets a crush. Ever. I'm too pragmatic for that. This is completely throwing me off. I've only seen Lucy twice for fuck's sake, and we've barely had a conversation. But God, do I want to see her again. I know nothing about her, except that I'm pretty certain she's not a stalker.

"You're never too old for anything," I say, moving on from my crazy thoughts. "But in this case, I think you're wrong."

Leaning against the armrest of the couch, I try to explain what happened without giving too much away. "It took her a

17

few moments to recognize me, and when I tried to help her in the pool, she flinched. She definitely wasn't trying to get closer. Wouldn't a stalker want to do that? Get closer, I mean?"

"Not if she's a smart stalker," Gran says, tapping her forehead.

I pat her leg and stand up. "You watch too many crime shows," I say with a laugh before taking a deep breath and pacing the room. "I don't even know what it is about her, but I can't get her out of my head."

"Hasn't it only been a few minutes?"

"No, I mean since we...since I helped her."

Grans eyes narrow, and I know she's thinking I lied about the one-night stand thing.

"I didn't sleep with her," I clarify, clasping my fingers on top of my head as my lips thin.

"Good," Gran says with a nod. "That makes it easier if you want to play hard to get."

"Gran!"

She raises her hands in the air. "I'm kidding. You're so wound up about this. She must really be something."

"We've barely spoken. She can't be something."

"Of course she can. It was love at first sight between your Pa and me."

She says this all the time, but it's bullshit, and everyone knows it. They hated each other when they first met. I raise an eyebrow so she knows I'm about to call her on it, and she laughs. "Okay, but it was *something* at first sight. We both knew there was more to come."

That makes more sense, and I like that outlook. Maybe there's more to come between Lucy and me. Or maybe there's not. But it feels like there's *something*. Guess I'll have to wait to find out.

When I get home from practice the next afternoon, I'm tired but hyped up. I should have stayed at the team facilities to train, but there's this strange energy running through me that I need to dispel, without the eyes of my teammates. So, after a quick meal to give me a boost, I head to the hotel gym. It's surprisingly well equipped for a resort and even has personal trainers on-site. Stretching out my neck as I push through the door, I freeze when my eyes lock on the very person I was planning to work out of my head. *Lucy.*

She's standing in front of the punching bag like she's ready to fight it. Knees bent, arms raised, she's about to beat the shit out of whomever she's picturing in front of her. She pulls her arm back and slams her fist into the bag with incredible force, and the sight of it sends blood pooling to the one place I definitely don't want it to be right now. But fuck if I can take my eyes away. On her next strike, she clips the edge and falters, cursing herself under her breath before repositioning and trying again. It's almost like she's teaching herself to box.

I watch her for another minute until one of the trainers gives me a strange look. Giving him a nod, I make my way to the weights.

With every intention of leaving her be, I work on my upper body until I can barely lift my arms, while Lucy continues to fight the bag. I know this because I happen to be facing the mirror, and she *happens* to be in my line of sight. She takes a step back and punches the air over and over in quick succession until her body sags, and she catches her breath.

Without any thought, I drop my weights to the stand and head straight over, abandoning my plan to leave her alone. *Maybe it's me that's the stalker.*

"And we meet again," I say as I reach her side.

Lucy jumps in fright before spinning on the spot and throwing a punch at my face. I jolt at the last second, so she barely clips my shoulder, but she still packs a decent punch. When our eyes lock, she hisses in a breath as her gloved hands fly up to her mouth. "Oh, God, I'm so sorry."

"Don't worry, it was barely a tap," I say, trying really hard not to rub the dull ache from her hit.

Lucy sags. "You're lucky I missed. What were you thinking sneaking up on me like that?"

"Not sure, to be honest. I just wanted to say hi. Turns out, the third time is *not* a charm." I nervously laugh and relish the fact that Lucy's lips finally pull up into a small smile.

"I'm hoping it wasn't me you were picturing with a punch like that," I joke, but it falls flat, and her smile fades. *Shit!* Wrong thing to say. "You've got a good technique. Have you been boxing for long?" I ask, trying to change the subject.

"I've actually just started, but I'm enjoying it. Do you box?"

I bite my lip and shake my head. "Nope."

Lucy's brows furrow, but the corners of her lips rise back up into the tiniest smirk. "So how do you know that my technique is any good?"

She got me there.

"I don't...really. But it looked impressive," I admit with a shrug as Lucy tries to suppress her surprised laugh and lightly taps my uninjured shoulder with her glove. Everything about her is sucking me in. Her infectious laugh, the way she looks up at me through her thick lashes, her voice. Everything. *What the fuck is going on?*

"Have you been here long? Or are you just starting your workout?" she asks, breaking my thoughts as her eyes scan the gym.

I'm not sure of the correct answer here because I can't tell why she's asking. Does she want to know if I've been watching her, or is she asking if I'm done so we can walk back together? She raises her eyebrows in question when I don't respond, then rolls her wrist, coaxing an answer. "I didn't think that was a difficult question."

"If I'm being honest, my answer is dependent on why you're asking."

Lucy laughs again but this time she doesn't try to hide it. "Why?"

I cringe because I am so bad at this. Maybe I should have left some time in my life to focus on women so I'd at least have better game. I haven't done anything like this since college, and even then, my girlfriend just kind of fell into my lap, literally. That's how we met, and it was very convenient.

I liked her. I even thought I loved her at one point. But I never had to work for it. I never wanted to. But now, I suddenly wish I knew everything there was to know about impressing a woman, and what the fuck is that? "I guess I was curious if you were asking because you wanted to spend time with me," I say, opting for an honest approach. Since honesty is what I live by.

Lucy bites back a smile, her eyes crinkling with humor. "Wes, are you messing with me?" *What?!*

"Why would I be messing with you?"

"In the past twenty-four hours, I've seen you on the TV, a billboard, and heard your name mentioned three times. According to hearsay, you're going to single-handedly turn San Francisco's losing streak around."

God, whenever I hear that, I usually cringe. That's not even close to being true. The team's in good shape this year, and I'm only a small part of that. I wish people would— Lucy starts laughing, pulling me from my thoughts.

"What's so funny?"

"Your face just answered my question. You're obviously not a fame whore. Even the mention of it made you look constipated."

"What?! That's a horrible comparison."

"Maybe so, but I'm right, aren't I? You're *not* a fame whore."

"I'm not an *anything* whore. So, do you want to get dinner or something?" I say, even though it's only three in the afternoon.

Lucy grins and finally removes the gloves from her hands before tucking a loose strand of hair behind her ear. "Or something sounds good."

Chapter Three

Lucy

T he "or something" became early evening drinks at the hotel bar. While I'd like to say Wes caught me in a weak moment and that's why I agreed, that's not the case. I haven't been able to stop thinking about him since I saw him again yesterday. And even though I had planned to steer clear of men for a while, I couldn't stop myself from saying yes, and really, what harm could a couple of drinks do?

"Alright, lovebirds, I'm off. You know the drill, right?" I ask Dylan and Summer as I head toward the door.

"We do, but I'm still not sure I like this," Dylan says, peering over the back of the sofa.

I roll my eyes, ignoring him and his overprotective brother vibes. I can take care of myself. Mostly. At least, that's what I'm choosing to believe. Summer smiles as she gives me a wave. "Have an amazing time; that man is heaven."

"Geez, do you want to go with her?" Dylan huffs as I walk out the door, and when Summer giggles, I have no doubt that conversation is going to lead to something I don't *ever* want to think about.

When I arrive to meet Wes, he's already there, waiting at the bar, deep in conversation with a kid beside him. He doesn't see me arrive, and although I thought I was fine with meeting him, I'm relieved. The second I laid eyes on him my heart began to race. I'm on a date. Even if we don't actually call it that. And that's something I didn't think I'd be doing for a while.

My ex, Greg, was an asshole toward the end of our relationship. He was possessive and jealous, yet wouldn't give me the time of day if he had better things to do. We'd been together for two years, off and on, and it's only been six months since we broke up. This is supposed to be my single time. And yet, as I look at Wes, my eyes focus on his inviting smile, his kind eyes, and the way he makes my heart flutter, and I suddenly want to throw caution to the wind and see where it takes me.

Inhaling a deep breath, I move toward him, stopping a few feet away before getting his attention with a wave, biting back a smile. He gives me a puzzled look but waves back before rising to meet me. "I don't usually bite, if that's what you're worried about."

"Nope, I wanted to avoid another run-in. Thought I'd greet you at a safe distance." I finally let my smirk break free.

Wes laughs as he jokingly rubs his shoulder. At least, I hope he's joking. *God, if I fuck up his game...*

"Hey, I'm kidding," he says, seemingly reading my thoughts. "I'm fine. No pain at all." He rotates his shoulder to drive his point home, and I laugh in relief.

"Okay, good. Who's your friend?" I ask, pointing to the extremely attractive—but young—guy Wes was talking to, as he watches us both with curiosity.

Wes gently presses his hand to the small of my back and motions toward him. "I'll introduce you before we sit."

Naturally, I stiffen slightly at his touch, but it's so subtle I don't think he notices, until he releases me and takes a small step away. *Goddammit, Lucy.*

The guy stands when we approach, and smiles. "You must be Lucy. Wes and I just met, and yet, I feel like I know you."

Wes grumbles beside me while I quietly laugh. "That's me. And you are?"

"I'm Grayson. Here to drown my sorrows since getting divorced."

"Sorry, what?" I blurt out and then cover my mouth as both Grayson and Wes chuckle beside me. *He looks seventeen; I can't help my reaction.*

"Sorry to hit you with the heavy. I thought it was only fair since I knew so much about you."

"Thank you. I guess. But...sorry, I realize this is completely rude...how old are you?"

Grayson's lips pull into a smile, but it doesn't reach his eyes. "I'm eighteen."

Eighteen! God, to be going through something so adult, so young. My heart breaks for him.

"I'm sorry."

"Don't be. I didn't mean to bring the mood down. You two go and enjoy your date. I've got a meeting with my agent anyway." He pays his tab and pats Wes on the shoulder as he walks past, before giving me a polite smile. And then he's gone and I have so many questions.

"Ahhh..."

"How about we sit and I'll tell you what I know?" Wes says, anticipating my question as he holds his hand up toward a booth.

Holding back my barrage, I nod. I couldn't think of a better idea.

The bar's pretty quiet, so the waiter arrives to grab our order as soon as we sit down. I ask for a margarita, needing to calm my stupid nerves—*although my brief interaction with Grayson certainly helped take my mind off things for a moment*—while Wes orders a water, making me cringe. "Shit. A bar wasn't really a great choice for you midseason."

He huffs out a laugh before smiling. "It's perfect, and I'm not really here for the drinks."

My chest heats at his warmth, and it's a new feeling for me. I've had guys' attention. A lot of it. And I've always been sucked into their bullshit, but I don't usually blush. Something about Wes's attention feels different.

"So are you on vacation?" he asks, interrupting my thoughts as he leans forward, giving me his full focus. My pulse quickens at his intense gaze, but it's not a negative feeling. It's definitely welcome.

"Before I answer that... Grayson?"

Wes smiles again. "Nice kid, but from the little I got out of him, he's been through a lot. Things might be looking up though. He's in a band and they just signed with a label here in San Francisco."

"Wow, that's incredible."

"It is. Maybe one day they'll be famous and we can look back on that one time we met their lead singer in a bar."

"Absolutely. I wish I'd known. I would have got his autograph."

Wes laughs, before turning his serious expression back on. "So, now...about you."

My smile fades ever so slightly when the topic comes back to me, but luckily our drinks arrive and Wes doesn't notice. "I'm actually here for a conference. One of those *let's put you up in a fancy place so you don't leave early* conferences," I joke. Although I'm not really joking. There are only really two sessions I want to attend, so if it wasn't here I probably would leave early.

"Are you living here?" I ask, quickly changing the subject again before he can comment. I came to that assumption last night while talking to Dylan and Summer, and I'm genuinely curious.

"I am. For now. I'm looking for a place, but I haven't found anything that feels right."

He shrugs as an unsure look crosses his face. It's actually adorable.

"I understand that. I heard you've been contracted for a few years, so you need to be comfortable during that time."

"Exactly!" he exclaims, excited that I get it. "If only my real estate agent understood that. She definitely thinks I'm high-maintenance."

"Are you?" I ask with a giggle as my mind goes crazy with images of what a high-maintenance Wes would look like.

He holds his thumb and pointer finger an inch apart and winces. "Maybe a little," he says, making me laugh even louder.

"There's nothing wrong with going after what you want," I say when I've calmed down a little, trying to ease his mind.

Wes stills for a moment before a smile lights up his face. "I'm glad you feel that way. Wise words. Something to live by."

Huffing out a nervous laugh, I steer the conversation in another direction, because I'm ninety-nine percent sure we're no longer talking about a house. "Am I allowed to ask who initiated the trade, or is that inappropriate?"

"You can ask anything you want..."

"Doesn't mean you'll answer," I finish for him.

"It doesn't mean I *have* to answer. But for you, I just might. Actually, I want to."

His lips pull into a lopsided grin as he lifts his shoulder, and my heart skips a beat. The raw honesty isn't something I'm used to, and I find it endearing. But of course, instead of being genuine in return, I joke, "Guess I need to start thinking of more interesting questions."

"Guess you do." Wes grins, lighting up his whole face while heat radiates through my chest. There's just something about him that makes me feel so much more at ease than I've felt in a long time. Maybe ever.

The conversation continues to flow easily, and I find myself really enjoying his company. Not that I thought I wouldn't. But I wasn't sure what to expect. When my phone buzzes in my pocket, I'm shocked to discover we've already been here for two hours. Rejecting the call, I smile and signal for Wes to continue his story.

"And then he said—"

My phone buzzes again, and I mentally facepalm, realizing a fault in my plan with Dylan and Summer. We never decided what to do if I *didn't* need a bailout. I sigh and smile apologetically. "I'm sorry, I'll just be a sec."

Holding my breath, I prepare myself for his negative reaction, but when he smiles without a hint of annoyance, I relax, even though I'm a little shocked.

My call to Summer connects and I rush out, "I'm good, talk soon," before moving to hang up.

"Lucy, wait!" Dylan's voice comes through the line, but I hang up anyway. Summer will talk him down.

Shoving my phone out of sight, I look up to find Wes's eyebrows raised as he does nothing to hide his amusement. "Was that what I think it was?"

"Absolutely not," I lie unconvincingly, only smiling when Wes chuckles.

"I guess I should be happy you said you were good."

"It's definitely a positive for you," I agree with a smirk, hoping he doesn't notice just how positive of a sign it is. How much I'm out of my comfort zone just by being here.

"Anyway, you were telling me a story," I say, bringing the conversation back to where we left it. On safer topics.

"I was, yes. But it's not important. I now feel like I'm running against a clock. You may have said you're okay *now*, but is another call coming? I don't know." He raises his hands in question and sucks his lips into his mouth, a grin trying to break free. Everything he does confirms that I made the right decision in meeting him today.

"That was the only one planned," I say to reassure him and then laugh when he jokingly wipes at his brow. "Are you always this honest and forthright?" I ask.

"Honest, yes. Forthright, no. I try not to lie, but I'm usually not as open." He tries to hide a nervous laugh as he runs a hand through his thick dark hair, and I find myself reaching forward to clasp his arm. Our eyes lock, and a moment passes between us. Wes sucks in a breath while my heart pounds in my chest.

"I appreciate the openness. It's refreshing," I say, pulling my hand back and breaking whatever strange trance we were in.

Wes smiles softly, as though he understands the significance of what just happened, before he straightens up. "Okay. Can I get you another drink?" he says, changing the subject.

Thankful for the shift, I offer him a grin, shaking my head. "I'm good. I'm not a big drinker."

He nods before he heads to the bar, and as he walks away, the strangest feeling takes over me. I may barely know him, but there's just something about the way he looks at me that makes me feel completely at ease, and that's crazy, right? We've just met. Well, if you don't count the fact that I jumped him at the beach that day.

When he returns with water and a beer, Wes slides the water across to me before taking a sip of his beer.

A laugh escapes me before I cover my mouth to stop it. "Sorry. Do I make you nervous?" I say, motioning to the beer. *Did I do something to push him to drink?*

Running a hand down his face, Wes laughs before blowing out a breath. "Like you wouldn't believe."

Why would I make him nervous? I'm the one that's nervous.

"You're right, I do find that a little hard to believe. You're gorgeous, you're an NFL star, and you're wealthy. There's no way you've never spoken to girls before." *There's no way they don't throw themselves at you.*

"Oh, don't worry, there's been a...few women...here and there, but it's always in the off-season and always *just* sex." His nose crinkles as he says that and an uncomfortable feeling takes over me at that revelation, but I keep smiling as he continues. "Sorry, I'm not sure why I said that. It's like I have no filter around you." He shakes off his thoughts. "Anyway, it's been a long time since I've tried to get to know someone. I've never really wanted to." He shrugs like his words are no big deal, while they hit me square in the chest.

"But...you want to now?" I ask, my voice cracking a little.

"Like you wouldn't believe," he repeats, and we laugh, the nervousness clear in both our voices. Could that be why he makes me feel comfortable? Because, like me, this is all new to him, and we're both just taking things as they come, but wanting to try? Whatever it is, it feels right.

"So, how come you avoid women during the season? That's a long time to go without," I ask, though I'm not sure why I want to talk about his sex life.

"I'm too focused to even think about it...normally. I live and breathe the game. I still spend time with close friends and my gran, but random women aren't even on my radar."

I want to ask about his gran, but the mention of friends sparks a memory for me. "That's right; your friend Carter was traded too. They talked about you being a package deal."

Wes's face scrunches before he speaks and I cringe. I should know better than to trust the media. "Yeah, that's not exactly what went down," he says with a frown. "But it's good to have him here. You seem to know a lot about me for someone who didn't recognize me right away."

I laugh because he's right. "It's actually football in general that I keep up with. I'm a huge fan. My brother plays for Denver."

"No shit?"

"No shit." I nod.

Wes grins before shaking his head in disbelief. "Who's your brother?"

"If I told you that then you'd know my last name," I say with a little bit of humor to hide the fact that I'm actually worried about that for some reason.

"Right, and you're not ready for that?" he asks without judgment, giving me even less of a reason to be worried.

"Not quite," I say honestly, twisting my hair between my fingers, offering him an apologetic smile.

Wes reaches forward and hesitantly pulls the hair from my grasp before tucking it behind my ear, sending my heart into an erratic beat.

"It's okay," he says with a genuine warmth I'm not used to. "I'm more than happy to put in the work and earn that information." He smiles but then it drops and his brows crease. "Although, I've only got a week, you said. And with a game this weekend, I have even less time." He runs his hands down his face, joking like it's all too stressful for him, and I laugh.

"I'll be at the game. Maybe we can meet up after?" I offer. *What?! He's never going to agree to that.*

His hands drop from his face, and a smile brightens his features. "Works for me. And what about tomorrow? Are you free tomorrow?"

Sucking my lips into my mouth, I try to hide my giddy grin but it shines through. "There's no playing hard to get for you, is there?"

Wes laughs. "I was actually told to play hard to get in case you were a stalker. All you did was wave, and I fucked that idea right off. Please tell me you're not a stalker."

"I'm. Not. A. Stalker." I say it robotically like I'm just repeating his words back to him, giving him a cheesy grin when his eyes narrow.

"You're not giving me much confidence here, Lucy. You keep showing up where I am. You know a hell of a lot about me and football in general, and you keep trying to get in my pants. It screams stalker."

I bark out an obnoxious laugh before burying my face in my hands, peeking through a gap while I continue to giggle. Wes drops his serious facial expression and laughs along with me.

"You wish I was trying to get in your pants," I say with an exaggerated eye roll.

"Actually, it's nice that you're not." He shrugs and it has an instant calming effect on me. As though in the back of my mind I've been nervous that's what he wanted but I hadn't realized it until now.

"Good. I'm glad we've had that conversation because..." I pause, not sure what I was going to say. I'm not at all here to get in his pants, and I'm happy he's not trying to get into mine. But I'm not sure what to say because...he wants to get to know me. But why? And am I ready to get to know anyone?

Wes reaches out and mimics my earlier affection, gently placing his hand on my arm. My pulse spikes, but I don't shy away from his touch. "I have no expectations, Lucy. None. I just want to get to know you. I don't know anything past that."

His words penetrate my soul, and I believe every one of them. And while I may be wrong—I've definitely fallen into this trap before—this time, I don't think I am.

The rest of the night flows effortlessly, and when it starts to get late, Wes walks me to my door. He doesn't go in for a goodnight kiss or even a hug. Instead, he takes a step back and waits for my move.

"Thanks for tonight," I say and then pause, taking a deep breath before I leap. "I can probably meet for a late lunch tomorrow. If you're free," I continue, reaching for the door handle.

Wes smiles. "I can make a late lunch work. Two p.m.? Same place?"

"Sounds perfect."

He waits until I'm inside before he starts backing away, and when he's a few steps down the hall, I offer him some faith. "My brother's name is Dylan. Dylan Mathers," I whisper-yell and watch as Wes's eyes light up and his smile brightens.

He nods as I move to close the door, and just before it clicks shut, I hear, "See you soon, Lucy Mathers," followed by a soft chuckle.

Chapter Four

Wes

I can't keep the smile off my face as I walk away, and I'm still smiling at practice the next morning.

"You're acting weird, and I don't like it," my best friend, Carter, says, lining up beside me for the next play. He pulls at the scruff under his chin, eyeing me suspiciously as I shake my head with a grin. And when I turn my focus back to the field—where it should remain—he frowns at me for not giving him an answer.

"I'll get it out of you at lunch," he huffs as our quarterback calls the play.

I take off in a run, prepared to block for our running back who is *supposed* to have the ball. But he doesn't. They switched up the play. Why? I have no idea. Maybe they're trying to ensure we're all paying attention. And clearly, I'm not. *Goddammit.*

"That was abysmal," Carter yells when I run back to my position. He's right. That was awful. And I should be mad about it, but I'm not.

"Johnson!" Coach booms, and I flinch, because *he's* definitely mad about it. "Where's your head today?"

"That's what I'd like to know," Carter mumbles beside me.

Gripping my neck, I smile apologetically before shaking out my shoulders. "Sorry, Coach. Won't happen again."

This isn't me. I don't lose focus for anything anymore. And I'm still new here. I need to prove myself. But fuck, it's hard to get a certain brunette out of my mind. Maybe the other guys are onto something...hooking up during the season would definitely make it less of a big deal when it happens. *This* is a first for me, and it shows.

I pull my head out of the clouds and pay attention to the remainder of practice, so Coach lets me off the hook. Carter, however, does not.

"Alright, we're going to lunch, and you're going to spill," he says, falling into step beside me as we walk off the field an hour later.

"No can do," I say without looking his way, knowing I'll be getting some kind of death stare in return. "I've got plans."

Carter's steps falter, and he pulls me to a stop. "Are these *plans* the reason you're so cheery?"

"N*ope*," I lie unconvincingly. "Just having a good day. Aren't I allowed to be happy?"

"You absolutely are. As long as you tell me why."

I bark out a deep laugh and shake my head. "I already told you. It's just a good day."

"I'm calling Grandma Katie," he threatens with a grin, and I shoot him a glare.

"Fuck off. No, you're not."

"Ahh, so there is something. I knew it." He claps like a giddy schoolgirl before his smirk rises.

"You're such a fucker," I grumble and then jump away when he tries to slap me on the back.

"I know." He shrugs.

After a quick shower, I get changed in record time and make a dash out to my truck to meet Lucy. Unfortunately, I'm not as fast as I thought because Carter's leaning against the driver's door, waiting for me with a huge grin on his face.

"For fuck's sake, I met a woman," I say, knowing he'll never let up.

His smile drops as his eyebrows shoot up into his hairline. "I thought you were going to say you got laid. 'Meeting a woman' sounds much more serious than that."

"It's *not* serious, and we haven't even hooked up. At all."

His brows furrow in confusion. "When did you meet her?" he says with a frown.

His reaction is not what I was expecting. I thought I'd get some light teasing, or maybe he'd even ask to meet her. But this is weird. "Two days ago," I say, massaging my forehead in slight frustration.

"Hmm," he says, but offers nothing else.

"Why are *you* acting weird now?" I ask to avoid punching him like I want to.

He gives me a look that screams "are you fucking kidding me" and then shakes his head incredulously. "Maybe because I'm worried about you. Are you sure you're ready for something like that?"

"For lunch?" I ask, playing dumb. I know what he's worried about, and it's easier to joke than to seriously consider his question.

"Don't be a dick. You know what I mean." *Unfortunately, I do.*

I sigh, running a hand down my face. "I'm just getting to know her. That's all."

"Nah, it's more than that. I can tell. I haven't seen you like this since..." he trails off.

Once again, he's right, but I'm not about to admit that.

"She's only here for a week...for a conference. It's just a bit of fun."

Carter visibly relaxes, and I smile. I should be grateful he's looking out for me, but it wouldn't hurt for him to want me to find someone.

"So can I meet her?" he asks with a cheesy grin now that he feels better about the situation. Without giving him an answer, I roll my eyes and flip him off, before jumping in my car. *Bye, Carter.*

I finally arrive back at the hotel at one forty-five, and after a quick hello to Gran—where she once again questions me for stopping by unannounced—I make it to the bar with a few minutes to spare. This time, Lucy's already waiting. Leaning against the wall near the entry, she has her eyes on her phone as her thumb flicks across the screen. She's nibbling on her bottom lip and has the faintest of smiles on her beautiful face. My heart races as I watch her. Everything about her draws me in, and I can't bring myself to move, let alone look away. So, when her head lifts, she catches me staring.

With the most adorable expression, she releases the lip she has trapped between her teeth, and straightens before raising her hand in a wave.

Walking toward her, I ignore the fact that she busted me checking her out and smile.

"How was practice?" she asks when I reach her side, not at all affected by my ogling.

"It was tiring, long, and *slow*," I say honestly, unable to hold anything back around this girl.

Lucy laughs, and I add the sound to my memory bank, along with the others, before gesturing to the door. "Should we go in?"

She nods as I hold it open for her, signaling for her to go first.

"How's the conference going?" I ask when we're settled in a booth.

Lucy brushes a few loose strands of hair behind her ear, and eyes me with a sassy grin. "It's tiring, long, and *slow*," she repeats my previous answer, and I can't stop my ridiculous belly laugh.

It's hard not to notice that things between us already feel different than they did yesterday. In a good way. I mean, yesterday was great. Everything felt natural and comfortable. But today...today it feels like we know each other. Like we've known each other for a while. I don't know how I got that feeling from the smallest of conversations, but it just feels right. *God, when did I become such a sap?*

Mentally shaking off my thoughts, I ask Lucy about her day and listen intently as she fills me in on all the "boring details" as she calls them, before filling her in on mine. We talk until our food arrives and only stop to take our first bite, then we're back into it.

"So my brother was here last night, and I may have told him I met you." She lifts her fork as she talks, laughing shyly.

I raise an eyebrow in question but smile to ease her nerves. "Oh, yeah?" I say, trying hard not to give away my own. *What did she say? What did he say? Has he heard rumors about me that he filled her in on? God knows there are plenty out there.*

"Yeah." She laughs. "He reminded me that you play with his friend Luke." *What?! So they didn't really talk about me?*

Luke...Luke... Fuck. Am I supposed to know him? I'm slowly learning everyone's names, but there are a lot of them.

"Luke?" I ask with a confused grimace.

"He's a rookie this year. Hothead. Bit of a loose cannon but a great player." Lucy laughs and then adds, "In more ways than one, I've heard."

My brows crease while I decipher her meaning, and when it clicks into place, I laugh. "Ah, so he's the opposite of me then?"

"Definitely. There's no "off-season only" bullshit for him. In fact, I'd wager when it comes to that rule, you're in the minority," she sasses, and I like this new version of her.

Tapping my knuckles on the table, I bite back a smirk. "You think it's bullshit? Are you saying I *should* be out having sex during the season?"

Lucy's face scrunches before something seemingly comes to mind and she smiles wide, her eyes lighting up with mischief. "I don't know. Maybe. Whatever." She shrugs, and the cutest blush coats her skin.

I release a held breath and smile. I want to ask why she's blushing, hopeful that it means she wants to explore something with me. Even if it doesn't lead to sex. But whatever her meaning, I'm thankful I didn't fuck it all up with the mention of sex on the second date. *Date? Jesus. No wonder Carter didn't believe me when I said it wasn't serious. I don't even believe me.*

I open my mouth to ask, but Lucy cuts me off, asking if my chicken is good, obviously wanting to change the subject. I burst out laughing and shake my head as she grins. "The pasta is delicious," she adds with a giggle. "In case you were wondering."

"I wasn't," I deadpan jokingly and smile when she laughs. "Believe it or not, I've actually had it before."

We talk for another hour, right up until I have to leave to get back to the stadium. I'm already pushing it for time or I'd stay longer.

We walk together until we reach the conference rooms, and while the urge to hold her hand is strong, I ignore it, enjoying the comfortable silence instead.

"This is me," she says, and I take note of the session name on the door—"Best practice and workplace relations." Unfortunately, it gives me no indication as to where she's come from, but I'll happily suck up any information I can about her. *Maybe next time I see her I should actually ask.*

Knowing there will be a next time, my focus shifts back to Lucy, and I grin. "Enjoy the session and remember...no matter how boring it gets, you can't sleep because people *will* notice," I joke, referring to a story she was telling me about a colleague falling asleep this morning.

Lucy covers her face in her hands and laughs. "I felt so bad for him. The red mark on his head was huge. But at the same time, that's what you get for falling asleep with your head in the palm of your hand...of course, it was going to drop."

"Let's hope he's learned his lesson and you have an uneventful afternoon."

"Fingers crossed." Lucy smiles, crossing her fingers in front of her. "Now, I better go, or I'll be late."

"Right, yes. But I'll see you after the game tomorrow, yeah?" I work hard to keep my nerves at bay as I await her answer.

She exaggeratedly sighs before rolling her eyes. "Yes, I suppose that can be arranged," she huffs before her lips pull up into a grin.

And my answering smile cannot be stopped.

"Can I get your number? You know, so I can text you when I'm done," I ask, not sure I can last until late tomorrow to talk to her.

Lucy hesitates for a second before pulling her phone from her pocket. "Sure, that makes life easier."

We exchange numbers and then say our goodbyes, agreeing once more to meet up the next day. When I finally jump in my truck, I have thirteen minutes to make the twelve-minute drive. *Talk about cutting it close.* I've never been fined once in my NFL career, but for Lucy, I don't mind risking it.

After reviewing opposition tapes, we talk strategy, and I'm mentally drained by the time I get home. I practically fall into bed fully clothed, but can I sleep? No. My phone is screaming at me to pick it up and text Lucy. Okay, maybe it's my brain and not my phone that's wanting that to happen. But either way, I give in, pulling up her number to begin.

Wes: Thank you again for lunch. Hope your session went well

I toss and turn for thirty minutes waiting for a response before cursing myself and giving up. I'm almost asleep when the bell chimes, signaling I have a text. My eyes shoot open, and I grab my phone, bringing the screen to life...and find nothing.

No message. No call. Not even an email to explain the tone. *What the fuck is wrong with me?* I'm losing my mind over this girl. Dropping the phone back to the bed, I smother myself with a pillow and yell out in frustration just as the noise sounds again, only louder this time. I blow out a breath but pick it up anyway, fully prepared to find the screen blank once more. Only it's not.

Lucy: Thank you. You'll be pleased to know my head is bruise free. I managed to stay awake

Since we've already established I'm not playing hard to get, I text her back immediately.

Wes: Phew! I've been worried

Lucy: Your concern is much appreciated :) Did you make it to your team meeting on time?

Wes: I did. *Just.* But even if I was late, it would have been worth it

The three dots appear and then disappear a few times, but it's not unexpected. It hasn't escaped my attention that she's not a huge fan of me talking about us in any kind of positive light. Or talking about an "us" in general. If only I knew why. Yes, I could very well ask her, but I know we're not in the right place for her to want to share that just yet. But I'm hopeful we'll get there.

The dots stop, and I'm almost sure she's not going to reply when a text comes through.

Lucy: I'm glad you made it all the same. I'm going to head off to bed. Hope you have a good sleep ahead of the game tomorrow

I will now.

Wes: Thank you. See you soon. Goodnight, Lucy

Lucy: Goodnight

My heart pounds in my chest, and all we're doing is texting. What is it about this girl that has me twisted in knots? And where exactly do we go from here?

Chapter Five

Lucy

S ummer and I push through the crowd to get to our seats not long before the game begins. We're running late, which is not uncommon when the two of us get talking, but it's annoying all the same.

"Logan called to say he's in Heartwood to see Liam this weekend," Summer says as we sit down, talking about her childhood best friend and the little brother he only recently found out existed. "I tried to convince him to come to the game but he said it's too hectic and..." Something gets her attention and she trails off mid-sentence.

When my gaze follows hers, I notice the teams are already warming up, so when she waves toward the field, I know she's found Dylan. This'll be the first time I've seen him play in the pros, and I'm pretty damn excited about it...and proud. My little bro. The annoying little shit I used to boss around. The guy that became one of my best friends and my protector. I've always expected big things from him, and he one hundred percent delivered.

"Did you find him, or did he find you?" I ask Summer as I watch Dylan run in our direction.

She bites her lip to hide her grin, and I know the answer. I swear he has a built-in radar when it comes to her. I mean, I know he arranged our seats, so he probably has the numbers memorized, but it's also safe to assume his eyes have been scanning the stadium since he stepped out onto the field.

"I'm ready for you to be my sister, Summer," I joke because it freaks her out.

She blushes while shaking her head. "We have plenty of time for that. We don't need to rush."

"Does Dylan feel the same?"

"Stop it." She laughs. "Where's Wes?" Standing up, she makes a point of exaggeratedly scanning the field, changing the subject completely. "Anyone know where the new guys are?" she says to the supporters around us.

"Sit down. Geez." I grip her jersey, pulling her into her seat, and she squeals as she falls.

"Oh, I'm sorry. I thought we were the type of friends that tease each other," she sasses, bouncing her eyebrows.

My lips pull into a smirk as I shake my head. "We are. I just don't want him to get his hopes up."

Summer frowns, her expression turning serious. "What's happening there, anyway?"

With a sigh, I lift my shoulders in a small shrug. *I have no idea.* "I don't know what I'm doing, Sum. I want to get to know him. I'm completely drawn to him for some reason, but at the same time, I don't think I have anything to offer right now. I don't know how much I can give him."

"I know you've been with some awful guys, but not all of them are assholes, Lucy. Just look at the two people closest to you, Dylan and Joel."

"I know."

She's right. *If only it was that easy.*

"He seems nice." She shrugs...and again, she's right, but I'm still not sure what to do.

"He is nice. He's doing all the right things and trying to get to know me. We're, um...actually meeting up again after the game."

"Lucy!" Summer exclaims and pulls me into a hug. I love her excitement, but I also hate it. I hate the person I've become lately, but I can't seem to bring the old me back. I need to try because this isn't the life I want to live. I'm a strong, independent woman, and I'm getting stronger. I want to be the Lucy I used to be. Well, parts of her anyway. The Lucy that always chose asshole boyfriends can stay the fuck away.

When Summer pulls back, she holds me at arm's length and smiles. "You've got this. Just take it one step at a time, but judge him for who he is, not because he's a guy in general." *Again, if only it was that easy.*

Wes is a hell of a player, and difficult to look away from. In fact, if I'm completely honest with myself, seeing him on that field has me feeling things I wasn't sure I'd feel again anytime soon. My heart races as I watch him run across the field, taking in the power in his legs as he pivots. I flinch when he slams into the opposition but find myself loving his confidence, his force, and his strength. The reserved Wes is gone; in his place is a man in full control. And yet, when he takes off his helmet and smiles up to the crowd, the guy I know shines through.

It's anyone's game at halftime, and I'm struggling to decide who to cheer for. San Francisco is my team, always has been, but Denver has Dylan. Summer does not feel my pain; she's Denver all the way. "I'm happy to be a turncoat. After all, who knows how long Dyl will stay in Denver. My loyalty is with him," she'd said as she painted the Denver colors on her face. Something I wouldn't dare do considering where we are, but she doesn't seem to care.

As the guys run off the field, I notice Wes scanning the crowd, looking for something, or someone...*me*. He has no hope considering I never told him where I'd be sitting, but he's trying and I almost want to stand up and wave. Almost. But I'd prefer not to draw attention to myself.

"Are you still heading home tomorrow morning?" I ask Summer before the second half begins.

"Yeah, sorry. My Monday afternoon class is draining. If I miss too many, I lose marks, and I've already missed one after going to Denver for a long weekend."

"I get it, and it's okay. It's been fun. I appreciate you coming."

"Anytime." She smiles. "Maybe next time you won't ditch me for a guy."

I'd worry if I didn't know she was joking. But she absolutely is. Her time's been taken up with Dylan.

Denver gets ahead late in the second half and manages to stay in front for the win. My heart hurts for Wes, but I'm so happy for Dylan. He may have only played a few minutes, but he played, and I couldn't be prouder.

Summer and I meet him after the game for a quick chat and congratulations before I sneak away. If Summer wasn't distracting Dylan, I'm sure I would have been questioned, but thankfully, she is.

Wes and I had texted earlier this morning to make arrangements for after the game, and agreed to meet at the beach for a walk in a couple of hours. Taking my time to get ready, I smile as a giddy nervous energy runs through me. It's a new feeling. All my past relationships have begun after a hookup. Things just kind of progressed without me giving it much thought. Whereas this—the excitement...the anticipation...the nerves—it's a first, and I kind of like it. It's definitely helping me to focus my energy on the good in life rather than the hell I've been living in lately.

I'm halfway through getting ready when my phone starts ringing, and Wes's name pops up on the screen, bringing a smile to my face. I don't know why, but I'm confident this is not a call to cancel our plans.

"Can't wait another forty minutes to see me?" I say, instead of a normal greeting.

"No, I can't. Are you ready yet? I'm already on my way to meet you."

A huge grin adorns my face as I shake my head. "How? Don't you have the media to deal with?"

"I volunteered to go first. Something I've never done." He pauses before whispering, "I think I made a few of them suspicious."

I start to giggle as a feeling of weightlessness takes over. Everything feels so easy with him.

"Okay, what about the lecture from your coach after the loss?"

"Mmm, yep, that was brutal, but it's done. And before you ask, yes, I promise, I showered."

I bite back my next smile even though he can't see me. "You need to at least give me twenty minutes," I say as I run the brush through my hair.

"You don't need it. You're always beautiful. I'll give you the two-minute drive plus some walking time. I'll meet you at the beach in ten."

With that, he shocks me by hanging up, and I'm not sure how I feel about that considering the type of guys I've been with. Guys that wanted everything their way. A small pang of unease takes over until my phone rings again.

"Fuck! I'm so sorry. The call disconnected. If you need more time, it's okay. You can take it."

I sigh silently in relief and then laugh at the assumption I made. He's proven himself to be one of the good ones in a few short days, and yet, I can't trust anyone. *God, I wish I could change that.*

"I'll be there in ten," I say, abandoning the makeup I'd planned and heading for the door.

"Great. See you soon," he says excitedly as I hear the buzz of traffic in the background.

When I pull up in the parking lot, Wes is casually leaning against the wooden railing at the entrance to the sand. He looks up at the sound of my car and squints when my headlights shine in his face. After cutting the engine, I turn the lights off and watch as he blinks a few times, re-adjusting to the dusk night surrounding us, then smiles when our eyes meet. Jogging over to my door, he opens it before I've had the chance and reaches for my hand.

"Nine minutes; I'm impressed."

My eyes widen, and as hard as I try, I can't keep the smile off my face. "You timed me?" I say, allowing him to help me out of the car.

"Nope, I was counting down."

I push at his shoulder and giggle like a schoolgirl. *What is he doing to me?* "Shut up. There's no way you were doing that."

"You're right." He laughs, rocking back on his heels. "I have no idea how long you took, but I'm happy you're here. Now, what are your thoughts on ice cream?" he says, pointing toward a van that's just pulled into the lot.

"Love it." I practically skip over to the window to order, not even waiting for Wes to follow.

"So, I did some research," I say after we've been walking for a little while. The conversation has once again been easy, and I feel so relaxed around him.

Wes takes a step in front of me before turning around and walking backward with his eyes on mine. "Oh yeah, what about?"

"You and Carter," I say with a raised brow as Wes's face flashes with intrigue before he smiles, motioning for me to proceed. "I noticed he didn't get much game time today, so I may have consulted the trusty Internet to see what that's about."

"You could have just asked me." He laughs. "I think we've established that I'll tell you just about anything."

"We have. And I need to use that to my advantage a bit more," I joke, sort of. "But in this case, you'll soon learn I'm not the most patient person on the planet."

Wes laughs again before moving back to my side. "Guess that makes two of us after my phone call tonight."

"You're right. Hmmm, maybe we need to cut this relationship off before it's even begun. We're too similar."

Wes's laughter stops and a warm smile lights up his face. *What's going on there?* Ignoring his reaction, I jump back into our previous conversation. "Anyway, as I was saying... I discovered that Carter was actually traded *before* you. And you were a last-minute change to San Francisco's roster."

A tiny smirk starts to form before Wes schools his features. "No way, we were a package deal. We never do anything without the other. He's actually just over there," he mocks, pointing behind me, because that's pretty much how the media perceive them.

I bark out a laugh and lightly punch his abs, abs that I wouldn't mind seeing again.

"Hey! Put that weapon away," he jokes, waving his hand at my fist. "I know the power that thing has."

"Well, I wouldn't have to use it if you hadn't been lying."

"Lucy Mathers, *you'll* come to learn that I never lie. I may joke, but I'll never lie. Not to you, not to anyone. There's no place in this world for lying."

I nod, because he's right, but I can't help wondering if there's a story there.

"That aside, you're correct. While Carter and I have been friends for forever, and would love to always play together, it wasn't planned that way. He was traded early and then when San Francisco lost a tight end at the last minute, my agent got me a deal. It was luck, but we're once again on the same team."

"That must be nice."

"It is; I just wish people would see his real potential. I'm hoping they'll nurture it here. They seem to be a supportive team."

My lips pull into a smile, but I try to hide it. "You, Wesley Johnson, are a good man."

"I try." He smirks, bouncing his eyebrows, before moving in close and slowly draping an arm over my shoulder, giving me a chance to step away.

But this time, I don't even flinch.

Another hour passes in comfortable conversation, and before long, darkness surrounds us and a cool night breeze sweeps in from the ocean.

"As much as I don't want to cut the night short," Wes starts. "But should we start heading back? You're not doing a good job of hiding the fact that you're cold."

What? "I'm not cold," I say honestly. Sure it's getting cooler but...

"Damn, I was kind of hoping I'd have an excuse to put my arm around you again."

I laugh but don't offer any other response to that. "How about we just walk a little more, and then we'll turn back. I promise the destination is worth it."

Wes's brows rise as he turns his head to the side. "Consider me intrigued. Let's keep moving."

Our hands brush accidentally while we continue our walk, and it's impossible to ignore the electric current that runs through me. Wes makes me feel a lot of things, but the most important one is...safe. He makes me feel safe. While I'll never completely forget my past, it's easier to push it to the back of my mind when he's looking at me like I've hung the moon. This is crazy. We only just met, and yet...we didn't. I can't deny the connection I felt when I kissed him that day. It's something I'd never felt before. And the need to kiss him again, just to experience that, is strong.

When our fingers brush a second time, I give in to my reservations and link our hands, giving him a squeeze. Wes gives me a sideways glance as he raises my hand to his smiling lips, pressing a kiss to my knuckles. "Just letting this bad boy know I have no hard feelings," he says, drawing attention to my fist.

Huffing out a laugh, I pull him to a stop and smile when I see we've reached our destination. "I think this was the spot," I say, nervously nibbling on my bottom lip.

Wes looks around, confused, until his eyes lock on something behind my head. "You mean *our* spot?"

"Do I? I mean, can you really have a spot with someone you just met?"

"Hey, don't lessen our relationship; we met ages ago," he jokes, pulling me closer until our bodies crash together. I flinch on instinct, but only because he caught me off guard. So when he tries to pull away, I hold on tightly, hating the fact that I made him question his moves.

Despite my attempt to keep him close, he takes a step back until our bodies are no longer touching before gently brushing my hair behind my ear, sending my heart into overdrive. "I like you, Lucy. And I'd love to kiss you again...more than anything right now. But I'm going to wait for you to make the first move. When you're ready." His eyes bore into mine while he speaks, making sure I understand his meaning. I do. One hundred percent. He's letting me set the pace. He knows something's wrong.

Taking my own step back, I watch our arms stretch between us until I'm too far away and his hand drops. Giving him a small nod in acknowledgment, I pause before launching myself at him, slamming my lips to his. The same lips that were the last to touch mine. Despite everything that's happened between now and then.

"Fuck!" Wes hisses against my mouth before he recovers from the shock and lifts his hands to frame my face, tilting my head up to deepen the kiss.

Keeping one hand on my neck, he moves the other into my hair, holding me tightly in place. He's strong and yet I trust him completely. I know that if I were to try and pull away, he'd release me in a second. But I have no intention of doing that. Instead, I lift to my toes slowly, making sure my breasts brush against his chest as I rise.

Wes groans, and when I gasp in return, he sneaks his tongue into my mouth, the feel of it sending my pulse racing. Something ignites within me that I haven't felt for a while, and my body aches for him.

Our tongues twirl slowly as my hands start to explore his body, running along the contours of his rock-hard abs before moving up along his solid back. My fingers play with the strands of his thick hair at the base of his neck, and he groans into my mouth before breaking away, moving his lips to my neck and shoulder. As he sucks on the sensitive skin just below my ear, I can't stop the moan that escapes me, and I intertwine our fingers, squeezing his hand, before my mouth seeks out his once more. When I bite down on his lip, Wes jolts, pressing his obvious erection into me, and I apparently lose all reason. *Oh, God.* Wrapping my spare arm around his neck, I move closer, pulling him down into me as my tongue pushes back into his mouth.

"Wait, Lucy," Wes murmurs against my lips. "We have to stop."

I freeze instantly—never wanting to do something against his will, or anyone's—and step back.

"I'm sorry, I—"

"You have nothing to apologize for," he rasps, a little out of breath. "That was *everything*. But if we keep going, I can't guarantee I'll keep it G-rated, and there are a few reasons that shouldn't happen. We're on a public beach for one."

My eyes scan the area, and sure enough, there are still quite a few people scattered around, despite the late hour. I laugh nervously as Wes pulls me in close again with a smile on his face. Palming my cheek, he presses a chaste kiss to my forehead. "What the fuck is it about you, Lucy Mathers? You're driving me crazy."

Burying my face into his chest, I audibly sigh, because I know what he means. I barely go a second without thinking of him, and we hardly know each other. *What is this?*

After making our way to the parking lot, we drive back separately to the hotel, but Wes waits beside his car to walk me to my door. This time, instead of taking a step back, he takes my hand in his and moves toward me, pressing his lips to my knuckles.

Without permission, a smile lights up my face as I shake my head. This guy is smooth, that's for sure. *Please, let this be real.*

Pulling me closer, he drops his forehead to mine and releases a deep breath. "I know I said I'd let you steer this ship, but now that I've tasted your lips again, I'm not sure I can go back. Please, tell me I can kiss you again, and then keep kissing you whenever I get the urge?"

My smile morphs into a smirk. "Is that likely to be often?"

"Most definitely." He grins with a nod, standing motionless until I say...

"Permission granted."

After rushing out "Thank fuck," Wes palms my neck and tilts my face up toward him, molding his mouth to mine. The kiss is soft and unhurried, like he's trying to explore every part of me. It's a kiss that packs emotion and has my heart pounding in my chest, begging for release. Begging me to finally give it a chance to roam. *To trust there are good guys out there.* Because with Wes, I want to believe in that.

When we're once again breathless, he moves away, and I feel the loss everywhere. He smiles shyly before taking another step back, and then another, until he's out of arm's reach. "I'm going to go. But I'd love to see you tomorrow. If you're free."

My hand comes up to my lips, and I nod before reaching behind me to open the door.

Wes smiles in acknowledgement and waits for me to step inside, before turning and jogging down the hall as I shut the door behind me.

I still feel a tingle on my lips long after he's gone, and my mind buzzes with what that means. Can I truly move on from everything and put my faith in Wes? Something tells me I can.

Chapter Six

Wes

H er walls are coming down. Right before my eyes, I can see the girl from the beach coming back to me. I say that like I know her well, but in all honesty, it feels like I do.

The girl I met on the beach appeared confident and carefree, and while Lucy definitely has those traits at times, she also comes across more guarded and protective of herself than she was back then. Not that that's a bad thing; it's just different from what I remember.

It also has my mind working overtime to figure out if I just got a different version of Lucy that day, or if something happened between then and now to affect her. Either way, she's opening back up, and it's beautiful to see.

For the past twenty-four hours, I've kept up my promise to kiss her often. At least, as often as I can around both our commitments. And she lets me, every chance we get. When she's with me, I don't question what I'm doing because it feels right, but when we're apart, it's hard to forget the simple fact that she's going home in two days, and I don't even know where her home is.

When the afternoon rolls around the next day, I check my watch for the millionth time and groan when I see Lucy still has two hours left of her conference for the day. The thought of keeping myself busy for that long pains me, so when a stupid idea comes to mind, I jump at it, not even bothering to think it through.

Twenty minutes later, I watch sneakily through the window as the young uniform-clad resort employee walks confidently into the conference room. He discreetly hands the presenter a note and then backs away with a smile.

As he exits, I slap a twenty-dollar bill in his hand, along with a signed cap, watching him as he disappears down the hall.

I can't hear what's happening inside, but I watch as the presenter reads the note before signaling for Lucy to collect her things and come forward. I know what the note says—I wrote it—so I expect her eyes to dart to the window in five, four, three... Yep, there they are, sooner than I thought. Her brows furrow in question, and when the presenter follows her eye line, I duck out of sight, probably causing more confusion.

Lucy steps outside moments later with her lips pulled into a line. She's trying to hide a smile, but the corners of her mouth seem to be disobeying her request, lifting up ever so slightly.

At least that's what I thought was happening. But when her lips lower into a very obvious frown, my chest tightens.

"Is it my dog? Did something happen to Mitzy?" she says in a whisper, causing my heart to pound as I take in her words and expression. *Fuck!* This backfired. I'd written a note to excuse her from the remainder of her session due to a family issue. She'd told me the last talk of the day didn't really apply to her anyway. I thought I was being funny.

Lucy eyes me expectantly.

"Ah, fuck... I—" Gripping the back of my neck, I grit my teeth and shrug. I'm about to spew out some epic apology when she bursts out laughing. *What?*

"Oh, Wes."

The laughter draws attention, and the presenter turns our way again, causing me to duck for a second time. Of course, Lucy laughs even harder.

"Stop it! You'll spoil my plan."

She nods, covering her face with her palm until her giggles dissipate, then turns to the presenter, giving him a terse nod before hurriedly walking my way. When I begin to rise, she pushes me back down and smiles as she looks back through the conference windows.

"Okay, you're good now," she says after a moment, allowing me to stand. I've just reached full height when she whispers "shit," links our fingers, and takes off in a hurried walk, pulling me down the hall and scrambling to get me into a doorway, out of sight.

What is going on here? I feel like I'm a school kid trying to skip class as Lucy peers around the wall and then springs back toward me, crashing her body to mine. I'd laugh at how unreal this felt if she wasn't standing flush against me, her breasts pressed to my chest, my cock straining against her stomach. *Fuck! Don't think about that. Bad thoughts, bad thoughts. No, wait! Pure thoughts, pure thoughts.*

"My boss is heading this way; he's not going to be happy to find me slacking off with you."

That'll do it. The thought of getting Lucy in trouble plagues my mind, and my brows pull together. "Fuck, Lucy, I'm sorry."

Her eyes find mine, and her lips pull into a smirk. "I'm not, but you need to get me out of here."

I huff out a quiet laugh before spinning her around and pressing her into the wall this time. She yelps in surprise, and it's the cutest little sound, but I don't have time to think about it. Lucy doesn't need to ask me twice. I'm getting us out of here.

Gripping her hips, I lean ever so slightly toward the corner and peer around. Sure enough, there's a guy hovering outside the conference room, who I can only assume is her boss. He looks down the hall in the opposite direction, and then his head turns our way.

I dart back in and press my body to Lucy's, just like she did mine. She bats her eyelids as she gazes up at me with a sassy grin, and I can't stop myself from pressing a chaste kiss to her nose and mouth before peeking around the corner again. He's still there.

With time to kill while we wait for him to move on, I link my fingers with Lucy's and bring her hand up between us.

"You know, I figured out what you do," I whisper, a cocky grin on my face.

"Oh yeah?" she asks, before sucking her bottom lip into her mouth, making me bite back a groan. *Focus, Wes.*

"Well, at least, I know it's something in the field of fitness and health."

"Close enough then," she says, biting back another smile and loving the fact that I haven't quite figured it out.

"How long did you study at college? That might help narrow it down."

"I'm twenty-four and I just finished. You do the math."

Twenty-four, huh? I bank that information in my "things I know about Lucy" file and consider her words. Her age doesn't help because she may not have started right away, and—

Ahem.

A throat clearing cuts off my thoughts—alerting me to the fact that her boss is now closer than he was before—and I freeze. "We're going to have to run," I say seriously, peering around the corner again, stealthy Wes in play. Lucy quietly cracks up beside me, and I raise a finger to her lips to silence her, getting a suppressed smile and a nod in return. She's loving this.

Signaling for Lucy to get ready, I check what her boss is up to one more time and, when the coast is clear, grab her hand and run. *Exactly like school kids skipping class.* Yes, I'm a thirty-year-old professional football player running through the halls of the resort laughing like a school kid. But run like hell I do. I give it my all. *What is this woman doing to me?*

Lucy giggles as we make our escape, clenching my hand tighter, following me through the maze of walkways.

I laugh along with her, but it's slightly forced. This moment has my heart beating out of control. And it has everything to do with Lucy and the blind faith she's showing me right now. I wanted to earn her trust, I wanted her to be comfortable around me, and in this second, I have no doubt that I've succeeded.

Lucy looks over her shoulder as we turn the corner and then stops, her laughter bursting out once more.

"Okay, you've broken me free from class, bad boy. What should we do now?"

I freeze. *Fuuuck.* With her erratic breathing, flushed cheeks, and the quick rise and fall of her chest, my mind has no choice but to go where it shouldn't. *What should we do now? I'll tell you.... We should go back to my room so I can hide you away from the world and slowly peel your clothes from your body, piece by piece, kissing every inch of your skin, as I—*

"Wes? Are you listening?"

Fuck! No. "Yes?" *At ease down there. You are not getting lucky tonight.*

Lucy raises an eyebrow in question, then giggles again. The sound of it is so light and carefree that I'm almost taken aback. Sure, she's laughed before, and she was absolutely in hysterics as we escaped her conference, but this...this has a softness to it that feels more real than the rest. Like she's finally at ease.

She clears her throat, and I realize I've been busted lost in thought once again. "Sorry, you wanted to know what we're doing?"

"Well, yes, but I asked... Never mind." She shakes her head and holds back a smile. "What's the plan?"

I stare out at nothing, thinking it through before answering. "Can I...cook you dinner?" I ask with a lift of my shoulder like it's just a random idea, when in reality, I've been thinking about getting uninterrupted time with her all day.

Her brows furrow, and she nibbles on her bottom lip, drawing my eyes there. Not that I let them linger. Now's not the time to be distracted. Instead, I wait patiently for Lucy's response, hoping it's a yes but almost certain it's a no. She may be more comfortable around me, but I'm not stupid enough to think she'd want to come to my place after only a few days.

Her mouth curls up in the corners, and she frees her lip from her teeth as she sighs. "That actually sounds perfect. But it's only four p.m." She says the last bit with some sass, and I have to hold back my own sigh of relief.

"Good cooking takes time. Are you not familiar with a decent home-cooked meal," I joke and then instantly regret it. I know nothing of her home life, but I know she's been through something. "Sorry, that was—"

"You may have age on your side. But you did not just challenge me in the kitchen," she says, and I rush out a laugh. *Thank God.*

"I don't think I challenged you at all. But I'm assuming by that comment that you're already judging me." My brows pull as I mock annoyance, not that it fazes Lucy at all. Her challenging expression remains as I continue. "Also, I never told you my age."

"Google is a wonderful thing, Wes Johnson. And while my brother may have the baking gene, you better believe I can cook."

The sass, the confidence...it's something she's given hints to, but it's finally shining through. My heart jolts as a sense of pride washes over me. Pride that I helped to bring this part of her back. Because I finally feel like I'm seeing the girl I met on the beach.

"I guess you can be my assistant then." I shrug, trying to put off the vibe that I'm not at all affected by the playfulness she's showing me.

"Hmmm. What are you making? Maybe I'll just watch and mock you."

"So that's a yes to me cooking?" I say, ignoring her verbal jab.

"It's a yes," Lucy says with a small laugh before a shy look flashes across her face, and she brushes her hair behind her ear.

An hour later, Lucy moves around the counter and rips the salt from my fingers before backing away with her hands tucked behind her, her eyes alight with mischief. The sun gleams through the window, creating a halo effect behind her, and I have to fight myself to concentrate on the issue at hand and not on the fact that I want to kiss her right now.

"Give it back, Lucy," I warn after snapping out of my thoughts, my tone only making her move a little faster.

"I'm putting it on the table where it belongs."

"You're not going to need it."

"Everything needs it."

We've been arguing over salt for the last ten minutes. Lucy doesn't believe me when I say she won't need to add anything extra to this meal. I've been helping Gran cook since I was a teen.

She shakes her head in skepticism but stops walking, giving me a chance to explain.

"Come here, and I'll prove it," I say, holding up a spoon full of my gran's famous stir fry sauce. Famous to me, anyway.

Lucy pops her hip, crossing her arms across her chest. "Let me guess; I'll close my eyes, ready for a taste, but feel your lips touch mine instead of that spoon. I know your kind," she sasses with a flirtatious grin.

I almost drop said spoon as I choke on a laugh. "That thought hadn't crossed my mind, but now that you mention it, I like the idea."

"Ugh, fine. Give me a taste, but no kiss."

I pout with puppy dog eyes as she walks over, but she remains unaffected until a smile lights up her face at the very last second. Lifting up on her toes, she presses her mouth to mine, smiling as she whispers against my lips. "Now, where's this magic sauce?"

When we've finished eating, Lucy sits back in her chair and pats her stomach. "For the record, it could have used a pinch of something else, but I can't put my finger on what." She stares at the salt shaker on the table in front of her as she taps her chin in thought.

My eyes narrow as I watch her, waiting for her to laugh, but she holds strong.

"For the record, I think you're wrong."

At that, she laughs. "Agree to disagree?"

"Nope." I refuse to believe that wasn't the best sauce she's ever tasted. "Maybe you need another taste."

"I do, do I?"

"Yep, one sec and I'll get it."

I dash back into the kitchen, and like the corny sucker that I've suddenly become, I spread some of the sauce across my lips before moving back to the table. Lucy's brows furrow when she sees the lack of spoon in my hands, but when her gaze lands on my lips, she squeaks out a laugh before covering her mouth to hide her grin.

"Okay, I'm ready," she says with as straight a face as she can muster.

I curl my finger in a come hither motion, and my pulse spikes when she rises from her seat. Now that she's walking my way, I'm not exactly sure what I expect to happen with this plan, so I stand still and watch it unfold. When she reaches my side, she pushes me down onto my chair and straddles my lap, her core lining up perfectly with the semi I now have pressed against my jeans.

Leaning back slightly, Lucy stares at my mouth as she runs the tip of her finger under my bottom lip, sending a shiver down my spine. I have to physically stop my eyes from closing as she moves closer and whispers in my ear. "Is this what I'm tasting?"

Fuck! I almost wish I'd been more creative with the sauce placement. I give her a nod, unable to form words as I try my hardest to keep my cock at bay. But when she sticks out her tongue and licks her way across my top lip, before sucking the bottom one into her mouth, I'm done for.

It's impossible to hold back the groan that rips from within me, but that's the least of my worries. My pants tighten as my length hardens beneath her, and by the way Lucy jumps, she definitely notices it.

"I'm sorry. I didn't mean..." she trails off and moves to stand up.

"Wait! I'm not sorry, unless it makes you uncomfortable."

Lucy pauses, and her eyes glaze over as if she's lost in thought, perhaps processing her feelings on what just happened. When her eyes meet mine, I notice a spark of something new, something I haven't seen since we first met—fire.

"I've never felt more comfortable with a man in my life," she says with a shy smile, her honesty shining through.

Framing her face in my hands, I breathe out an audible sigh before pressing my lips to her forehead. That one simple sentence holds so much meaning, and I'm not sure what to process first.

Lucy grips my tee in her hands as her forehead meets mine, and when she sucks in a breath, I hold my own as I wait for her next move.

"You're not going to hurt me, right?" she rasps, and my heart breaks for this girl. *What has she been through?*

I could easily assure her, and it would mostly be the truth, but I think this warrants more than that.

"I'm not going to lie and say I've always been a gentleman. I know I've hurt people, and I've been hurt, but Lucy..." I tilt her face until our eyes meet. "Something about you makes the idea of hurting you feel impossible. Something I can't even fathom. So no, I'm not going to hurt you."

Her eyes dart between mine, searching for something, maybe sincerity, so I hold my gaze. Never once wavering. I mean every word. And when she gives me the smallest nod before burying her face in my chest, I know she believes me. I'm stunned for a second, but as soon as I recover, my arms wrap around her, pulling her tightly against me.

I'm not used to this. My life is football, and Gran, and occasionally Carter. I've even had a girlfriend before, a serious one. At least, one I thought was serious in my earlier years. But this connection, right here, is new to me.

I've never wanted to protect someone so much in my entire life, and I don't even know what I'm protecting her from.

Lucy pulls back after a few minutes and straightens in my lap. "I wish I'd kept kissing you that day. Instead of running away. I should have stayed, kissed you again, and spent the night getting to know you."

My heart pounds in my chest as I try to read the meaning within her words. But when I can't, I try a different approach. "Why don't you stay a bit longer and get to know me now?" I ask, wanting more than anything to get to know *her*.

Her eyes flash with something like pain, but before I can question it, her expression morphs into one of calm and she smiles before whispering, "I would love that."

Chapter Seven

Lucy

W e talk for hours about everything...*anything*, and curl up on the couch to watch a movie. I must fall asleep at some point, because the next thing I know, I'm opening my eyes to a dark and quiet room and there's a blanket over me.

Sitting up in a bit of a daze, I'm trying to decide what to do, when Wes walks back into the room.

"You're awake?" he says with a genuine smile, not even at all bothered by the fact that I passed out on our date.

"Yes, sorry about that," I say with my voice coming out all raspy, and of course, I yawn at the end.

Wes shakes his head. "No, it was getting late. I should have walked you home hours ago. Come on, I'll take you now."

My chest tightens at his words and a feeling of panic takes over. I'm not ready to leave, even though I am tired. I meant what I said about wishing I'd stayed to get to know him that night. My life would be very different right now if I had. I'm not making that mistake twice.

"Is it okay if I stay?" I ask as my fingers pull nervously at the bottom of my shirt.

Wes looks surprised by my question but blurts out "yes," so quickly that I almost laugh. *Almost*. While the decision to stay here was an easy one, it doesn't mean I feel completely confident about it.

When his eyes dart between the bedroom and the sofa we're currently sitting on, I sense he's about to be the gentleman he claims *not* to be, so I beat him to the punch.

"I'm fine with sharing," I say, sitting tall. "But we can put pillows down the middle if you're worried," I add, using humor to hide just how nervous I am. I'm not sure what I'm asking by staying over, but considering the thumping in my chest has returned to normal, I know I made the right choice. I trust Wes, completely. And maybe that's wrong of me, but right now, it doesn't feel that way.

Wes's brows furrow as he looks toward the bedroom once more. Is he hiding something or just not interested in having someone in his space? I mean, it's not like this is a hotel room for him. It's currently his home. I probably wouldn't want a semi-stranger in my bedroom either.

"Mind if I have a moment to tidy up?" he says with a wince, and I can't stop the laugh that escapes me.

"I'd welcome it," I joke and love when his lips thin into a smirk, his eyes crinkling as they do.

"I'll be right back."

Barely five minutes pass before the bedroom door opens again and Wes pokes his head out, his eyes immediately finding mine. "Okay, it's somewhat decent," he says, and I laugh again before following him into the room, unable to keep my gaze from roaming around, desperate to learn everything I can about him. But his room looks a lot like mine. Almost identical apart from a few minor details. There's no personal belongings, no photos. The only new information I learn is that he seems to like blue, with shades of the color scattered around the place. Blue suitcase, blue shirts in his closet, various blue baseball caps.

Wes takes off his watch and gently places it in a box beside his bed. It's then I remember his sponsorship deal with Tag Heuer and make a mental note to find out what he really thinks of the brand. I'm always curious.

When he looks my way with raised eyebrows and a playful expression, I realize I'm still standing in the doorway and push off the wall, hesitantly stepping inside, making my way over to the bed.

"Do you want the pillows between us?" Wes asks, and I giggle while shaking my head.

"I don't need them."

He simply nods in answer, before his eyes rake over my body and he frowns, his gaze flashing toward the dresser. "What about something to sleep in?"

"*That*, I need. I kind of have nothing with me since you kidnapped me from class." I wink, making Wes chuckle as he pulls a tee from the top drawer, throwing it my way.

"You're tiny, so my shorts will swim on you, but we can try and roll them up," he says, reaching back into his drawers.

"No, that's okay," I say, and Wes freezes, his hand hovering in midair. "The tee is enough, but thank you."

Somehow the idea of standing in front of him wearing only his tee and my panties has my heart beating erratically for reasons I didn't expect. I'm not nervous or panicked. The idea actually thrills me.

Wes, on the other hand, looks positively terrified as he visibly swallows, turning with wide eyes to gaze at the bed. I bite back a smile and walk toward what I assume is the en suite. "Can I change in here?" I ask, pointing to the door.

He nods again but doesn't meet my eye.

Stripping off my clothes is fine, but the moment I slip the tee over my head, sans bra, I freeze, suddenly acutely aware of the situation I've put myself in. I barely know Wes. It's been less than a week, and for some reason, I'm standing in his bathroom half naked. Am I crazy? Yes. But that has nothing to do with this situation. Do I believe Wes when he says he would never hurt me? Also yes, but then again, I foolishly believed all my other ex-boyfriends, right? *Didn't I?* Come to think of it, deep down I never did. I just accepted it because on their good days, things were amazing, I was worshipped. It was easy to forget the bad.

This doesn't feel at all like *that*. Wes hasn't given me any reason to doubt his words. Not even a single red flag. And I trust him, one hundred percent. Why? I have no idea. Call it gut instinct, but I do.

Taking a deep breath, I stretch Wes's tee at the hem, trying to cover more skin. But when it doesn't help, I close my eyes and gather my strength instead. I can do this. This is my choice. I'm in control.

Pushing open the door, I find Wes sitting on the edge of the bed, hunched over with his face in his hands. When the door creaks, his head flies up, and his eyes meet mine. For a split second, his gaze drops to my bare legs before darting back to my face, and when our eyes lock a second time, his are ablaze with want.

Now it's my turn to nervously swallow.

My heart races as I tiptoe barefoot across the room. Why I'm on my toes, I don't know. Maybe it has something to do with the room being so quiet and not wanting to disrupt that. Or maybe it's something else.

Stopping when I'm next to the bed, I watch as Wes stands, pulling back the covers so we can both get in. "Last chance for the pillows," he jokes, but it's clear as day that he's still secretly hoping it's an option.

I shake my head with a soft smile before making myself comfortable on the mattress, curling my knees up as I face his side of the bed. Wes joins me but keeps his distance, and we're both silent for a beat.

"I'm a sleep talker. Always have been," he admits without looking my way, and I laugh out loud, internally thanking him for breaking our silent tension.

"I've been known to throw a punch here and there," I joke and am rewarded with Wes's gaze shooting to mine as he rolls over to face me. "Fuck! I've felt that left hook. I'm regretting this decision right now."

"No take backs."

"Damn. Okay, punches I can handle. You don't kick though, do you? Do I need to cover my junk?"

I laugh again, playfully shoving at his chest. "I promise not to touch your junk," I say and instantly regret it when Wes raises a hand in defense.

"Hey! I never said you couldn't touch it. I'm just against kicking," he says, bouncing his eyebrows while reaching out to stroke my arm. I *walked right into that one.*

Biting back a smile, I shake my head and ignore the way his touch coats my body in goose bumps. Wriggling over, I place a gentle kiss on his cheek before retreating back to my position. "Goodnight, Wes."

Wes laughs, kissing my head in return before we both settle into our sides of the bed, our fingers connecting as we do. "Goodnight, Lucy," he says before closing his eyes. His actions speak so loudly, I know I can trust him, making it easy to fall asleep.

Sometime during the night, I feel Wes's hand grip my hip, and I can't say if I'm dreaming or if it's real. We're walking side by side along the beach, but instead of waves crashing, it's eerily silent. *What's going on?* When his hand squeezes, I startle awake, and my eyes flash open. *Dream then.* Although...

"Fuck, sorry," Wes whispers, as his hand disappears from my body. *Maybe only half dreaming.*

With lightning speed, I reach behind me and clasp his wrist, wordlessly moving his hand back to where it was. I'm confused between what's real and what's not, but I know I want him to touch me and I haven't wanted that lately.

Nothing more happens after that, and I slowly drift back to sleep. I'm balancing on the edge of a dream once more when Wes's hand twitches and drops from my body. I feel the loss immediately, so like last time, I reach for it and secure it back in place. Wes inhales deeply and stills for a second before slowly moving his hand up and down my leg, hesitating every few seconds until I wriggle to let him know I want more, my entire body coming to life as I feel his touch everywhere.

His fingers brush against me from my waist down to my thigh with a featherlight touch, but there's a roughness to his skin that has my body breaking out in shivers. And when he moves back up along my side, wordlessly repeating the movement a second and third time, I'm completely on edge. Especially when on the fourth go, his fingers spread out, and his hand shifts to the inside of my leg.

My breath hitches as he moves closer to my core, but I don't dare speak. His caress is driving me wild, and I'm not ready for him to pull away if I do.

The hairs all over my body stand on end as I anticipate his touch, hoping he'll continue on his path as my core pulses with need, and I have to fight not to clench. The tips of his fingers dance along my skin toward the apex of my thighs, only stopping when they hit the lace of my panties and he sucks in a breath.

"Fuck, Lucy..." he rasps before trailing off. The sound of his voice sends another shiver through me, further increasing my desire to have him.

Several seconds pass with him unmoving, and when it becomes clear that he's hesitant to go any farther than my panty line, I cover his hand with mine and take the lead.

Moving our joined hands between my legs, I put pressure on Wes's finger as we journey over my mound. He groans and shuffles himself closer to me, giving himself extra reach, and then takes back control, sliding my panties to the side before running his finger through my heat.

"Oh, God. Wes."

My hips rise off the bed as his fingers explore me. I need to get closer. I need more. He's barely touched me and I'm a writhing mess, squirming with pleasure. And when his finger finally slips inside me, a collective moan rips from the two of us before we both still, our frantic breaths being the only sound to break the silence.

Adding a second finger, Wes scissors them inside me, so slowly that I almost cry out in desperation. I don't know if he's teasing or worried, but either way, he has my nerve endings on full alert, the slightest touch sending my body to heaven and my pulse skyrocketing.

With his fingers buried deep inside me, he readjusts his position until he's hovering on top of me, his weight resting on his elbow. Brushing my hair off my face with his free hand, he gently presses his lips to mine as his fingers start to pump, increasing the speed as he goes.

"Oh, fuck, Wes..." I'm panting against his lips, not wanting to break our connection but unable to stop the words spilling from my mouth.

Wes sucks on my lip before releasing it with a pop, sending another bolt of electricity through to my core. "I got you," he says, giving me another chaste kiss. "And I don't want to let go."

My heart stills, and I cry out as everything hits me at once. He doesn't even know it, but his touch, his kiss, his words...everything he does is erasing the darkness from my past. And when he curls his fingers inside me, I'm done for.

"Yes, yes!" I call out as my release rips from within me and my body spasms uncontrollably.

Wes's movements slow, but he doesn't stop until I practically beg him to. Until his touch has me thrashing around, unable to take it anymore.

He drops to the bed beside me as if he's the one who's spent, and then licks his fingers before wrapping his arm around me.

"Sorry I woke you," he rasps, and I burst out laughing, rolling onto my side, bringing us face-to-face.

"I've never been *less* sorry," I whisper, my hand on his chest. "And I'm not ready for this to be done."

Chapter Eight

Wes

I never intended to take things that far, but when Lucy's hand landed on top of mine, all my good intentions went out the window. I knew my touch was affecting her. I could feel the blood pumping through her, pulsating toward her core, the way her skin pebbled with goose bumps as my fingertips feathered along her body, and when her breath hitched... *fuck!*

I've spent the last few days fucking my hand so I could avoid taking things too far too quickly, but all that went to shit the second she moaned my name.

I need inside her more than I need my next breath, but I also need her to initiate it. I'm not blind; I know we have a connection. I've seen the fire in her eyes. But I can also see the walls she's erected, the guard she has up, the hesitancy. I need to be one hundred percent sure she wants more before I show her *exactly* how much I want it.

We're both silent for a moment as her words hang in the air. *She's not ready for this to be done.* Does she mean tonight? Or does *this* mean us? I'm kinda hoping it's both. She peers at me through hooded eyelids and I'm caught in her gaze. The rise and fall of her chest, paired with her flushed cheeks, has me in a daze. This girl is tugging at my heart, and she doesn't even realize it. I've known her for a week. Actually less than that. No one has ever had this hold on me, and all I know about her is her name. *Basically, I'm fucked!*

Breaking whatever trance we're in, I pull her into my arms and press a kiss to her head. "You're so goddamn beautiful, Lucy. Thanks for picking me on the beach that day."

She giggles and tries to hide a yawn before speaking through it. "Honestly, it was slim pickings. I picked the best of a bad bunch."

"Well, consider me honored," I joke, settling Lucy's head on my chest before running my hands through her hair. "You need to sleep."

Her head shoots up in protest, but I gently push it back down. "Sleep. We can explore more of what you want in the morning. My practice isn't until eleven."

She sighs but gets herself comfortable against me, running her hand along my skin until it rests on my hip before wrapping her leg around me. I continue to rake my fingers through her silky strands as I hum quietly, something my mom used to do, and within minutes, Lucy's peacefully asleep again, with no idea how much having her in my arms is affecting me.

I'm losing my mind, and I can't for the life of me figure out what's different about this girl.

My internal alarm wakes me at five a.m., and despite having little sleep, I feel well rested. After my middle of the night fun with Lucy, I passed out cold and slept better than I have in years. Waking with her tiny frame still curled into my body and her leg entwined with mine is a place I always want to be. She has her hand splayed over my naked chest and her face tucked into my shoulder. She's so close, her eyelashes brush against my skin as she dreams.

I don't want to move, but I also want to surprise her with breakfast and convince her to spend the day here, even though I have to disappear for practice. The idea of kissing someone goodbye and then returning to her welcoming me home is something I've never really thought much about, but right now, I'm almost desperate to make it happen. Which I'm sure has everything to do with knowing we're on borrowed time.

I gently lift Lucy's hand and place it on the pillow beside her head before slipping out of bed. She groans in protest, still fast asleep, and the sound sends a message of attention straight to my cock, as if my morning wood wasn't bad enough. *Looks like I'm going to need a quick shower before breakfast.*

Lucy only sleeps for another hour, then joins me in the kitchen as I'm flipping the last pancake. My chest tightens as I watch her rub her sleepy eyes and brush her messy hair behind her ears, still dressed in only my tee. My college football tee I might add. Something I never even let my college girlfriend wear.

She smiles when she catches me staring, and a slight blush brightens her cheeks. "You made pancakes?" she asks, licking her lips as she gently tugs at her hem, trying to stretch it to cover her legs. *Don't hide away. Everything about you is beautiful.*

"They'll be ready in a sec," I say, instead of my thoughts. "Take a seat, and I'll bring them over."

Lucy lightly pads into the kitchen to join me, ignoring my instructions, and immediately grabs a strawberry. After dipping it into the maple syrup, she slowly raises it to her mouth, pausing as the liquid touches her. Her eyes spark with mischief as she coats those lips in the sugary goodness, just like I did last night.

"I think you need to taste test this syrup. You don't want to serve something that isn't perfect," she says as the tip of her tongue sneaks out to test a sample.

I bite back a groan and nod. "No, we definitely don't want that."

Leaning forward, I run my tongue along the seam of her mouth so lightly that she moves forward as though desperate for more. And when I pull back, she dips the strawberry into the bowl again and smears the liquid across my cheek, following the trail with her tongue. Clenching my fist, I bite back another groan and will my eyes to stay open, trying to maintain my composure. But when she seductively sucks the strawberry into her mouth and picks up another one, it's on...

Barely a few minutes later, maple syrup coats my face, neck, and hands as Lucy sucks my finger from base to tip. Gripping her face in one hand, I pull the other from Lucy's grasp and run a syrupy finger down her cheek and neck then along to her collar bone as low as her tee allows. I want nothing more than to rip my shirt clear off her and continue my path of destruction, but instead, I opt to lick every inch of her that I can see, loving the taste of the sweetness mixed with her skin. She squeals and tries to pull away, but I hold firm, pulling the neck of the tee she's wearing down to run my tongue along the top of her cleavage. My hands bunch in the material as she hisses out a breath and pushes me away.

"Okay, enough. I need to shower." She giggles, and the sound takes over me. I'm already more worked up than I should be, considering I have to leave shortly for practice, and now there's talk of a shower. *When did my shorts get so tight?*

Lucy stares at me as she sucks her lips into her mouth, holding back a smile. And when she raises an eyebrow in question, I realize I haven't responded to her statement.

"Shower...right. Yes, of course. I'll get you a towel."

Well, that was smooth. I don't mean to sound so disappointed, but I guess I was pretty happy with getting messy, and now she wants to be clean.

Lucy laughs before slowly licking the syrup off her fingers, her gaze unfocused, as though she's lost in thought. It's so erotic I have to clench my fists again to stop myself from throwing her over my shoulder and taking her to bed to devour her. From the innocent look on her face, I'd say she either has no idea what she's doing to me, or she's a damn good tease. But I'd easily wager it's the former when she blinks a few times and her chest flushes.

With a shy smile, Lucy walks away as I stand frozen for a second, needing a moment. But when I hear the shower running, I spring into action, remembering she needed a towel.

Towel in hand, I adjust the bulge in my pants and knock on the bathroom door. "Want me to bring it in or leave it by the door?" I ask, my voice coming out raspy.

"You can come in. I'm decent."

The first thing I see when I walk inside is the mirror, and reflected back at me is a very *decent* and very *naked* Lucy. *Fuck me!*

I quickly look away in case she hasn't realized I'd be able to see her, but when she giggles again, I know that's not the case.

I feel her presence behind me before I've had the chance to turn, and then her hands wrap around my waist as she kisses the middle of my back before resting her head where the tingle remains from her touch. "I need you to join me," she says in a sultry tone, and if I wasn't already rock-hard, my cock would have instantly stood to attention.

My eyes close as my body sinks into her. "Need?" I ask.

"More than you could possibly imagine." *Fuuuck!*

Detaching her hands from my body, I spin around to face her, not wanting to waste another second. I couldn't hold back even if I tried.

Backing her into the shower, I don't even bother removing my clothes as I follow her in, framing her face in my hands. She's practically panting as I stare in her eyes, wanting to make sure I understood her meaning—needing the confirmation. While the desire reflected there should be enough, it's the slight nod she gives that has me crashing my mouth to hers and pushing her back against the tiles as the water cascades over us.

Lucy moans when I suck her bottom lip into my mouth, running my tongue over the edge. She grips the hem of my tee and attempts to peel the soaked top from my body but gives up after a few tries, moving to my shorts instead. I reluctantly release her face and quickly undress, enjoying the breathless thank you Lucy gives me.

As soon as I'm naked, my focus returns to her, and I bend to suck her nipple into my mouth, loving the way she arches her back and breathlessly moans as she scrapes her fingers through my hair, pulling me closer until I have no choice but to suck harder.

"Yes, oh, God." Her raspy voice sends a bolt of electricity straight through me, and it takes everything in my power to stop myself from gripping my length, wanting for it to be Lucy's touch that gets me off.

Running my free hand from her shoulder, across her collarbone, and down her chest, I give her other breast some attention, massaging and pinching before moving on. She hisses at me when I flick her nipple, but it turns into a drawn out moan when I continue my path, only stopping again when I reach the warmth between her legs.

"Fuck, Wes," she whimpers as I run a finger through her heat, immediately pushing it inside her. *Fuck, alright.* There's no way I could have waited any longer.

After pumping in and out a few times, I'm about to add a second finger when she grabs my wrist to stop me, making my heart jolt, along with my body. "Fuck, did I do someth—"

"No, God no," she rushes out. "I want more. I..."

She trails off and bites her lip, but I'm almost certain I know what she's trying to say, so I take a chance on it.

Walking her backward until she hits the bench seat, I thank God for luxurious hotel showers. Her ass hits the tiled surface, and her brows pull in confusion until I drop to my knees in front of her, spreading her legs wide.

Biting my knuckle, I groan at the sight of her stripped bare, glistening in front of me. This feels like a privilege. Having her vulnerable like this is something I will never take for granted. She's perfect, and in this very moment, she's *mine*.

Lucy stares down at me through lust-filled eyes, her thick hair stuck to her face as drops of water stream down her chest, pooling at the crease of her waist. Everything about her is mouthwatering, and it's almost my undoing. But I hold strong. This is her moment.

My pulse spikes as I plan my next move, and when I run my palms along the inside of her thighs, toward her core, Lucy's breath hitches, and she clenches in front of me.

Fuuuck.

Spreading her legs farther, I practically face-plant into her, eliciting a groan from both of us as Lucy clenches again and her legs tighten around me in a vise-like grip.

"This...this isn't what I meant, but oh, God, don't stop."

Wasn't planning on it, baby. And I knew exactly what she meant, but I'm not ready for that.

I lick, and suck, and tease her with my fingers until she's flailing uncontrollably, with her legs locked so tightly around me that I'm lucky my blood's still circulating. When I look up from my position between her legs, my mouth still working her into a frenzy, she grabs my head in her hands and cries out in ecstasy. Her cheeks flush, as her mouth drops open and her head falls back against the wall.

I groan against her core, and her body arches, squeezing my head even more as she bucks against me. And fuck, I don't ever want this to stop. Watching Lucy lose control is something I'll never tire of.

After a few more seconds, she pushes me away and stands up, leaning against the wall to support herself on wobbly legs. "Sit...now," she demands, and I almost laugh at how adorable she is, looking all hot and sated. But since she said *now* and looks all growly, there's no chance I'm going to take my time and risk pissing her off and missing out on whatever comes next.

Pushing off the floor, I sit as instructed and rest my palms on the seat at my sides. Lucy's gaze moves from my chest down to my hard length, and we both watch as it twitches from her attention. Begging for her touch. For anything she'll give me.

Biting her lip, Lucy closes her eyes and releases a quiet moan as she softly wraps her hand around me.

"Fuck, Luce. You're killing me," I grate out, causing her eyes to flash to mine, a little dazed, like she'd forgotten there's a man attached to the appendage. Without a word, she lets go and crawls onto my lap, running her soaked core back and forth on top of me, her eyes focused on our connection. *Yep, she's trying to kill me.*

Another groan rips from within me, and I almost come on the spot. I need her now. She's had me worked up since the second she licked maple syrup off my face, and now I'm ready to explode. And yet, when she grabs my length again and lifts herself up, I grip her waist to still her, stopping her in her tracks.

"We need protection."

Her face falls, and I know I'm an idiot, but I want to keep her safe.

Letting go of her hips, I grab her face in my hands and wait for her to look at me. "This is one hundred percent about protecting you. I want nothing more than to fuck you bare, but we should wait until you fully trust me for that."

Lucy's eyes widen and she nods. "For some unknown reason, I trust you more than I've ever trusted anyone I've been with. I'm on the pill. I need to feel you inside me. *You*, not some rubber."

"Holy fuck, Lucy. I'm all clear, I promise."

I barely get the promise out when she sinks down on top of me, and, "Jesus Christ!" I groan, once again gripping her hips as she wraps her arms around my neck before we both still for a second, as though both needing a moment to process what's happening.

I've never felt anything like this. I mean, I've never been bare before, even with my exes, but that's not what I'm referring to. Every nerve ending in my body is firing, not just the ones in my cock, and my heart is thumping so hard, I'm pretty sure she can hear it. I've never been a corny motherfucker, but my thoughts are going there...Lucy feels like she was made for me. I twitch inside her, and she moans, squeezes me back. Both tiny movements, but it's enough to end our cease-fire, and within seconds, she's slamming down on top of me while I pump up into her, frantic and needy. It's not at all how I pictured our first time, but it's fucking amazing, and I wouldn't change a thing.

"Fuck, Lucy. I can't get enough of you. I'm buried so deep, but I need more."

She cries out in pleasure and pulls my face to hers, sucking my lip into her mouth. My body jolts as a spark runs through me, and I have to still her again to calm myself down. She laughs as I squeeze her hips, desperately trying not to come before she reaches her climax for a second time. And when she laughs again, I growl before I start moving, slower this time, shooting a fake glare her way. "Stop laughing. You're fucking sexy when you're happy, and it's not helping my cause."

Her eyes brighten, and her laughter stops, replaced by a warm smile as she presses her lips to mine and rocks against me, matching my slow pace.

We continue like that, connected in every possible way until we're both panting. The water flowing over us has long ago turned cool, but neither of us seem bothered by it.

When I feel her tighten around me, I press my thumb to her core while lifting her up to change our angle, pumping harder as I do. "Yes, that's it." She pants and moans, cursing until her walls squeeze me so tight that I explode inside her at the same time she screams out my name.

"Fuck, Lucy. Fuck!"

She falls into me but continues to pulse as we both come back down to earth. And when I wrap my arms around her, holding her firmly against me, I almost sigh in contentment.

"Thank you, Canada," I whisper, referring to the maple syrup, and chuckle when Lucy bursts out laughing.

Burying her face in my neck, she shakes her head as she whispers back, "I'm not sure I'll ever look at pancakes the same."

Chapter Nine

Wes

I race out of my truck, right on time for practice…again. Seconds later and I would have been fined. I'm pretty certain Coach will let it slide, as long as I don't make it a habit, but Carter is going to ream me. He knows what I've been through, and he knows the hard work I've put in to prove I'm not really the person I was painted to be. That football comes first. That it's always come first. And he's right. Yet, as I walk into the locker room, bag carelessly tossed over my shoulder, I can't bring myself to care. Okay, obviously I care, but I made it on time. I'm here. That should be enough.

Just as I suspected, Carter's tapping his wrist when I reach our side-by-side lockers. His expression screams disappointment, but when I simply shrug, it turns to disbelief.

"I don't like this, man," he says as I drop down on the bench seat in front of him.

"I never asked for your opinion."

"No, you didn't, but you fucking should. Remember last time? Or do I need to refresh your memory?"

I can't stop my eyes from rolling as I pull my sweater over my head. "I was a rookie. A kid. This is different. I won't let it get to me like that."

His eyes widen as he gives me a pointed look. "Is it different? Are you or are you not late because of a girl?"

"I'm not late. In fact, I'm going to be ready before you are." I gesture to the sweatpants he's still wearing as I roll mine down my legs. "And this is completely different."

"I'm just looking out for you."

"I know. But you don't have to worry. She'll be gone in twenty-four hours and then life will be back to normal. You'll have me all to yourself again. Because that's what this is really about, right?" I'm talking complete shit to get him to shut up, but if it works, I'll be happy. Only the words burn me to say. Twenty-four hours? That's it. Fuck, I feel sick.

Carter eyes me curiously, so I add a wink for extra emphasis, and laugh when he slaps me in the chest. A laugh that's definitely a little forced.

"I have other friends," he mumbles under his breath as we continue getting ready, and his sulking makes me laugh for real this time.

"Of course you do."

I'm wrecked when practice is done and dragging my feet as I walk across the parking lot. My head's in the clouds, or more specifically, back on the field, running through the easy play I kept fucking up. Is Carter right to be worried? He's right about my mind not fully being on the game, but I'm certain it's because things with Lucy are up in the air. And if I talk to her and sort out my feelings, and hers, it'll be better.

I'm almost at my truck when a pap shoves a mic in my face, making me jump. "Jesus. Chill, man. If you have a question, asking it from a distance will get the same result."

"Really?" he asks, not believing a word out of my mouth. But I'm telling the truth. Just not in the way he thinks.

"Yep, really. I'm not going to answer any of your questions, no matter where you're standing. You can talk to me after the game like everyone else." I keep walking, ignoring his annoyed stare.

"What if it's about your personal life?"

That pulls me up short. I wish I hadn't reacted. I wish I'd just kept walking. But that small hesitation, the tiny pause in step, tells him everything he needs to know.

"Yeah, that's what I thought. Answer my question, and I'll leave you and your new girl alone." *Fuck!*

I turn to face him with a bored expression. It's fake boredom because I'm desperate to know what he has to say, but I think he's buying it. "What's the question?"

"Are you dating the sister of Denver's new wide receiver?"

What the actual fuck? This guy's done his research. Dylan's not even on the media's radar yet. I know, because I looked him up.

"I can confidently say that I'm not," I answer truthfully because we haven't defined it. If he'd asked if I was sleeping with her, that would have been different.

"Okay, let me rephrase." *Fuck!*

"Nope. You got your question. I did exactly what you asked."

"I've got photos, man. So we can do this the easy or the hard way."

My fists clench by my thighs, but my face remains composed. I can't give in. No matter what he claims to have. Lucy and I haven't done anything other than kiss in public, and there's been photos of me kissing in public before. It's no big deal; it'll blow over. Yes, it's usually during the off-season, but still, a kiss is nothing.

"Write what you have to. I'm sure it will be a lie no matter what I say."

"But—"

"Are we all good here?" our offensive coordinator calls out from behind us, cutting off the crap about to spew out of the pap's mouth. "Come on, Dave. You know the drill. There's a time and place for questioning my players."

Dave turns around. "And I usually respect that, but this isn't football related."

Coach has his hand on his hips, his bullshit radar on high alert. "*Everything* is football related. On your way."

I'm surprised when Dave listens and heads to his Porsche. The flashy car he probably paid for by ruining the lives of others.

"You too, Wes. On your way."

"I'm gone," I say with a nod, definitely ready to be out of here.

I've just opened my door when Coach calls out again. "And whatever he's looking for, sort it. I'm not stupid. I know something's going on. Don't let it fuck up your game."

After serving him another quick nod, I jump in my truck and out of his judging sight. People keep assuming the worst and it's pissing me off. I've got this. I'm in control. *I think.*

Lucy doesn't welcome me home like I'd hoped. She never agreed to that caveman plan. But she's knocking on my door, not even five minutes after I've walked through, so I'm happy all the same.

"How was practice?" she asks, flopping down on the sofa with her legs over the armrest. I smile at how comfortable she's become around me, as bit by bit I break down those walls.

"Practice was practice. I'd rather hear about you. What did you get up to?"

"Well, I had the farewell lunch for the conference, and now, I'm stuffed full of decent food and resting on your couch."

"Sounds like fun."

"It's my idea of a good day. Good food, soft couches, hot men. Can't complain." She shrugs, closing her eyes in contentment.

"Hot men, huh?" Raising my eyebrows, I pull my lips into my mouth and bite back a smile. Partly because I don't want her to know how much she's affecting me, but also because I know she's about to sass me.

"Yeah, this guy at the conference is...smoking!" *And there it is.*

"It's nice to have someone decent to look at while you're working. I've got that with Carter."

Lucy bursts out laughing as she shakes her head. "Ugh! I don't want to go home. I'm not ready."

"Then don't. Stay here..." *Forever, if you want.* Whoa! Where did that come from?

Lucy smiles, completely unaware of my silent request to keep her.

"Unfortunately, my time is up. I have to check out in the morning. But don't worry. I'm not going to disappear on you. In fact, I have a surprise that you're going to love." She's full of confidence until the last word leaves her mouth. After that, her forehead creases, and she worries her bottom lip before releasing it. "At least, I think you will," she continues, this time a little nervously.

"If it has anything to do with today *not* being the last time I see you, then I'm all for it." As my words hit her, she relaxes into the seat. I'm not sure why she's nervous when I've been like a damn moth to a flame around her. Surely she knows I'm not ready for goodbye either. But either way, I smile before pulling her to her feet for a kiss.

We spend the afternoon lazing around and finish the day off where our story began.

"Well, this is very romantic," Lucy says as we walk hand in hand along the water's edge, the sun setting on the horizon. She's not wrong. It's pretty epic. I've lived here for a few months and never once taken the time to appreciate how truly beautiful it is. Although, the vision beside me is even better.

"I have been known to find it in me, every once in a while. If I dig down deep enough."

Lucy laughs, nudging me in the side. "I guess I should thank you then, for putting in the effort."

"Only for you, Luce. Only for you." I nudge her right back.

We walk in silence a little farther, ankle deep into the fresh waves, until Lucy cries out and practically leaps into my arms. "What was that?"

I fight to hold back a laugh as I catch her. "What was what?"

"Something swam across my foot." She's leaning away from my body, searching the water for the culprit, and when she looks back at me, I lose the battle, laughing out loud.

"I'm going to go out on a limb here and say you are not from the beach."

She jumps out of my arms and positions herself at my side, away from the ocean. "Actually, you're wrong. I grew up pretty close to the beach. Doesn't mean I like things attacking me in the dark." I feel something brush along my toes and know exactly what she felt. Reaching into the waves, I subtly lift the seaweed into my hand and hide it behind my back as Lucy continues her rant. "I mean, it could have been anything. And I, for one, don't want to find out."

"So you're not interested in what I have behind me."

Lucy freezes before her hand flies to my chest, stopping me from stepping closer. "Don't even think about it."

I couldn't hold back my responding grin if I tried. "But don't you want me to put your mind at ease?"

"Nope. I'm perfectly happy in my blissful ignorance."

She takes a subtle step back, then another, and when I follow with my own step, she takes off in a run, giggling as she does.

Holding the seaweed in front of me, I make chase, catching up to her in an instant, but letting her stay ahead, enjoying my view from behind her. "I'm coming for you," I joke, trying hard to keep my distance as she calls over her shoulder.

"Stay back. I don't want whatever that is near me."

I laugh out loud as I snap at her heels. "You really should take a look at it, Luce."

She spins as she moves, continuing to jog backward. It's dark now, so while her gaze is laser focused on the grassy mess in my hand, she hasn't quite figured out what it is. Recognition hits at the same time she stumbles, and the laughter makes it hard for her to balance. I abandon the seaweed and leap toward her, catching her in my arms right before she hits the sand.

"My hero," she laughs out, gripping my biceps for dear life.

"But also your tormentor." I laugh back.

Her face turns serious for a second, and she shakes her head. "No, that's not you."

She blinks a few times and then smiles, pushing to her feet. "That was a close one." She laughs again, but this one feels a little forced. "I think I've had enough excitement for the night."

I want to laugh along with her, but I'm still reeling from her reaction to my joke comment. *What did she mean?*

"First a sea creature attacks me, then you chase me with seaweed, and that almost fall... Yep, I'm all beached out."

"There were no sea creatures," I chuckle, snapping myself out of my head.

Lucy shrugs before turning away from the ocean. "Agree to disagree," she says, reaching her hand back for me to take. I link our fingers and let her pull me along, only stopping once we're on dry sand to tug her back toward me and wrap her in my arms.

"Despite your near death experience, today was fun. Thank you."

Lucy laughs into my chest, giving me a squeeze. "You're a good guy, Wes." Running her hands up my body, she secures them around my neck, her gaze following the movement until she's peering up at me through her long lashes. "I'm so happy to have met you."

This feels like a goodbye of sorts, but when I try to ask about it, she cuts me off. "I didn't mean anything by it. Just wanted you to know."

I give her a piggyback the rest of the way—to avoid any more incidents—and when we're back at the resort, we have dinner together again.

Unlike last night, we keep it light, and when it's done, she decides to head home. With practice scheduled for early tomorrow, plus my need to keep the ball in her court, I don't argue. Though I do insist on walking her to her room.

"You know this is a *see you later* situation, not *farewell*, right?" Lucy says as we reach her door. She plays with the ends of her windswept hair, and I mentally sigh in relief, not having realized how much I needed to hear those words.

"Glad we're on the same page. Are you ready to tell me where you live?" I ask, acting the picture of cool even though deep down this question has me on edge. I want this girl. I don't even want to contemplate not seeing her again. But I'm not a huge fan of long distance, so I'm hoping the travel is on the shorter side.

Lucy beams up at me as she shakes her head. "Tomorrow, I promise. It's all part of the surprise."

That's gotta mean she's close, right? I could handle Los Angeles or San Diego. Both are beachy, and she mentioned growing up near one.

"Tomorrow then. But at least tell me this...are you flying or driving home?"

"Driving," she answers quickly.

Fuck, yes! My heart thumps in my chest at the very possibility that this may all work out. The car she's been using must not be a rental because she's driving. I have a truck. I don't have a lot of spare time, but we can make it happen.

"And do you enjoy a good long road trip?" I ask, trying to get as many clues as possible.

Lucy smirks. "Hate them. I'd definitely opt to fly." Yes!

I don't even bother to act chill this time as a megawatt smile lights up my face. "Good to know, Luce. Good to know."

Holding my arms out wide, I love when she steps into them, perfectly folding herself into my chest. "Has that put your mind at ease?" she asks, looking up at me.

"I was never even worried," I joke and she barks out a laugh, clearly not believing my bullshit.

"So, we'll talk tomorrow?" she says with a hint of vulnerability, despite her teasing.

"Just try and stop me," I reassure her before dropping my mouth to hers in a slow and gentle kiss.

Our lips brush lightly, our tongues tangling, exploring, molding into one as my hand moves into her hair, cupping her head to increase the pressure between us. Lucy moans into my mouth, and my pants once again tighten. Like every sound she makes is my undoing.

Gripping my shirt, Lucy bunches the fabric between her fingers, sucking my lip into her mouth. And the kiss turns frantic. We make out in front of her door until we're both desperately in need of a breath, but intake only enough air to keep going.

Voices get louder in the halls as a group walks our way, and we spring apart like we've been caught doing something wrong. Lucy giggles as her fingers brush over her lips, a look of pure lust in her eyes. I smirk back at her, my chest rising and falling in sync with hers as we both catch our breath, waiting for the intruders to pass by.

The second they're gone, I pull her into my arms, wrapping her in a hug. "Talk tomorrow," I reconfirm before taking a step back.

"You'll be begging to get rid of me by the time we're done," Lucy jokes as she opens her door.

Her glowing smile is my parting gift and something I'll be picturing every day until we see each other again. Which will be sooner rather than later if I have my way. Because while she may have said it as a joke, us being *done* is not even an option I'm considering right now.

Chapter Ten

Lucy

Falling back onto the bed, clothes in hand, I groan out loud. There is no part of me that wants to leave right now. Which I know is stupid, because I only live about thirty minutes away. But in the last week, I've grown accustomed to being close to Wes, and that's definitely going to change when I'm gone. I won't be able to meet him in the halls or catch up between our commitments.

Pulling out my phone, I shoot him a text because I seem to have this inability to stop thinking about him.

Lucy: Why didn't I get a late checkout, or I guess the better question is why didn't I pack last night?

He replies almost instantly, and I smile.

Wes: You were too busy being romanced

Lucy: I think you mean attacked

Wes: No, I definitely mean romanced

I laugh out loud as I throw my clothes at my bag, watching as half of them hit the floor. Not that I care. My heart is so full and happy that nothing could bring me back down to earth. I didn't think I had it in me to let someone else in, especially someone I just met. But getting to know Wes has been the best thing that could have happened. I'm not healed by any sense of the word, but I'm getting there, and I know he's the one that's going to break down my walls.

The hotel room phone rings, and I jump at the sound. It's the wakeup call I'd set in case I slept through my phone alarm. Which is always a strong possibility. But this time, I'm up, despite the fact the clock on the bedside table reads seven a.m., and I don't have to check out until ten. Sleep just isn't an option right now with the nervous energy running through me.

Staring up at the ceiling, my mind drifts back to Wes as I picture him on his way to practice. He's probably been up since five and feels fresh as a daisy...or something. I don't know. Point is...I'm sure he's not feeling tired and shit like I do.

When my cell vibrates again, I preemptively laugh at whatever he's about to say. I know it's going to be seaweed related. I can sense it. There's no way he's going to let that one go.

But when I look at the screen, it's not Wes, and my heart stops as I read the name in front of me. *Greg.*

My chest tightens, and my stomach churns. I don't want to read this, but at the same time, I need to know what he's got to say.

Greg: I saw the photo of you and that football player. Is that why you left? Or are you still playing hard to get?

Fuck! I don't even know what to process first. What photo? And why won't he leave me the hell alone? My phone chimes again, and it's a link to an online news article.

Wes Johnson at it again. Is San Francisco about to lose their new tight end for a girl?

What?

There's a photo attached of us kissing on the beach. It's impossible to make out our faces, but in the small accompanying photo, we're standing side by side, and it's clear to see it's the same people. I'm described as Dylan Mathers's little sister. And while they are wrong about their facts, whoever this writer is has taken the time to look me up.

Sucking in a breath as my heart thuds in my chest, I fight to stop myself from falling apart. Having Greg contact me is bad enough, but this... this makes me feel sick. Not to mention, I have no idea what the headline means.

I scan the first few lines of the article but have to stop when it makes me feel worse. Sources say Wes is arriving late to practice and messing up his game. And apparently, it's not the first time. I'm so confused, but I'm not about to believe an article when I could just ask Wes myself.

My thoughts swirl as I try to process it all. Lifting my phone to call Wes, I curse when I see another text waiting for me.

Greg: I'm coming over

Oh, God, oh, God. A chill runs through my entire body as moisture fills my eyes. *Don't cry. Don't cry. I'm okay. I'm not at home. He can't find me.* It's been over a month since I've seen him. He's been quiet. I thought he was done. *Why won't he leave me alone?* I don't want to go home. But I don't know where else to go.

Slowly lifting myself up off the bed, I call down to reception and ask to extend my stay. Luckily, it's midweek, so they offer me an extra day.

Picking up my suitcase, I dump everything onto the bed, searching for my toiletries. I've got Tylenol in here somewhere, and fuck, my head is hurting.

I feel uneasy and slightly on edge. My mind is whirring, my hands are shaking, and I'm downright jittery. When I finally locate my toiletry bag, I step back, tripping over something on the floor. My heart just about lodges in my throat as I imagine someone grabbing ahold of my foot. And while I know it's irrational and over-the-top, I can't control the way my heart races as I move toward the bathroom, dropping my hands to the sink as I stare at myself in the mirror. *I'm strong. I'm capable. I won't let anyone hurt me.*

Mindlessly rustling around in the bag, my eyes lock on my birth control pills and I freeze, with my hand hovering in midair. "Fuck! Fuck! Fuck! No, no, no."

Silent tears fall down my face as I stare at my bag, a panic taking over me. I've been on the sugar pills. I should have my period *right now*. I shouldn't have been able to have sex with Wes. How did I not notice that? And why hasn't it come? Fuck, this can't be happening. I can't even remember my last period. Was it last month? The one before?

I'm stressed, and I've only just started with this particular brand of pill, so more than likely it's just my body adjusting. Right? That's it. It's fine. *I'm fine.*

There are so many possibilities for my lack of period. It's *fine*.

I repeat the words over and over, but the tears continue to fall, and deep down, I know I'm lying to myself. *How the fuck could he do this to me?* Bile rises in my throat, as an aching throb fills my head. And when my body convulses, I drop to the floor, curling up into a ball.

I cry for what feels like hours, until the need for confirmation takes over. After pulling myself together for just long enough to focus, I grab my purse and head for the nearest pharmacy.

Sinking down onto the sand, I bury my face in my hands, letting the tears return. I did a test in the gas station bathroom across the road, and just like that dirty stall, my life's about to be a mess.

"Are you okay?" a soft voice asks from above me, breaking my thoughts. I frantically wipe my face before looking up into weathered eyes full of warmth and concern, and my tears once again fall.

"Not really," I say honestly, jumping slightly when she rests her hand on my shoulder, giving it a comforting squeeze.

"I'm a little old to sit down beside you," she says, unperturbed by my physical reaction to her. "But there's a bench over there if you want to talk about it."

I laugh between sniffles and find myself nodding without giving it any thought, completely out of character for me.

Brushing the sand from my legs as I stand, I smile at my savior. She's warmly smiling back at me, but I can see the concern etched in her expression and can only imagine what she sees when she looks at me.

"Come on, let's sit. I'm Katie," she says, motioning the way.

"Thank you, Katie."

Tears start to well again, but I brush them away before fol-lowing her to the bench seat and taking my position beside her. We both stare out into the ocean, silently listening to the waves crash against the shore, watching the rhythmic way the water flows. At least, that's what I'm doing, and the kind woman beside me lets me have my moment. She doesn't say anything, doesn't ask me to talk—she's just a comfortable source, patiently waiting for me to be ready.

Taking a deep breath, I close my eyes and let the words flow for the first time. "I'm pregnant."

Katie pats my leg softly but still doesn't speak, as if knowing there's more to it, more I need to get off my chest. So I continue. "The baby is my ex's. And he..." I can't say the rest. I can't talk about what happened. But she doesn't need to know the details. The tone of my voice and the tears in my eyes are enough to tell her this isn't something I wanted to happen.

Wrapping me in a hug, she rubs her hands up and down my arms as I cry, letting me completely lose my mind, never once letting go. She whispers soothing words of encouragement, and I take it all in. It's the exact reaction I'd have expected from my mother if she hadn't distanced herself from us emotionally after my father died, something that I'm sure has led to my hardened shell and the fact I don't let anyone in.

Katie stays with me for what feels like hours without me giving her any real information. She lets me cry, tells me it's going to be okay, offers to help in any way she can. And she's so freaking patient.

She's a complete stranger, and she's giving me more support than my own mother has in years. But I can't keep her here any longer. She has a life to get back to.

I sniff a few times and run my hands down my face, attempting to clear away all the sadness displayed there. Smiling over at her, I'm about to tell her I'm fine when she beats me to it, shaking her head.

"You've got me for as long as you need me, but is there someone we can call?"

My brows furrow as I consider her question. Dylan's my emergency contact, my one call from jail, my go-to guy. But he's not ready for this, and I'm not ready to tell him. He'll fly off the handle. He means well, but I can see his anger at the situation overshadowing the need to comfort me. Summer would be the next obvious choice, but I can't expect her to keep this from Dylan—it's not fair. And she shouldn't have to deal with that fallout. After those two, Wes comes to mind, and my stomach twists in knots. He doesn't need this right now. I don't even know what I'm going to do with my life. I can't bring someone else into the mix.

When I think of the next person, I don't even hesitate. "My friend Joel. He'll be here in a heartbeat," I say, knowing he's the best option.

Just over an hour later, I hear Joel's motorcycle pull into the parking lot, and feel a weight lift. "Lucy?" he calls out in concern as he jogs toward us, his eyes bouncing between me and the kind soul by my side. As soon as he reaches us, he engulfs me in a hug, holding me tightly without asking why. I'd probably cry if I had any tears left, but I don't, so what he gets is me shaking uncontrollably and murmuring into his chest.

"Shhh. It's going to be okay. I promise you. It's going to be okay," he whispers into my hair as he rocks me back and forth, over and over.

I feel so safe in his arms, and while it doesn't change my reality, I can't seem to pull away. But after a few more minutes,

Joel does it for me. "Thank you for... She's gone," he says, searching around for Katie.

What?

My head shoots up to see we're now alone. Katie's nowhere in sight. She stayed until I had someone to look after me, and for that I'll forever be grateful.

"Come on. Let's get you home," Joel says, rising to his feet, pulling me up with him.

He walks toward my car but stops when I squeeze his hand. "Actually, can we go back to the resort? All my stuff is there."

When we're back in my room, Joel makes a sandwich as I sit on the couch with my arms wrapped around my knees. He's talking or singing, I don't know; either way, it's not getting through to me as I stare out into space. I'm having a baby. A *baby*. With someone I despise. And no one even knows what he's done to me. I have no fucking idea what to do, and—

"*Lucy.*"

Huh?

Tilting my head, I shoot Joel a blank stare, not really caring if he tells me what he wants or not.

"Wes messaged," he says, eyeing me in question, waiting for my reaction. But when I simply shrug, he shakes his head and reads the message aloud, forcing me to focus.

Wes: Are you home yet? By the way, where is home?

"What do you want me to say?"

I feel sick as I run Wes's words through my head. I'd been joking about not telling him I lived so close, with grand plans to surprise him, but now...

"Tell him I'm home safe and leave it at that," I say, ignoring the second part of his text as Joel frowns, typing the response.

And when he hands me back my phone, I throw it across the room, not even flinching when it breaks.

"Why'd you lie? Or more to the point...why'd you make *me* lie?"

"It's complicated."

Joel shakes his head, his expression difficult to read, but I'd say it's a mix of concern and disappointment. "Don't do that, Luce. Don't push him away. I've been on the other end—"

Oh, god... "Delilah! Shit, I'm so selfish. I didn't even think. I just knew calling Dylan was a bad idea, and you're like a brother to me and—"

"Lucy, stop," he says, cutting me off as he drops to the couch beside me.

Joel and his girlfriend, Delilah, have been through so much, and I shouldn't have called him. *God. How could I do that?*

"It's okay," he continues. "I'm okay. *Delilah's* okay. We're both worried about *you*. And you're right, I think we need to work out a plan before we tell Dylan. He hates Greg. He's not going to like the fact that he's about to be in your life forever, even if it's just as a baby daddy."

My stomach churns as I think about Greg being in my life in any capacity. *Oh, no, it's...*

"I'm going to throw up."

I make it to the bathroom seconds before dispelling the contents of my stomach and find Joel right behind me, pulling the hair away from my face.

"How long has this been going on? Is this how you figured it out?" he asks, his tone soothing.

"Actually, that's the first time. I'm kind of hoping it's a one-off."

Joel chuckles softly, and I manage a smile through my nausea. "Yeah, I guess that's wishful thinking."

It only takes a minute before my stomach settles, and we've just walked back to the living room when Joel's phone starts to ring. He pulls it out of his pocket, cursing under his breath before silencing it. "Make sure I'm there when you tell Dylan. You're going to need the support."

He's half joking, but if he knew everything, he'd be just as upset as my brother. One of the reasons it's best to keep it to myself.

By late afternoon, I'm ready to go home, or at least check out of the resort. Joel helps carry my bags as I walk like a zombie to the front desk.

"Why don't you follow me to my place? You can stay the night. Our couch is pretty comfy," he says, his face twisted as though he's trying to hide the fact that he's lying. At least about the couch.

I try to smile, but it's forced. Instead, I nod because what choice do I really have? I can't go home with Greg's threat hanging over me, and I have nowhere else.

Joel wraps his arm around my shoulder after I've dropped the room keys back and leads me to the parking lot.

When we're a few feet from the car, he stops suddenly, a resigned sigh leaving his lips.

"What's going on? Why'd—"

"Lucy?"

Shit.

My head snaps up, and I step out of Joel's arms as though I've done something wrong, watching with a lump in my throat as Wes pushes off my car and steps toward us, a blank expression in place.

"I'd ask if you actually live here, but since you have your bag..."

My shoulders drop at the disappointment in his tone.

"I'm sorry, I..." I trail off because I don't have an excuse. He's not stupid, and deserves better than whatever was about to come out of my mouth.

"You lied," he rasps, shaking his head. And while that's not what I was about to say, I guess it's the truth, so I offer Wes a small nod.

"I see." *He hates liars.*

Joel's hand lands on my shoulder, and my eyes flash to his when he squeezes. "I'll give you two a minute."

My heart jolts at the thought, and I find myself shaking my head. I don't know what to say to Wes. I don't know what I want, but the thought of Joel walking away right now has me irrationally panicked. I grab his hand as he moves, keeping him in place, and feel awful when I notice Wes flinch. He steps forward, and my eyes widen with nerves, hating myself when his face drops at my expression. "What's going on, Lucy? Has something happened?"

Joel squeezes my hand in encouragement, but I can't do it. I can't drag him into this mess. It's *my* mess.

"I'm fine. I just didn't expect to see you."

Wes recoils like he's been slapped, and his eyes flash to Joel's, jumping to the wrong conclusion.

"No," I rush out. "It's not what you think."

"What do I think?"

"Joel's just a friend."

"Okkkaaay," Wes draws out, looking away, clearly confused.

"But I need to go."

His eyes snap to mine and narrow as he focuses on my features. "Where? Where are you going? Where's home?" His voice raises slightly. "Were you ever going to tell me?"

"I don't know!" I yell, once again lying through my teeth. I had every intention of telling him where I lived, but now...now I honestly think it's better he doesn't know.

Wes nods as though he accepts my answer, but I can see the hurt in his eyes.

Holding his gaze just about kills me, so for the briefest moment, my eyes flit to my car behind him. It's so quick, but he sees it, and his shoulders drop in defeat before he steps aside, no longer blocking the path. "I'll get out of your way. I don't want to add to whatever's going on. I just want you to be okay. I hope to hear from you soon."

He walks toward the glass doors of the resort without another word, not even looking back, and my stomach drops.

"Wes!" I call out, not ready to say goodbye. But when he turns around expectantly, all I can offer is an apologetic frown. He shakes his head and huffs out a laugh before walking away and out of my life.

The second the doors close, my body gives out, and I fall into Joel's arms as fresh tears take over. I hate what I've just done. I will never forget this moment. But my life's about to change, and the less complicated it is, the better. This is the right thing to do for both of us. I know it.

So why does it feel so wrong?

Chapter Eleven

Lucy – Summertime, almost five years later

"Come on, Katie. Uncle Dylan will be here any minute, and if we're late, we'll miss out on ice cream."

I hear her rushed footsteps down the hall as she runs toward me. *Of course, ice cream got her moving.*

"I'm heeeeere! Where is he?" She stands before me with her shoes in her hand and an expectant smile on her face. "Quick, Mommy. Put these on," she says, shoving the pink boots in my direction.

I raise an eyebrow, and she laughs. "Pleeease."

As soon as I bend down to help her, there's a knock on the door, and Dylan pokes his head through without waiting for a response. "Where's my favorite little girl?" he says with a beaming smile.

"Uncle Dylan!" Katie screams, jumping to her feet, shoes abandoned. She takes off in a run and throws herself into his open arms, snuggling her face into his chest. He was traded to San Francisco last year, and the move has been a godsend. We've loved having him closer to home.

When Katie was first born, Joel kind of took on the father figure role for her, without even being asked. He was there for me from the second I called him, and his support has never wavered. On top of that, Delilah and Summer have been my guardian angels. They're always showing up randomly for one reason or another, making sure we're both good. Even after Summer moved to Denver, she'd still help as often as she could. Then I've had Logan and Dani, and Cory and Nate. And Thomas...

But Dylan and Katie...they have a special bond that can't be rivaled. Just like Dylan and I had when we were kids.

"Hi, little bug. Are you ready for a fun day?" Dylan asks, bending down to talk to Katie face-to-face.

She nods dramatically as she grips Dylan's shoulder, giving him the smile she's reserved just for him, letting it light up her features. "Is Aunty Summer coming?"

Dylan ruffles her hair. "Not today, bug. She's resting. But your mom's coming with us."

Katie shrugs, unfazed by that information—she could take it or leave it—and I can't help but laugh. This beautiful little soul is my whole world, and she'd rather be with my little brother. *Kids.*

"Can you please go and get your water bottle?" I ask Katie, then watch as she runs away. "You're going to have to stop calling her your favorite soon," I whisper, turning to Dylan with a stern expression, arms folded in front of me.

Dylan mimics my stance, crossing his arms over his chest as he stands up. "Actually, I'm not. She'll remain my favorite girl for a while yet," he says, fighting a smirk, and his meaning hits me.

My hands fly to my mouth as tears prick my eyes. "It's a boy?"

"It's a boy." He nods.

Unable to hide my excitement, I squeal and pull Dylan into a hug, squeezing him so tightly that he pushes me away. He and Summer got married a year ago after deciding to try for a baby. It wasn't all smooth sailing, but three months ago, it finally happened, and I couldn't be happier for them both. And for Katie. Even though she's got plenty of other kids in her life, she's going to love having a cousin.

"Oh, Dylan, I can't wait to meet your little man. How's Summer feeling?" I ask, reading between the lines of his earlier "she's resting" comment.

"She's still struggling, but says today's better than yesterday, so that's a bonus."

"It definitely is."

Katie runs back into the room with her water and backpack in hand, pushing my legs toward the door. "Let's goooo!" she whines, like it's our fault we're still standing in the doorway, never mind the fact she's still without shoes.

"Okay, little bug, let's go." Dylan smiles and nods, always letting her get away with everything.

Ice creams in hand, we pull up at Katie's favorite park, and Dylan collects the football from the truck. He's been teaching her how to play, and she's obsessed, telling me regularly that she wants to be a football player like Dylan when she grows up. And she very well could be, because I have to admit, for a four-year-old, she's pretty freaking good.

I curl up on the grass with my latest read and listen to the sounds around me. I don't need to be here. Dylan's more than capable of looking after Katie alone, but I'm catching up on lost time. We've always been close, and having Dylan in Denver was hard for me, especially when Katie came along.

Although, at least that meant he was in another state when I told him the news about my pregnancy and the anger that Joel and I predicted hit with full force. That wasn't a fun day. *And he doesn't know half of it.*

While I may not have seen him as often as I liked when I moved from our hometown to the city, he was still only an hour away. It wasn't that easy when *he* moved, and now, sometimes, I just need him around. He settles me.

The sun dips as the afternoon rolls on, and I'm just about to call it a day when my phone rings, and Dani's name flashes on the screen. She and I have been friends since we both worked together for Heartwood University's football team years ago. While I left to have Katie, she's still working there. She's also married to Logan. It's a long complicated story, but despite me warning Dani to stay away—with Logan being Summer's playboy best friend at the time—Dani was apparently his undoing and he completely changed his ways.

"Hey, Lovely, are you back from your vacation?" I ask with a smile. She and Logan headed to Australia for an action-packed getaway. Logan lived there for six months during his time as a pro surfer and talks about it all the time. So, of course, now we all want to visit there. *Maybe one day.*

Dani huffs out a laugh and sighs. "What vacation? I spent the weekend catching up on laundry, and today, I'm back at work. It feels like it never happened."

I frown even though she can't see me. "That's a shame. I was really hoping you'd come back relaxed, despite how much you had planned."

"Me too," she laughs again. "Maybe next time. And maybe if we went in warmer weather. Anyway, I want to catch up with you properly, but right now, my call regards work."

Sitting up straighter, my brows furrow as my book falls from my lap. "Okay," I say, curiosity lacing my voice.

"How do you feel about coming back?"

My breath hitches, and my chest fills with a mix of nerves and excitement. This is something I've been thinking about and debating for the last six months. Katie's starting preschool at the end of the summer, so I'll have a bit more time. And I could definitely use the money. *And the adult interaction.* But at the same time, it makes me nervous to think I won't be available for her as often as I am now. I'm currently only working casually for a local clinic, when someone's free to watch Katie, and it worries me to commit to more. I'm all she's got.

"Ummm." I hesitate.

"You don't have to decide right away, but you should give Aaron a call, and at least go in for a chat. They're in need of someone urgently, and your name has been thrown around multiple times."

"Why didn't Aaron call me himself?" It's odd that Dani's the one asking me this, considering she's in the marketing department and I worked with the fitness team. Aaron was my boss when I worked for the college before Katie was born. We got along well, so there's no reason he couldn't just pick up the phone.

"His wife told him not to bother you. Said that you'd contact them when you were ready."

I huff out a laugh as I run my hand through my hair. Lola always did have my back. She took one look at me when I announced I was pregnant, grabbed hold of my hand, and dragged me into a spare room. She sat me down and told me that if something was wrong or I'd been hurt, she'd help me get justice. After telling her that wasn't necessary, I shared more with her that day than I've told anyone, though not everything. Not the part I feel so stupid about. Not the part that hurts the most.

Since that day, she's been checking in on me regularly. She swears that Aaron doesn't know a thing. And since my family don't either, I've been able to push it from my mind. *Mostly.*

"I'll call him now. It's the least I can do if they're desperate."

Dani sighs. "You don't owe them anything, Lucy. You had a baby. No one faults you for that." I know she wants to say more, but she's holding back, so I deliver my usual response.

"They took a chance on me with that promotion, and a few months later, I told them I was pregnant. I owe them."

"Do I need to get into equal opportunity and all that?"

"Nope, you don't. I'll call them. And I'll make a decision based on what's best for me and Katie, not them. Will that make you happy?"

"Very much. Thank you." I can practically hear in her voice the proud smile she's undoubtedly displaying.

She hangs up, and my body tenses at the thought of what I'm about to do. I need to calm down. It's just a phone call. And yet, it feels like a life-changing decision. I haven't really kept up with the Heartwood U Football team, other than the things I've heard though Dylan or his friends. And while Dani keeps me up to date on some things, mostly gossip, we tend not to talk shop when we catch up. We have other things on our minds these days, and most of the time we have two kids running around between us.

Aaron's phone goes to voicemail when I call, and because I'm still not sure what I want to say, I hang up without leaving a message. He calls back less than a minute later and doesn't even let me speak before he's talking. "Please tell me you're ready?"

I laugh as I watch Dylan swinging Katie around in the air. *That's the million-dollar question, isn't it?* "I'm ready to at least *talk*, if that's what you mean."

"I'll take it. Come in any time you like. I'll drop everything."

He's lying, but I appreciate the enthusiasm, so we lock in a time for me to visit the following day.

"What's with the smile?" Dylan asks as we walk to the car a short time later. Lifting my hand to my mouth, I check, and sure enough, there's a smile there. I hadn't even realized. *Maybe I want this more than I thought.*

"I have a meeting with Aaron tomorrow, about potentially going back to work."

Dylan's eyes light up, like they always do whenever I'm happy. He's seen me at my worst and never wants me back there. "That's great, Lucy. Let me know what I can do. Summer and I can help with Katie, and you know Delilah will offer the same."

I'm certain she would, but she's got enough on her plate right now with her and Joel looking into fostering a child.

"Cory and Nate are on summer break now too, so you've got their help if you need it," Dylan adds, referring to our teacher friends. I have options; I know I do. I just need to decide if going back to work full-time is the best thing for me and Katie right now.

When Katie's in bed later that night, I draw myself a bath and contemplate my future as I sink down into the bubbles. Going back to work isn't an easy decision, but it has its benefits, especially financially. We get by, Katie's never without, and heaven knows Dylan spoils us both, but he's about to have his own little family to take care of, and maybe it's time I did something for me.

I love being a physical therapist; I wouldn't have spent six years studying if I didn't. I've missed it like crazy. Well, I miss it when I have the time to think about it. Katie keeps me busy, but she's a good kid. I've never had any concerns with her.

"Can I do this?" I whisper to myself before closing my eyes and dipping my head under the water, letting my mind swarm with thoughts, pros and cons and every little thing it can conjure. I don't move from the bath until the water turns cold, and by the end, there's one thing clear as day. I *think I can.*

Chapter Twelve

Wes

I throw the clipboard across the table and drop my head into my hands. "Are you fucking kidding me? Why did I sign up for this?"

Four sets of eyes flash up at me, and I realize that probably wasn't the best thing to say. To these people, this team is their life. But I just started in this role and all I know is the information presented in front of me. The document telling me our best player, our quarterback, just transferred to another college...for a girl. A *fucking girl*. Well, it doesn't say that's the reason, but it's common knowledge. Good luck to him, I say. Yes, I've let girls fuck with me before, but come on...she's just going to break his heart into a million pieces and he'll miss out on a championship. *Trust me, I know.*

"Is there any way we can talk him into staying?" I ask, hoping we can change his mind. Our offensive coordinator raises his eyebrow, his expression the answer I need. It's done. There's nothing we can do but move on.

I want to call him a dick, but he's actually a nice guy. They all are. It's a good team and that pisses me off even more.

I huff out a sigh. "All right, what options do we have?"

"Your ex-teammate's little brother could step up?" one of the guys says, acting like he knows me.

But what?! "Who?"

I get a glare from the team manager and it's probably deserved. I should know the entire roster by now and I mostly do. I just don't have their siblings memorized.

"Bennett," he says with a pointed look.

Bennett. Now that I picture the kid, it all makes sense. I should have known the two of them were related. First time I saw him he had his arms around two girls, something I've seen several times with Luke.

"Okay. One for the list. Anyone else I should look at?"

It should be as easy as moving our backup into the position, but he's not ready. He's great but he's not a superstar. We lost a superstar, and we need a replacement.

After bouncing ideas around for a while and getting nowhere, our recruitment head suggests we seriously consider the freshman we just secured, but I'm not sure a seventeen-year-old is the right choice for us. Nonetheless, I add him to the list, and by the end of the meeting, I'm over it. *What a fucking mess. All for a girl.*

As soon as I get back to my office, I drop down onto my chair and throw my feet up on the desk, the motion sending paperwork flying to the floor. Not that I worry with my care factor set to zero right now.

Closing my eyes, I lean back until I'm pretty sure the desk chair's at a breaking point and sigh. This was always my plan after retirement. I always wanted to coach. Sure, I'd planned on spending my time as the receiver coach, not the head coach, but it's coaching all the same. And Heartwood U is a good college with a great football team. *Why can't I be happy?*

I'm lost in thought when my office door slams open and I flinch, causing my chair to crash to the floor. "Jesus Christ!" *I am going to murder someone.* Rubbing my head, where it just connected with the wall behind me, I wince at the pain. "This better be good. I've had a shit start to my day and—"

"That's a bad word," a little voice says from somewhere in the room, and I freeze. *What the fuck?*

Scrabbling to my knees, I look over the desk and see a tiny little human staring back at me. "I won't tell." She shrugs.

Who the fuck let a kid in?

I stare at her in bewilderment, not really knowing what I'm supposed to do. Am I meant to report a missing child? Do I have some sort of duty of care here? Or can I politely tell her to leave?

She smiles over at me, rocking on her heels with her hands locked behind her back, and I soften...a little. Because even I have to admit it's *fucking* adorable, and anyone that doesn't think the same would have to be heartless. I have a heart; it's just frozen over at the moment.

My lips pull up into a grin, and when she notices, her eyes light up as she opens her mouth to talk.

"Katie, where are you?" Dani, our marketing manager, calls out before popping her head into the room, her words sending me reeling. "Ah crap. Sorry, Wes. Katie, please say goodbye to Mr. Johnson and come with me. Your mom will be done in a few minutes."

"Bye, Mr. Johnson," she repeats with a tiny wave before skipping out the door. I wave back absentmindedly even though she doesn't see it. Dani does though, and she offers me an apologetic yet confused grin.

As soon as she closes the door behind her, I fall into a heap on the floor, my head crashing back into the wall. *Katie. Fucking*

Katie. My eyes sting as I rub them, before shoving my fists in the sockets to stave off any emotion threatening to come. I do not need this now. Or anytime, really.*Could this day get any worse?*

Why the fuck would I ask myself that question? Of course it can get worse, and it did. On top of everything else, I've got the university president on the phone to complain about some scandal between a player and one of our *much older* trainers. *Fuck my life.* And with that in mind, they're going to enforce a ban on dating within the workplace, including players dating staff—a given—and staff dating staff, because, and I quote, "we need to set an example," or some shit. I personally don't care, but I'm pretty sure my defensive coordinator is going to have a thing or two to say about it since rumor has it he's dating our travel planner. *Can't wait to see that blow up.*

The rest of my day runs somewhat smoothly by comparison, but by the time I get home, I'm in desperate need of a beer. The only bonus about no longer playing professional football—I don't have to worry about my food or alcohol intake.

I'm sure I'm just overly stressed because I never signed up for this responsibility. When I signed my name on the dotted line, I was accepting a role as the receiver coach for the Heartwood University Lions, nothing more. But of course, shit happens and now I'm the interim head coach and everything is fucked-up.

Thank God my private life is lacking because I don't have much more head space for anything else.

Beer in one hand and chicken salad in the other—because okay, I do still think about my food intake a little—I fall onto the couch and sigh.

It's been one hundred ninety-two days since I blew out my knee during a championship game. If I wasn't so close to retirement, I would have worked my ass off to get back on that field, but considering I was already pushing my limits, it ended my career. I'm certain I only had a year left, max, but I wanted to go out on my own terms. With all the retirement fanfare and all the glory. Instead, I hobbled off the field, never to return again. *And it's fucking sucked.*

I've had a shit year all around. Quite a few shit years if I really want to complain. It's like I'm continuously losing things—my job, my mind...*her*. But losing my gran, Katie, was hard. *One* of the hardest things I've ever been through, and I'm definitely not over it.

Katie. Fucking Katie. I'd been doing so well to not lose my cool at work...on top of everything else. Actually, scrap that, I'm constantly losing my cool at work, but I've never been emotional. Today I came close. Hearing that little girl's name had my heart lurching in my throat. Obviously, I know there are other people out there with the name Katie, but it's the first time I've come across one since my gran passed away. And I was not at all ready for it.

I don't know what to do with myself for the next hour, so I alternate between working out and vegging out. Both have their positives and negatives, but neither put me in a good mood. Nothing has lately. I don't want to get into a big *woe is*

me spiel, but I could use a break from things fucking up in my life.

My leg muscles burn as I squat down, balancing the weighted bar across my shoulders. I can already tell that my fitness levels are dropping. The motivation to train like I used to just isn't there. But I push through it and finish up my last rep with a grunt.

Dropping to the floor, I take a deep breath before starting my next routine—the one I fucking hate, the one I'm pretty sure everyone hates—burpees. I'm busting out my thirty-seventh rep, already exhausted from the rest of the set, when my phone vibrates on the counter. I ignore it, knowing that if it's someone important they'll call back. I've never been one to rush to the phone. I don't give a fuck if your house is on fire, you've called the wrong person.

The vibrations stop as I drop down into my next move, but the phone buzzes again, seconds later, stopping after one ring. *Dammit.* Pausing mid rep I stare at my phone with a scowl, waiting for what I know is coming. And right on cue, the phone vibrates again. *Fucker.* I have no doubt in my mind that it's Carter. He knows that the third time is usually a charm for me, and he's trying to cheat the system.

Jumping to my feet, I take my time moving to the kitchen, and answer on the last ring. "Yup." I puff into the phone, unable to give him anything else until I catch my breath.

Carter laughs. "How was your day, sweetie?"

"Fuck off. What's up? We spoke yesterday."

"You know I can't go a day without speaking to you."

"Carter," I warn.

He chuckles to himself, and I hear the phone rustle as he moves around. "Okay, okay. I want details on the QB? All you texted was 'I've got no quarterback.'"

I drop my head back with a sigh, running a hand through my already mussed hair. "It's a fucking nightmare. He's moved for a girl and now we're scrambling to find his replacement. I'm running some plays with a few kids tomorrow to see who's the best fit. But if I'm being honest, I don't think we'll be playing in any championships for a couple of years. That kid really fucked us."

"Damn, what about Bennett's little brother?"

"What the fuck? How do you know about him?" I ask incredulously, but then the answer hits me and I laugh. "Bennett?"

Carter still plays for San Francisco and is set to have his best year this coming season. He's a little younger than I am, so probably has a few years left. Something I'd be jealous about if he wasn't finally getting the support and recognition he deserves.

He barks out a laugh at my realization of Luke's bragging. "You know it."

"Yeah, well, he's on the list for tomorrow."

"Luke will be pleased. He never shuts up about the fact that you're coaching his little bro. What's he like?"

My mind bypasses football because I know that's not what he's asking. "Worse than Bennett from what I've seen."

"Big call, man. Big call."

I never knew Luke in college, but I think it's safe to say he hasn't changed much, and his brother seems to be following in his footsteps. But as long as he doesn't give me trouble, I don't care what he does with his personal life. That's all on him.

Carter's car starts in the background and I huff quietly, thinking about where he might have been. Probably a training session at the team gym. The thought makes me sad. Even though I just finished my own workout, it's not the same. That team became my family and I miss them, even Luke.

"So what else is new?" Carter asks, as "Eye of the Tiger" plays softly through the phone. I'm so lost in the song that when he repeats the question, I answer honestly instead of keeping my mouth shut.

"I met a little girl named Katie today," I say and immediately wince.

"Ah fuck," Carter curses under his breath but loud enough I hear it. "You okay?"

"Yeah, yeah, I'm fine. I don't know why I told you that."

"Because it affected you," he says, his jovial tone long gone.

"You're probably right. Life fucking sucks."

"I agree *that* sucks. Losing Katie sucked hard. But your life is good. You're just a grumpy bastard. A grumpy bastard that shouldn't be alone tonight."

I huff out a laugh, shaking my head. "You and I both know there's a good chance I won't be alone."

Carter groans with a laugh just as keys jingle in my front door and it slowly opens. "You're right. I should have known."

My lips pull into a grin as I turn around and relish in the smell of takeout from my new favorite diner. "Took you long enough," I say, hanging up the phone.

Chapter Thirteen

Wes

I *hate* Monday meetings with a passion. As if Mondays weren't bad enough just by existing.

"Are we done? I have things to do," I bark out before biting my tongue. It's been almost a week since we lost our quarterback and we *still* don't have a replacement. Rising to my feet, I move to leave—"Actually, one more thing"—and drop back down with a groan. Will this ever end?

Our fitness director, Aaron, keeps talking despite my clear annoyance. "We've got a new physical therapist starting to-morrow—well, she's not really new," he drones on as I rest my face in my hands, waiting for his announcement to be over while trying really hard not to walk out midspeech. I've been told that's rude, but sometimes it's necessary. "Some of you may remember her, so if you see Lucy in the halls, please make her feel welcome."

"*The fuck!*" My head shoots up and I glare his way. This has to be a joke. The world is trying to mess with me.

"What do you mean 'the fuck'?" Aaron asks, an uncharacter-istically sour look on his face. This guy is always nice, but from day one it's been obvious we weren't going to get along—there's just something about him. Probably because he's *too* happy. I don't know. I don't care.

"I'm a little put off by the fact that I *just* started as interim head coach and the team seems to be falling apart. First you

125

lose your coach, hence me, then a QB, a trainer, and now a physical therapist? What's going on?" I'm acting crazy, I know. But I'm not wrong.

"We haven't lost any trainers," Aaron says with a frown, before abruptly announcing, "Meeting adjourned."

Since he doesn't actually have authority to make that call, no one moves until the big man in charge repeats his statement.

What?! That was weird. I'm not going to argue though. Pushing back my chair with a loud screech, I stand to leave. Again.

"Not you," Aaron demands, motioning for me to sit. My fists clench beside me, ready to argue, but when my boss gives me a nod, I'm forced to comply. *Fucker.*

When the room has cleared out, Aaron taps his pen on the table and continues. "We haven't lost a trainer. It was our PT caught with one of *your* players."

I don't like the way he says "your" but I let it slide. Maybe this guy isn't as nice as he seems.

"Right, okay. So you hired *another* female to replace her. Isn't that asking for trouble?"

Aaron's eyes flare, and he slaps his palms on the table. If looks could kill I'd be six feet under. He's about to tear me a new one when the boss man steps in.

"Come on, Wes. Since when are you sexist?"

Uh. Since never. I just popped my sexism cherry, and I feel pretty shitty about it. Not that I admit that. Instead, I square my shoulders and face off with both of them.

"Since I have my defensive coordinator threatening to quit if he's forced to choose between his job and his girlfriend, now that the bullshit no dating rule is in place." *And since you decided to hire a girl named Lucy and I'm fucking pissed about it.*

Fuck my life.

"Run it again," I yell at the two guys I've been working to the bone. We need a decision by the end of the day. Summer training is about to start, and I'd rather not have to admit we're missing a crucial player.

"That's it, Mini B. Nice one." I clap his performance and nod to the offensive coordinator, Sean. This kid is good.

Mini B's eyes narrow as he jogs back to position. They all think I'm an asshole, yet I always give credit where credit's due. Compliment aside, he's not a huge fan of the nickname I've given him now that I know his brother, but I'm sure it'll grow on him. Or I'll tire of it. Either way, he's fine.

"Alright, Rookie. You're up."

We're down to the rookie and Mini B for the starting quarterback position. Rookie is fucking phenomenal for his age. He has raw talent that can't be rivaled, at least in speed and skill. Calling the plays though... He's still got a bit to learn. I have no doubt that after a year as a backup, he'll be the number one player on everyone's radar. The scouts were right.

Mini B, on the other hand, has a mind for this game. Despite being a wide receiver, his ability to call plays and predict movement is up there with some of the best, and he has this *born leader* feel about him. But he's also cocky as fuck, so I'm torn.

We practice for another hour before calling it a day. The boys smile as they walk off the field, but I know I pushed them hard and they'll be cursing me in the locker room.

Sean joins my side and we both sigh in unison. It's weird but neither of us comment.

"What are you thinking?" he asks, looking my way.

"I hate to say it, but I think we have to go with Mini B."

Sean laughs. "I think you're right. I mean, Trevor *is* amazing." *He means Rookie.* "But I'm not sure he's ready."

"Same sentiment, different shirt," I say, shrugging a shoulder before walking toward my office. Sean laughs a little hesitantly as he follows me, like he's never heard me joke before. *That was a joke, right. Because we're wearing different shirts? Uh whatever.* "Let's sleep on it," I say over my shoulder. "But I think we've got our QB," I add and then disappear out of his sight.

Carter calls when I'm on my way home later that day. I haven't answered his call since we spoke last week, and judging by the voicemails he's left, he's not happy.

He pranks me twice and then lets the third one ring until I answer.

"You've got a dependency problem," I say as a greeting.

"Fuck off. You hung up on me midcall because your *lady friend* came over and then haven't answered the phone all week. I was worried you'd been murdered in your sleep and we'd never find the body."

I laugh, because while I haven't answered his call, I've texted, so he knows that's not true.

"No such luck," I joke. "I'm— What the fuck was that?" I yell, blaring my horn when some fucker cuts me off.

"How's the QB hunt going? Random outburst aside, you don't seem as pissy as usual, and you answered your phone."

"I think we found our guy."

"Thank fuck. Tell me it's not Ryan."

"Who's Ryan?"

Carter sighs. "Jesus, Wes. Do you know any of your players' names?"

"I know surnames." I'm completely bullshitting him because I know it annoys him. Ryan and Mini B are one and the same.

"Ryan Bennett."

"Ooooh, yeah, sorry, it's him."

I smirk to myself when he groans, knowing Luke is going to be insufferable, and Carter will have to put up with it. But it's nice that he's proud.

We're still talking when I pull into my driveway and notice a familiar truck idling down the road.

"Any lady friends over tonight?" Carter asks jokingly, like he always does, knowing there's only one other person that would ever be at my place. I could be an asshole, but it's been a couple of weeks since we've actually seen each other, so I do the right thing and give him the answer he wants.

"Nope, my best friend's coming over. In fact, he'll be here any minute."

"You better mean me, asshole."

"I can see your truck, fucker. Get inside."

Carter and I drink until the early hours, taking advantage of the off-season, even though I have work in the morning. I'm on my third shot—*God knows why we moved to shots*—when Lucy comes up in conversation. Carter likes to torment me with her every now and then, and I usually laugh it off, but today it hits too close to home.

"Trust me, you do *not* want to mention her name."

Carter raises an eyebrow and leans in close. "Why, is it your anniversary or something?" he whispers and then laughs. The fucker laughs and I almost deck him.

"No, asshole. A new girl starts tomorrow who happens to be named Lucy."

"Get out of town. A Katie *and* a Lucy, within a week."

"*Get out of town?*" I say, leaning back with a smirk.

"I also could have gone with *shut the front door.*" He shrugs as I laugh, grateful for the small respite.

"You're funny, but they both suck, and so do you. As does new Lucy."

Carter pauses for a second before looking to the ceiling. He's seemingly lost in thought until he has some kind of epiphany and starts clicking his fingers in front of me.

"Did that hurt?" I ask before he can fill me in on his excitement.

"What if *new* Lucy is *old* Lucy!" he exclaims until he realizes he shouldn't be excited by that prospect and his brows furrow.

I have to admit, the thought crossed my mind.

After everything went down all those years ago, curiosity got the best of me, and I looked Dylan up online. He attended Heartwood U. Grew up in *this* town. If Lucy had still lived here when I met her then she'd only have been an hour or less away from our hotel. And yet, I never contacted her.

Sure, she may have moved since college, or high school. But did I throw my laptop across the room in annoyance anyway? You bet I did.

"I considered that for a second. But then someone mentioned that her surname was Kelly, and my theory went right out the window."

Carter raises an eyebrow as he stares me down, clearly waiting for me to catch up on his thoughts. Umm... *Oh Fuck, unless she's married.* A sharp pang runs through me, and I almost grip my chest from the pain. Goddammit, it's been years. *Get the fuck over it.*

I'm on edge the next day, because despite spending most of the night trying to convince myself it was a coincidence—that this Lucy wasn't the same as *my* Lucy—I failed. Of course she'll fucking be the same. That's the story of my life.

I should have marched my ass over to the therapy rooms first thing this morning, but I'm too chickenshit to find out the truth. I'd rather live in denial.

Fuck, that girl really did a number on me. To think I had trust issues *before* meeting her, and now...

Running my hands down my face, I shake off my thoughts and try to concentrate. Unsuccessfully. For hours.

My boss raps his knuckles on my partially opened door in the early afternoon and gives me a pointed look. I pretend to finish reading the document in front of me, then look his way. "What's up?" I ask as though he's interrupting, when in reality, I have no idea what the document says. It could very well be a takeout menu.

"I want an update on the QB issue. You've got five minutes. I need a coffee first."

He disappears down the hall as I roll my eyes. He was the only one missing from the meeting when we collectively made the decision. If he'd bothered to check his email he'd get the answer, but he's the athletic director, so I follow him anyway.

"I've already emailed you about this," I say, walking into the staff kitchen behind him. "We've decided to go with—" I freeze.

Oh, hell no.

Sitting at the round table in the center of the room is my worst nightmare and dream come true. *Fuck, fuck, fuck!* I was really hoping I was wrong.

"Nope, no. Uh-uh. I'm done. I'm taking a personal day. Bennett's the new quarterback. Check your email. I'm outta here."

With that I turn around and storm out, needing to put as much distance between myself and that room as physically possible.

Chapter Fourteen
Lucy

I'm frozen, sandwich raised halfway to my mouth, shocked to see Wes standing in front of me on my first day back at work. When my brain finally catches up with my vision, a soft smile starts to form. That is until he speaks.

"Nope, no. Uh-uh. I'm done. I'm taking a personal day. Bennett's the new quarterback. Check your email. I'm outta here."

With that, he's gone and I can't breathe. *What the fuck just happened? Why is he here?* My eyes flash to the other man in the room. He's somewhat familiar, but I can't place him. He frowns as he looks between me and the door Wes just vacated, almost as confused as I am.

I'm about to apologize, though I've done nothing wrong, when it hits me. Wes is here.

My chair falls to the floor as I aggressively push it back before running for the exit. *Wes is here.*

"Wait!" I call out as I round the corner, coming to a screeching halt when I find the hallway empty.

Did I just imagine that? That was Wes, right? I mean, it's been a long time, but his face is still at the forefront of my mind. I *know* him. Although, he'd be difficult to forget with all the billboards anyway.

Someone taps on my shoulder, and I jump, completely lost in my thoughts.

"Jesus, sorry. What are you doing?" Dani asks, her forehead crinkled in concern. I must seem frazzled as I frantically look left and right, searching in all directions, unable to move.

"Do you know Wes Johnson?" I ask, without looking her way. "Sorry, of course you do. Everyone knows him. But do you know that he's *here*?"

I whisper the last part and Dani laughs.

"Yes, to both. He's the interim head coach here. Didn't you know that?"

My eyes widen in shock. *Why didn't I know that?* I knew he'd had a career-ending injury. I saw it happen. But... "How did I miss that?" I say, whether to Dani or myself, I don't know.

"No idea. It's been all over the media. Why are you being weird?"

Dani doesn't know about my time with Wes. Only a few people do. The article Greg sent me back then never saw the light of day. A reporter friend had told him about it, but somehow it disappeared, as though it never existed. As though our time together *never existed*. And while I was a little relieved...fuck, it hurt.

"I...I've just always been a big fan," I lie. Dani and I are close friends. I tell her most things. But this is Wes's workplace, so until I talk to him, it's best if I keep things on the down low.

I'm sure Dani picks up on my strange tone, but she doesn't say anything. Instead she smiles. "Well, you're in for some luck because it's almost impossible to miss him around here. But you know what they say about meeting your idol?"

"Don't?"

"Exactly."

What does that mean?

A colleague calls Dani away, and she heads toward her office, leaving me alone with my thoughts. I've met Wes; he's completely different from his football player persona but in a good way. Why would she hint at something bad?

I wander the halls on my way back to our rooms. Since training doesn't start until next week, I've got a bit of time on my hands, and despite Wes saying he's going home, I seek him out. It's not in his nature to shirk his responsibilities like that. At least that's what he once told me, so I'm almost certain he's still here.

And I'm right.

When I pass by the coaches' offices, a voice booms inside the one with his name taped to the door. "What the fuck do you mean?" Wes yells, and with no response I'm going to assume he's on the phone.

"I don't need this today. Where?"

More silence.

"Ah fuck, okay. I'm on my way."

The door slams open before I've had a chance to step away—I wasn't expecting him to move so quickly. Jumping back, I press myself against the opposite wall and flinch.

Wes stills, and his eyes lock on mine before raking over my entire body, causing a chill to run through me. I'm wearing my favorite skintight leggings and a team-issued polo. Nothing special. And yet, the way he looks at me, the way he drinks me in, you'd think I was naked *and* beautiful. My heart pounds in my chest and I stop breathing.

"Wes?" I whisper without moving a muscle. Scared that even the slightest twitch will have him scampering away.

His eyes snap back to mine, flashing with anguish before he shakes his head and scoffs. "I've got to go."

I expect him to rush off then, but he doesn't move a muscle until I take a tentative step forward.

"Fuck," he hisses before running a hand through his dark messy hair and walking away.

"Wes, wait!"

He pauses but doesn't look back. "I don't have time for this."

"Is something wrong?" I say, taking another step toward him with a lump in my throat.

Wes's shoulders stiffen, and he finally turns around, anger in his eyes. "Do you care?"

I flinch at his comment and my chest aches. "Always," I croak, my voice clogged with emotion. It's not a lie. I care. I cried for days after walking away from him, and only half of it was because I was pregnant. The other half—him.

Wes huffs out a laugh and departs without another glance my way. I consider leaving him be. I do. But I've never been a hold back kind of girl.

"Wait!" I call again as I run after him.

He pushes through the glass doors to the parking lot before I've reached him and continues to ignore me as he approaches his truck. The same truck I remember.

"Wes, stop, please."

Pausing with his hand on the door handle, he peers over his shoulder with a scowl. "*What*, Lucy?"

"You look worried. Can I help somehow?"

I'm not sure what I'm asking. Or why. But I can't walk away without offering something.

He spins then and stares at me blankly, stepping into my personal space. "No, Lucy. You can't help. This is a personal matter and we're practically strangers."

Ouch! My chest burns from the lack of emotion in his expression, and I almost believe his words until he blinks and his eyes remain closed a beat too long.

"I'm sorry. I'll leave you be," I say as he jumps in his truck and slams the door before pulling out of the lot. It's not until he's out of sight that I release a held breath. Can I blame him for being angry at me? No. But pretending we're strangers isn't going to work. Not when I still have his touch, his taste, his smell etched into my mind. I've never regretted walking away that day; I did what was best for both of us. But that doesn't mean I haven't wished things could have worked out differently. I'm just not sure where to go from here.

I'm about to head back inside when someone calls my name. My stupid heart jumps, thinking Wes has come back, but it's not even his voice.

When I turn around, Greg's best friend is jogging toward me. My heart thuds again but for a different reason entirely. I've had nothing to do with Greg since the day he sent me the article about Wes. I changed my number. I moved, for God's sake. Seeing his friend *now* makes my spine curl.

"Bry, how are you?" I play nice, even though I want to throw up.

"Lucy, it's been so long. Are you back working here?" Brighton asks and I internally cringe. Do I lie? And why the hell is he here? He lives an hour away.

"Potentially, we'll see. I'm just putting the feelers out." That would have been the truth if he'd seen me last week so we'll go with that.

Brighton smiles. "Nice one. My brother's kid is on the cheer team. I'm picking her up from practice." *Guess that answers my question.*

"Oh, perfect. It's a great college."

Brighton smiles but doesn't say anything back. He blinks a few times like he doesn't believe I'm actually standing in front of him, and that's unnerving.

"Well, it was good to see you. I've gotta run or I'll be late," I say awkwardly, pointing toward the doorway, making Bry snap out of whatever weird mood he's in.

"Yeah, yeah. Me too. Good seeing you, Luce."

My lips pull into a forced smile before I walk away from our awkward conversation. When he's out of sight, my skin covers in goose bumps, and an uncomfortable feeling swirls inside me. I'm not sure if anything will come of that interaction, but if it does, it won't be good.

Within ten minutes of finishing work, I arrive at my local gym. The need to work out and physically hit something is strong. The negative energy flowing through me needs to go. As soon as I'm changed, I head over to the punching bags and find Joel and Delilah stretching beside them. Joel's hands are taped, and there's a pair of gloves at his feet, making me eye them both suspiciously.

"Summer thought you might need company since she can't be here. Del's here to work out, and I'm here to box."

Summer and I completed a self-defense course together just before I got pregnant. Actually, it was after I became pregnant but just before I knew it. From there I developed a love of boxing and now spend most of my time honing those skills. Summer often joins me when she wants a sweat session, but hasn't been coming all month.

"It's been weeks since she last came, Joel. I'm okay."

"Maybe we want to get fit." He shrugs. Raising an eyebrow, my eyes trail over his ripped arms busting out of his tight tee, before moving to Delilah's equally fit body.

"Yeah, I'm sure that's it."

Delilah cracks up laughing as Joel shakes his head. "You're right. Joel's full of shit. We wanted to talk kids. More specifically babies."

My face alights with surprise and I bite back a smile, trying not to get excited when I could be wrong in my assumption.

"Go on," I say, waving a hand toward them.

Joel laughs. "Delilah and I got approval to be foster parents. We're on the list."

"Ahhh!" I throw my arms around them as tears well in my eyes. It's been a long road to get them to this point, and my heart fills at this news.

Taking a step back, I clap my hands together and grin. "What do you want to know?"

"You talk and box. I'm going for a run," Delilah says, squeezing my arm as she walks away with a smile on her face.

Joel and I do just that. We box and talk until it's physically impossible to do either, and we breathlessly fall to the floor. I think I've discovered more about myself and raising a child than Joel has, but hopefully he got something out of our chat.

"I think you broke me," he says from the floor beside me. He's an absolute mess, but I'm not sure he's referring to boxing.

Letting my head fall to the side to look at him, I respond with as little effort as possible. I'm just as fucked. "I could say the same about you," I huff out. "I didn't know you could box."

"I'll let you in on a secret if you don't tell anyone."

My brows furrow as I nod.

"Summer asked me to do this last week. I didn't want you to show me up. So I've been coming every day since she mentioned it."

I laugh because that's such a Joel thing to do, although it's normally Delilah he'd be messing with.

"I don't know how Delilah puts up with you."

"Me either. I'm one lucky son of a bitch."

"Hey, your mother is lovely," I sass, knowing he doesn't mean it literally.

"She really is," Delilah says, joining us again. We both turn to look at her but neither of us move. We can't.

"It's a figure of speech, Luce." Joel rolls his eyes and I laugh before turning serious.

"You're going to make an amazing foster dad, Joel. I have absolutely no doubt. And Delilah...ah, you're going to be perfect. I'm really happy for you both."

Joel's lips pull into a warm smile as he flops a hand over his face. "Me too. I'm nervous as anything, but excited for it all. Except for that shit explosion thing you decided to mention...*in detail*. That doesn't sound fun."

"Wow, you really have no clue, Joel," Delilah adds, shaking her head.

"Yep, sometimes you have to laugh or you'll cry," I joke, although it's not really funny. I've cried a lot. Being a mom has been the hardest and yet most rewarding thing I've ever done. And, while it took me four of the nine months to get used to the idea of being pregnant, the second Katie entered this world, she was my everything. Would it have been nice to have her father in the picture? Of course. But I wasn't going to let that happen. He didn't deserve me and he definitely doesn't deserve her.

"Well, I'm glad that little bug grew out of that stage. Especially since I'm spending the day with her tomorrow."

I want to say a smart-ass comment. He's left it wide open for one. But I can't. Instead I pull him into an awkward floor hug and press a kiss to his cheek, before rising and hugging Delilah.

I don't think I could have done this parenting thing without my friends. They've all treated Katie like one of their own, and I couldn't be more grateful. I'm often asked if I'm a single mom—when people don't see a ring, or hear me talking about all the things Katie and I do as a duo—and while technically I am, I always say *no*. I have so much love and support in my life, that I've never once felt like I was doing this alone.

Looking a little less disheveled after a shower, we're all smiles as we walk to our cars. "I'll see you in the morning when you drop Katie off," Joel says as he waits for me to get in mine.

Delilah snorts. "Actually he won't. He's never up early if he doesn't have to work. But I'll be up and can't wait to see Katie."

I smile. "Either way, I really appreciate it. I'll have everything sorted out by next week."

"No rush. We love spending time with her. And what else am I going to do on my day off?"

I could list a hundred things for him to do, but I don't, because I'm grateful he's choosing to help me. They both are. With this job being so last-minute, it hasn't been easy to get my shit together, but I'm getting there. My life may be a mess, but it's mine and I wouldn't change it.

Although as I drive away, an image of Wes springs to mind and I have to wonder...maybe sometimes a little change isn't a bad thing.

Chapter Fifteen

Wes

The clock ticks over to nine-oh-eight and I need to get my ass into gear. I have a nine fifteen meeting with my staff, but I can't bring myself to leave my truck. I'm sensing a pattern where Lucy is concerned. Only this time I'm not pushing the boundaries so I can see more of her. No, this time, I don't want to see her at all.

My chest tightens at the memory of running into her yesterday—not the kitchen, that's a complete blur. But when I opened my office door to rush out and found her there, all doe-eyed and panicked, I couldn't look away. She's as perfect as I remember. If not more so.

The swell of her breasts peeking out of her unbuttoned polo and the curve of her hips completely sucked me back in. I knew it was wrong, but I couldn't stop myself from running my eyes over every inch of her body, needing to get my fill after all this time. Allowing my heart that one moment to pound as I watched her shallow breathing and the subtle clench of her legs.

Knowing I affected her just as much as she did me was really fucking satisfying. I took in as much as I could in those few seconds, drinking in the same long golden-brown hair falling in waves over her shoulders, her lightly sun-kissed skin and perfect freckles, her bare lips, her...lack of a wedding ring. Yeah, I checked. Not that it matters, I just needed to know. *But does that mean she's divorced? Why the name change?* And why do I care?

Shaking off my thoughts, I stroll into the meeting at nine twenty-one, and nobody seems to notice. They're all getting settled and talking about random shit like their kids or a TV show they binged the night before. And even though I'm the one that's late, I make a big deal out of it.

"Let's start? We're already ten minutes behind."

As usual, the meeting goes over the allotted time—*who schedules these things?*—and I'm itching to get out of this stuffy room. I love the idea of coaching, and I'm excited to start with the team, but the meetings and politics, I can do without.

"And last, Aaron asked his new staff member to pop her head in and introduce herself—"

"Is that really necessary?" I bark out but he ignores me.

"She should be here any... Ah, Lucy, hi."

Fuck me. I groan louder than I mean to and bury my face in my hands. These guys know I hate meetings so will assume I'm pissed due to the time, not the person standing in the doorway. The person I can't get out of my fucking head.

"Hi, I'm Lucy. I recognize a few of you from when I was here almost five years ago, and..."

She keeps talking but I tune her out, my mind drifting back to when we first met. Did she work here then? I'm guessing yes, as it was about five years ago. At least I now have confirmation of how close she really lived. We could have easily made things work. Only an hour drive to see each other. An easy commute if I spent the night. Hell, I could have even lived here. *What the fuck, Wes? You knew her for a week!*

A week! I knew her for a goddam week and she caused irreversible damage. Imagine what any longer will do.

Lucy waits in the doorway as everyone departs, shaking hands as they pass. I hang back, hoping she'll leave when she sees I'm the last one, but it's wishful—or stupid—thinking.

"Wes, right? The head coach? Nice to meet you," she says as I approach.

Is she kidding me with this?

I stare at her blankly, waiting for her to laugh, but she holds strong, keeping her hand out in front of her, ready for me to shake. *Not happening.*

"I'm Lucy," she continues.

"Excuse me, I have another meeting to get to."

I move around her to exit, but she grabs my arm as I do, digging her nails into my skin, leaving her mark. *As if she hadn't already done that.* "We're going to have to start over, now that we're working together," she whispers, with a fake smile in place.

"We don't *have* to do anything," I say, staring at the tiny hand she has wrapped around my bicep, refusing to look her in the eye.

Of course she argues. "It will make our life easier."

"Will it? Enlighten me."

I don't look up, but I sense her rolling her eyes. "Neither of us need this tension. We can be civil. We're both *professionals.*"

Damn. Pulling out the big guns. "Fine. Nice to meet you, *Lucy.*"

I pull my arm free and walk away, not once meeting her gaze, and as soon as I'm in my office, I breathe. My arm burns from her touch, and I want to rip it off but at the same time, I welcome it. *How does this woman still affect me so much? And why?*

I pace the room, wearing a line on the carpet until the offensive coordinator arrives for our meeting, snapping me out of my mood. "Bennett's here. Are you ready to make his year?"

"Yeah, let's do it." Anything to distract me from my beautiful nightmare.

For the next few days, I avoid Lucy like the plague. If I see her in the halls, I turn around. If I hear her name mentioned, I hum to block out the noise. Usually something like "Maneater" by Hall & Oates or "Black Hole Sun" by Soundgarden, because my brain clearly likes to fuck with me and those are the songs that pop into my head. *Talk about issues.*

On the odd occasion I can't avoid her, she smiles and cheerfully says hello, to which she usually gets a nod in response, and once I even grunted.

I don't want her in my space. I'm finally starting to feel like myself again after Gran died and my career ended. I don't want something else fucking with me. *Thank you, universe.*

When the weekend finally rolls around, I'm out of there without looking back. Several people invite me to Friday night drinks, but I can't do it. I need to separate myself from this place for the entire weekend. After all, it's the last full weekend I'll get off. The air in the building has been stifling, and I need a break. So from Friday evening until Sunday night I chill, I rest, and I drink myself stupid...alone.

I'm hungover as fuck when I wake Monday morning, but I have to suck it up and be at work in a little over an hour. Stumbling toward the kitchen, I do a double take when I pass by the living area.

Facedown on my couch is a very naked, very fit looking woman with her ass in the air. Her long blonde hair hides her face, but I'm pretty certain I've never seen her before.

She starts to stir and rolls onto her side, giving me a full view of her body. And while I'm sure she's very nice to look at, I groan before turning away.

I do not need this right now.

I know I was plastered last night, but I don't think I was *that* drunk to forget going out and hooking up. Which can only mean one thing... "Alright, Gray, where the fuck are you?"

The toilet flushes, and I'm blessed with my second naked human for the day. *Yay, me.* He scratches his head as he walks, swaying with each step that he takes. I might be hungover but Grayson is still drunk...or *something. Please don't let it be something.*

A million things run through my head, but there's three that stand out... Why am I always the one they call? Why do his bandmates insist on dropping him at my door? And why the fuck did I give him my key?

I watch him move toward me—like he doesn't even realize I'm here. And when he next stumbles, his eyes roll into the back of his head and he falls to the floor. My heart stops, but the rest of me springs into fight mode, running over to catch him before his head hits the tiles.

I lift him quickly, but almost drop him again when I hear a loud bang and the blonde cries out. *This is too much.*

Ignoring the naked woman now on my carpet, I try to rouse Gray. He's the only one I care about in this scenario.

"Grayson. Grayson, wake up." He doesn't move. "Come on, fucker. You're scaring me."

I slap him a few times until he finally begins to murmur, and my heart starts beating again. This is so much worse than I thought. We are way past the point of me being able to help him.

"What's wrong with him?" the blonde asks, now awake after her fall. Unfortunately for her that means she's getting the brunt of my anger.

"What the fuck did you give him? What did he take?"

"Ha, if he's taken anything, it never came from me. He's the ringleader where that's concerned."

What? Jesus! I thought we were past this? How have I been so blind?

I instruct her to keep him awake while I quickly dress. I don't even take the time to piss. I can't afford it if I'm right and he's taken something.

When I walk back into the living room, he's sitting up unassisted, playing with the girl's hair. My entire body deflates as the tension leaves me. He's okay. *Sort of.* But he's about to meet my wrath as my concern quickly morphs to anger now that he's fine. "You're going to rehab," I demand.

We've been here before. He beat it last time; he can do it again.

Gray laughs as though I'm joking, and I want to pummel him. But of course I don't, because then he'd never listen to me.

"I'm not kidding, Gray. You told me you were clean. I know you drink too much, but I've ignored it, thinking that's better than the alternative. That's on me. But I can't ignore *this*. You can have all the sex and rock 'n' roll you please, but I draw the line at drugs. You need help."

"It's a one-off; it's not like last time," he tries to bullshit me.

My naked house guest laughs and shakes her head, confirming his lies. Never thought she'd be on my side against the famous rock star, but I'll take it.

"You need to talk to someone. You're already on thin ice with your label."

Gray scoffs. "They need me more than I need them."

I hate that he's right. It makes it hard to get my point across. But I'm about to argue anyway when my phone rings. I know it's going to be someone from the media team asking where I am. But despite the fact that I'm supposed to be sitting down with some journalists in thirty minutes, I don't answer.

"I have to go. Stay here. I've got plenty of food. We'll talk when I get back."

The blonde looks at me expectantly and I groan. "Look after him, will you?"

She nods with a smile as I walk away, instantly regretting my choice to leave.

By the time I get to my office, I'm a disheveled shell of my usual self. I gave in and called one of Grayson's bandmates on the way here. This guy has a good head on his shoulders, not that Grayson doesn't—he just lost his way for a while. I have no doubt that Zach will look after him. He'll be angry but he'll be there. I just can't expect him to take full responsibility. After all, like Gray, he's practically a kid.

The newspaper interview is harmless, but I'm on edge the entire time. When I'm finally able to check my phone, I relax, seeing a message from Zach to say that Grayson's okay. While I might be relieved, I'm still so fucking angry at the situation. *What are you thinking, Gray?* I have the strongest urge to knock some sense into him, if only I could guarantee it would work.

I've just rounded the corner to my office, intent on grabbing my keys and hitting the gym to work off this frustration, when I come face-to-face with Lucy. In a dress. Looking so beautiful it hurts. *Not now, Lucy. Please.*

My chest tightens as I scowl. "Whatever you're selling, I ain't buying," I say, moving around her.

"Wes—"

"No, Lucy. If you need to talk to me, as the *head coach*, you make an appointment," I bark, completely unnecessarily, before walking away.

Chapter Sixteen

Lucy

"What's your problem?" I whisper-yell, chasing Wes down the hall. There're a few office doors open, so I try hard not to draw any attention to us. Not that there is an *us* anymore. And maybe there never was.

Wes doesn't respond. He just tosses me a look over his shoulder that says "are you kidding me with that question" and continues on his way. Like the conversation is over. But boy is he in for a shock. I get that things didn't end well with us, but it takes two to tango. He never called, never messaged. He walked away that day and never looked back. Something he wishes he could do now.

As he storms into his office, pushing the door closed to shut me out, I jam my foot in the gap to stop it and let myself in, slamming it behind me.

"Do you mind? I've got shit to do."

"I don't really care how busy you are. We work together, Wes. I'm not putting up with this attitude for the foreseeable future."

"Colleagues don't have to be friends, Lucy. We may need to discuss players from time to time, but we don't need to discuss our weekend, chat about the weather, or anything else outside of our specific roles. I'll treat you how I treat everyone else, and you can treat me how you want. Deal?"

"No." Plain and simple. I'm not letting him get away with this shit.

"No? Just like that?"

"Just like that." I smile innocently, trying hard not to laugh at the shocked expression on his face. This is a side of him I've never seen before, but then I suppose I only knew him a week, and yet I act like we had some epic love affair and I'm jaded.

I sigh and change tack. "Look, I know things ended strangely with us. And I don't think either of us is to blame—"

"I fucking hate liars," Wes states, slamming his fist on his desk, cutting me off. "I was honest with you about that from the start. Lying is and always will be a deal breaker for me." He pauses but I don't say a word. The pained look on his face tells me he's got more to say. More he needs to get off his chest.

"My dad told me nothing would change between us when he left—lies. My first agent said he'd always have my back—lies. My college girlfriend spun lies with practically every word that came out of her mouth. Even my mom told me she wasn't *that* sick, and she fucking died, Lucy. She *died...*

"People sugarcoat everything thinking they're doing the right thing. But for who? *Who* does it benefit? Certainly not the person being lied to."

He pauses again and this time I can't speak, even though I want to. I don't know what to say. "For some fucked-up reason I thought you were different," he says after a moment. "And in hindsight that was a ridiculous notion because I barely even knew you. You told me all that shit about a surprise and...actually, I guess that wasn't a lie, because God, did you surprise me. If you want to know my *problem*, think back to our time together and the lies you spilled. You'll get your answer. Now get the fuck out of my office."

151

I don't move. I can't. I stare at him in shock as my pulse races, trying to unpack everything he just admitted. I'm angry at him, *for* him. My heart pounds with rage while it shatters with heartache. He did tell me he hates liars, and I lied by omission. But he never gave me a chance to explain.

Wes stares back at me until it becomes apparent that I'm not going to leave.

"Fine, I'll go," he says, moving around me toward the door. The hinges creak as he pulls it open and I panic. I have to say something. Without turning around, words spill from my mouth. "I was *hurting*, Wes. You knew something was wrong and you left. You *left*." My voice wavers as the door slams shut. *But is he in or out?* "I saw it written all over your face," I continue. "You even *asked me* if something had happened." Silence surrounds me but I don't stop, hoping like hell that I'm not talking to an empty room but too nervous to turn around and find out. "You were right. I'd just had some news and I was dealing with it. Or at least, trying to deal with it. I shouldn't have lied to you, Wes. But I cared about you. A lot. And if you'd bothered to check in with me, I would have eventually told you everything. We both fucked up. Don't make working here hell just because of our past." When the last word leaves my mouth, I chance a look over my shoulder and see he's still standing there facing the door. One hand rests on the handle, his back hunched over as his other hand clenches by his side.

"Wes—"

"Fuck it!"

He snaps out of whatever moment he was locked in and turns around, abruptly storming toward me. He looks positively mad with his eyes narrowed and lips pulled into a frown, so I take a few steps back until my legs hit his desk. "Fuck, Wes. I'm—"

He grabs my face in his hands and slams his lips to mine. It's not the reaction I was expecting, nor should it be, but I can't for the life of me stop myself from kissing him back.

Gripping his shirt, I pull him into me, leaning back against the rich mahogany as Wes groans before running his tongue along the seam of my lips, begging for entry. Entry I grant him easily, needing him just as much.

When our tongues touch, a spark runs through me, straight to my core, and I have to fight to stop myself from grinding against him. Especially when his hardness presses into me. But I can't stop my moans. It's been too long since I've been touched like this; I can't control it.

With another groan, Wes runs one of his hands along my neck and into my hair, clenching the strands in his fist as he angles my head to deepen the kiss. A strangled squeal escapes my mouth, and I buck into him involuntarily, causing us both to cry out. When Wes rips his mouth from mine, I'm certain I've just broken the Lucy trance he was in, until he grabs my waist and lifts me up, setting me on the desk. My legs fall apart instinctively and my dress rises up to reveal my *soaked* satin panties. Wes's eyes darken, and he bites his lip as he stares between my legs, fixated on my core.

It's been a million years since someone looked at me like that—looked at me at all—and the last person to do it is standing right in front of me, making me melt.

He blinks a few times before stepping closer and taking my lips in another bruising kiss. He leans into me until I have no choice but to rest back on my palms and wrap my legs around him, wanting him as close as physically possible.

We kiss like that for a while, our tongues exploring, our bodies subtly moving in rhythm until I'm a writhing mess. *I can't take it anymore.* Sucking Wes's lip into my mouth, just like I did all those years ago, I internally cheer at the effect I have on him. He grunts as though he's in pain and grips my thighs, pressing his fingers into my skin before sliding me to the edge of the desk and sinking down on top of me. I don't even wait for him to start moving before I grind up into him, seeking the friction I so desperately need, moaning when Wes grunts again.

I'm not sure how long we stay like that before Wes repositions us slightly, allowing room for his hand to roam high up my dress, to the thin strap of my panties. Twisting the elastic in his fingers, he continues to grind into me, as he pulls tightly on the material causing it to rub hard against my core. The pressure and motion cause so much friction that I cry out in ecstasy as my head falls back against the wood. "Fuck, Wes. Yes."

He groans with his speed increasing until the desk starts to move as he pounds against me. Changing the pace once more, he kisses his way down my chest, nipping gently at my cleavage, making my body flush. My heart rate increases beyond what should be physically possible, and I'm not sure how much more I can take as my legs clench in anticipation. I'm so close to my release, I can feel the tingles shooting through me. I just need a little... "Oh god!"

Wes leans forward, and the rough denim of his jeans rubs me exactly where I want it. "Yes, that. Keep going."

He bites my bottom lip, and the spark it causes sends me flying over the edge.

I clamp a hand over my mouth to stop myself from screaming just as his office phone rings behind me.

I've never seen someone move as quickly as Wes does when he jumps away from our moment, almost ripping my panties as he goes. The elastic snaps back and I flinch, ready to say something until I sit up and see his expression. Suddenly that little sting is the least of my problems.

With both hands in his hair and his face contorted in pain, he squeezes his eyes shut, as though he's trying to block out the world...or specifically, me.

"That shouldn't have happened," he rasps, and it would hurt, if I wasn't expecting it. "I need to work. You should go."

He moves toward the phone, but my hand shoots out to stop him. "Wes," I whisper, my heart skipping when his eyes meet mine and his gaze softens.

"I'm sorry. I lost my mind for a moment. It won't happen again," he huskily whispers as he lifts the handset of the phone, finally shutting off the noise.

"This is Wes," he states plainly, void of emotion, until he hears what the other person has to say.

And that is my cue to leave.

"Again? Fuck! How did that shit get out?"

I leave quietly as Wes yells down the line, and if I'm looking for any positives from that call coming in, then at least I know he's grumpy at the world; it's not just me.

I only make it a few steps away from his office when I re-member I originally had a purpose for being there and curse. Running my hand through my hair, my fingers get caught in the knots and I panic to think of the state it's in. The state I'm in. Too bad. He's the one that caused it, so he can deal.

Wes is still on a call when I enter. He's got the phone in one hand while the other massages his temple. *Ugh! That's not a good sign.*

His eyes shoot up to mine and his brows furrow as I walk toward the desk, grabbing a pen and paper before settling into his chair so I can write a note. He subtly adjusts his jeans as he watches my every move, continuing his conversation. A conversation that suddenly becomes one-sided with Wes dishing out uh-huhs, yeses and nos. I don't even think he's paying them any attention.

When I've finished listing the players we need to discuss, I put everything back in its place, pushing the chair under his desk. And without a backward glance, I leave the room, not even giving him the satisfaction of waving goodbye.

I, however, get a lot of satisfaction from feeling his gaze follow me out.

When I get back to my office, Aaron is waiting for me. I startle at the sight of him, my face flushing red when I remember what I've just done and that I haven't been to the bathroom to clean up. *Can he tell?*

He smiles apologetically and waves a piece of paper in front of me.

"Sorry, you look like you rushed to be here for this. I was just inviting you to a dinner we're hosting at my place this Friday. These are the details."

"We?" I ask with a smirk.

"Okay, Lola. I'm just there for support."

I laugh out loud, probably louder than necessary because I'm a tiny bit uncomfortable with the current situation. "That's what I thought," I say, as I subtly pull at the end of my dress to make sure it's sitting properly. *Why didn't I check that before?*

"Tell Lola I'd love to come but I'll have to play it by ear. I'm already asking a lot of my family, so it might be hard to find a sitter."

Aaron's smile doesn't waver. "Bring her with you. My two will easily keep her company."

My brows furrow as I consider it for a second. Katie's not shy, but she's never met Aaron's kids. Wanting to keep an eye on her will definitely distract me, but at the same time, it can't hurt to get out more. "Let me think about it. Can I let you know in the morning?" I smile as Aaron walks over and pats me on the shoulder.

"Take all the time you need. I'll count you as coming, but if you can't, it's no big deal. We can rain check."

A throat clears loudly behind us, and we jump apart for no reason except that it came out of nowhere. Aaron's subtle eye roll at whoever's behind me draws my attention to Wes. The last person I'd expect.

He's standing in the doorway, casually leaning his shoulder against the frame with his arms folded across his chest. He raises an eyebrow when he catches my gaze and pushes off the woodwork, walking toward us.

"You done? I need Lucy."

Aaron frowns. "Actually, can you wait a moment—"

"Nope, things to do."

Wes turns to leave and I mentally curse him. When did he become such an asshole? I hate that we legitimately have things to discuss, and it needs to be before training camp starts this week. "Wes, wait!" I call out before turning to Aaron. "Was that all, or do you need me to come and see you when I'm done?"

"That was all," he says with a smile before walking away, making room for Wes to enter and get himself comfortable in my chair—just like I did his—with a cocky smile in place. That's

157

new, and it's hot as hell. I'm not sure how I feel about it. He's the air of confidence, and for a brief second, when he crosses his ankles in front of him, I get a glimpse of the easygoing Wes I once knew, causing my heart to flutter.

"Okay, hit me with it," he says, pulling me from my reminiscence. "Who should I be worried about?"

Chapter Seventeen

Lucy

Wes is somewhat civil over the next few days...

"Get the fuck out!"

...At least he is with me.

It's day two of our training camp, and lying on my table is one of our key wide receivers, injured after what I'm told was a stupid mistake. And Wes just found out.

"Seriously, everyone get the fuck out. I need to talk to Lucy and Silvers alone."

Trey Silvers, the player in front of me, grimaces at Wes's tone, and I don't blame him. Wes is a big guy so can be intimidating *without* the booming voice. That's an added bonus. Right now, he's taking up a large percentage of the doorway, and his posture alone demands attention. And he definitely has it. From me anyway. I have to fight to take my eyes off him, until I notice *his* attention is on Trey and I'm free to drink him in. He's every bit a football coach in his tight team-issued tee and black sport shorts. His toned legs would usually catch my eyes, but it's the ball cap that gets me. It's pulled low on his face, casting a slight shadow over his features, and the tips of his dark hair curl out of the sides, like it's a haphazard mess underneath. I never knew I found that sexy until this very moment, and suddenly I want to rip off the cap and run my hands through it, gripping it in my fists, just like he did with mine. *Dammit.* I blink a few times to rid myself of *that* visual, and swallow a lump in my throat, just as Wes's focus shifts to me.

"Tell me this is an easy fix, Luce," he asks, calmer than I expected.

I smile and thank my lucky stars that I can give him the answer he wants. "It's a mild..."

I pause when I catch Wes glare at the word mild, letting him sweat a little.

"*Very* mild sprain. He'll be good in a week tops."

"A week!" he yells before taking a deep breath and repeating himself at a reasonable decibel. "A week...okay. Is that the best we can do?"

"It's worst-case. Let me do my job and we'll see."

He nods before walking out the door, cursing at someone in the halls. Trey's eyes flash to mine and his brows furrow. "I expected a lot more yelling," he says, despite only knowing him for a few days.

I shrug by way of answer before getting back to work. *So did I, Trey. So did I.*

When I'm all done with Trey, I switch on my music and start tidying up.

"I Knew You Were Trouble," by Taylor Swift comes on and I dance around the room, letting my mind drift with the music. When the chorus hits, I raise my fist to my mouth and mime the lyrics like I'm Tay. Like this is my song. As one of my favorite pastimes, nothing beats losing myself in an addictive tune to get the heart pumping. Except maybe boxing. Boxing will always be my favorite escape.

Waving my arms in the air, I close my eyes and sway my hips as the music takes control of my body. It makes me want to go out. Hit up a club. Something I haven't done in years.

The song ends and "Perfect," by Ed Sheeran comes on, completely slashing my vibe. Don't get me wrong, I love this song, but I can't do romantic love songs at the moment. They all remind me of a love lost, a love I never even got to experience and all the choices I've made.

Bending over, I drop my elbows to the table and sink my face into my hands, taking a few deep breaths. My life is good. I have Katie, amazing friends, the job I've always wanted. But there's also this underlying heartache and worry that I fear will never go away. And I shouldn't be letting it get to me.

Standing tall, I change the song, swiping through a few until I find something I can handle. "Smells Like Teen Spirit," by Nirvana pops up, and I'm one hundred percent down for it, rocking out until my next appointment is due.

Aaron pops his head in around lunchtime, a hesitant expression on his face. "Is the kid from this morning okay? I don't need another reason for Wes to come at me."

"He'll be fine... but why is that?" I ask, curiously.

"Why is what?"

"Why does Wes '*come at you*'?"

He sighs, shaking his head. "Doesn't he do that to everyone? I didn't think I was special."

I cough out a laugh because he's right. "No, I suppose you're not. It appears to be a trend." *But is it the real Wes or is there more to it?*

My lips morph into a frown as I process that notion. He's like a completely different person from the Wes I knew before. But maybe he's not. Maybe I just caught him on a good week.

I work on a few more players in the early afternoon, in a preventive capacity, and also spend some time watching and taping the team practice. I like knowing the players, seeing how

161

they move and anticipating if we might have issues. It helps me to be ready.

My day flows quickly, and while I'm exhausted by the end of it, I'm also feeling on top of the world. God, I missed this. I spent six years of my life training for this very thing and barely got to experience it.

I'm packing up for the day when there's a knock on my door. *Damn, I was so close.* Looking up from my position on the floor, I catch Wes's eyes on my ass before they quickly move to my face, and I no longer mind the interruption. My cheeks flush at the intensity of his stare, and my heart races, but I try to ignore it.

"Hi, Wes. How was your day?" I say, standing up with a smile. I've noticed that the nicer I am, the more it annoys him, and I kind of get a kick out of that.

"Tiring, and stressful, and...it doesn't matter. I just wanted to check in on Silvers. Now that he's not here, has your response changed?"

I mentally roll my eyes and sigh. "Nope. He'll be as good as new next week. I've got to say I'm surprised it took you this long to ask. Bet that question has been burning a hole in you."

His lips twitch like he wants to smile but he doesn't. "He's not my only player, Luce. I've got other things to do."

"Yes, I know. You're busy busy. Are you going to Aaron's dinner party tonight?" I say, though I shouldn't have asked. I know he's not. But I couldn't help myself.

Wes glares at me and he scoffs. "We both know I'm not. Are *you*?"

"I'll be there, yes. It's nice to spend time with colleagues outside of working hours. You know...to bond a little."

"I couldn't think of anything worse."

My eyes narrow as they bounce between his, trying to find any inkling that he's joking, that he hasn't really turned into such a bitter man. But there's nothing there. It's not some ruse or act that he's trying out. He really is grumpy.

Wes visibly shakes as though he's affected by my scrutiny before taking his cap off and running a hand through his hair, settling it at the back of his neck. His lips purse for a second and then he shakes his head again. "Have fun *bonding*, Lucy. Hopefully, I'll have no *need* to see you tomorrow."

I huff out a laugh, completely understanding his meaning. If only his delivery was different.

"Thanks, I hope I don't see you either," I lie...again. Even though he hates it. Only this time, I'm pretty sure he thinks it's the truth.

I'm still staring at the doorway long after he's gone, completely lost in thought, wondering what it would have been like to have seen Wes after all these years and not have him hate me. Would something have happened between us? Something more than a quick—fully clothed—romp on his desk. It pains me to think that I'll never know, that in another world, maybe things could have been different.

My phone rings, breaking me from my thoughts to see Logan's name lighting up the screen. He must be here. God, I'm lucky to have such great friends. I laugh off my craziness and snap myself out of my daze before answering the call. "Are you out front?"

Logan laughs. "I am. I tried to call Dani, but she's not answering. Can you detour via her office and tell her to get her sweet ass down here?"

Logan and Dani are a total opposites attract couple. If you met them both individually, like I did, you would never expect them to work. But they do.

I smile at the frustration in Logan's voice and decide to leave it alone. "I will. How's Katie?" Logan picked Katie up from my mom's so she could come with me to Aaron and Lola's tonight. I decided not to ask anyone to watch her, hoping she gets along with Aaron's twins.

"Katie's fine," Logan says, and I picture him rolling his eyes. "Why don't you come out and see for yourself? She's currently chatting up a football player."

I toss out a small laugh. "I bet she is." That girl will talk to anyone. Hopefully he's a patient kid. "I'll be right there."

"*After* getting Dani," Logan reminds me.

"Yes, *after* Dani," I confirm and hang up, heading toward Dani's office.

Ten minutes later, Dani and I exit the building with tears of laughter in our eyes. She walked in on one of the players in a state of undress and just finished describing it in detail. It seems to be a habit of hers.

"I thought they were all gone," she cries out between breaths, clearly frazzled as I laugh some more.

"Mom! Mom!" Katie runs toward me and leaps into my arms as Logan joins us with a questioning look. I move out of earshot so Dani can repeat her story without little ears listening in, but can't stop my chuckle just thinking about it.

As we approach my car a truck revs beside it. A familiar one that's been there the entire time I've been outside and yet I'm only just seeing. *Shit!* My eyes lock on Greg sitting inside his metallic-blue Ford pick-up, and I freeze, my feet completely rooted to the ground. It's not until he smirks at me that my instincts kick in and I move back to Logan, placing Katie in his arms.

"I'll get the car started. Can you get her in her seat?" I whisper as Logan eyes me curiously. Something on my face must convince him not to ask questions because he walks toward my car without another word. Katie immediately starts tickling him, none the wiser that she has anything to be concerned about, while inside, I'm on the verge of a panic attack.

Greg jumps out of his truck as I approach my driver's door, and rushes to my side. "You're here. I didn't believe Bry. But there you are. In the flesh."

"Yep, I'm here. But I really have to go."

"Wait!" He reaches out and grabs my forearm, his fingers digging into me in a bruising hold. "We need to talk."

"I have nothing to say."

His eyes flash to my back seat and he smirks again. "I beg to differ."

When my eyes follow his stare, I see Dani helping Katie into her seat just as Logan joins my side. I should have known he wouldn't leave me alone. "Greg, good to see you again. Everything okay here?" he says, wrapping an arm around my shoulder with a polite smile in place.

"Everything's great," Greg says, taking in the size of Logan compared to him. "I'll be off, but we'll talk soon, okay?"

Getting back in his truck, he drives away without waiting for an answer, while I'm left reeling.

"What—"

"Thanks, Logan," I say, cutting him off before stepping out of his hold. I know he has questions, but I don't have any answers right now. "We better go so we're not late." I need the distraction.

Chapter Eighteen

Wes

"**N**o, run it again!" I yell before blowing my whistle and repeating myself. "Again!"

Out of the corner of my eye, I see Silvers hobble out of the tunnel after leaving Lucy's office with a frown still in place. *Shit!* Is it worse than Lucy said? I could ask him directly, but something tells me he'll lie. Instead, as soon as I get a small window, I rush off to Lucy's room, needing to know the truth. A week I can handle, a month would be bad, but not the end of the world. Anything more and we're fucked. With a new quarterback we need our best receivers.

Music plays as I round the corner to Lucy's office. Her door's ajar, so I peek through the opening instead of making my presence known. And the sight is breathtaking.

She's dancing to some Taylor Swift song and she's absolutely stunning. I'm struck motionless, mesmerized by the way her body moves with the beat. Hypnotized by the sway of her hips, the curve of her body, and the way she runs her hands through her hair, giving me flashbacks of when I did the same.

With her lips pulled into a smile, she's playful, happy, and *free*. A version of Lucy I wish I'd seen more of.

Leaning against the doorframe, I watch like a creep until the song ends and "Perfect," by Ed Sheeran comes on next. Lucy freezes, snapping me out of my daze, as her head falls into her hands on the table, giving me the perfect view of her ass. An ass I now desperately want to slide between. My shorts tighten, and I have to clench my fists to stop myself from moving toward her and doing just that. *This fucking woman.* What I wouldn't give to have her naked again, spread out before me, begging me to take her. *Fuck!*

Scanning the halls, I quickly adjust myself in my shorts before my gaze moves back in the room, trying to focus on something else, anything else, but it's pointless. I'm drawn to her in more ways that I'd like to admit. I'm fucking addicted. Have been since the first time our lips touched. And like always, my eyes seek her out, but this time when I see her, I really *see* her and I'm no longer worried about *my* feelings. She's not hunched over to catch her breath like I first thought. She's taking deep breaths and quivering on the exhale, clearly lost in thought. I want to go to her. I want to engulf her in my arms and protect her from the world. But I don't. I'd rather not get caught up in another emotional roller coaster that comes with caring for Lucy Mathers, or Lucy Kelly as it may be.

I'm about to sneak away when she suddenly stands tall and darts across the room, stopping the song in its tracks. The opening notes of a few more songs begin but she skips them all until she finds "Smells Like Teen Spirit," by Nirvana and visibly relaxes before starting to dance once more.

I release a held breath, push off the door, and walk away, suspecting she needs this moment to herself. I'll come back after to check on Silvers.

***

The rest of the day runs relatively smoothly. The boys start to get into a groove, and I find myself yelling less. *Slightly less.* Some of the younger receivers even step up in Silvers's absence, obviously wanting to prove themselves while he's out. And while that's somewhat of a relief, I still need him to be game ready as soon as possible if we have any chance of winning. He's one of our best.

I'm on my way to my truck after departing Lucy's office for the third time today and once again, I didn't want to leave. Especially knowing she was going to Aaron's house. I don't know why, but that guy rubs me the wrong way. He's too happy and... *Ah shit!* I'm fucking jealous. It's got nothing to do with Aaron at all. I'm jealous because that jerk-off and Lucy have such an easy relationship without a complicated past, while I flip between hating her and wanting to pull her into a goddam hug, forgetting everything that's happened. Something I'm actually trying to work through.

I'm almost to my truck door, pissed off at the realization I've just come to, when I feel a small tug on the end of my shirt. Turning around, I find the little intruder who busted into my office last week. *Katie.*

"Remember me?" she asks with an expectant grin. She's all dressed up, as though she's heading to a party, and I've gotta say, she's cute. Her long strawberry blonde hair falls in ringlets over her shoulder, and she's gripping a little handbag that hangs across her body. She almost looks familiar, but I can't place it.

I squat down until we're eye level and nod. "Katie, right? How could I forget you and your beautiful name?"

Katie beams up at me, and I can't stop my return smile. *Smile. Fuck, when was the last time that happened?*

"My mom named me after a *lovely lady with a big heart.*" Katie sings the last part, clearly proud of her moniker. My heart clenches and I swallow a lump in my throat as she smiles brightly. This little girl has no idea how much she's affecting me.

"My grandmother's name was Katie," I admit. "And she's *exactly* like you described."

Katie bounces on her toes in excitement, as a man on the phone behind her—presumably her dad—gives me a funny look. Not that I blame him since his daughter *is* talking to a stranger.

I'm distracted by his glare, so it takes me a moment to process Katie's next question, but when I do, my heart almost breaks. "Can I meet her? *Please.*"

Shit! A tight feeling swarms my chest as a shiver runs through me. I'm about to answer, or at least I'm about to change the subject, when Katie's dad calls out. "Katie, come on. We've got to meet your mom near the door."

Her smile widens and she runs toward him, jumping into his arms before throwing me a quick wave over her shoulder.

Slowly lifting myself from the dirt, I head to my truck and slide in, all while trying hard not to let my feelings take over. My head falls to the backrest and I close my eyes with a sigh. I can't think of a single reason I would ever have introduced Katie to my gran. I don't even know her. But fuck it would be nice to think that I could.

Despite telling Lucy that I hoped not to see her the next day, it's now the next day and I'm purposely seeking her out. For no reason. It's eight fifteen in the morning, so it's unlikely she'll have any new information for me, but since I lay awake for hours last night with visions of her running through my mind, I know I won't be able to concentrate unless I stop by. So here I am.

Rapping my knuckles against her door, I wait approximately two seconds before pushing it open, "Lucy, I just..." I trail off when I find her lost in a daze. She's staring out the window, completely in her head, having not even heard my knock. It would probably be comical, if her face wasn't pulled into a grimace and her eyes weren't wide with panic.

"Lucy, what's wrong?" I move into the room without waiting for her to answer and join her side. It's not until I lightly touch her arm that she flinches and jumps away from me, bringing me back to when we first got to know each other.

"Fuck, sorry. I just wanted to see if you were okay?"

Lucy's brows furrow and she frowns. Her gaze is still unfocused as she rubs her arms like she's cold, only it's really fucking warm today. Her current state is actually scary, especially after having to deal with Grayson for the last few days.

"Lucy. What's going on?"

Her office phone rings and she jumps again, the only difference being that this time she jumps toward me, not away, tucking herself into my chest, with her arms locked tight around her body. A feeling of rage hits me. She's scared. She's fucking scared. But of who? "Lucy, I want to help, but I need to know what's wrong."

Her face snaps to mine and her eyes widen before she steps away, shaking her head as she huffs out a laugh, her face flushing a light shade of pink. "God, sorry. I had a late night at Aaron's and I'm tired. I obviously drank too much. Maybe I'm still drunk." Her shoulders lift in a shrug as my brows pull together. She doesn't look hungover or drunk. Tired, maybe, but her eyes are clear and she looks pretty well put together. Still, I'm not about to question her on it and cause further embarrassment, so I nod and accept her excuse. That being said, I'm not leaving until I know she's okay.

Her phone rings again, and she glares at it for a second before making her way over. Her hand shakes as she picks up the receiver, and my chest tightens with worry.

"Lucy speaking."

The person on the line responds and Lucy lets out a sigh of relief, her entire demeanor changing. "Hi Dyl, you're up early. To what do I owe the pleasure?"

Her brother. *Thank fuck.* A wave of tension leaves my body as I watch her relax. I'd heard Dylan had been traded to San Francisco after I left. It's nice to know she has someone nearby who cares for her. It definitely puts my mind at ease.

They chat back and forth for a minute, and by the end, Lucy's calm. I'm still reluctant to leave, but I feel a little bit better than I did before.

After hanging up the phone, Lucy turns my way. Her eyes flash with shock when she sees I'm still standing by the window. "Oh, Wes, I'm sorry. You probably wanted me for something, right? Is it one of the players?"

"No, well, yes...no." Lucy frowns in confusion, understandably, but I hadn't come up with an excuse for being here yet and now I don't even care what it was.

"The players are fine. At least, they were when I left them yesterday. I'm still here because you looked a little spooked when I first came in."

She starts shaking her head before I've even finished speaking and rushes to speak herself. "Like I said, I'm just a bit off after a late night. But thank you for the concern. You've got things to do, I'm sure. No need to worry. I'm good."

I bite back a groan because she's clearly lying, despite knowing how much I fucking hate it. And now, I'm going to spend my day fixated on figuring out who she's trying to protect with her bullshit. Is it me? Is it her? Or is there someone else involved?

Once again, I don't move, causing Lucy to nervously giggle. Except I don't think she realizes it comes across as nervous. "Wes, I'm fine. I promise. Go, do your thing. We can talk later if you need to."

Does that mean she needs to?

I nod as I make my way to her door, and I'm about to turn back when Aaron arrives, moving around me to get in. "Good morning. Don't tell me we have more injuries already?" he says with a look of concern.

"Nope, Wes was just checking in for an update," Lucy says, smiling at him but not quite meeting his eyes. *Fuck, is it him?* I take a step toward him with my fist clenched by my side but freeze when Lucy gets my attention, ever so subtly shaking her head. *It's not him.* I relax my hands and nod in return before walking away.

While it's a relief to know that Aaron's not the cause, my heart aches knowing that there *is* someone out there that's hurting her.

And I want to burn the world down to find out who.

Chapter Nineteen

Lucy

Wes walks out the door and I almost double over. Since the moment I snapped out of my thoughts and realized he was in the room with me, I've been on edge. The tension is wound so tight, I'm on tenterhooks waiting for it to snap. I'm not stupid, I could see that he'd figured out something had happened, so when he took a step toward Aaron, fist ready for action, I had to stop him. I had to admit he was right, even though I desperately wanted him to believe everything was okay.

My nod seemed to work, and thankfully, Aaron is none the wiser as he picks up a book on my desk, no doubt waiting until he knows Wes is out of earshot before he speaks.

"I think you can guess why I'm here," he says when the coast is clear.

I offer him one word, curious to see how much he knows. "Lola."

"She's worried as hell but won't tell me why."

Nothing then. That's good.

"Tell her I'm fine. Actually you don't need to. I'll call and tell her myself. Honestly, I'm okay. It was silly. I'm fine."

Aaron's brows furrow and his lips pull into a line before he releases them and speaks. "I know I'm a guy and we're not supposed to know these things, but Lola's clued me in on the fact that *fine* does not actually mean *fine*."

173

I roll my eyes and laugh, though it's fake. "I promise, I'm good. Not *fine...good.*"

I'm actually neither. I'm not *fine* at all and I'm definitely not *good.* But I can't think about that until Aaron walks away. He eyes me suspiciously for a moment and then shrugs. "Good enough for me. I did as asked. I checked in. If you want to talk about it, please call Lola."

I exhale quietly and a sense of relief takes over. "Thank you. I will."

Aaron departs, and I practically fall in a heap. It's nice to have people checking up on me, and since Lola knows a little about my past with Greg, she's probably one of the better people to talk to. But I spent a long time trying to move on from what happened. It took all that I had to bury my past. The last thing I want to do is talk about it. I'm secretly hoping it will all blow over, but as I think about last night, I'm not so sure that it will.

I should have known that Brighton would tell Greg about me. I should have prepared myself for that. But I didn't. And seeing him there put me in a strange mood for the rest of the night. So instead of having fun at the dinner party, I wanted to curl up and disappear. I couldn't shake the weakness I felt all over again, the pain radiating through my chest. From. One. Look. That's all it took to send my world crashing down. I knew we couldn't hide forever, and yet I did nothing to prepare for it. This is all my fault.

My day's busier than yesterday, so when Dani stops by on her way in, I already have a player with me, giving me an excuse not to talk to her. I can guarantee she's checking up on me too.

As soon as I saw Katie secured in her car seat last night, I drove away, leaving Dani and Logan staring at the car. Then I refused to discuss it at the party. So of course she's here now.

And she's not the only one worried about me. Wes *happens* to wander past several times throughout the day but never once comes in. I start to expect it though, and every time I hear word that they're taking a break on the field, I wait for him to appear.

By the end of the day, I'm once again wrecked and ready to go home. I feel worse than I've felt in a long time, but I guess emotional exertion will do that to you. The look in Greg's eyes when he grabbed me hasn't left my mind for even a second. And as I pack up my things to leave, the panic grows. It's dark out, and most of my colleagues would have left for the day. Dani rushed off hours ago for an event, and even Aaron's long gone.

Taking a deep breath, I open the office door and my heart leaps as I startle, my hand flying to my mouth. I'm not alone. Wes leans against the wall opposite my room, with his phone in hand and his ankles crossed in front of him.

He looks up from his typing when he hears me and pockets his phone before pushing off the wall, spinning his keys around his finger. "Come on, I'll walk you to your car."

With that, he sets off toward the parking lot, only pausing once to let me fall into step beside him.

We walk silently, side by side, with our hands occasionally brushing, but neither of us draws attention to it. A warmth fills me as my heart beats wildly in my chest. Wes is walking me to my car. The guy who just last week wanted me gone, *figuratively*, is now my protector. And that means more to me than he'll ever know.

When we reach my door, he stays close, waiting for me to get seated, before taking a step back. I open my mouth to thank him, but he shakes his head like it's no big deal and offers me a weak smile. "Goodnight, Lucy," he says as he backs away, only turning around after I've started my car. *Talk about mixed signals.*

I don't want to leave. I want to get out of the car and talk to him, but instead, I drive away with a thankful smile on my face.

The journey home is uneventful, but when I pull into my driveaway, I groan and run my hands down my face. Summer's waiting patiently on my doorstep, with her hands in her lap, undoubtedly ready to fire questions at me. She looks beautiful with her radiant pregnancy glow and tiny bump. It definitely suits her.

My lips pull into a soft grin as she looks my way and stands. I should be thankful that she's the one greeting me instead of Dylan, but either way, I know I'm going to have to spill.

Katie's at Mom's again today. She's having dinner there and they're watching a movie before Mom drops her home. A calculated move on my part. I wasn't sure what today would bring, and didn't want to risk Katie seeing me if I came home an emotional mess. Which I would have, if not for Wes.

Taking a deep breath, I step out of the car and walk straight into Summer's open arms. She hugs me tightly, rocking me back and forth, as I anticipate what words are about to come from her mouth.

"Heads up, your brother and Joel are inside."

That was definitely not it.

I groan again, and bang my head on her shoulder a few times before pulling away.

"Guess we should get this over with." I sigh.

Summer grabs my arm as I move, pulling me back toward her. "You don't have to tell them anything. Logan called me and said he was worried about you after something happened before the dinner party. Unfortunately, I was on speaker in the car, with both of the boys there. I'm sorry. All he said was that Greg showed up, so naturally we're worried about you."

My shoulders drop and I blow out a breath. "I probably should have told you all the full story," *or most of it,* "a long time ago. I'm sorry."

"You know we're here for you, Lucy. And while I think I always knew there was more to it, none of us would ever push you to share more than you want to."

When I'd first found out about Katie, I told everyone that Greg had threatened me verbally, but nothing more. That was my reason for wanting to join a self-defense class too. They all seemed to buy my lie so easily, never liking Greg to begin with, so I let it go and tried to move on.

I'm not sure what to say to them now as I walk inside, but I have to say something. I'm not sure I can avoid it anymore. Especially if he's back in my life.

Dropping onto the couch, I press the heel of my hand to my eyes and try hard not to cry as I think about what went down. Taking a deep breath, I tell my friends what happened.

"I saw Greg last night. At work."

"Motherfucker," Joel says from beside me, making me giggle even though it's not funny.

Somehow I'd managed to walk out of our building last night without seeing a truck that would have once gained all my attention. The very truck that Katie was conceived in. I should have seen it the second I stepped out into the night. Bile rises in my throat just thinking about it again now. How I've become so complacent lately.

"Seeing him was so unexpected that I kind of froze and probably acted a little rash."

"What did the fucker do? Did he say anything?" Dylan practically growls, like I'm holding back.

"Nothing happened. He just said hello," I lie. I can still feel the burn where his fingers wrapped around my arm, and my heart still pounds from the encounter.

"So why is Logan worried?"

"Probably because I got nervous and practically threw Katie at him. Maybe in the hope Greg would think she was Logan's daughter."

"Why don't I believe you?" Dylan asks as Summer and Joel look between the two of us.

I pause, not knowing how much to tell them about the past. It's been years since I've seen Greg. He shouldn't still hold this power over me. But while I'd love to say I'm over it—that I've moved on, that I'm stronger and more confident now—after last night, I'm not so sure. Greg knows I'm here. He knows where I work. And I'm ninety percent sure he's going to use that information to force me to talk to him. I should tell them that but instead I show them my arm.

Dylan jumps up immediately. "I'm going to fucking kill him. I don't give a fuck what happens. He's a dead man walking." He doesn't even let me go into any detail; the bruise is enough. Summer grabs his hand and pulls him back onto the couch, trying to calm him down as I look to Joel for help, only to find his eyes just as murderous.

I give him a soft smile but he shakes his head. "I have to agree with Dylan on this one, Luce," he says with a huff.

"You're being stupid. Both of you," Summer says as she rolls her eyes. "Neither of you are going anywhere near him. You should be focusing on Lucy, not that fucker."

All eyes flash to Summer's when the word fucker leaves her mouth. She *never* swears. Looking at her stomach, she grimaces and pats her baby bump. "Sorry, little man, but it was necessary."

Dylan visibly softens, and a small smile touches Joel's lips. When my gaze locks with Summer's, she gives me a sympathetic grin and winks, letting me know she has my back when it comes to the guys.

I knew they'd react this way, despite neither of them being fighters. It's why I never told them what really happened back then. But I do now. Well, most of it anyway, except about the night Katie was conceived. That's not something I'm prepared to talk to anyone about. But I tell them about the way Greg treated me before we broke up, and that he kept contacting me after I met Wes, and when I finally get to finish my story, which actually ends at the beginning, Dylan stares at me in shock. "You knew Wes before the conference?" he asks, trying to get his head around everything.

"Not really, no. But I *had* kissed him, so I guess you could say we weren't strangers."

Joel huffs out a laugh as Summer sighs. "I really wish things had worked out with him, but I understand why you left without pursuing it."

"You know my thoughts on that," Joel adds. "But if I'd known the whole story, I probably would have been easier on you."

"I'm sorry I didn't tell you. I was scared and I don't know, maybe a little ashamed."

179

That gets Dylan raging again. "Ashamed! Lucy, that fucker... He hurt you and I..." his voice cracks as he trails off, rubbing his hands into his eyes to stop the tears. My own eyes fill as I rush toward him, pulling him into a hug.

"God, Lucy, I'm sorry. So sorry I wasn't there," he whispers into my neck, his voice full of emotion. "What can we do now?"

"There's nothing we can do. We just have to hope he doesn't find out about Katie."

"But he saw her last night?" Summer asks, her face white with panic.

"He did, but it was from a distance, and then she was with Logan. I can only hope he doesn't think more of it."

"We won't let anything happen to either of you, Luce. You know that, right?" Dylan says, making sure to lock his eyes with mine so I really listen.

I nod because it's true. I have a lot of people looking out for me; I should always feel safe. And yet, why am I surrounded by so much unease?

Chapter Twenty

Wes

Getting my legs to work and walk away from Lucy, when I was convinced something was wrong, had been fucking hard. Just like it had been hard in the parking garage almost five years ago. I'd known then that something was wrong, and yet, I'd let my stupid pride stop me from calling her and checking in, even though I thought about her all the time. I categorized her as a liar, just like everyone else in my life, and never gave her a chance to explain. Not that she ever tried.

But now...*now* it's different. And knowing I'm not going to see her until Monday is eating me alive. I think it's safe to say I'm not over her. Yes, I've continually tried to tell myself she's out of my head, like she's out of my life, but my fierce need to protect her would suggest otherwise. Seeing her today, with fear in her eyes, took me straight back to that day in the pool when she'd flinched away from me and to the subsequent times following that. Sleepless nights were spent contemplating why she'd reacted that way, and no matter how many times I wanted to find another reason, I always came back to the same one—someone had physically abused her, and it had definitely been recent...back then. So now, I'm left wondering if this is something new, or if that *someone* is back in her life. Either answer kills me, making me want to keep her close to chase the fears away. A clear contradiction to how I felt about her last week.

I'm still angry. Angry at the way things ended between us. Angry that she's back. But a little part of me is coming around to the fact that I may be partially to blame. After all, I didn't even *try* to contact her after walking away. I've thought about her often since that day. It's safe to say she's the only one that ever made her way into my soul. And I barely knew her. There was just something about her. Something that ate away at me for years because while I hated her for lying, I still fucking cared. Like now. *Why do I care?*

When I'm still wide awake at four a.m., with no sign that sleep will come, I throw on my workout gear and run to the local gym. Lately I've been working out at the stadium whenever I have time and giving myself Sundays off, but today it's necessary. Not only to wear me out enough to sleep, but to burn this weird energy I have running through me—before I use it on *something*, or rather, *someone* else.

My quads burn as I push against the leg press for my third set. I need to do this more often or my muscles are going to disintegrate. *Fast.* Especially with the extra junk I've been putting into my body since I was injured. *Pizza, anyone?*

"Pump up the Jam," by Technotronic fills the room as I look around. There are only a few people working out at this hour on a Sunday, so I'm thankfully left alone. But when the clock ticks over to six a.m. it's a different story.

"No way! Johnson's at my gym." A kid, probably around nineteen, approaches while I'm cooling down. He has long, dark hair pulled up into a man bun and a thick gold chain around his neck, but that's not what has me stopping to pay attention. It's the fact that he's wearing a jersey with my name on it. To the gym. At six a.m. on a Sunday. *Am I being punked?* My eyes dart around the space but I can't see any cameras. Not that that's reassuring. This can't be real.

"I can't believe you're here, man. Look what I'm wearing."

He spins around to show me his back, not realizing he's standing in front of a mirror. I'm about to respond with some kind of dismissal when he cuts me off.

"Is it really you?" he whispers in awe, and that's enough to change my mood. I bark out an incredulous laugh, shaking my head. These are the fans that make everything worth it. The excitement in his eyes. The passion. I used to love this. When did I become so bitter about it? About everything?

A trainer walks between us, breaking my thoughts as he calls out to the receptionist.

"Can you put Lucy K down for a boxing sesh at two thirty?"

That gets my attention.

"Done. You gonna finally ask her out this time?"

What? A feeling of unease takes over as my chest tightens. *Fuck!* She's one of the *reasons* I'm so bitter. It all started with Lucy, and yet now I'm shooting daggers at some guy who may or may not want to ask her out.

"Man, that fall. I've never seen anything like it. I prayed you'd get back up. We could use you this season," my number one fan continues to talk, completely unaware of my inner turmoil. I almost tell him to shut up so I can hear the guy's response, but I don't. Instead, I plaster on a fake smile and give him the chat he so clearly wants—and deserves since he's still wearing my name.

Looks like I'll be back this afternoon.

At two twenty I sit in my truck like a stalker, suddenly wondering what the hell I'm doing. How did I go from wanting Luce out of my sight, to now creeping on her from inside my truck? A truck that she'll easily be able to recognize.

Nope. I'm leaving.

Aggressively throwing the gears into reverse, I raise my hand to the back of the passenger seat just as someone knocks on my window, scaring the fucking life out of me. Slamming on the brake, unnecessarily, my hand flies out to brace myself as though I'm expecting an impact. *What the fuck?* Talk about fight response. I side eye my window and groan when I see Lucy standing there with a big smile on her face, completely different from the girl I watched drive away yesterday.

Still facing forward, I roll down the window and sigh.

"Lucy."

"Whatcha doin'?" She laughs.

"Practicing in case I'm ever in a collision," I say as I turn to finally look at her.

"I got that part, but what are you doing *here*?"

"A workout. What else?" I'm blunt but it's better than her discovering I was stalking her.

"Finished one or about to go in?"

Now's my chance to leave. Tell her I'm finished and drive away with my dignity intact.

"About to go in." *Dammit.*

Lucy bites her lip and stares off into space before her eyes light up with a smile. "How'd you like to be my punching bag today, Wes?"

That's exactly why I'm here. "Couldn't think of anything worse."

She's kicking my ass. Literally. Okay, not literally because it's boxing and that's an illegal move but *technique* wise, she's beating the shit out of me. All while Mr. *I might ask her out* flirts at every opportunity.

"Hold up. I need five," I say reluctantly as I hunch over with a wince. While I will say there are moments where I'm going easy on her, most of my pain is due to her talent. It didn't take long to realize that the girl who accidentally punched me in the arm five years ago now has some skills. Some serious skills.

"I've gotta say it's an honor to have you in my ring, man," the guy says, moving to Lucy's side. "But you really suck." I shoot him an annoyed glare, but he ignores me, instead focusing on Lucy and adding, "Like really suck," just to drive his point home. He's bullshitting of course. I'm not that bad. I just lack the finesse that Lucy has. I take more of a haphazard approach. I don't argue though.

"I get it, thanks," I say with a fake smile. "I never had much need to learn boxing during my NFL career. Funny that."

Lucy and the douche-face laugh together as I groan, straightening myself up to go again. "Come on. Let's do this."

I bounce from foot to foot like I see them do on TV and wink at Lucy when she smiles. Pulling her arms up to her face, she hides a blush behind her gloves, making my pulse spike. Take that, douche, you're not getting the girl on my watch.

As if reading my thoughts, he wraps his arm around Lucy's shoulders and her face scrunches, visibly uncomfortable. Not that the dick notices. "You've got this," he says, awarding him a scowl from me as I open my mouth to argue. Lucy shakes her head again, just like she did with Aaron, and I retreat. Douchebag continues on.

"Alright, you two. Try again. Remember we're only sparring. You look a little murderous there, Johnson."

I'm sure he's not wrong considering what I want to do to him, and I'm about to show him *exactly* how well I can throw a punch when Lucy socks me one in the left shoulder.

"The fuck, Luce. I wasn't ready."

She bites her bottom lip with a flirtatious grin and peers at me all doe-eyed. "Oops, my bad." *Is she playing this up for dickwad?* I don't even care if she is.

I try to bite back a smirk, but fail. She looks so fucking sexy trying to act all innocent, it makes me want to throw her over my shoulder and spank her. *Fuck!* Now is not the time for that thought.

"You ready this time, Wes?" Lucy asks, distracting me from my inappropriate thoughts.

"I'm ready."

We spar for another ten minutes with Lucy's fists connecting six times compared to my four, all of which were hesitant as opposed to her power punches.

Taking our time walking toward the changing rooms, Lucy laughs about one of the numerous moves I pulled to hide from her swing. I silently watch as she animatedly recalls my flinch in great detail, enjoying the way her eyes sparkle while her lips pull into a grin and the way her hand grips my bicep and stays there as she talks. She's the most carefree I've seen her since she started at Heartwood U, and it makes my heart swell. Especially after what I witnessed yesterday.

What I wouldn't give to see her like this every day, even those days I wish her gone.

She releases her hold on me as we reach the doors, but when she takes a step away, my hand shoots out instinctively, grabbing her wrist to pull her toward me. She yelps in surprise but allows it to happen. And when she's pressed against me, my spare hand sinks into her hair, guiding her lips to mine. Lucy sighs as I groan into her mouth while connecting my fingers with hers. It all happens in an instant, moving from soft to heated so quickly, I couldn't stop it if I tried, and the next thing I know, I'm moving us through to the men's changing rooms and into a shower stall, never once breaking the kiss.

Blindly flipping the lock on the door behind us, I spin around until Lucy's back is to the wall and take a step toward her. But she's having none of it. She shoves at my chest until I break away and then drops to her knees on the tiled floor.

Nope, no. That's not happening. I move to lift her up, but she wriggles out of my grip and yanks down my athletic shorts and compression pants in one go, watching my length spring free. I close my eyes and groan before stopping her in her pursuit and tossing her a towel. "If you insist on being down there, at least make yourself comfortable," I grumble quietly as if I'm the one hurting.

Lucy peers up at me through her lashes, smiling as she lifts her knees, and slides the towel beneath them. The look alone has me twitching and it shouldn't. I shouldn't want this again. But fuck, I do.

Leaning forward, she runs her tongue along the ridge of my length and across the tip before sucking me into her mouth without warning. I bite down on my knuckles to stop myself from grunting, not really sure if we have company. And thank God I do, because in the next second I'm hitting the back of her throat at the same time the door swings open and some men start talking as they enter. I groan around my fist, and it's not at all quiet, but I can't stop it. When I try to pull out, assuming we'll stop now that we're obviously not alone, Lucy grips my ass and locks me in place with a wicked grin on her face. *Who the fuck is this girl?*

She deep-throats me again, and I can't hold back a curse, glaring down at her to knock it off. Making eye contact is the wrong move because I almost explode like a teenager at the visual. *Almost*. Her playful expression is gone, replaced by so much heat and desire, my balls tighten as I lock the image away in my memory bank, for obvious reasons. *She's enjoying this.*

Losing my mind, I pump into her over and over, watching as she closes her eyes and moans before digging her nails into my ass. *And I'm fucked*. It's been a while, and the fact we could get caught is surprisingly thrilling. "I'm going to..." I trail off my whispered words—she gets the point—and wait for her to pull off. But she doesn't. She sucks harder with her hand also pumping me, until I see stars and lose all control.

When I come back down to earth, Lucy stands and wipes her mouth on her sleeve before picking the towel up off the floor. She throws it back on my bag and leans forward to whisper in my ear. "And they say chivalry is dead."

I shake my head as the smallest smile appears on my lips, making Lucy's eyes light up in happiness.

The bathroom is now eerily quiet, and I have no idea when that happened, too caught up in my release.

Lucy reaches for the lock but I stop her, my brows furrowed in question. *Does she think we're done here? Not a chance.*

She laughs silently as I reach for her pants, shaking her head before lifting up to my ear once more. "Now we're even," she whispers. "Thanks for the workout session."

With that she's gone. And I'm left wondering who the hell that was and what the fuck just happened.

Chapter Twenty-One
Lucy

As soon as I get to my car I take a deep breath and squeeze my legs together. I lost my mind in there, completely reverting back to the *"need to please"* version of Lucy. The version I had no idea existed until I was pregnant and reflecting on my relationship with Greg.

The only difference between then and now is that this time I *enjoyed* it.

Where I'd usually be counting down the seconds and praying my boyfriends would quickly find their release, with Wes, I got off on the sight of him falling apart. He makes me feel powerful. Like I'm one hundred percent in control. And I was. He was at my mercy. And when he smiled at the end... *my heart.*

So, why did I run? I can only guess it's because of my fear that it will all come *crashing* down.

I still haven't moved from my spot in the parking lot several minutes later when my phone vibrates with a text from an unknown number. My pulse spikes, higher than it already is, and this time it's not a good thing.

Holding my breath, I unlock the screen, preparing for it to be Greg.

Unknown: You're killing me, Luce. Why do I still want you so fucking badly?

My heart stops. While that could easily be Greg, I know deep down that it isn't, and my lips automatically form a smile. I take a chance, and hope that I'm right.

Lucy: I don't think you are allowed to look up staff phone numbers for personal use

Unknown: How do you know I haven't kept it all these years

Because I changed it.

Lucy: I just know

Quickly saving the contact to my phone, I drive out of the lot, desperate for a shower since I never took one at the gym. I'm more sweaty than usual from wearing a three-quarter sleeved top to hide my bruises. But when I arrive home to see three more messages, I abandon that idea.

Wes: Always so smart

Wes: Why'd you run? You can't tell me it shouldn't have happened...

Wes: Because I'm finally thinking it should

I drop onto the couch, sweaty clothes and all, and slowly release a sigh. I don't know what to make of that. Have I thought about a second chance with Wes over the years? Yes. But it was a dream. Something that was never going to happen. I have Katie now. She's my priority, and I'm not sure if I'm ready to start dating, or whatever he wants. I'm not sure I'll ever be. But I know he's impossible to stay away from. And if anyone is going to make me take a chance on a relationship, it's Wes.

Katie arrives home from her swimming lesson with Dylan as I'm finally getting out of the shower. *Perfect timing.* He always took her swimming when he came to visit and asked if he could take her to her lessons when he and Summer moved back. At least until the season starts, although obviously we'll have to change her day so we can go to his games.

"Hi, Sweetie. How was swimming?" I ask, bending down for a hug. Katie runs into my arms before looking over her shoulder at Dylan.

"Uncle Dyl had to dive in."

What? My eyes flash to his as he grimaces. "They had a new instructor. She hadn't really worked with three- and four-year-olds before, I've since been told. But she kind of ran this activity that had the kids holding a pool noodle to float, with Katie in the middle. And it sank. Four kids on one noodle. Is she insane? I'm so..." His gaze moves to Katie's when he pauses. "We can talk about it after."

My eyes flit over Katie's entire body, checking she's okay, but since she's beaming up at Dylan like he's a hero, with a big smile on her face, I let out a held breath as I nod.

Though, I can see Dylan's really worked up about it. Understandably. I would have been murderous if I'd been there. I'm a little murderous right now. But she's okay. The swim school, on the other hand, is in for a tongue lashing.

"You're okay, right, bug?" Dylan says, kneeling in front of her.

She nods and finally turns back to face me. "I went under the water, Mom."

That doesn't really answer Dyl's question and freaks me out even more.

"Did you cough?" I ask, trying to remain calm.

"Yes, Uncle Dyl made sure I did." *That's good.*

"And did you keep swimming or get out?"

She's already shaking her head before I finish asking the question, so I make a note to ask Dylan whose call that was. Is she going to be scared of the water? Or was it Dylan that kept her out?

"How about we go for ice cream?" I ask, dropping the topic. *For now.*

"Yeah!" Katie cheers, jumping up and down at my offer of a treat. I'm not a strict mom, but I try to limit the sweets. It's how Dylan and I were raised so I've kind of just continued it.

Katie's scare though...definitely calls for ice cream. I just wish I knew how worried I should actually be.

Summer arrives not long after Dylan and Katie, and we spend the afternoon and evening together. After a long wind down period, I finally get Katie to sleep and walk back into the kitchen to find Dylan's head in his hands and Summerstroking his back with a concerned expression. "What happened?" she mouths when she sees me.

"Dylan?"

He peers up at me with a look of complete exhaustion. Like it's taken everything he has to keep himself together until now.

"What if she'd drowned, Lucy? What if I hadn't been there? Two kids went down and the instructor grabbed the other kid."

Summer gasps as her gaze shoots to mine. They obviously haven't discussed what happened. And while I have to fight to keep it together, she's okay. Because of Dylan.

"You were there, Dylan. She's okay."

"But what if I wasn't? What happens when the season starts or when our little guy comes along and I don't have as much free time. It's just *you*, Lucy. You're on your own."

I can't help but laugh as I realize why all this is getting to him. He's worried about both of us. His family. It's a fear he's always had since our father died when we were young. He'd always been concerned that if he went pro with the NFL he wouldn't be around when we needed him. Like our pro footballer father. But he shouldn't be worried.

"Dylan, I've been doing this by myself for years while you've been in Denver. Well, not entirely alone because I've had our found family. But I get by. It'll be okay. Thank you for being there today though. And for jumping in."

Dylan shakes his head. "It's not okay yet, Luce. She says she's fine; you know because she's your daughter and that's what you do. But she wouldn't get back in the pool."

My face scrunches because I was afraid of that, and also, he's not wrong. I'm acting that way right now when in reality my heart hasn't stopped thumping since he first told me what happened. But if I make a big deal around Katie, it will become bigger in her mind. And if I make a big deal around Dylan, he'll feel worse. I'll have to take her again soon so it doesn't remain a fear. But for now, I'm just happy Dylan was there.

"We'll get her back in. You did good, baby bro."

Dylan huffs out a laugh as he burrows into Summer's shoulder, and the look she gives me eases my mind. She's got him. He'll be okay.

A short time later, when Dylan takes out the trash, Summer approaches me in the kitchen. "Dylan struggled a lot in Denver, being away from you and Katie. I never wanted to tell you because there wasn't really anything we could do about it, but you know what he's like...he loves to hold on to guilt. And now he's nervous about becoming a dad himself. Keep an eye on Katie, but don't worry about Dylan. We've been through this before; we'll get through it again."

My heart breaks for my little bro, and like always, I thank the world for being so lucky to have him.

"Maybe he should talk to someone. I'm sure Joel can offer recommendations."

"He is. He'll get there," she says and I think she's finished until her soft smile turns wicked. "You know...if he knew you had Wes, he'd probably feel better."

I scoff, because I've given her no details on anything Wes related except that I work with him. Also... "That's a bit sexist."

"I'm kidding, Luce. I was trying to see if there was a...*you and Wes*. You tell me nothing these days. But I've noted that you didn't deny it."

I huff out a laugh. "I'll tell you when there's something to say."

Summer nods with a smile. "Good. I'll be waiting."

I'm late to the office Monday morning because Katie refused to go to my mom's. Not that I blame her; it's been a huge adjustment for her. She's gone from spending almost all her time with me to only seeing me morning and night. And the guilt of that is doing a number on me. Add to that, yesterday's pool incident... If I'm being honest, I didn't really want to leave her today either.

It's just one of those days, and hopefully once she starts preschool she'll feel better. *Hopefully.* At the very least, she won't notice I'm gone as much.

I'm tired and emotional when I finally walk through the glass doors from the parking lot. The image of Katie's crying face is etched into my mind, and it's a struggle not to let my own tears fall. I want to turn around, get back in my car, and pick her up. To spend the day at the zoo or museum. To draw, paint, or sing. Anything she wants. But I signed up for this. I need to be here.

Aaron's walking out of his doorway as I pass, but I barely acknowledge him. I just want to fall in a heap at my desk until my first appointment arrives. But no such luck.

"Everything okay?" he asks, and I know he's thinking about Friday night.

"Everything's fine, just the typical Monday morning exhaustion."

He laughs, seemingly believing me. "I'm with you there. Listen, I don't want to bring this up," he says, taking a step toward me. "But I saw you and Wes walking to your car Saturday night when I came back to get some paperwork."

I frown, unsure where this is going because that particular interaction was innocent.

"You know there's a nonfraternization policy, right?"

What?!

"I never read that," I say and then grimace. That was not what should have come out of my mouth. "Not that it matters because I have no plans to have a relationship with anyone here. Especially Wes."

"I know, I know. Your daughter is more important. I just thought I'd tell you."

"Thanks." I *think*. "I appreciate it. Although you might want to tell HR to add it to their contracts because I just signed one and it wasn't there."

"Agreed. I've been told it's a work in progress."

I nod before walking away, pulling out my phone before he's even left my office.

Lucy: Did you know about the nonfraternization policy?

Lucy: (Laughing Emoji)

Wes: Yep

Okay, then. So what? He just doesn't care?

Lucy: I think some might consider what we're doing to be fraternizing

One of our linebackers knocks on my door as soon as I've pressed send, so I don't get to check Wes's response until after he's gone. But the second he leaves the room; I pick up my phone, smiling in anticipation.

Wes: Won't happen again. You can relax

What?! My insides twist at his words before I've even processed why he would say it. We hooked up yesterday, and while I wasn't convinced of it happening again, he definitely alluded to it. What's changed between now and then? Or is this hot and cold attitude he has the real Wes, and no one ever knows which version they're gonna get?

I really thought I was making progress, but obviously not.

Chapter Twenty-Two

Wes

What. The. Fuck?

Lucy has a daughter? I stand frozen, just outside her door, as Aaron's words run on repeat through my mind. *"Your daughter is more important."* What?!

Lucy. Has. A. Daughter.

Since when? She's never *once* mentioned that. Maybe she *was* married. Or maybe she *is* married...and doesn't wear her rings. I've been trying to push the surname change out of my mind, in fact... *Holy Shit!* Dylan's brother-in-law is Thomas Kelly, Seattle's quarterback. Thomas *Kelly*. Did she fucking marry Thomas? Is he married? Jesus, I've never wished to have kept up with gossip sites more than I do right now.

With one hand running nervously through my hair, I snap out of my daze and walk away, reaching for my phone. Bringing up my search engine, I type in *Thomas Kelly's wife* and am about to click go when it occurs to me that it *doesn't fucking matter*. Husband, no husband. She's lying *again*. Yes, it's a lie by omission, but at this point, that's enough. I don't have the emotional energy to waste my time on people like that. Especially after how badly it fucked me up last time.

God, I wish I hadn't walked past her office. I could have stayed blissfully unaware. Then again, I guess it's better that I know.

And she has the nerve to text me about the nonfraternization policy. As if she's not hiding a huge fucking secret.

I can't do this again. I'm spiraling, just like I did years ago. And it's the same woman involved. *Fuck my life.*

I spend the rest of the day on the field with the team, and by the time we're finishing up I'm well and truly ready to crash. But I can't. The big guy, a.k.a the athletic director, a.k.a Bossman called another meeting for six p.m.—Six P.M.—and my teeth grate as I storm to the room, loudly dropping into a spare seat.

"We have a fundraiser at the end of the season and..."

Bore. Major bore. I don't plan on being the head coach by the end of the season so I don't need to pay attention here. He's talking...alumni and beneficiaries and...I'm out. I might be required to be there at the event, but since the guy filling in for my proper role isn't here, I know I won't be required to help when I'm back in my original receiver coach position. So, instead of listening, I picture all the ways I could be spending my time, rather than this hellhole.

I'm on a beach in Hawaii surrounded by white sand, beautiful women, and... loud as fuck, drunk teenagers. *Nope that won't work.*

I'm running down the field toward the end zone. The crowd roars, I'm almost to victory...until I'm hit from the side. *Fuck, that won't work either.*

Relaxing in a bar for a drink... *nope.* Watching Netflix... *nope.* Dancing... *hell no.*

"... He has this built-in ability..." The AD's still waffling on but... wait, that's a song.

"Invisible Touch" by Genesis, one of my favorites. I could be rocking out in my living room, singing it loudly, out of tune... *also nope... that one reminds me of Lucy.*

Lucy... Lucy... My time could be spent pushing her against a wall and stepping between her open legs. I could be gripping her long ponytail and angling her head to accept my kiss. I could be inside her. I could... *fuuuuck.* My shorts tighten to the point of being uncomfortable, and I have to subtly adjust myself. That spiraled quickly. I don't even *want* to be doing that. Any of it. I just want to get the fuck home and be done with today.

"Is this meeting really necessary...in August?" I snap out of nowhere.

All eyes turn to me and Bossman scoffs, "Got somewhere to be, Wes?"

"Yep. Home. It's been a long day. The team's struggling, and I need some fucking rest if I'm going to function tomorrow."

"You're free to leave," Bossman says with his arms folded over his chest, like he's challenging me, like I'm not actually free at all. Too bad I don't give a shit.

"Thanks, Boss." I throw him a half wave and hightail it out of there, already pissed about that time I'll never get back.

Wallet, phone, and keys in hand, I head straight for the parking lot. I need a beer and carbs. Loads of carbs.

When I reach the exit, the guy I saw with Katie the other night is entering with another kid. This one looks to be about ten, and the two of them laugh as they shuffle around me. I grab the door they just came through right as it shuts and hear my name before I get the chance to exit.

"Was that Wes Johnson? Can I talk to him?" the boy asks, obvious awe in his tone.

I keep walking without even listening to the man's response, something I never do. Is it rude? One hundred percent. But I'm done for the day. And I don't really want to risk snapping at an innocent young kid if he keeps asking me questions. So, out the door I go, pretending not to hear him.

Apparently, that was the wrong thing to do, because not even an hour later, I'm sitting on the sofa with my feet up and a text comes through.

Lucy: What the hell, Wes? That boy you ignored WAS one of your biggest fans

Fuck my life. Of course Lucy knows that guy and his kids. He probably went to Aaron's staff dinner party. They probably all hang out on weekends. Fuck!

For the rest of the week, I avoid Lucy like the plague. In fact I avoid everyone unless it's absolutely necessary. So by Saturday night, I have Carter breathing down my neck.

"Open up, dickhead. We're going out." He's pounding on my door and I know he won't give up until I let him in.

"I'm not in the mood," I grumble as I open up, standing aside to let him through.

"Well, get in the mood. We're going to Jaded."

Ugh! Big night then.

I groan but reluctantly move toward my bedroom to get ready. I could fight it, but I know Carter, and he'll just drag me there if I try.

When I'm somewhat decent looking, I find him waiting for me in the kitchen, two whiskeys in hand. "Pre-game?"

I'm not a huge drinker—past few weekends aside—but I'm going to need it to get through tonight. I wasn't joking when I said I wasn't in the mood. *What am I thinking?*

"Too late," Carter says, as if reading my mind. "Drink up and let's go."

I knock back the drink in two gulps—bad idea—and then follow Carter to the waiting Uber. I'll give him two hours, tops, and then I'm done.

Three hours later, I'm still out and I'm not even mad about it. Jaded is owned by a music friend of Gray's, and it's a popular hangout for those of us in the public eye, because the guy on the door is under strict instructions to vet the people he lets in. Having said that, it's one of those establishments you have to know about to actually find. From the street it looks pretty dark and dingy, so they don't often get walk-ins. But with the candlelight style lighting and deep-red accents, it's a nice place to relax and get lost in.

Carter's off flirting with some chick he met five minutes ago, while I'm talking to the bartender who is so freaking lovely. *Lovely? What the fuck.* Ah well. He is.

"And then she waltzes back into my life like she's meant to be there and *dammit!* because she probably is, but I was finally starting to forget about her."

He wipes the bar top in front of me—where I just spilled my whiskey after half yelling dammit—and smirks. "Did you really start forgetting her, or were you just telling yourself that?"

I huff out a laugh. "The latter for sure. Man, if you saw this woman…" I bite my knuckles with another groan before spinning on my swivel stool. I've been doing this every few sips just to check in on Carter, and sure enough, he hasn't moved. I'd say he's going to be stuck to this chick all night. As my stool moves slowly back to its starting position, something catches in the corner of my eye and my jaw drops. "Fuck me, am I drunk?"

Pushing off again, I do a second loop, ignoring when my new friend says "yep," and search the crowd. Sure enough, Lucy's sitting in a booth with a group of girls, laughing. *Laughing.*

I twist my head to keep watching her while I continue to turn, only looking back at the bar in the last second.

"That was weird," the bartender says as he mixes a cocktail for the girl next to me, and I nod, because he's right. *What are the chances?*

I take a quick look over my shoulder and smile. "Hey man, I think I'll make this one a double."

"You should go over there," the bartender says, signaling toward Lucy. I don't look where he's pointing because I've hit stalker level already since I first noticed her. *She has a kid. Why isn't she home looking after her?* "Or you could chat with the lovely lady approaching you now," he adds, pulling me from my thoughts.

Subtly rolling my eyes, I hold back a groan as a woman sits down beside me. "Wes Johnson in the flesh."

"That's me. And you are?"

"I'm Lucy. My friends and I were just talking and—"

"I'm sorry, what?" My eyes almost bug out of my head, while the woman freezes, her eyes flashing away, clearly confused. Her face tinges pink and I almost feel bad. "What did you say your name was?"

"I...uh...Lexi?"

"Lexi?" I repeat.

"Yep?"

Why the question?

"Maybe because you're being a douchebag," my bar friend says, alerting me to the fact I'd said that out loud and I'm definitely acting like a douche.

Lexi walks away without another word, and this time, I do feel bad. A little. *But come on! The world is clearly messing with me... Or I'm just bad at hearing.*

When I turn back to the bar, I notice my man has graced me with another whiskey, and fuck do I need it.

I drink doubles for the next thirty minutes and I feel amazing.

"I'm going over there," I announce and almost fall off my chair when I throw my hands in the air.

"Uhhh. Are you sure that's a good idea? Isn't she pissed at you, after you were a dick to that kid?"

Fuck, I told this guy everything.

"Guess we'll find out."

Mr. Barman laughs, and I realize I really should have gotten his name, but it's too late now. Lucy, here I come.

I approach slowly because it definitely makes me look cooler and stare at Lucy as I move. Dressed in a black, off the shoulder dress, Lucy looks beautiful as she laughs along with her friends, something that stops the second they see me.

"Ladies. How are you this fine evening?"

Now that I'm here, I recognize the blonde as the girl from the hotel. But I don't know the others. They're all smiling at me, except Lucy. She's positively mad. "We're great. We were just discussing how big of an ass you are to little kids."

Ouch!

"Fair call. I deserve that." I shrug as I lean against the booth for support.

Lucy crosses her arms over her chest and frowns. "What are you doing, Wes? Why are you here?"

"Here, here?" I ask, pointing to my position on the floor. "Or here at Jaded?"

She rolls her eyes while her blonde friend chuckles. "What do you want, Wes?"

"You," I say plain and simple, because it's true. I've never wanted anything so badly in my entire life. *She has a kid.* Fuck if I care right now.

"You told me we'd never fraternize again," Lucy says, throwing my words back in my face. Technically, I didn't say that, I texted it. But either way...

"I lied." *Fuck!*

"You. Lied." *Yep. What a hypocrite!*

"You're right. I'm sorry. Let me make it up to you." I have an idea.

Lucy eyes me suspiciously as I back away, waving at her like a giddy school girl. I'm not entirely sure what I'm doing, but I'm too drunk to care.

Chapter Twenty-Three
Lucy

Summer bursts out laughing, while Delilah and Cory just stare in Wes's direction. They wanted to take me out for a girls' night, trying to get me out of my funk. I was reluctant to come, and now I'm convinced I shouldn't have. Thank God Dani couldn't make it because she actually knows Wes, and I can picture her reaction.

"Ahh, who was that?!" Delilah asks, practically standing in her seat to see more of him.

"That was Wes Johnson. He and Lucy had a thing," Summer says before filling the others in on what went down. Well, the parts she knows anyway.

Burying my face in my hands, I shake my head. God, he looks hot tonight. His muscles are bulging in the button-down shirt that he's *rolled up at the sleeve*, and his hair...it's all mussed like he's been running a hand through it and all I want is to do the same. *But I hate him, right?*

He's a grumpy asshole who told me we're done for no reason and is mean to little kids. Yep, I hate him.

So why the hell am I all smiles as he shimmies toward me while "Dance With Me," by 112, starts to play. I have to suck my lips into my mouth to stop myself from laughing. *I'm mad, remember?* But when all three of my friends dissolve into giggles and Delilah wolf whistles, I'm done for.

205

Wes mouths the words to the song as he dances in front of me. This is a side of him I've never seen before. I mean, I didn't even think he drank. But if Wes is a funny drunk, rather than his usual grumpy self, I'm here for it.

He holds his hand out when the chorus hits, and I place my palm in his, not even pretending to hesitate. I want to be close to him, desperately.

"You go, girl!" Summer calls out as Wes pulls me to the dance floor while I bury my face in his chest as I laugh.

Grabbing my waist in one hand, he pushes the other into my hair, forcing my gaze up to his. "None of our shit matters right now, Luce. It's just you and me. And you are a fucking vision."

My heart races and I nod, despite his words confusing me. The way he's staring at me, like I'm the only one in the world, makes me want to forget everything too.

His splayed hand moves around to my lower back, pressing us closer together as his head rests on mine. There's some deeper meaning to his words. I can sense it. But I feel so good in his arms that I choose to ignore it, getting lost in Wes instead.

We dance like a couple of drunks after our little moment, even though only one of us is drinking, and when the girls announce they're leaving, Wes asks me to stay.

Pulling out my phone to check the time, I see a message from another unknown number waiting for me.

Unknown: We need to talk.

I swallow a lump in my throat and inwardly curse. I shouldn't be here. I should be at home, protecting Katie. "I don't think that's a good idea. I have to get home to my..." I trail off, taking a step back but keeping our fingers connected. "You said we were over," I add, because suddenly I'm shy. And backtracking. I've just been grinding against Wes for an hour, and now I'm thinking things through. Where was my rational brain earlier?

Wes frowns as he stares down at my phone. He shakes his head before pulling me in close and whispering in my ear. "You're right, I said that. And you're better than a quick fuck. Have a good sleep, Lucy."

He steps back and releases my hand. *What?*

"Is that what this was? Is that what you wanted all this time?"

"Isn't that what this is? Isn't that what *you* want? After all...you all but admitted that you have someone waiting at home. Is that who the message was from?"

What?

"Is that what you really think of me?" I ask, quickly looking over my shoulder to make sure the girls are a distance away.

Wes sighs, running a hand through his hair, exactly what I wanted to do earlier. "Wouldn't it be great if I could say yes," he admits. "Wouldn't it make our lives so much easier if I believed that?"

What is going on?

"Wes, I—"

"Go and look after your daughter, Lucy. I'll see you on Monday."

Holy shit! A shiver runs through me as Wes turns and walks away, leaving me frozen to the spot. *He knows.* He knew that entire time? Was he messing with me? Or too drunk to care? God, what must he think of me for keeping that from him. *I'm a liar.* After everything he confessed to me, telling me everyone he's ever cared for lied to him, I do it anyway. Granted, I had no reason to bring Katie up in conversation, but considering me being pregnant with her was part of the reason things didn't work out back then, I probably should have at least mentioned it. How the hell am I supposed to face him now?

I purposely avoided Wes on Monday, but today we have a full team meeting. So, while I can pretty much guarantee Wes will be shitty about attending, he has no choice. He's the head coach. *At present.*

After arriving early to prep my office for the day, I make it to the meeting five minutes before it begins. When I'm still alone at nine a.m., I have to wonder if I messed up the time, until the door slams open and Wes stomps in.

"Are you fucking kidding me? Where is everyone?"

I gaze in his direction with a blank expression and offer no reply. Guess we're back to being mad at each other. Although, I'm not really mad, because I now realize I might be the one in the wrong.

Wes drops into a seat on the opposite side of the room and leans back until the front legs lift up off the carpet. "There better be a good explanation for this," he mumbles to himself as I continue to ignore him. Instead, I focus on my nails. I really need a manicure. I wish I could do that dip stuff...my friend does it and wow, it's just—

"Lucy?"

Oops, guess I was focused a little too much on my hands. "What, Wes?"

"Did. You. Get. A. Notification. About. A. Time. Change?" He says it slowly as if I need help keeping up.

"Obviously not or I wouldn't be here." I roll my eyes and pull out my phone, checking my texts and emails. *Shit!*

"Actually...there's one here. It's been pushed by fifteen minutes. Guess everyone will be arriving soon." I shrug with a smile, watching as Wes huffs and crosses his arms over his chest.

For five minutes we sit in silence and it's deafening. I can see Wes's mind working while he broods. His eyes occasionally flick to mine, but just when I think he's going to speak, he huffs and looks away.

"Okay, let's get it out in the open. Yes. I have a daughter."

"I don't care."

"Are you sure about that?" I laugh because I'm so nervous, I don't know what else to do.

"Positive."

Great. This is going to be fun.

"She's wonderful. Thanks for asking. She may only be four but she has a huge personality and...why are you looking at me like that?"

Wes stares at me with a puzzled expression before shaking his head and frowning. He begins to say something but pauses before starting again.

"Why didn't you mention her?"

Good question.

"I guess I was warming up to it."

"And she's *four.*"

"Yeah, she's—"

A few people stagger in, including the AD's personal assistant. She pauses when she sees us both settled in our seats, and a look of horror crosses her face. "Oh no. Are you two early or did you miss the memo?"

Wes almost growls. "What do you think?"

She cringes and looks my way.

209

"I got the email but hadn't checked it. It's fine. Please don't worry about it," I say, hoping to wipe the panic from her expression.

Wes continues to scowl as the others walk in and get seated, and when the meeting starts, the first thing on the agenda is the nonfraternization policy. *Oh shit!* I huff out an incredulous laugh, as Wes's face falls into his hands.

Wes avoids me the rest of the day Tuesday, and I find myself growing anxious about it. I want to call him out on his reaction to finding out about Katie. He's being childish, and I have the strongest urge to be childish right back, until we can both laugh about it. But at the same time, I should probably leave him alone. I need to focus on Greg right now. I can't be distracted by Wes when he's back in my life.

By Wednesday lunchtime I'm sick of being alone with my thoughts, and since I don't have any players scheduled today, I'm going insane. After trying many things to distract myself, I pop my head into Aaron's office in the hope of finding something to do. "Anything to report?" I ask as I enter his office.

He looks up from the papers he's rustling through and smiles. "Nope. All smooth sailing here. How about you?"

I internally deflate but manage to plaster a smile on my face. "All good with me. Just wanted to check in," I lie.

"Good to hear. Lola said you haven't called her and actually asked me to stop by your office. This saves me the trip."

My shoulders stiffen as he indirectly mentions one of the topics I'm trying to get out of my mind. I don't want it to be a big deal. Because if others think it's an issue, it becomes an issue. I still haven't responded to Greg's text. The last thing I need is to have more people worried along with me.

"Please tell her I'm all good and I'll try and catch up with her on one of my lunch breaks this week." I walk backward toward the door as I talk, hoping that I can escape before he asks more questions.

"Okay, Luce. I will. Enjoy the rest of your day. Here's to it remaining injury free."

Is it wrong that I hope someone needs me? Yes, it absolutely is. Either way, I raise my crossed fingers as I depart, and when I arrive at my room, it's empty. *Damn.*

I settle at my desk and check my phone—yet another avoidance technique—and see three missed calls from my mom. Panic courses through me because she never calls me at work, and she's with Katie.

I call back immediately, and the fifteen seconds it takes her to answer are excruciating.

"Lucy, thank God."

"What's happened? Is Katie okay?"

Mom sighs. "Honestly, I don't know who's more dramatic, you or your brother."

My face scrunches. "Excuse me?"

"Katie's fine. I would have texted or left a voicemail if she wasn't."

That's reassuring. Mom's been great. I shouldn't complain. But she relaxed on the whole mothering thing after Dad died, so I do worry about how she'd react if she was ever in a situation she wasn't prepared for.

"Okay, that's good, but you're calling me at work?"

"Oh yes, I'm on my way to drop Katie off."

"Where?"

"At your work."

My head drops back and I look to the ceiling, taking a deep breath before I respond. "Why?"

"Sam got off early from work and wants to take me to the city for the afternoon. He forgot I had Katie, but he works so hard. He deserves the break."

Ah, what? I only dropped Katie there a few hours ago. "But you're watching Katie because I'm at work."

I should have known something like this would happen.

"I know," Mom continues, like my statement was obvious but meaningless. "Katie's a good kid. I'm sure she'll just color quietly in the corner."

I almost bark out a laugh because she can't be that clueless, right? She raised Dylan and me. We were four once. Instead, I massage the bridge of my nose, closing my eyes, trying to bring about calm. I can do this. "Okay, Mom. I'll see you soon."

"You will. I'm just pulling up."

She hangs up before I can respond, and that's probably a good thing because she would have definitely heard my over-dramatic sigh and commented on it.

I quickly rearrange my room to give Katie a play space and text Aaron to let him know what's going on. *With a little white lie.*

Lucy: My mom has to help out a family member unexpect-edly, so is dropping Katie here. Hope that's okay?

Aaron: Of course, the guys will love it

Lucy: Thank you. I promise not to make a habit of it

Aaron: I know you won't

Hmm, not sure what that comment means but I don't have time to process it because Mom starts calling again. I'm guessing she's finally realized she has no idea where my office is, nor is she on the approved security list.

"I'll meet you at the front desk in five," I say instead of a proper hello and then hang up, rushing off to meet her.

At five p.m. I'm exhausted and so is Katie. I've got to admit, despite thinking my mom was crazy for suggesting she'd play quietly, she actually did. My little angel.

"You've been amazing today, Katie. How about I pack up my things and then we go and see your favorite person?"

Her little face lights up and she bounces in the seat. "Del?"

I can't help but laugh. I was actually thinking about Dylan, but her favorite person does change on a regular basis.

"I'm sure I can arrange that."

The company Delilah is working for just designed their very first children's clothing line, and Katie loves getting to play dress-up in the samples Del brings home. She often asks to wear the dresses when she plays football so she can "look pretty while playing."

"Yes!" she cheers as she rises from her seat.

"Wait, can you stay there for ten more minutes while I pack up?"

Her face falls as though ten minutes is a lifetime, but then she flops back down and goes straight back to drawing.

Today could have been a nightmare, but thankfully it wasn't. Let's hope it doesn't happen again.

Chapter Twenty-Four

Wes

I'm ready to leave for the day when my phone buzzes on my desk, making me startle. Like always, I ignore it and continue packing up my things. But after it rings another two times, I give in and answer. "Yep?"

"Son, we need to talk," my father says, completely ignoring my rudeness. I clench my fist and inwardly groan. *What now?*

"I'm kind of in the middle of something. Can I call you—"

"Now, Wes."

Squeezing my eyes shut, I take a deep breath and sigh because I know exactly why he's calling. "How much do you need?"

Dad huffs. "I hate doing this. You know I do. But I just don't have anything to give."

So it's not him that needs it? Ever since I was traded to San Francisco and my earnings were released, Dad's been asking me for money. I used to say no, but when Gran died, I gave in.

"What's it for, Dad?" I ask, wanting him to admit it.

"Does it matter?"

I huff out a laugh because at the end of the day, he's right; it doesn't matter at all. "I hate this."

"What else am I supposed to do?" *Treat me like a son, instead of a bank.*

My free hand runs down my face and I sigh. "Okay, Dad. What do you need?"

215

"I reckon ten thousand should do it for now."

My hand drops. "For now? What the fuck, Dad?"

"Hey, watch your mouth."

"Who's asking whom for a favor? I'll say whatever the fuck I like," I cry out with my voice now louder than it needs to be. My gaze flies to the door, but thankfully it's shut.

"Can you help or not?"

I feel for my old man, I really do. He's the only one left in my family that has ever given me the time of day. His wife—my stepmom, I guess—and her kids have never bothered with me. Despite the fact that they actually got to grow up with my father around them, they're pissed because they believe I somehow lucked out with my genes, when in reality I worked my ass off to play football when my mom could barely afford the gear. All because my dad—*who financially supports them*—paid the bare minimum in child support. But we made do. There was no luck about it.

"Yep. I always do," I tell my dad, because it's true.

I donate a fair chunk of my money each year to various charities. I'd much rather the ten grand go there, but Dad would just end up taking on another job or remortgaging his house, and I can't let him do that knowing I have the cash to help.

He sighs in relief. "Thank you."

"No sweat."

"No, I mean it. I love you, son."

"Yep. Love you too."

If only you dished out those words more often, maybe then I'd believe them.

I take a moment to calm myself down before leaving. And as I move through the halls, I walk past Lucy's office with my phone raised to my ear, pretending to be lost in conversation. Suffice it to say this isn't the first time I've done this; it works well to avoid having to talk to her.

I round the corner to the safe zone, just as Lucy's voice stops me midstep. There's an edge to it, a fact she seems to be trying to hide.

"You can't come here. It's my work."

She pauses as I take a few steps back toward her office just to make sure she's okay. She's in the hallway now, pacing back and forth, so lost in her call that she doesn't even notice me a few feet away.

"No, you don't need to do that. She's not even here."

Just as she says the words, I hear giggles coming from her office, and I have to wonder if that's the "she" Lucy is referring to. Because if I heard it, chances are the caller did too. Lucy's eyes slam shut and she quickly mumbles something before hanging up and immediately dialing someone else.

"Where are you?" she says, clearly panicked this time.

"Sorry, hi. Where are you? I need you to come and get—"

She runs a hand through her long brown hair and drops her head back, staring at the ceiling. "Okay, shit."

Her head then rolls forward to her chest, and she sighs before straightening up, her eyes flashing toward her office. "It's okay. I've got this," she says before hanging up.

I move to walk away—*she said she's got this*—but I pause again when I'm racked with guilt. "Ah, fuck."

Hearing Lucy move back into her office, I take off in a run to catch the door before it shuts completely.

"I know something's wrong. How can I help?" I say, stepping into her room.

Lucy's eyes widen in surprise and flash toward something on my left before coming back to me. "Wes, I—"

"Hello, again," a familiar voice says from behind me, cutting Lucy off.

I turn toward the voice and freeze. There in front of me is Katie. *Katie.* The little girl with the same name as my grandmother, the little girl who happens to be four years old, the little girl who on close inspection has *my* light brown eyes.

Fuck. *Fuck!* I feel sick. I'm going to throw up.

"Wes?" Lucy asks in a small voice, just above a whisper, but I don't look at her. I can't. It at least snaps me out of my downward spiral, though, and I do what I have to do, for now.

"I heard you on the phone. I'm happy to wait here if you—"

"No! Ah, no, that's okay." Her eyes flash to Katie's again. She's smiling but it's clearly forced. "We'll be fine."

Nothing about this situation is fine. She's not fine. But something tells me it's Katie she's worried about. *Why?*

"Is it Katie's..." I mouth the word "dad" at the end and tense up as Lucy shakes her head. *Of course it's not. Because I fucking am.Shit, shit, shit.*

Swallowing a lump in my throat, I put on my best smile.

"Katie, your mom still has some packing up to do. I was thinking you might want to come and see my office. I've got lots of football stuff." I wince because what four-year-old is interested in football? "Or we can watch something..."

Her huge, cartoon-like *brown* eyes widen, just like her mother's *blue* ones did, and she smiles brightly. "I love football!" *Guess I was wrong.*

Lucy's entire body deflates as though all the tension just left it as she mouths "thank you" and then starts the charade of actually packing up.

"Uhh...we'll be in my office until you're ready."

Lucy kisses Katie on the head before we both walk away, leaving her completely alone, waiting for God knows who. And that doesn't sit right with me. I have to do something. I shoot off a quick text before we reach my door and pray to God he comes through for me.

"So this is my office," I say awkwardly as Katie's eyes bounce around the room. When she spots my signed footballs, her eyes light up.

"These are my prized possessions. A couple are signed, and one's a championship ball. Over here I have my..." I pause because I'm talking to her like a tour guide showing her around. Gripping the back of my neck, I take a deep breath. *I can do this.* "What I mean is that...yeah, this is my stuff." I shrug.

Katie walks over to the balls and grabs one in her grubby little hands without even asking. "Don't do that!" I rush out, and she freezes with the ball midair before releasing her grip, the ball and her gaze both dropping to the floor. *Shit! Shit! Goddammit. Fuck!*

"I'm sorry. It's fine. We can play with this one," I say, picking it up off the carpet. "How about catch?"

Katie's eyes rise to mine and she gives me a small yet slightly wary nod. I try to meet her smile with as big a grin as I can muster, but apparently I look funny because she bursts out laughing. Laughing is good. *Right?*

We play catch for a while. And even though my teeth are clenched the entire time, praying nothing happens to my precious ball, Katie does warm up to me. And she has a pretty good arm for a kid.

"Are you sure you're only four?" I ask, in awe of her skills.

"Four and a quarter," she states matter-of-factly, causing my chest to tighten and my entire body to break out in a cold sweat. Four and a fucking quarter. *Holy shit.*

I have to consciously make an effort not to study her too closely—so I don't freak her out—but that's exactly what I want to do. Well, not the freaking out part. But I want to see what similarities or differences I can find. I mean, the natural talent she's displaying should be a giveaway, but she's also Dylan Mathers's niece so I can't lay sole claim to that. Or any claim just yet. But it can't all be a coincidence, right? *Fuck!*

I want nothing more than to storm down to Lucy's office and demand she tell me the truth, but I'm also terrified to know.

Katie seems like a good kid, but then again, it's been five minutes, so how could I possibly assume that? I don't know what she's like with her mom and... Wait, didn't I see her with her dad last week? Is that her stepdad, or am I just fucking delusional? I could ask her, but then what if I'm not her dad and he died or something? *God, someone slap me, please.* My thoughts are out of control.

"Can we draw?" Katie asks suddenly, pulling me out of my chaotic thoughts.

"We can do whatever you want," I blurt out foolishly, trying to control my wandering mind.

Katie's eyes crinkle in happiness as a smile lights her face. And while it's adorable...fuck, I should know better than to offer a kid the world if I don't plan on delivering.

I don't know how long we've been playing when I hear a commotion from down the hall. "You need to leave!" Carter's voice booms, and I take off in a run until I remember my purpose and skid to a halt.

Katie's laughing at the drawing I did for her when I return, like she didn't even hear the yelling or notice me run off. So after squatting down beside her, I chuckle like I never left. "Yeah, it doesn't look much like a horse, does it?"

On the outside, I'm calm and collected, playing with Katie like nothing is wrong. But in reality, I'm on edge.

Lucy wants me here. Katie needs me here. But fuck, I want to be with Lucy. I need to know she's okay.

Chapter Twenty-Five
Lucy

My heart clenches as I watch Katie and Wes walk away. The sadness I managed to overcome all those years ago rises to the surface. Why the hell couldn't he have been her father? Why didn't I stay and get to know Wes the day I first kissed him? Why didn't I tell him everything after I found out? Why have so many years passed without Wes being in my life, when there's something telling me he's meant to be there? And while I'm at it with the whys... Why the fuck is Greg on his way here now?

After Katie's been gone for a few minutes, I step into the hallway, trying to listen for any clue as to how she'll be with Wes. His office isn't that close, but considering most people have gone home, it's dead silent in the building, so I'm hopeful. As if hearing my prayers, Katie's laughter travels the distance to my ears, and I sigh in relief. At least that's one less thing to panic about. The second, though, should be here any minute.

As soon as I push through the door to the foyer, I see him. He's pacing back and forth with his hands moving around animatedly, like he's delivering some big speech, and I huff out a laugh. If he thinks he can talk his way back into my life...

Slowly moving forward, I'm standing in his direct line of sight when he spots me, a smile adorning his face.

"Lucy," he sighs like I'm a sight for sore eyes, while I wish him gone.

Rolling my eyes at his bullshit, my hands settle on my hips as I try to appear confident. "Why are you here, Greg?"

"Why do you think I'm here, Lucy? You have a daughter. She's four. I did the math."

"You're not the only guy I've ever slept with, Greg. And you know for a fact I was with someone else. You confronted me about it."

Greg's eyes narrow as his teeth clench, but then his gaze flashes up to our second-floor offices, and he smiles. *What the fuck?*

"Please, Lucy. No more games," he says, taking slow steps toward me with his hands raised in the air. "Have you done a DNA test with the football player?" he asks, saying the words *football player* like it pains him.

I want to say yes. I want to tell him Katie is Wes's, but guilt swirls inside me and I can't. It was one thing keeping Greg from his daughter when we'd lost touch, but straight-up lying is a lot harder.

"I haven't," I rasp and cringe when I see that my answer gives him so much pleasure.

"So, it's possible that she's mine?" His face lights up and he reaches out to touch me but thinks better of it when I flinch away, my eyes flashing to the security guard near the office entry.

"I guess it's possible."

Greg drops to his knees in front of me and grabs my legs. His grip is tight enough that I can't move without risking a fall on my ass, but also loose enough that it wouldn't be considered

223

as a negative gesture. Even though it is. *It one hundred percent is.* And I feel sick to my stomach.

"Get up, Greg," I say, my voice void of emotion.

Greg shakes his head. "I don't care if there's only a fifty percent chance she's mine. I will be there for her and raise her like she is. Give me a chance to prove myself to you both, Lucy. Take me back so we can be a family." My stomach churns at what he's asking. Is he really that messed up to think that would ever be a possibility?

"Get up, Greg," I whisper-yell through my teeth, my skin prickling with disgust.

Greg shakes his head again, more violently this time. "Not until you agree to let me see her."

"Please, Greg. Just stand up."

"Where is she?"

His grip tightens but he's still smiling, portraying a romantic to the outside world.

"Get up," I repeat, much louder this time. I'm trying so hard not to use the words *let go*, as though asking him to do that is like admitting that I think he's the one in control.

Greg's eyes flash with impatience before he schools his features once more. Then he laughs. Like this is some big joke. "I'm not moving until you agree to give me a chance."

He runs one of his hands up the inside of my thigh, stopping just as he gets to my skirt. The feel of his hand so close to my core sends a shiver down my spine as my skin crawls. Yep, I'm going to be sick. The instinct to use my self-defense training kicks in and my knee itches to move, but I hold back. As long as he's focused on me and Katie's with Wes, I'm okay. I can handle this. *God, I hope she stays with Wes.*

"It's not going to happen, Greg. Katie and I are fine on our own."

"You named her Katie? *Fuck!*" he yells the last part, finally losing his cool, though I don't know why. Closing my eyes, I mentally curse myself for giving him too much information as I contemplate what to do next.

Both our voices start to rise after that, and I chance a look to the second level of the foyer, hoping they haven't carried up into the offices. That's the last thing I need.

When no one peers over the balcony I figure we're safe. Although, I don't know why I'm worried; no one's here and I'm hoping Wes is too focused on Katie to notice.

I'm about to try to wiggle free from Greg's grip when it tightens on me, seconds before Carter freaking Williams steps into my peripheral vision. I expect him to walk on by, but when he stops, I'm shocked.

"I think you need to let her go and walk away," he says calmly, and all I can think is *what*?

Greg scoffs but finally releases me before standing up. "This is none of your business, man."

Carter takes a step forward, and Greg tries not to cower. I almost cower. He's a huge guy—not The Rock huge but he's close. And intimidating.

"Lucy's a friend. So it's one hundred percent *my* business. I don't want to cause trouble. I just need you to walk away," he says calmly again, and I have to stop myself from reacting. *We're friends*? I mean, I'm not about to call him out on it, but we've never even met.

"We're just having a conversation, and don't think I don't know who you are. You're Carter Williams, one of San Francisco's offensive tackles, best friend to Wes Johnson. You're the guy that after all these years might finally get a shot. *You* should walk away. You don't need bad publicity."

Carter laughs, and I have to admit he sounds a little un-hinged. "Why are you making threats if it's just an innocent conversation?"

"It's just the kind of guy I am."

"So I gathered."

Greg gets up in Carter's face, and to his credit, Carter doesn't even look rattled as Greg spits out, "What's that supposed to mean?"

Instead, Carter takes a subtle step in my direction, placing me behind him. "You should leave."

Greg stands his ground. "I'm not going—"

"You need to leave!" Carter yells, and even I jump at the demand in his voice. My eyes shoot to the second story once more.

Looking over Carter's shoulder, Greg meets my eyes and his features soften. *That's weird.*

"Can we talk soon? Please?" he asks, with a relaxed tone.

I say yes because I don't know what else to do, and then watch as he stalks out of the building.

Carter turns to me the second Greg is out the door and sighs. "Are you okay?"

"Yeah, I'm fine. He didn't hurt me." *This time.*

Carter stares at me for a minute, probably trying to see if I'm lying, and then ever so slightly nods before walking to the glass sliders leading to the parking lot. "I'm going to double-check he's gone. You head on up. I'm on the approved visitors list."

I return his nod and walk as fast as I can toward the elevator, suddenly desperate to see Katie.

When I reach Wes's office, he's huddled on the floor with Katie, both intensely drawing. Leaning casually against the frame of the door, I watch them for a moment, enjoying the peace, until Wes looks my way.

"Are you—"

"It's all good." I wave him off, preferring to stay in this new reality where Wes and Katie have some kind of relationship.

Katie looks up at that moment, and I smile. "Hi, sweetie."

She smiles but immediately goes back to her drawing, leaving me to talk to Wes.

"So Carter's lovely. If not a little over-the-top."

Wes huffs out a laugh. "Shit, I thought you needed help. What did he do?" His eyes flash to Katie's for a second before coming back to mine, like he's checking she's okay. I may be back in the room, but he's still keeping an eye on her.

"He was fine," I say, when I have his attention again. "I just didn't expect him to come in guns blazing. Actually, I didn't expect him at all. Thank you."

Carter appears at that moment with a megawatt smile. "My ears are burning."

Wes rolls his eyes, and when he meets Carter's stare, Carter flashes him with a look of something I'm not expecting...pity. *What's that about?*

I look toward Wes at the same time Carter moves across the room to join Katie on the floor, drawing my attention away. "You must be Katie. I'm your mom's friend, Carter. It's nice to meet you."

Katie says hello and starts showing Carter her drawings, while Wes rises and signals for me to join him in the hall, out of earshot. *We need to talk.*

I let out a slow breath and flop back against the wall opposite his office door, resting my head against the brick. "Okay, say what you have to say."

He doesn't look happy about whatever it is.

"Are you ever going to tell me what's going on? Or do I need to ask Carter? I'm sure he has more information than I do now." His tone has more bite than it did seconds before, and I'm confused as to why, but...

"Now's not the time."

Running a hand down my face, I give him a soft smile, trying to make sure it appears genuine but not convinced that it actually is.

Wes blows out a breath and scratches his head. "I just have one question, but can you promise...no more lies?"

My eyes close for a second before I school my features and nod. I can do that. *Maybe? I hope...*

Wes is about to speak when Katie calls out, "Mom!" interrupting our conversation.

I frown apologetically. "Wes—"

"Never mind," he says, cutting me off. "Go. Something tells me you wouldn't have been honest anyway."

What?

My shoulders drop as he walks away—actually *sulks* away is probably more accurate—and with a fake smile in place, he thanks Katie for playing with him before lightly grabbing Carter's arm. "Let's go."

I watch them both leave, unsure about what just happened but too frazzled by other things to do anything about it now.

When I finally get to bed that night, I'm wrecked. Physically and emotionally. Physically because it's late—on top of being worked up and unable to sleep myself, Katie was up late for the same reason, too wired to sleep after her excitement at meeting two famous football players today. And emotionally because I'm desperate to know what Wes was trying to ask me. And why he got so mad. Does he want to know about Greg? No, that can't be it. He seemed upset about it, like it directly affected him. Maybe he's still pissed off about my lies. Either way, I've wasted enough time trying to figure it out, and I'm done. If he wants to be moody, that's his problem. But I'm not putting up with it any longer.

Wes spends the next day snapping at me any chance he gets, and it doesn't take long until I'm at a breaking point. I haven't even had a hint of a smile since he left Katie and me in his office while practically dragging an apologetic looking Carter out the door, and I need answers.

I'm making a cup of late-afternoon coffee in the break room when he walks in. As soon as he spots me, he sighs before running a hand down his face in frustration. I put on a smile and continue my personal pledge to kill him with kindness. "Good afternoon. Lovely weather we're having."

"I've been looking for you," Wes replies, completely ignoring my pleasantries. "We need to talk."

Ugh! When he says it like that it no longer interests me, especially if I'm just going to get barked at. But I agree anyway. And as I step through the door, Wes holds it open for me, only releasing it when I'm completely out of harm's way.

"Look, I'm happy to talk, but I can't deal with this hot and cold anymore."

Wes stares at me in complete confusion. "When was I hot?"

I almost laugh, but bite my lip to hold it off. *He's serious.* "Just now. You held open a door for me. Plus you looked after Katie yesterday, and I know you were worried about me. That's confusing. And, let's not forget last Saturday night."

"Okay, I get it. My life is fucking confusing. Half the time I don't know if I'm coming or going, but I do know this… I might be pissed at the moment, but I can't stay the fuck away and I still fucking care. A *lot*. So, it is what it is. And that's all I'm saying on the matter."

Alrighty then. Why the hell does that make my heart skip a beat. Stupid, stupid heart.

Wes turns on his heel and walks toward his office, assuming I'll follow. And of course I do. Because having him pissed at me is driving me insane. Despite the fact that I enjoy pushing his buttons, I'd really prefer to just move past whatever hang-up he has.

A little part of me wants to push back, prove to him that he pisses me off just as much. It's what I'd do if it was Dylan. But another part of me desperately wants him to pull me into his arms and tell me it's okay.

After closing his office door behind me, I lean against it and contemplate my next move. How do I play this? Do I smile and flirt? I've never been great at flirting, so maybe that's a bad idea. Maybe I should stamp my foot and—

"So, Archer says the PT is working, but he still doesn't look great on the field. I've noticed he occasionally flinches when his left foot moves a certain way. And as much as he thinks he's hiding it, he's fooling no one."

Huh? Wes eyes me curiously when I don't say anything and then continues on. "What I need to know is do we need different treatment, or is he talking shit about being ready?"

Again, huh? Did he really drag me here to talk about work and not us? We're not going to finally clear the air? My deer in the headlights stare must give away my confusion because he clenches his jaw and his nostrils flare. *Oops.*

"Are you even listening to me? Luce, I need my players to be game ready. I'm not blaming you. I just want to know what's going on. Is that too much to ask?"

Fuck! That snaps me out of my daze.

"No, it's not too much to ask at all. And Archer is definitely not game ready, no matter what he says. In fact, my report to the offensive coordinator *clearly* states that he should be on a lighter training schedule for at least another week and—"

"For fuck's sake. Does anyone take shit seriously around here? Am I expecting too much? Yes, my college days were a while ago, but I definitely feel like we had a lot more structure and processes that had to be followed. Fuck!"

He runs his hand through his hair and down to his neck, and I follow the movement because it's easier than looking into his eyes. Eyes that I know are begging me for answers. About this, about us.

"I haven't been here long enough to really make an assessment, but I agree that things are slipping through the cracks because of the staff turnover."

Wes nods, seemingly agreeing with me, so I continue, "I know you only see yourself as an interim coach, but you could really make a difference. Despite pretending otherwise, it's obvious you care. And the guys need that."

I peer up at his reaction and find him staring back at me with a look that's difficult to decipher. It's sort of a cross between appreciation and disgust, if you can show those at the same time. Wes sure can.

"And if I don't want the role?" he asks, but it's not in the bitter tone I would have expected.

"No one is forcing you. I just happen to think you'd be great at it. Or any role you took on in life." I shrug because I'm not really sure what I'm saying.

Wes sinks into his chair and drops his face into his hands. He's quiet for a moment until he looks up at me with a look of pure anguish. "Thank you, Luce. I appreciate the update on Archer. I've got it from here."

In other words, you're dismissed.

Pulling open the door, I'm out of the room in record time, without another word. I don't want to say any more in case it's something I regret. But when I'm a few steps down the hall, I hear Wes curse out loud and stop, suddenly pissed off. Why did I walk away? Wes is the one guy I've felt like myself around. The only guy that's ever let me speak my mind and been proud of it. It's time he got a bit of that now. Turning quickly, I stalk back toward his office, ready to give him a little dose of no-bullshit Lucy.

Chapter Twenty-Six

Wes

God, she's so infuriating. Why can't she just tell me I have a kid without me having to ask her? Without me having to make up stupid excuses to see her, hoping she'll spill. "Fuck this."

My chair rolls back, crashing into the wall, as I push it away to stand and rush to the door. "Lucy, stop!" I call out, pulling the door open right as Lucy barges in, yelling "I've had enough!" and crashing straight into me.

I try to stop myself from propelling forward, but I'm too late, and we both almost fall from the impact. My hands grip her shoulder and the doorframe to steady us before I take a step back. An unwarranted scowl is on my face.

"What, Wes? What do you want? I don't care about your work issues right now. I—"

"I don't give a shit about that either. I want you to finally tell me about Katie."

Confusion flashes over Lucy's features before it's replaced by anger. "I have a daughter, Wes. Is it really so hard for you to wrap your head around that?"

"No, that part is crystal clear. It's the rest that's messing with me."

"The *rest*? You're going to have to spell it out for me because I have no idea what you're talking about."

"Is she mine?" I demand, my hands flexed at my sides.

"What?"

"Is. Katie. Mine?"

"What?" she repeats.

Is she kidding me? Pinching the bridge of my nose, my face scrunches as I speak through gritted teeth. "For fuck's sake, Lucy."

"Is that a joke?" she says with her head tilted to the side, a look of bewilderment crossing her features.

"Why would it be a joke?" I ask, although I'm beginning to doubt myself based on her reaction. Except... "She has my eyes."

Lucy huffs out a laugh. "She *doesn't* have your eyes, Wes. Come on..." She trails off and I can see her mind working right up to the moment she realizes I'm right.

Her eyes widen and she shakes off whatever thoughts she had whirring in her head. "Her eyes are brown, Wes. Half the population has her eyes. I promise, she's not yours. That's why I left."

"What?"

"I found out I was pregnant the last day you saw me, and I panicked. I lost all ability to make rational decisions. I lost my mind, Wes. And even if I had been thinking clearly, you didn't need that in your life. Someone was about to publish an article that said you were falling back into some old patterns because of me and I don't know... I was struggling. It was a lot for me to process and then you..."

"I what?"

Lucy looks to the ceiling before her eyes meet mine again and she whispers, "You just left."

My heart aches as I step forward and pull her into my arms, needing to be close to her. She's right; I left. And while I'm pissed at her for lying, I've regretted it every day since. What am I doing?

"I'm sorry, Luce. I'm so fucking sorry."

I press a kiss to her head but she pulls away, staring at me with her ocean-blue eyes.

"You thought I would keep that from you?"

"I don't know, Luce. You make me crazy. I overthink *every-thing* when it comes to you. I've been like a fucking detective trying to piece together clues of your life in the years since I last saw you. I had no idea why you left, and I guess, I just needed to find a reason."

"But why would I leave? If she was yours, why would I leave?"

She has a point, and I hate myself for not thinking of that. "I'm sorry, Lucy. I..." I trail off as she blinks up at me, hooked on my every word. I'm not sure why I keep fighting this when I know I have feelings for her and that's never going to change.

"Luce..." I breathe out causing her eyes to close as she nibbles on her bottom lip.

Seconds later, our mouths meet, and I'm not even sure who moved first. Lucy moans as she grabs my shirt, pulling me closer, while my hands move from her waist to her face, tilting her head toward me.

Still thinking about her bottom lip, I suck it into my mouth and run my tongue along the seam, until she opens up and allows me to explore. For the next few minutes we make out like our lives depend on it. Tongues swirling, hands roaming, bodies molding.

My fingers run through her hair, gripping her ponytail as she slowly starts grinding against me. "Fuck, Lucy." I groan against her lips before walking her backward to the wall.

Bad idea.

The second her back hits the bricks, she pushes me away, trying to break out of my hold with a dazed expression on her face.

I spring back immediately, panic coursing through me. "Are you okay?" I ask, my chest tight with nerves.

"What?" she whispers, unfocused, as though still under some kind of spell. *Fuck, what did I do?*

"Are you okay?" I repeat louder, seemingly snapping her out of it.

"Yes, I'm fine," she says, standing up a little straighter. "Yes," she repeats again, with more conviction as a confident expression replaces her doe-eyed look. "I stopped because I shouldn't be kissing you. I struggle to resist you at times, but you were an asshole over something that wasn't even true. I just need some time. And maybe you need to work for it."

With that she pushes off the wall and walks straight out my door. The confident sway of her hips has me wanting her even more, but I can't help the small smirk that rises to my face as my eyes follow her out. She's right. I fucked up and I should work for it. But I've never worked for anything when it comes to women. Never wanted to. Maybe it's time I forget about the outside bullshit and focus on what's important...because when I do that, I have no doubt that she's the only thing that'll come to mind.

Pulling my phone out of my pocket, I bring up Lucy's contact and send her a text. The first of many.

Wes: I'm sorry

Wes: But also...you lied. So you need to give me a slight pass for the attitude

I'm only half joking with the last text and I know she'll read it exactly as intended.

Lucy: Okay, you can have a small credit

Wes: Appreciated (wink emoji)

Wes: Do I get bonus points for the door opening and general care for your well-being, too?

Lucy: Don't push your luck

A smile pulls at my lips because while I may try to pretend otherwise, this girl is under my skin, and I'm no longer sure I want her gone.

Chapter Twenty-Seven

Lucy

It takes Wes one attempt at "working for it" for me to realize he's never had to do it before. His text messages last night should have clued me in, but I wasn't exactly thinking straight because...*what the hell*? He thought Katie was his daughter? That I would have run off and kept that information from him—all this time, even after seeing him again. What kind of person would do that? *Oh right...me.*

My chest tightens as the guilt takes over, and I once again feel sick at the fact I've kept Katie away from Greg. But these are two completely different situations. Apart from being a moody asshole at times, Wes is a wonderful man. The kind of man anyone would want as the father to their children. But Greg... I can't even put into words how much that man unnerves me. The thought of having him near Katie terrifies me. I know it's not exactly ethical to have kept them apart; I'm not stupid. But Katie is my number one priority, and right now, I don't trust him with her.

The situation with Wes is different. And despite Wes's attempts to get back into my good graces being a bit comical, this isn't a joke. I asked him to work for it because I wanted him to actually stop and think about what he wants. I have a daughter. He seems to be pissed off at me on a regular basis. And as much as I've tried to convince myself otherwise, I have feelings for him. It's not as easy to just mess around and see what happens. I need to take Katie into consideration and can't afford to be moping around with a broken heart.

So here I am, staring at Wes with a confused expression on my face because he just handed me a coffee and said, "Are we good now?" *Yep, that's one of his attempts.*

Pair that with the donut he left on my desk this morning with an "I'm sorry if I made you mad" note, and you've got yourself the Wes Johnson guide to groveling.

"Well?" he asks me when I don't answer.

"Well, what?"

"Are we good now?"

I can't help it; I burst out laughing before walking away. We're in the staff kitchen for God's sake, and there's a nonfraternization policy in place.

Wes follows me, just like I assumed he would, and when he enters my office he has a smile plastered on his face, though it's definitely fake. He's trying hard not to be grumpy, so I guess I should give him credit for that.

"Are we here to make out?" he says after closing the door, shocking the hell out of me. My eyes bulge until the corners of his lips pull into a smirk and he subtly bounces his eyebrows, making me laugh again. "Oh Wes."

"I know, I know. I'm not very good at this. I'll keep trying."

"What are you trying to achieve exactly?"

"Huh?" He takes a step forward, forcing me to step back.

"What is it you're trying to get out of this?"

Stepping forward again, he moves into my personal space and leans in close. "*You.*"

Cue the butterflies. I am absolutely swooning right now. But he doesn't need to know that.

"Okay then," I say, pushing him back. "We're not quite there yet. But, as you were." I somehow manage to keep a composed expression, watching as Wes chuckles before walking away without another word. And it's not until the next day that I get his third attempt. And that one involves cake. He definitely knows I like food, but I need something more. Something deeper.

We have a practice game on Saturday, meaning the day is so busy, I don't see Wes at all. I may be finding his daily attempts to grovel hilarious, but I've grown attached to them, and if I'm being honest, I'm a little off today. I'm not only missing the attempts, I'm missing him. And I hate that. *Ugh, when did I allow those feelings to seep back in?*

At five thirty, Logan arrives with Katie, after taking her and Liam out for the day. Liam has Katie's hand tightly in his hold as they enter my office, and I can't help but smile at the protectiveness he's already showing at nine years old. Just like Logan does for Dani and even me in some ways.

"Lucy, can I take Katie to find Dani?" Liam says with an excited smile on his face. "I know the way."

I pretend to consider it for a second before giving him a smile and a nod. It's not far to Dani's office, so I have nothing to worry about. I *hope.*

Katie squeals as Liam leads her away, and despite not needing to be worried, I stand in the doorway and watch them until they round the corner toward the marketing rooms.

"She's fine," Logan says from behind me, drawing my attention. "Liam's a cautious kid. He's not going to let her run off or anything."

"I know, I'm just...never mind." I smile as I walk back into the room, busying myself at my desk.

"You're worried about the douche," Logan says, reading between the lines.

"Yes." I sigh. "I know he can't get in here, but he's always on my mind."

"Understandably, but you know we'd never let anything happen to you or Katie. Dani and I are just around the corner; Dylan and Joel are only an hour away. Actually I should say Summer and Del because I'm pretty sure those two would kick his ass for you. Maybe more than the guys would."

"You're right. Especially about the girls. Summer would even kick *your* ass if I told her to."

I wink as I continue to pack up my things.

Logan laughs. "No doubt. In fact, she'd take great pleasure in that. Jokes aside though, you're safe." He pauses for a second before adding, "Plus I hear there's a certain ex-NFL giant who'd do just about anything for you."

My jaw drops as my eyes flash to Logan's mischievous grin. *How the hell does he know anything about Wes?*

"Summer," he laughs, answering my silent question.

I'm about to play down our relationship when Katie comes barreling into the room, practically bouncing off the walls in excitement. "Wes wants to take us to the park to play football tomorrow, and then out for ice cream! Can we go, Mom? Can we go?"

I bite back a nervous smile as I shake my head. *Of course he does. Well played, Wes, well played.*

"You know Uncle Dylan loves playing football with you," I say because playing football isn't a new thing for her.

"But he's not Wes, Mom. He's just Uncle Dylan."

Technically she's not wrong but poor Dylan.

"What about swimming? You promised we'd try again this week."

Katie pauses and gives me a look that almost breaks my heart. "Can we try next week?"

Ugh. I have to get her back in the water, but forcing the issue isn't going to work.

"Okay, sweetie. I'll talk to Wes."

"Yes!"

She hugs my legs and then takes off running again, back where she came from, and like before, I watch her until I see Dani walking her way. Only then do I relax.

"What were you going to say about Wes?" Logan says knowingly, pulling my gaze away from the hallway. "Or should I say *deny* about Wes?"

"Ha ha. There's nothing going on. He's just a nice guy who happens to know that Katie likes football."

"If you say so," he says with a smirk.

As soon as Logan is gone, I dial Wes's number, fumbling when he answers on the first ring with a simple hello, as if he *wasn't* expecting my call. *Yeah, right.*

"You answered that pretty quickly."

"Why wouldn't I? I'm hopeful that this call might hold some good news for me."

"Or it might be me putting you in your place for using my daughter to get what you want," I deadpan.

There's silence until Wes curses under his breath, forcing me to hold back a laugh, waiting to see how this plays out.

"Fuck, I'm sorry. It wasn't premeditated or anything. She popped into my office and started talking about football, and I genuinely wanted to take her. I mean, getting to see you is a great bonus, but that's not why I asked. I'm new to all this kid stuff, but I'm trying."

He's trying? My heart. Now I feel bad.

"It's lovely, Wes. And Katie's very excited. We'd love to go with you."

He releases a breath, and I can picture him running his hand through his thick hair. "Thank fuck."

"Tomorrow then?" I say and my heart races like I'm agreeing to a date. I know that's not what this is, because this is about Katie, but I'm definitely excited to be spending any nonwork time with Wes.

"Yes, tomorrow," he says and when I'm just about to hang up, he adds, "You could have walked over to say all this. I would have liked to see you."

My lips pull into a giddy smile—something that Wes seems to elicit from me—but I fight it.

"You're right, Wes. I could have. Have a good night."

"You too, Lucy." He chuckles as I hang up the phone.

Katie and I wait for Wes in front of the house the next day, with her car seat at my feet. Even though he offered to pick us up and take us out, I still feel like it's a chore for him to do it, so I'm trying to make it as easy for him as possible. I know I shouldn't feel like that, but I already get so many handouts from family and friends that I feel guilty whenever people do something nice for me.

Wes pulls up in his truck and immediately jumps out to meet us. I don't really take in his appearance until he's walking our way, and when I do, I'm locked in place as desire runs through me. *Kill me now.* He's wearing gray sweatpants that mold to his muscular thighs—and almost have me drooling—a fitted black tee, and a San Fran baseball cap. *Um, what?!* Is he trying to mess me up in front of my daughter?

I can't stop myself from staring as he approaches. The way he moves has me mesmerized, and I'm struggling to concentrate.

When he reaches our side, he lightly flicks me underneath my chin and then squats down to Katie's height, handing her a kid-sized football as he says hello. She's got a hundred of them at home, but she still lights up, just like my heart does. I'm giddy again, and it's not until Wes's eyes meet mine that I realize what just happened... Was he closing my dropped jaw? *Jesus!* That's embarrassing.

When his laughter touches his eyes, I know he's read my thoughts, but without saying a word about it, he helps carry our things to his truck with a smile in place. And I'm not complaining about that.

"Do you want me to install the seat?" I ask after he lifts it into his truck. His forehead creases as he stares at the contraption, seemingly processing what to do.

"Nope, I'm good," he says after a beat, and sets out to get it done.

Fifteen minutes pass and it's not only me laughing at Wes's frustration, but Katie's joined in too. "Why don't they make these things easier to install? I must be missing a part. Is it still in your car?"

"Nope," I say, pulling my lips into my mouth.

"Okay, so do you know what I'm doing wrong?"

"Yep."

"Are you going to tell me?"

Pushing between his rock-hard body and the door of his truck, I work my magic and have the seat installed in a couple of minutes, all while Wes watches me with great interest.

"Now if you could just pull this as tight as you can, we'll be on our way." I hand him the tightening strap and step out, biting back my triumphant grin, until Wes grumbles and my laugh escapes me.

"I'm going to beat it next time," he huffs out.

"It's not a competition." I laugh in return.

True to his word, Wes devotes most of his attention to Katie throughout the day, and he should—he absolutely should—but I'm sure she wouldn't mind if he threw a tiny bit my way. And neither would I. Instead, I watch on from the sidelines—where Katie relegated me to—and try not to embarrass myself by openly drooling again.

My phone vibrates on the grass as Wes throws Katie in the air, and I'm laughing as I reach for it, completely unaware of the pain it's about to bring me.

Unknown: Can we talk? This is my work number. I'm doing pretty well for myself and I'd like to support you and Katie. Greg

My heart jolts. I'm not sure why I keep thinking he'll give up. I may have tried to insinuate Katie wasn't his, but he's not stupid. I should have expected this.

I don't respond, and the phone continues to vibrate until I have two missed calls and another text.

Unknown: Please, I just want to get to know her, and make up for the lost time and my lack of support

What is he even saying? Does he want to pay child support? I ignore his message again and avoid looking at my phone for the rest of the day, vowing not to let it get me down on an otherwise perfect afternoon.

After playing catch, Wes and Katie drop down on the blanket I've laid out and both go for their water bottles. Wes sighs dramatically after taking an abnormally large gulp, and I have to bite back a laugh when Katie mimics his every move.

"You're really good, kid," he says, smiling at Katie, and from the lift in the corner of his eyes, I can tell he's holding back a laugh too.

"I'm going to play when I get big," she says, stretching her arm up as high as it will go, and then adds, "This was way better than swimming."

Wes's confused eyes briefly flash my way before they're back on Katie. "What do you mean?"

"I don't want to do swimming and Mom said I could skip it."

His eyes meet mine again, and this time there's a hint of concern there. I shake my head to tell him it's fine, but his brows furrow for a moment before he smiles. "I love swimming. Why don't you want to go?"

"I just don't like it anymore," Katie says with her arms crossed in front of her. In other words...conversation over.

Wes nods and replies, "Okay, good enough for me." But I can tell he wants to ask me about it.

"Who's ready for ice cream?" he adds, changing the subject and smiling when Katie's mood instantly lifts.

We eat way too much ice cream and get take-out sushi on the way home, my idea of balancing out the good with the bad. Katie starts fading as soon as her plate is clean, and even though you'd think that would mean an easy bedtime for her, it won't. It's like she gets a second wind as soon as the word *bed* is mentioned.

"All right, Katie. Say goodnight to Wes."

"But Mooommm."

"No buts. You've had a big day. It's time for sleep. Wes is going home now. Aren't you, Wes."

He widens his eyes almost comically, clearly not expecting me to say that, but when he sees my expression, he recovers. "Yep, I'm off. I'm so tired," he says with an exaggerated yawn, as he raises his hands over his head. His T-shirt rises and a sliver of skin peeks out along with that V. It's so mouthwatering, I have to fight to keep my eyes on his face. "I had a lovely day. Thanks, Katie," he continues, completely unaware of the effect he has on me. "Can we do it again?"

Katie yawns right back at him, as do I—those things are contagious—then she nods. "Yes, please."

"Perfect. I'll plan it with your mom. Goodnight."

"Goodnight."

We head off toward the bedrooms, and even though I thought I made myself clear that I didn't want him to leave, I throw a quick glance over my shoulder to make sure that he hasn't.

As soon as our eyes meet, he smiles and nods, putting my mind at ease.

I need him here tonight, for so many reasons, and that smile is everything.

When I finally finish getting Katie off to sleep, I find Wes staring out my kitchen window. "Sorry about that," I say as I approach. "Katie wanted you to help. It took some bargaining to win her over."

He spins around quickly with a furrowed brow, as if processing my words before shaking off his thoughts and smiling. "Sorry, I was in my head. What did you say?"

Releasing a breathy laugh, I move around him, pouring myself a glass of water. "It doesn't matter. Thank you for today. It was fun."

"You're welcome. Katie's a great kid."

"She has her moments. But I've always instilled it in her to behave around others. So, at least we know she sometimes listens."

"Meaning she only gives *you* hell?"

"Something like that." I smile.

"Sounds exactly like how her mom is with me," he jokes, and I smile until a thought comes to mind.

"I still can't believe you thought that I'd keep her from you, Wes," I say, bringing down the mood but feeling the need to talk to him about it.

He grimaces before running a hand through his hair. "I didn't want to believe it. But Luce, I barely trust myself anymore, let alone other people."

"And why is that? Why do you have trust issues? You've mentioned a little bit but—"

"Going straight to the big questions, huh?"

I smile apologetically, biting my lip with a nod.

"Okay, fine. But if I'm stripping, then you're stripping."

"What?"

"We're both going to bare our souls."

I swallow a lump in my throat because, God, that makes me nervous. I've got so much bottled up, but at the same time, this talk is needed. If we're ever going to move past everything that went wrong between us then we need to figure out why. "Okay," I say with a nod.

"Okay."

Chapter Twenty-Eight

Wes

N ow that I've suggested we share all our secrets, I'm at a loss for where to start. It's not that I have lots of them, but it's a part of my life I don't usually talk about.

Lucy leans back against the counter with her water to her lips, peering up at me through her lashes. Her telling me I had to work for it—for her—really made me stop and think about what I wanted, and she's it. She's what I want. I've just been struggling with how to move forward from all the shit in my life.

When the silence between us shifts toward awkward territory, I finally clear my throat and look down at my hands, clenching and unclenching my fists. "I know I've mentioned this before, but I despise lies. I seem to attract liars for some reason, and it just got to a point where I had to say enough...that I deserved better, and refuse to let those people into my life. My father aside—I just..." I look up to see Lucy's remorseful eyes and her lip trapped between her teeth as she nervously bites it. *Shit*. I probably should clarify... "This isn't about you. Not yet, anyway."

She huffs out a laugh. "Even so, I'm sorry for lying."

"Thanks, but you weren't the only one to mess up back then," I say seriously, very aware that I walked away first.

250

Lucy laughs but it's a little forced. "You're right, but let's not play the blame game," she says with a soft smile before motioning for me to go on.

"I had a girlfriend in college," I start after giving Lucy a quick smile in return. "For all of college, actually. She was always really supportive of my football career, and understanding of my, uh...obsession with it. At least I thought she was. But not long after I was drafted, I found out she'd cheated on me with another player on the team, and—"

"Bullshit!" Lucy exclaims, cutting me off, and I laugh at her reaction.

"Nope, that happened. And then I found out she'd actually been cheating all through college. Kind of hedging her bets on who would make it big and earn the most money. I—"

"Are you fucking kidding me?" she says, cutting me off again. "What kind of a person does that? I hope you dumped her ass there and then. The nerve. If I could... What? Too much?"

Her question snaps me to attention and I realize I've been staring at her with my jaw on the floor. My pants also feel a little tighter because *my God...*

"Badass, protective Lucy is hot. So fucking hot. And you could never be too much. Don't ever think that."

Lucy blushes, which only makes her more beautiful, something I didn't think was possible. She brushes her hair behind her ear, giving herself the chance to briefly look away with a shy smile. I'm not even sure what brought on her reaction, but I can't stop staring at her.

"Protective Wes is pretty good too," she says when she looks up again, causing me to laugh.

"You ain't seen nothing yet," I joke. "Actually, in honesty, I wasn't aware I'd ever been protective." *Out loud.*

"And that makes it so much better. But I've seen it a few times." She shrugs as though it's no big deal, but it is. I'm glad I've made her feel protected, because I have no doubt, I'd do pretty much anything for her.

"I care about you, Luce," I let her know in case it's not obvious. No matter how pissed I was at her, I've never stopped caring.

"I know. I've never once questioned that."

She knows. I feel an ache in my chest that I almost want to rub. I have no idea what's causing it, but I think it's safe to say it has something to do with the iridescent blue eyes staring back at me and the incredible woman they belong to. A woman I've foolishly been pushing away. I almost want to laugh at how stupid I've been, pretending she doesn't affect me. And I'm about to say something to that effect when she gets in first.

"Anyway, sorry. We were talking about your ex."

Yup, we were, but I'm definitely happier now that the conversation has moved on...

"You broke up with her immediately, right?"

...but Lucy clearly needs answers and she deserves them.

"I did." I sigh, running my hand down my face. "Even before I found out about the college stuff. But that wasn't the end of us."

Lucy hisses, and I chuckle despite this part of my life being anything but funny.

"Her family started making my life hell. Suggesting that because she'd been with me through college—before I got 'too big for my own good' as they put it—that she was somehow owed money or something. They actually said she'd settle for fame. As if that was something I could give her.

"It got to the point of being borderline threatening. Her brother would be waiting for me before practice, or her father would be blowing up my phone. The coaching staff agreed to let me start late and leave early, to see if it died down without having to call in authorities, or the media circus that would follow. But the media found out anyway which only encouraged my ex's family even more."

Lucy gasps, her hand flying to her mouth. "Jesus. So you were never actually in trouble with the team?"

"No. I mean, yes, it affected my game, but they were understanding about it."

"Why didn't the media know that? The article I read painted you in a pretty bad light."

I blow out a breath because she's not wrong. The writer of that article did not fact check.

"The media did. At least, they found out pretty quickly. Once our PR team got involved, the stories died down after only a day or so. The article you saw was one guy latching on to a story he must have read years ago. That's why it was never released. Though I still don't understand how you got hold of it."

"I'd like to know that too. My ex sent it to me, but it's not like he's close with anyone in the media. At least, he wasn't when we were dating."

I shrug, because even though it's a loose thread that's been driving me crazy, I don't have any answers.

Lucy looks to the ceiling before biting her lip again, hesitation clear on her face.

"What is it?"

"That explains why the media thought you were having issues back then, but what about with me? Why were they saying you'd fallen *back* into that pattern?"

I grimace and rest my face in my hands, subtly kneading my temples. This is the part no one knows. The part I've kept hidden from everyone.

"I lost *some* focus again, briefly, but I knew I'd eventually find a balance between you and football, so I was fine with it. I wasn't letting it get me down like last time."

"You lost focus?"

"Yeah." Taking a deep breath, I push off the counter and grip the back of my neck. "I have trouble quieting my mind. It's been that way since I was a kid. It's why I try to focus on one thing. Dedicating all my time and energy into my football. When something else comes along it can take me a beat to find cohesion in my head, but as soon as I do, I'm fine. It's why I struggled back then, and it's why word got out that I was struggling again with you. I just didn't have you long enough to reconcile it all before it was over."

Taking a breath from my outpouring of information, I chance a look at Lucy and find her staring back at me with glassy eyes, her lips sucked into her mouth, as though she's staving off the tears. *Dammit!* I do not want her pity.

"Lucy, I didn't tell you that so you'd pity me or feel bad, I—"

"No, that's not..." She reaches out and grabs my hand, linking our fingers. "I don't feel either of those things. I...have you ever spoken to someone about it? Maybe seen... God, I don't know. I treat the body, not the mind, but—"

"Thank you," I interrupt, giving Lucy's fingers a squeeze as I smile. "My mom took me to see a psychologist as a kid, but back then they blamed it on me being a boy and having a small attention span. These days I imagine I'd be diagnosed with something. After a bit of research, I'd guess it'd likely be ADHD. But that's not the point. I'm sorry if that article led you to believe you were messing with my life, because that's not the case. I was more than happy to have you in it."

Lucy looks away and sniffs before her gaze comes back to mine. I hate that I'm hurting her. It wasn't my intention, but once I started there was no going back. It's as if her knowing everything will somehow make all my hurt go away.

"I'm sorry too," she says, mimicking my hand squeeze. "I could have handled that situation better. I was freaking out, and I didn't want my mess to become yours."

"Oh, but what a wonderful mess she is," I say with a wink and relish Lucy's entire face lighting up.

"She's more than wonderful. She's my world, and while I'm not sure I'd do anything differently if I was faced with the same choices, I still think about what I missed out on because of how I handled things. More specifically what *we* missed out on."

My lips curl into a smirk as I pull Lucy closer, until our bodies touch. "You thought about me?"

"Yeah, I thought about you," she whispers as her spare hand grips my waist, lighting me up inside. From the moment her lips first touched mine, Lucy's every touch has awakened me, and this is no different. Being without her is not an option anymore. In fact, it's never been an option, so why the fuck did I take so long to realize that?

Letting go of her hand, I lift her up and seat her on the counter before stepping between her open legs. Her breath hitches as I brush a lock of hair away from her face. "You're so beautiful, Lucy. And while I may always wish things had turned out differently between us, I'd never want you to change a thing either. Katie's perfect; you're perfect. And I want to get to know both of you properly. Catch up on the last few years. I want to know everything. At least, anything you're willing to share."

Lucy nods as a lone tear escapes, running along her slightly flushed cheek until it hits her lips. She wipes it away and then shocks me by pushing me back and dropping her feet to the floor. "I'm sorry, I know I said I'd bare my soul if you did, but I can't. I...I don't want you to think less of me."

"What?" *This took a turn I didn't see coming.* "Lucy, that's not going to happen. Unless you're about to tell me you've been lying about Katie's paternity and she really *is* mine."

That gets me a tiny laugh, but I can tell she's still nervous.

"No, she's definitely not yours. But I have been lying about her, just not to you. Don't you hate liars in general?"

Fuck! I'm not at all happy about my truths making her panic about her own. "No, I don't hate *liars*. I hate *lying*. There's a difference and it all depends on context."

Lucy blows out a breath and closes her eyes. When she opens them again I see the moment she decides she's going to tell me. And the pain that comes from that breaks my heart. I can't stand seeing her upset like this.

"I was—"

"Lucy, stop." Reaching out, I clutch her shoulders and pull her into a protective hug. "You don't have to tell me anything. It's okay."

She mumbles something into my chest until I move back and give her some breathing room.

"You're right; I don't. But I want to. You stripped, and now it's my turn."

Swallowing a lump in my throat, I nod, suddenly nervous. Maybe I'm not ready for this.

"When you found me in the parking garage that day, I'd just found out I was pregnant," she begins, unaware of my worry. "Something you already know. But what you don't know, and the reason I wasn't handling it so well is because..." She pauses and an unease takes over me, fearing what she's about to say. I have a feeling I know, but fuck I hope I'm wrong. My heart thuds in my chest as I wait for her to continue, but when she doesn't, I step forward and pull her into my arms once more, silently rocking her back and forth until she takes a deep breath and steps back.

"My ex and I had a complicated relationship. I recognize now that he was really good at emotionally mistreating me but then building me up enough that I never noticed, even when people were pointing it out. And I hate that. I've always thought I was a strong woman but I let him..." She trails off and I feel like the air's being squeezed out of my lungs, as I watch this beautiful soul break in front of me.

"Anyway, we had broken up a couple of months before Katie was conceived."

She pauses again, and her gaze drops to the floor.

"I swore I'd never sleep with him again, but I..."

My heart lodges in my throat. Her posture and expression—well, the features I can see—scream guilt, and though it pains me to think she went back to that manipulative asshole, we're all allowed moments of weakness.

Stepping forward, I lift her chin until she looks up at me, and my world stops when her eyes once again well with tears.

"Lucy, you did nothing wrong. You—"

"I didn't want to."

"What?"

"I said no."

"*What!*"

Grabbing her face in my hands, I sink down until we're eye level, my gaze locked on hers. "Lucy, did he force himself on you?"

"No, no. It wasn't like that. It wasn't rape if that's what you're thinking. We'd slept together many times before. I just didn't want to do it *that* time."

The fuck?

"Lucy, that's *rape.*"

I want to fucking murder this guy, but I also never want to leave Lucy's side.

She shakes her head back and forth, over and over, fear in her eyes. "No, it's not. We were in a relationship before then. He just—"

"Lucy, he *raped* you."

"No. No. No." She shakes her head frantically before burying her face in her hands. "It's my fault." *Fuck!* Maybe that wasn't the best way to handle that.

After stilling her, I press a kiss to her forehead and lower my voice, trying to sound somewhat calm while I really just want to rip some fucker apart.

"No, Luce," I say, just above a whisper. "Nothing about this is your fault. And even if you don't classify it as rape, he still hurt you and that's not fucking okay. I'm guessing this means you didn't report it?"

"They wouldn't have done anything. I had no proof."

I hate that she's probably right. They wouldn't have done anything. But someone should. *Her ex is a dead man.*

"Did you have bruises? Anything you could have shown them?" I'm trying so hard to keep it together but it's killing me inside.

Lucy shakes her head again as the tears start to fall. "I let him," she says through sniffles, clearly trying to fight it. "I didn't want him to hurt me, so I let him do it."

My heart shatters into a million pieces, and the fragments cut me like a blade.

Without another word, I lift her into my arms and carry her to the sofa before sitting down and locking her tightly in my hold. "I'm so sorry, Lucy. I hate that you have such an awful memory for what should have been a beautiful moment."

"I can't even regret it," she whispers, burrowing her face into my shoulder.

"I know," I whisper back, and we stay like that in our comforting embrace—for hours or minutes, I don't know—until she pulls away.

"Sorry, I don't know why I got so emotional just then. I've moved past this. I'm good."

"Lucy, you don't have to apologize, and you definitely don't have to move past it. Fuck, I don't even know what to say."

"You don't have to say anything. I shouldn't still be thinking about this. It's not like I have permanent scars."

"Not all scars are visible, Luce."

With a quivering lip, her chin drops and she shies away from me.

Reaching forward, I tentatively lift her face with a single finger, and she lets me. "Your strength blows my mind, Lucy. Don't ever hide away from who you are, because I happen to think you're incredible."

She sniffs again, as a hint of a smile graces her lips.

"Thank you. You're a little bit alright yourself."

My mouth pulls into a crooked grin, wanting to smile but also needing to ask one more question.

"Sorry to keep talking about him, but do you see him at all?"

Lucy wipes the tears from her face as she shakes her head. "I've only seen him twice since it happened—after work on the night of Aaron's dinner party, and when he came to the stadium. He's also messaged a few times to see Katie."

"What?!" I recoil, a sick feeling taking over. "That was him? But...I was there. You said it wasn't Katie's dad... I left you alone with him. *Fuck!*" My head drops back to the sofa and I take a deep breath. Lucy doesn't need me going crazy right now. "I'm sorry, I just... I would have gone with you if I'd known."

She blinks her eyes as fresh tears glisten there, then frames my face in her hands, giving me a smile. A *smile*. "You did one better, Wes. You protected Katie, and that means more to me than you'll ever know."

Actually, I think I'm starting to understand.

But still that brings me no comfort. I want to protect them both. I want that man gone.

Lucy snuggles into me after that, as though we're about to watch a movie, when in reality she just tore me apart. I feel sick, I feel murderous, but mostly, I feel like I've let her down. I should have been there for her when she found out she was pregnant. I should have *never let her go*.

As I mindlessly run my fingers up and down her back, I think about everything we've shared tonight. We both let go of so much heavy baggage, and I feel a deeper connection to her because of it. She's one hundred percent ingrained in my soul. I never meant for that to happen, and I'm not really sure when it occurred, but now that it has, I don't ever want it to change.

Fuck! This moment feels life-changing.

My hand stops moving, frozen in midair as realization hits. This *is* life-changing.

Lucy gazes up at me with a puzzled expression, seemingly aware that something just happened, without knowing what. Our eyes lock as I try to figure out how to put it into words. What could possibly be enough to convey every feeling I've got building up inside me. Nothing comes to mind, until..."Can I kiss you?" I ask, breaking our silence.

Lucy's lips pull into a soft smile as her brows furrow. "Since when do you ask?"

Since I realized your kiss means so much more to me than I thought it did, and I'm not sure you feel the same.

"Since you told me I have to work for it. We may have talked, but other than that, I'm not sure if I've done enough," I whisper to her instead of my actual thoughts.

Lucy's breath hitches and her fingers find their way into my hair before she lowers her face to mine. "Kiss me," she whispers, her eyes shining with need.

So I do.

Our lips brush once before I cup her jaw and pour everything I have into the moment.

Chapter Twenty-Nine

Wes

T his kiss feels different from any other we've shared. It's unhurried, it's explorative, and it's taking over my body and mind. Lucy's perched sideways across my lap and while I love it, I need to be closer to her; this isn't enough. I'm about to break our connection to reposition her when she lifts up, twisting her body around until she's straddling my legs, and then sinks down on top of me, never once separating our lips—like she can read my mind. My hips rise involuntarily as I groan into her mouth.

Massaging her tongue with my own, I push my hands into her hair, angling her face so I can deepen the kiss, as my thumb runs along her jaw, my fingers curling into her possessively. *Possessively. Shit.* I loosen my grip and begin to drop my hands until Lucy whimpers and forces them back where they came from, grinding into me at the same time. Fuck, this woman blows my mind, but this isn't how I wanted tonight to play out.

Despite Lucy's objections, I release my hold on her face and move my hands under her ass, lifting us both off the couch. Moving toward the hallway, I look out for any sign that I've found her bedroom while Lucy holds on for dear life, as if there's even the slightest possibility I'd drop her. There's not. Right now, I can't even fathom there being a reason big enough for me to ever let her go.

"Where are we going?" She giggles against my lips as her fingers dig into my shoulders. "I can walk."

Yeah, that's not happening.

"I have no fucking idea," I say honestly. "But this moment is bigger than a quickie on your couch."

Lucy's breath hitches as her legs clench around me, and I've gotta say that's a pretty awesome reaction.

"Next door on your left," she breathes out hurriedly, angling her body so she can watch where I'm going.

I push through the partly open door and pause, needing to take a moment. It's not like this is our first time, but it's our first time in almost five years and I want to savor it.

"Do you need further direction?" Lucy asks before sucking her lip into her mouth. My length twitches at the tone of her words, and I loosen my grip until she lowers enough to feel what she does to me. Sucking in a breath, her head drops back slightly, making me twitch again. I'm not one to take direction. But with Lucy it's different, and I need her to know that she won't ever have to do something she doesn't want to. In or out of the bedroom.

"For you, I'll do anything. If you want to drive this, drive it. You are *always* in control, Lucy. Even if I have you pushed up against this wall, slamming into you from behind. *You. Have. Control.* Don't ever forget that."

Lucy gasps before crashing her lips to mine and mumbling "bed" against my mouth. True to my word, I do as she says, lowering her to the mattress before moving to lie on top of her. She pushes me back and sits up, crossing her arms in front of her. Something I was not expecting.

"Get naked," she says, taking the *control* thing very seriously. It's hot but it's going to take some getting used to. I like to lead. This will be a challenge.

"Get naked," she says again, motioning for me to stand before delivering the words that are music to my ears. "And then I'm handing you the reins. *Every* part of me is yours."

Holy fuck! Those words don't just hit my ears or my cock, but my soul. Having Lucy's trust is everything.

I take my time peeling my clothes from my body, watching Lucy the entire time, reveling in the way her crystal-blue eyes darken as she squirms on the bed. And when I'm down to my briefs, I pause, waiting to see if her gaze travels or stays locked on my face. It travels. And it doesn't move from there until I'm pumping my length in my hand and moving over her, sucking the lip she was nibbling into my mouth.

"Your turn," I say, hovering above her, chuckling when her eyes flash to her body and then back to me, her brows furrowing adorably.

"Do you want me to undress myself?" she asks, uncertainty in her voice.

"Absolutely not. I've been waiting to do this for too long. I'm going to take my time until you're writhing beneath my touch. Begging me for more."

Lucy visibly swallows and nods, giving me the permission I so desperately need. And then my lips are back on hers, not wasting another second as I roll the waistband of her leggings down, letting my knuckles brush against her skin as I do. She shivers at my touch, and I harden more than I thought was possible. Taking my time is going to be a test for both of us, but worth it in the end.

Sitting up, I pull her along with me so I can lift her tee above her head. My lips immediately go to the swell of her breasts, pushed up by her baby-blue lace bra. Her chest flushes the most beautiful soft pink, contrasting directly with the icy color of the lace, and it's an image I'm almost certain I'll never get out of my head.

Laying her back gently, I release one breast from the cup of her bra, sucking the pebbled nipple into my mouth, as my hand squeezes the other, loving the feel of her filling my palm.

Lucy moans, and her chest rises as she quietly cries out. "God, yes. Don't stop."

Not a chance.

After giving the same attention to her other breast, I kiss my way down her stomach, leaving her bra in place. She shivers again as I feather the kisses along her skin. She's so reactive to my every touch that it takes everything in my power not to skip ahead and push myself inside her. But I hold strong. At least until I've pulled her leggings and panties completely down her legs and left her lying breathlessly in nothing but the lace of her bra.

My eyes rake over her entire body, needing to memorize it all, not at all convinced that something else isn't waiting around the corner to tear us apart.

She's so fucking beautiful with her flushed ivory skin pebbled in goose bumps, her hair billowing around her, and her chest rising and falling in shallow breaths. Being here with her is like a dream, something I never thought would happen. And I never want this moment to end. Especially when she blushes again, hiding her face behind her hands. Her raw vulnerability has my heart beating out of my chest, knowing what this moment means to us both.

I press a kiss to her core, enjoying the giggle it gets me, before moving up her body and taking her hands away from her eyes, pressing kisses to both of her palms.

"Please don't hide away. I'm staring at you because you're breathtaking, Lucy, and you shouldn't be shy about that."

"Oh yeah, my mom body and caesarean scar are perfection," she says sarcastically, thinking she's joking. And yet, they're exactly my thoughts.

"*Everything* about you is perfect, Lucy. *Everything*," I reassure her, running my fingers gently across the areas she just mentioned to make sure she knows I'm including them. "You couldn't be more perfect if you tried. Actually, that's a lie. You'd be more perfect if you were *mine*."

Her gaze softens and she opens her mouth to say something, but I stop her with my lips. Yes, I want her to be mine, but that's not a discussion for now. Right now, I need inside her more than my next breath.

Reaching for the condom I left on the bed, I quickly sheathe myself before lining up with her entrance. When my eyes lock on Lucy's, she's already nodding, as though anticipating my silent question. *Yes, she's ready.*

I push into her in one quick movement—I'm unable to go slowly anymore—but when she cries out, I pause. "Fuck." She's so tight that I'm struggling to focus on anything except the vise-like grip she has me in, but that didn't sound like a happy reaction, and I can't proceed until I know. "Are you okay? Did I hurt you?"

"No. God, no." Lucy shakes her head and half sits up, palming my cheek in her hand. "It hurt, but you didn't hurt me. And I was expecting the pain. It's been a while for me."

"How long is a while?" I rasp as Lucy takes a breath, pulling my head down until her lips meet my ear.

"You," she whispers and I almost explode on the spot. *Jesus Christ.*

"Shit, Lucy. Are you sure you want to do this? Are you r—"
"God, yes! Please."

She falls back to the bed, pulling me down with her until my elbows hit the mattress beside her. After wrapping her legs around my waist, she bucks up into me, the angle giving us a deeper connection.

Pumping into her, I follow her cues, listening to her moans and whispered words to guide my speed and intensity. When I feel her walls tighten around me, more than they already were, I grip her legs, pushing them toward her chest before slowly rocking my hips, hoping the new angle and friction are enough to send her flying.

I have my answer in seconds, when her body jolts against the bed and she quietly cries out my name before wrapping her arms around my neck and forcing my weight down on top of her. Abandoning my grip on her legs, I pump hard a few more times until my body stiffens and I follow her over the edge, sighing into her ear as my body comes down from the high.

"As. I. Was. Saying...Perfection."

Lucy giggles and the sound hits me straight in the chest. I don't let go of her as I roll to her side. Instead, I bring her with me until she's snuggled under my arm.

We're both silent—for how long I don't know—and I want to spend the night here, but I know that's wrong. Katie doesn't need to wake up to me taking over her space. We need to do this the right way and—fuck! *Katie.*

As if I've woken her with my thoughts, she calls out "*Mom,*" making me jump so quickly, I fall off the bed. *Oomph!* My gaze springs to the door, but it's still closed. *What the fuck?* Her voice definitely came from the room. Lucy's soft laughter fills the silent space as her head peers over the side of the bed, and she looks at me with an amused expression.

"Whatcha doin'?" she asks, her grin widening.

"Where's Katie?" I rush out, panicked, ignoring her apparent delight in my stress. *How is she laughing right now?*

"Ah, in her room," she says like it's an obvious answer before disappearing from my sight.

"But...what—"

An object flies into my lap, cutting off my question as Lucy reappears.

"You really *do* only focus on one thing in life. Are you actually confused right now?" she asks with a lightness to her voice, clearly mocking me.

I look down at the screen in my hand as it comes to life and Katie calls out again. A fucking monitor. I know what they are. *God, I'm a dumbass.*

"Apparently so," I joke as Lucy laughs again before jumping off her bed and pulling on her panties and a silk robe.

"I'll be right back," she says, motioning to the hallway. "There's an ensuite through there if you need it." She looks down at my junk as she points over her shoulder toward the door she's referring to, and it's my turn to laugh. *At myself.* Because I'm a fucking mess. What a way to end a beautiful moment.

I'm just walking back into the room, half-dressed, as Lucy gently pulls the door closed behind her and moves to my side.

"I'm sorry." She sighs. "I wish you could stay." She runs a finger up and down my chest, following the motion with her eyes until I lift her chin, forcing her to meet my gaze before giving her a chaste kiss.

"I completely understand. We need to figure out what this is before getting Katie involved. We didn't wake her, did we?"

Lucy giggles. "No, not at all. She wasn't even awake; she calls out in her sleep sometimes. And thank you. You're right about needing to figure all this out, but I do want to say that I'm—"

"Can I take you on a date?" I rush out, cutting her off. "Just the two of us. Before you say what you were about to say."

A shocked expression briefly crosses her face, but she recovers and nods again. "I'd love that. I'll just need to arrange someone to watch Katie."

"Take all the time you need. Any nonwork time I have is yours."

I brush a kiss across her forehead and then step back, reaching for my tee.

Lucy watches my every move with her finger between her teeth, making it very difficult for me to depart.

We say our goodbyes and I head to my truck, taking my time as I do. It's not until I'm seated inside that I realize I still have unanswered questions about her. Her surname for one, and whether or not the asshole supports her. Working full-time can't be easy on her and Katie, so my guess is he doesn't. All questions that will have to wait for our date.

But if she thinks I'm keeping my distance at work until then, she's absolutely mistaken. I've waited too long for this; staying away is not an option.

Chapter Thirty

Lucy

I barely sleep after Wes leaves, with my mind too wired after everything that happened during the last few hours. Wes's confession and honesty completely threw me. I don't know what I was expecting him to say, but I definitely didn't think he'd open himself up like that and leave himself so vulnerable. My heart broke for him. To lose your girlfriend and then be harassed like that. To be moving through life knowing your mind works differently to others but never being given the tools to deal with it. I mean, he's coping. He's an amazing man. But would his life be easier if he'd had help?

Then there was my confession and Wes's reaction to it. The emotion in his voice made me feel like he wanted to take on some of the responsibility of what happened, even though I didn't know him back then. The protective vibe he threw out had my heart racing, and when he handed me the reins... God, I almost died. He's nothing like any of the guys I've been with, and I have to wonder why that is. I can't help questioning what I did to attract all the wrong men when I was younger. And how I managed to finally attract the right one, only for it to be the wrong time.

We have a second chance, and for the first time in what feels like forever, I actually want to take that leap of faith, to risk my heart being broken just because if I don't, I may end up worse off. But at the same time, I'm terrified to bring him into my mess with Greg.

When Monday comes, I'm slammed with work and don't get to see Wes at all, which seems to be happening too often for my liking. But short of hunting him down on the field, there's not much I can do.

On my drive home, I call Dylan with a giddy nervousness running through me, but when he answers, all that subsides.

"Brother from the same mother, how are you?"

He laughs and I picture him shaking his head. "Sometimes I worry about you, Luce."

"Aww, I love you too, baby bro."

"Alright, what do you want?"

I knew he'd be on to me, but having him ask makes it harder for me to chicken out.

"I was wondering if you and Summer wanted to try an overnighter with a child before your little one comes along."

"A child?"

"More specifically, *my* child."

Dylan huffs out a laugh and then he's silent for a beat. And that kills me. *Why? Why is he silent?*

"That's pretty huge, Lucy."

Shit!

"I know. Sorry, it was a long shot. It's okay; you've got a lot going on and—"

"No, Lucy. I meant that's pretty huge for *you*. Won't it be the first time?"

I sigh because yes, it will be. But I was hoping he wouldn't bring that up so the guilt didn't take over.

"Yes, and it is huge. Maybe I shouldn't..."

"Lucy, you absolutely should, and we'd love to spend the night with Katie. You know that. Don't overthink this. I only have one concern."

I swallow a lump in my throat as there's a good chance his concern might make me change my mind.

"Is this for Wes? And do I need to have words with him before you go out?"

I'm so tense that when I burst out laughing I almost swerve off the road. "Nope, definitely not. You are not having words with anyone."

"But it is Wes?"

"Yeah, it is," I admit quietly.

"Good. I'm okay with that. Just promise me you'll take things slow and be careful. You're strong, Lucy. Always have been. But…"

"I know. And my days of choosing the wrong guy are over. I promise."

Dylan laughs. "That's not where I was going with that, but yes, you've made some questionable choices. Although, at least you never dated Luke, despite his attempts."

"There's still time," I joke and am blessed with my little brother's relaxed laughter. He's always acted like a protective *big* brother. Ever since we were young. And I love him to death for it.

"Thanks, Dyl. Talk to Summer and let me know what night works. We'll fit in with you."

"Will do. Love ya, Sis."

"Love you too."

I'm rushing back from a morning meeting the next day, already short of time for an appointment, when Wes appears in the hallway in front of me, a glint in his eye. *What's he up to?*

"Wes, I don't have time. I have to—"

He pulls me into his arms and cuts me off with a bruising kiss, right in the open, where anyone can see. And God, does it have my heart racing and my mind in a puddle on the floor. *What was I doing again?*

His hands cup my face as his tongue pushes into my mouth, molding with mine and sending a shiver right through me. His kiss is so intoxicating I don't want it to stop, but somewhere deep in the back of my mind I know I should...for some reason. Something to do with—

Shit!

I push him away and take a step back, scanning the halls as I do. "What are you doing?" I whisper-yell, with my hands on my hips as though I'm angry, when not two seconds earlier I was ready to jump him.

"Saying hello." He shrugs like it's no big deal.

"Your *hello* could get us both fired."

"Let them try. They can't fill the job I currently have, remember? They need me more than I need them. And as for you? If they fired you, I'd quit."

Ugh! I want to stay mad at him but it's hard when he says nice shit like that.

"What about the players? You'd be letting them down."

Wes's head drops back, and he grunts as though that realization just hit him. "Damn those fuckers for growing on me."

I can't help but laugh until I remember the other reason I shouldn't have been kissing him.

"I've got to go, but set up a meeting and we'll talk."

Wes gives me a look that screams "you're kidding me, right?" then laughs.

"Okay, Lucy. I'll book a time."

And with that he's off, leaving me frozen on the spot, needing a moment to process what just happened. He said he wanted a date, but are we a thing now?

The morning flies by, and when I finally check my phone at lunch, I have a message from Dylan.

Little bro: How's Thursday night?

A giddy feeling takes over me.

Lucy: Perfect. Thank you

Thursday night. Only two days away. Butterflies flutter around my stomach as a small smile plays on my lips. I feel like a schoolgirl with my first crush. It's been so long since I've felt this nervous anticipation. Actually, Wes is really the only guy to ever elicit these feelings. And we're back on track. Finally. *I hope.*

When the last of my duties for the day are done, I start cleaning my work space until I hear the rap of knuckles on my door, Wes's signature announcement. He pokes his head through the open space before I've answered, and his small smile almost takes my worries away.

"You didn't accept my meeting request. Too busy for me now?"

He raises an eyebrow as he walks farther into the room, and I bark out a laugh. The contrast between this Wes and the one from last week can only be described as black and white. He's a completely different person. More like the guy I met all those years ago. I'm about to tell him just that when Aaron enters the room, not even bothering to knock.

"Lucy, do you have the report on Easton, I... Wes." He nods by way of greeting before his eyes shoot to mine, a look of annoyance crossing his features. *Wes really has no friends here.*

"Don't you knock?" Wes demands, and I have to bite back a smile. *And that's why.* Guess he hasn't changed as much as I thought.

"Do you have a reason to be here?" Aaron counters, causing Wes to sneer.

"Same reason you have. I wanted Easton's report."

He's full of shit, sort of, but I've got to hand it to him for thinking on his feet *and* for not telling Aaron why he's really here, since he said he doesn't give a shit about his job.

"Wes, thanks for stopping by. I'll have the report ready Thursday evening." My eyes lock on his, hoping he understands my meaning, and when his face lights up with a smile, I know that he has.

"Thursday is perfect. I'll pick it up then."

"Thank you."

He turns to Aaron and his smile morphs into a smirk. "Aaron, always a pleasure. Bye, Lucy."

With that he disappears out the door, whistling as he goes. *Whistling!* He's a little shit because no one would be that happy about a report on a player that's barely injured, and since Aaron is staring at me like we've both lost our minds, I think it's safe to say he's definitely on to us.

"Thursday, really? Why's it going to take so long?"

"I've got some patients who have more pressing injuries and I need to get their reports done for third parties."

Aaron nods and departs, because that's a plausible excuse and not a complete lie, even though I will definitely have the report done by tomorrow afternoon at the latest.

With Aaron gone, I finish packing up and head to my car feeling happy about the direction my life's heading right now. It's only as I hit the fresh summer evening air that I check my phone. *Big mistake.* I never responded to Greg, and now it's too late.

Unknown: I'm here. See you when you finish work

Chapter Thirty-One

Lucy

My heart stops as soon as I see my car. Greg's leaning against the driver's door, looking calm and collected in fitted jeans and a black sweater. I'll always find him attractive, only now when I look at him, my insides squirm and my skin prickles—and not in a good way.

"I know she's my kid, Lucy," he says, not wasting any time with hellos. "And like I said in my text—I just want to get to know her. From what I've seen, she seems like a good kid. You've done a good job raising her without me, but you won't have to anymore."

What?! My panic spikes and I scan the parking lot hoping we're not alone. We are, but there's a camera pointed right at me, so if anything happens the security guards will see. *Won't they?*

"How do you know anything about her?" I ask, trying to appear unaffected.

"I was driving by your mom's and she was out front. She's adorable. She looks just like you, but I had the same hair color when I was younger."

"Nobody drives past my mom's place. It's not on the way anywhere."

Greg's brows furrow and he frowns. "Sorry, this is coming out wrong. I'm not saying any of this as a threat." *Feels like it.* "I just... I want to get to know her. Ever since finding out I have a child, I can't get her out of my head. And since you're ignoring me, I wanted to see her. That's all."

I sigh. That calms me a little, though it probably shouldn't. He seems sincere but then again, that's how Greg works. He always managed to suck me in, one way or another, in the past, so I need to stay alert when it comes to him.

"You can't just show up where she is, Greg. Even if she was your daughter—"

"She is."

"Even *if she was*, you can't do that to her. She needs to be eased into it."

"So can I see her? To ease her into it."

Closing my eyes, I take a deep breath. *It's okay. Katie's okay. Just be rational.*

"You know we'll never be a family, right?" I ask, instead of answering his question.

"Maybe not. But I still deserve the chance to be her dad."

Ugh, unfortunately that's true. It doesn't matter what he's done to me; I have no right keeping her from him, especially now that he knows she exists.

"How about we plan a time together? I'll bring Katie, *and* Dylan, and you can meet her."

"Why does Dylan have to be there?"

"For Katie. He comes or she doesn't."

He nods as a smile lights up his face, coming across as genuine. *Please let it be genuine.*

"I'll text you on your work number. But maybe sometime next week?"

"I'd prefer sooner, but I'll take what I can. Thank you, Lucy. I'm going to show you that you can trust me again. I will."

"You better hope so, because Katie will only be in your life if you do."

Greg presses a kiss to my cheek before walking away, and as soon as his back is turned, I exhale, my body deflating as I wipe all traces of him from my face.

This is my worst nightmare coming true. I have to believe that he'd never hurt Katie, but I'm terrified that he will.

Falling back against my car, I blow out a breath and still myself, until my pulse returns to normal. I don't want her to know him. But keeping them apart is not really my decision to make. The last thing I want is for him to go the custody route, because then anything could happen. *I could lose her.*

I'm lost in thought, my mind dangerously close to reaching its own personal hell, when I hear someone calling my name. It takes me a moment, but when I eventually look up from the ground, Dani's at my side, her expression full of concern.

"What's wrong? Has something happened?"

"Yep." I nod, still processing everything.

"And..." She raises her eyebrows, encouraging me to talk.

I run a hand down my face and sigh, not wanting to voice the truth but knowing I have to. "Katie's dad is back and he wants to see her."

Dani's hand flies to her mouth as Wes appears in my line of sight.

"The fuck?" he demands. "That's not happening. Where is he?" He spins around, scanning every inch of the parking lot as Dani's eyes narrow, moving back and forth between the two of us.

"He's gone," I state plainly, not wanting him to see my concern.

"But he was here?"

"Yep."

"Talk to me, Luce. I'm worried." Wes steps forward but stops when I subtly shake my head.

279

"It's fine."

"It's not fine."

Dani throws her hands in the air, a look of confusion on her face. "What am I missing? Is there more to it, Lucy?"

"Nothing," I blurt at the same time Wes says, "We're dating."

"Wes!" I exclaim before burying my face in my hands.

"What? Dani's your friend. She's not going to say anything."

Dani gasps, and I see her megawatt smile through the slits of my fingers. "Yes! I knew it. Why didn't you tell me? I mean, Summer let a little slip, but we didn't know it was serious."

"It's not," I say, finally looking up at her.

"It definitely is," Wes adds from beside me, and I huff out a laugh. He's being such an ass right now.

"It's *not*," I repeat. "Wes is taking me out on Thursday night for our *first* date. And we're keeping it hush-hush."

"At Lucy's request." He shrugs.

"So we don't get fired," I counter.

Dani laughs at the two of us while I just stare at Wes in disbelief. *Who is this guy?* His cockiness is so hot, but now is not the time for that.

"Well, I think it's great," Dani says with a grin, trying hard not to show how excited she is at the prospect. I have no doubt she'll be calling me as soon as we're both in our cars.

"Now we have that sorted. Did you say hell no to that manipulative fucker? He's not seeing Katie, right?"

"I can't really stop him. He has rights."

"Where's he been for the last four years then? You said you've only seen him twice. He abandoned her. Why's he back now?"

My face reddens as a pain hits me in the chest. "I, um…I never told him."

Wes freezes, his eyes widening in shock, while Dani wraps her arms around me sympathetically, already knowing this information.

"He hasn't done a paternity test though, right? So he doesn't know for sure?" she says, trying to make me feel better.

I nod with a sigh, because this is getting a lot bigger than I need it to be. I haven't even processed it internally yet. "Technically you're right, but he's not stupid. He's seen her. They may not look exactly alike, but the dates match and she apparently has the same hair color he had as a kid."

Wes huffs. "That means nothing. Come on, Luce. You can't be serious."

I'm about to object when Dani puts her hand up between us before turning to me. "Wes is right too. If his only *'proof'* is hair color, you don't need to let him see her."

"But what if he petitions for custody or something? You of all people know how that can turn out."

Dani sighs and nods, pain in her expression, knowing that all too well. She's about to speak when Wes grabs my hand, curling my fingers in his. "We won't let that happen, Luce."

I huff out a breath, because it's not that simple. "I can't afford to fight him, Wes. He says he has money. What if he does and I don't win?"

"If money's the only thing standing in your way, it's a non-issue. *We won't let that happen*," he repeats before pulling me into a hug.

I push him away, conscious of the fact that people are still leaving for the day, and we're standing out in the open. I can see he wants to argue, but instead he nods and steps back, always doing the right thing.

"Thank you," I say. "You're right. It's not going to happen. Because I'm going to let him see her. It's going to be fine."

Dani reaches out and squeezes my hand just as Wes mumbles a bunch of expletives under his breath. He means well—I know he's trying to protect me—but he doesn't get it. I'm terrified Greg will try to take her from me, and I can't risk it. If he says he's genuine, then for now I have to give him the benefit of the doubt. *For now.*

Thursday rolls around, and before I know it, it's time for my date. Wes and I have passed in the halls a few times since the parking lot, but we've always been surrounded by colleagues so have only ever exchanged a polite hello or smile. And now that our date's almost here, I'm nervous about it. What if we've both changed so much that we have nothing to talk about without Katie as a buffer? What if the spark we have turns out to be sexual tension and doesn't actually translate to a relationship in everyday life? Or what if he discovers he no longer likes me? I'm spiraling, I know I am, but for almost five years he's the only guy I've thought of, and I never expected to get this chance with him again.

At exactly five on the dot my phone buzzes on my desk. Though I'm almost certain it's Wes, my pulse still spikes, worrying it could be Greg. He's left me alone since we last spoke. And I can only assume—and hope—he's letting me set the pace. But if there's another reason for his silence, I don't know what I'll do.

Luckily, this time it is Wes, so I can relax.

Wes: Time to pack up, Luce. I'll be at your place for that report at six

I smile into my hand, as an instant calm takes over me. Stressing is only going to ruin our night. I need to let it play out.

Lucy: I'll be ready, report in hand

I rush home to get changed, thankful that Katie's already settled in at Dylan and Summer's but missing her all the same, and I've just hung up from calling her to say goodnight when my doorbell rings. Giddy anticipation takes over me again and only worsens when I open the door and see Wes standing there looking absolutely delicious in dark fitted jeans and a black shirt, with his sleeves rolled up once again.

He has one arm braced above his head on the door frame, making the veins in his forearm stick out, while the other holds flowers. *Flowers!* He's simultaneously making me swoon and want to drop my panties at the same time. Screw the date. Other than last week, I've had a five-year drought; we're staying inside.

Curling my fingers into his shirt, I drag him through the door, not even bothering to say hello. He chuckles but lets me pull him along without argument, an amused expression in place.

Taking the flowers from his hand, I gently place them on the kitchen counter with a rushed "thank you" before launching myself at him and crashing my lips to his.

He catches me easily, his fingers digging into the flesh of my ass, settling beneath the dress I conveniently wore.

He groans as he squeezes, his hand roaming my cheeks before pulling back from our kiss. "Fuck, are you not wearing panties?"

I huff out a laugh and roll my hips into him, smiling against his lips when he rewards me with another guttural groan.

"I am," I say between kisses. "They're just tiny."

Wes grunts as he lifts me higher and positions me on the counter, pushing my dress up to my waist. His eyes darken as they lock on my white silk thong before he rips the thin material from my body and throws it away, making my insides clench with need. "Oh, God."

Dropping to his knees, he spreads my legs wide, immediately running his tongue through my heat. "Holy shit, Wes. *Jesus.*"

A groan rips from deep within him before he stands up and leans over me, his lips barely a breath from my own. "As much as I want to worship every inch of you, especially here," he says, teasing my mound with his fingers. "I've been thinking about taking you again, every second since I was last inside you, and I need it... now."

I clench again at his words as my head drops back. *God, I need it too.*

"I'm good with that. Take me."

Wes wastes no time sheathing himself before pushing inside me in one quick movement. This time all I feel is intense pleasure, not a hint of the pain I felt last week. We fit. It's perfection. He's meant to be inside me. To be mine. Just like he wanted me to be his.

We both cry out as we start to move, and he sinks deeper and deeper with every push. I want to match his power, but I can't get enough movement in my current position. And I need it.

Lying back until I'm resting on my palms, I lift one leg on to the counter and use it to help with traction, to pump harder and faster until I have Wes grunting my name.

"Fuck, Lucy. You feel so good. Always so good."

He grips the counter edge with one hand, lifting my ass with the other, and the new angle has me unable to hold back a scream. "I can't. I...oh, God, Wes."

I try hard to hold out, loving the connection I'm feeling, but when Wes leans forward, a spark runs through me and my orgasm hits, catching me off guard. My insides contract and pulse, squeezing Wes's cock as he grunts, his hand gripping me tightly. "Jesus Christ!" Pumping a few more times, he curses the world before falling on top of me in a huff.

We're both silent for a few seconds until Wes sighs in contentment. "You, Lucy Mathers, were made for me."

Wrapping my arms around him, I huff out a laugh and then sink back to the counter, my head landing on top of the flowers. *Oops.*

I feel Wes's body move as he chuckles above me, and a satisfied smile graces my lips. I could stay here all day. But...

"Now, can I take you to dinner?" he huffs out, whining as though I've ruined his plans.

I giggle as I push him away so I can stand, straightening my dress as I do. "That would be lovely. I'm ready. Are you?"

Wes's eyes move to my crotch and he grunts, knowing I now have nothing beneath my dress. "You better be ready," he mumbles as he walks toward the bathroom to clean up.

Chapter Thirty-Two
Wes

I 'm in a world of pain knowing that Lucy's sitting across from me in a busy restaurant...with no panties. Somehow, I'm keeping up with the conversation, but fuck, it's a struggle.

"And then he finally moved back," Lucy says, talking about her brother, Dylan. "Pity you never played together. I think you'd have gotten along."

I nod, because she's right. We do get along. "We spoke a few times at events, but I could never bring myself to ask about you."

Lucy's eyes widen before confusion masks her shock. "You spoke?"

"Yeah, we shared a sponsor so I saw him a few times. Why do you look mad right now?"

She crosses her arms over her chest and huffs dramatically like a child having a tantrum. "Because he never told me."

I almost laugh at the adorable look on her face until her words register.

"Would you have wanted to know?" I'm not sure what I want her answer to be. Is it easier to know she wanted to find out about me, or better if she didn't...so I don't feel like we missed out.

"Yeah, I think I would have."

Fuck! The latter was definitely better. Years wasted.

"But I wasn't ready." She sighs, as her hands drop to her side.

At least that's something.

"And now you are?"

A smile lights up her face making me want to reach across the table and kiss her. Even more so, after she answers, "I am."

Pulling my lips into a grin, I nod and shelve that conversation for another time. "You know, the last time I saw your brother he'd just gotten married. He was so high on life I thought he was drunk."

Lucy laughs out loud before covering her mouth with her hand. "Yep, that's Dylan. The love he has for Summer is infinite. And I thought he was his happiest the day they said their vows, but you should have seen him when he found out Summer was pregnant."

"They're having a baby?"

"Yep, a little boy due around Christmas."

Well there you go. Good on him. "I bet Katie's excited."

"Over the moon." She smiles and then her nose crinkles in thought. "Although, I don't think she's prepared for Dylan's attention to be on someone else."

"Nothing ever prepares us for that." *And I know exactly how she's going to feel.*

"I suppose you're right," Lucy laughs, obviously not sensing the melancholy in my voice.

"And Summer is Thomas Kelly's sister, right?" I ask casually. As though this very topic hasn't been on my mind for a while.

"That's right. I guess you probably know him too?"

"Not really. I mean we've played against each other, but that's it. How well do *you* know him?"

Lucy's brows furrow at my questions, probably due to the slight rise of my voice, but she doesn't falter.

"I know him pretty well. We see each other on the holidays and the odd weekend here and there. He's a great guy."

A *great guy*. "And you have his surname?"

Lucy gasps but recovers quickly, turning it into a laugh. "Oh. Yeah, I do."

She grimaces slightly before biting her lip as a pensive expression crosses her face. I'm not sure whether to ask more or if that short answer meant I'm supposed to drop the subject, so I nod, lifting my glass to my lips, needing a moment to decide. But Lucy continues.

"Since I already saw Summer as family, Thomas suggested I use their name after I decided I didn't want to put Mathers on Katie's birth certificate. I guess you could say he lent me their name." She laughs nervously. "I registered Katie as Kelly and changed my name at the same time."

"*Lent* it to you?"

"Yes. I'm hoping one day I'll be able to change it again. To my husband's name." She shrugs as though it's a passing thought, but the words hit me like a gut punch. The feelings they conjure up are unlike any I've felt before. *Husband*. I've never really thought about marriage. Actually I have, but I've always thought it to be a bit of a sham. That little piece of paper does nothing for the relationship. One party can still walk away at any moment and start a new family with no consequences whatsoever. And yet, when Lucy talks about a husband, why do I suddenly want that person to be me?

After we've finished dinner, I desperately want to take her home to bed, but I don't. She deserves the full dating experience. *Not that I know what I'm doing.*

But I want it to be special.

To try.

For her.

As we walk silently through the lit-up streets of San Francisco, a sudden feeling of comfort takes over me, and I need to be touching her. Reaching for her hand, I entwine our fingers and squeeze, pulling her closer until our shoulders touch as we walk. We both remain silent, but it's impossible to miss the moment Lucy's lips lift and a shy smile appears. For someone so badass, it's like she doesn't see her worth. Doesn't realize how amazing she is.

When it comes to sex, she's this confident woman, but romance, that's another story, and I want to change that for her. I want her to see how amazing she is. If only I knew how to do this romance stuff myself. The one thing I do know is how I feel, and it's about time I told her.

Lifting our joined hands to my lips, I softly kiss each knuckle before pulling her closer to whisper in her ear, wanting to make sure she hears me loud and clear. "I like you, Lucy. A lot. I've wanted this for a long time. I've wanted *you* for a long time. You're so fucking special and I don't even think you realize it. The wait was worth it."

Lucy's breath hitches and she tilts her head back to look in my eyes, but before she can say anything, I reiterate my words. "*You* were worth the wait."

I catch the flash of a smile before she burrows her face into my chest, wrapping her arms around me. She's still for a moment until she looks up at me again, blinking through her long lashes. "I'm yours," she says, and my chest tightens. I never wanted any of this until Lucy first came along, and now that she's back in my life, I'm prepared to fight anyone that stands in our way.

Conversation starts up again, after our moment, and as we joke and laugh, I keep her hand firmly in my grasp, never wanting to let her go.

When it hits ten p.m., I invite Lucy to my place for dessert, just as my phone rings in my pocket—three times—distracting me from my question. *Ugh, why do my friends know me so well?*

"You should get that. They obviously want to speak to you," Lucy says, patting me on the arm. I know it's going to be one of two people, and whoever it is earned themselves an ass kicking.

After finally pulling the phone from my pocket, I see that it's Gray, just as a message comes through.

Grayson: At your place. See you when you and your woman get home

Dammit! I groan because there goes my plan.

Lucy's brows furrow as she watches me, and when I roll my eyes, she laughs.

"That was Grayson. You might remember him from our very first date. He was the eighteen-year-old kid, recently divorced."

Lucy's face lights up and she claps her hands together. "Of course, I remember Grayson. You kept in contact with him?"

"I did. And it's a long story, but he's at my house," I say with a lift of my shoulder like it's no big deal, but that's not true.

"How long of a story?" Lucy frowns, her expression full of intrigue. So I fill her in. As we walk, I tell her all about Grayson and how he's completely ingrained in my life. She gasps in some moments, laughs in others, her eyes locked on me the entire time.

"So in conclusion...he's at my house. Meaning my plans for the rest of the evening are foiled."

Lucy nibbles on her bottom lip and grins. "And what exactly were those plans?"

"Like I said, my place for dessert." I fake pout.

Lucy laughs out loud. "And what exactly were we having?"

"Chocolate cake for you... *You* for me."

Her laughter disappears as her pupils dilate and she squirms ever so slightly on the spot. It makes me want to push her up against the closest building and ravish her, especially knowing how easy the access would be.

"I don't have chocolate cake at my place, but the other is definitely on offer," she says, winking as she does, reading my thoughts. *This woman.*

I groan before linking our fingers again and moving us through the late-night crowd in the direction of my truck as fast as I can. I'm good without the cake. *Date over.*

When I wake the next morning, Lucy's in my arms. The soft sound of her breathing filters through my dreams, and her long hair tickles my chest where it's splayed across me. Brushing the strands away from her face, I study her features, taking in the way her lips curve up slightly as she sleeps and the dusting of freckles across her nose. I can't stop myself from pressing a light kiss to her forehead, gently enough that I don't wake her, content to just lie here and exist beside her.

I must fall back asleep at some point because when I wake again, Lucy's sitting up with my shirt around her shoulders, buttons undone. She's so stunningly beautiful, inside and out, that I have to pinch my leg to remind myself she's mine. When she notices my movement, her eyes light up as she looks my way. "Hey, handsome."

"Hey, yourself. I could get used to this. Waking up with you in my bed. Or me in yours as the case may be."

Lucy giggles but shakes her head. "Oh, my mornings are nothing like this. If you think us being together is going to lead to this"—she motions to us on the bed—"be prepared for a shock."

"Huh?"

"Have you forgotten about Katie?" She laughs again.

"Never." *As if I ever would. That girl has definitely found a place in my heart, just like her mom.*

"Then put two and two together," Lucy says, breaking my thoughts.

"Ahh, is she an early riser?"

"She usually sneaks in here at about five."

"I'm good with five. My alarm was set for four thirty when I played. I usually wake a lot earlier than this."

A sassy grin appears on Lucy's face, and her eyes sparkle with mischief. "Perfect! The sooner we have Katie comfortable with you staying over, the better. The two of you can entertain each other while I sleep in."

Reaching up, I grip her at the waist and pull her backward on top of me, tickling her as I do. "Is that how it's going to be?" I say, my fingers working hard to make her squirm.

She cries out, "Absolutely," as she fills the room with uncontrollable giggles, a sound I'll never get sick of and a moment I wish could last forever. Sadly, reality gets in the way and Lucy's alarm goes off, alerting us to the time. We reluctantly say our goodbyes to get ready for work, and I leave Lucy with a parting kiss to hopefully get her through the day.

As I drive away, I picture waking up to the sounds of two giggling girls, and a warm feeling consumes me at the thought of maybe one day having a family of my own. But not just any family—this one.

For the next week, Lucy and I talk every night, but we don't get time for another date. The stupid policy at work means that even though we spend all day in the same building, I'm lucky if I get a wink and a smile when she passes by. It's killing me. And with the season starting up, it's only going to get worse.

I'm anxious more today than any other with the knowledge that Katie and Lucy are meeting with Katie's sperm donor after work. I refuse to call him her father until he's proven himself to be one. The jackass has done no right in my eyes. Not that I have a say in the matter.

When it gets to four p.m. and I haven't seen Lucy, I track her down, uncaring of who sees us. I can't let her leave without her knowing I'm here if she needs me.

She's slipping out the glass door to the parking lot when I finally spot her, and I jog to try and catch up with her.

"Lucy! Wait up," I call as I get closer, only stopping my jog when I reach her. Knowing she's going to object, I press a quick kiss to her lips and then take a step back with a small smirk on mine, chuckling when she rolls her eyes as she huffs out a laugh.

"Sorry, I couldn't help myself." I shrug. "Are you heading to the park now?"

She blows out a breath, and I can see the stress plain as day on her face. "I am. Dylan's already with Katie, so I'm meeting them there."

I itch to pull her into a hug, but I keep my hands by my side, knowing she'll likely push me away. "I want to be there. You know that, right?"

She grins, reaching forward to connect our hands ever so slightly. "I know. But I've got Dylan. He's not going to let anything happen to either of us."

I can't stop my frown even though she's right. "Okay. Please call me when you get home."

"I will. I...thank you."

Not wanting to piss Lucy off, I quickly scan the parking lot to make sure the coast is clear before pulling her in for a proper kiss. My lips instantly mold to hers as my tongue seeks entry. And without resisting, Lucy moans as she sucks my tongue into her mouth, her hands clenching my shirt. The kiss may be brief, but it's full of emotion, both of us knowing how hard today will be.

"Call me," I say after I've broken our connection, my hand mimicking a phone to my ear.

"I will." She laughs, backing away until she hits her car, only then turning around.

Unable to leave, I wait until she drives away, an uncomfortable feeling settling in my chest.

Chapter Thirty-Three

Lucy

Dylan stops what he's doing and looks at me in shock. "You know I want to kill him, right?" *I sure do.* He's mentioned it a few times.

I held off on telling him that Greg would be meeting us today because I didn't want him to call in reinforcements. I'm sure if I'd given him a heads-up, everyone would be here. He'd probably even have Thomas fly in from Seattle. It's much easier this way. Although he does look a little mad.

"I do know that," I reply. "But I'm kinda hoping that means you'll see through his bullshit easier than I apparently do."

"Wouldn't Joel be better for that?"

I sigh, because yes, he would be, but Dylan doesn't get it. "Dyl, there are a lot of better options, but you're my brother, Katie's number one fan, and I need *you* here."

He nods before curling his arm around my shoulders, and while I'm happy he seems to understand, his silence concerns me a little. *I hope I'm doing the right thing.*

Katie, Dylan, and I run around the park until five thirty comes along—go time. Making my way to the parking lot, I wait anxiously, wringing my fingers, while Dylan and Katie continue to play behind me, close enough that Dylan can keep an eye on us both. I'm not ready for this, at all, but he wants to get to know his daughter, and what choice do I have?

Greg arrives a couple of minutes late and jumps out of his car as soon as it's in park. "I'm so sorry. I swear I left work on time; traffic was a nightmare."

The sincerity in his voice shocks me, but I recover enough to respond. "It's fine. It's barely been five minutes. Are you still working in the city?"

"I am, but not at the same joint. I've moved up in the world."

I figured as much when he mentioned money, but thought I'd ask. I'm about to ask another question to delay him, when Greg's eyes flash to the playground and then back to me, a small smile playing on his lips.

"Can I see her?"

I internally flinch and hope my anxiety doesn't show on my face. "That's why we're here," I say uncomfortably, forcing the words out. "You should know that Katie knows who you are. Or at least, she knows she's meeting her father today. She's excited. Don't mess this up."

Anger flashes across Greg's face before it subsides, replaced by hurt. "I'm not an absent father, Lucy. *You* kept her away from *me*. Remember that before you speak."

Keeping a straight face, I nod once and then head off toward Katie and Dylan, leaving Greg to follow. His words do everything to remind me that deep down, he's still the same guy, and I can't get sucked into the nice things he does. I need to be wary.

Dylan's the first to spot us when we approach, and his jaw locks when his eyes find Greg. If I wasn't one hundred percent sure that Dylan was smart enough not to ruin his career with an assault charge, I wouldn't have asked him to come. But thankfully, I'm confident in that.

Katie spots Greg a few seconds later, and she frowns briefly before smiling. Reaching for Dylan's hand, she waits patiently for us to arrive and then motions for me to bend down so she can whisper in my ear. "I thought it was going to be Wes," she says, her voice laced with disappointment. My chest tightens as I bite back a gasp, having no idea why she would think that.

When I straighten up, my eyes lock on Dylan's and there's no doubt in my mind that he heard what she said, with his expression almost mimicking mine. *And if he heard...*

I turn to find Greg staring at me with a forced smile and rigid stance. He absolutely knows what she said, and he's not too happy about it. Then again, I guess I wouldn't be either.

"Katie, this is Greg. Greg, this is Katie," I say, hoping to move on.

Katie nods Greg's way and then her eyes flash to me and Dylan. I hold my breath waiting to see what she does, and just when I think I'm going to have to intervene, she turns back to Greg. "Do you want to play football?"

I mentally facepalm because of all things to say, that was possibly the worst, but at least she's trying. Plus, she doesn't know that Greg thinks I left him for a football player all those years ago.

Greg, to his credit, gives Katie a huge smile and asks her to lead the way. All while Dylan fumes as he watches them walk to the field.

Hip checking him on the way past, I manage to get a tiny smile in return, but it's obvious that he's struggling to keep his cool. And I can't say I blame him.

Katie and Greg play until it starts getting dark and I have to call it a day. Katie objects as usual, and by the time Dylan and

I finally get her into my car, I'm emotionally drained. I've been on edge ever since Greg arrived, but I didn't realize how tense I was until he was gone.

I can't wait to talk to Katie about her thoughts but know it's going to take her some time to process things. If I ask her now she'll just shrug or tell me she doesn't know, but if I give her an hour, she won't shut up about it.

After closing Katie's door, I turn to find Dylan pacing in front of me. It's what he does when he's worked up about something. "I'm sorry, Dylan. I know that was difficult, but I really appreciate you being here."

"You're sorry?" he asks, confused. "You shouldn't be sorry, I'm sorry. I can't even imagine how you're feeling right now. You're my hero, Luce. Always have been. Your strength. My God...you're just...amazing. And don't let anyone ever tell you otherwise."

He pulls me into a hug as tears prick my eyes, and I mumble a thanks into his chest. My phone starts ringing but I ignore it, enjoying the comfort from my baby bro. Having him here made a world of difference, and he wasn't even needed.

Katie and I grab take-out dinner on the way home, and when she's all tucked into bed, I finally ask about Greg.

"Was today okay, sweetie? You had fun with Greg, right?"

"It was good. He's nice."

"He is." *Can be.* "Do you want to see him again?"

Katie shrugs and shifts her attention to one of the many stuffed toys she has in her bed. "If I do, I don't think we'll play football. He's not that good."

I bite back a laugh and lie down next to her, wrapping her up in my arms. "I'm sure we can find something else for you to do together."

"Like karaoke?"

This time I do laugh. Katie's been obsessed with karaoke ever since finding out Dylan once sang to Summer.

"We can ask. But for now, it's time to close our eyes."

"Can you stay in here until I fall asleep tonight?" she asks, and while I'd normally ask her to try on her own, tonight I easily agree.

"Of course. I love you."

"Love you too."

Katie takes a little while to drift off, so in my exhausted state, I pass out next to her. It's not the first time and it definitely won't be the last, but when I wake I'm a little disoriented. By the time I make it to my room it's three a.m. and I'm still so tired, I could probably sleep for a month.

Double-checking I've set my alarm on my phone, I see a message from Wes and wince. Actually two missed calls and three texts. *Shit!*

I don't even bother reading the messages before I dial his number, not even worrying about the time. He answers within seconds.

"Lucy?" he rasps, clearly awakened from sleep.

My heart pounds in my chest as I prepare to hear the disappointment in his tone, or worse, for him to scold me.

"I'm so sorry, Wes. I know I said I'd call you, but Katie wanted me to stay beside her until she fell asleep, and I crashed with her. It's no excuse but today was emotionally taxing, and I can't believe I forgot. I'm so sorry. Please don't be upset. I'll—"

"Whoa! Lucy, slow down. It's okay. I've been worried about you but I'm not upset. Why do you think I'm upset?"

"Because I said I'd call you and I didn't."

Wes huffs out a soft laugh. "Yes. But only because I wanted to know you were okay. Today killed me, but I understand."

My pulse slowly returns to normal, as the tightness in my chest subsides.

"So, you're not angry?" I ask, confused.

"Fuck, no. Why would I be angry? Luce, are you okay?"

Sighing, I bury my face in my hands and try to stave off the tears. "I am now," I say with a sniff, and it's not a lie; hearing his voice is instantly calming.

"God, Luce. I wish I was there."

"I wish you were here too. But it's three in the morning. You should be asleep."

"I don't give a shit about sleeping. Tell me all about it. How did it go? Did he do anything he shouldn't have?"

My lips pull up at the edges, and all the stress leaves my body. I've never had this. My family cares for me, obviously, but I've never had someone to talk to about my day. To help unpack my emotions. Someone to share it all. My insides fill with butterflies because maybe Wes is my guy. The one for me. And because I have Wes asking to listen to my troubles, those troubles disappear.

"It was actually okay. They seemed to get along and he was good with her. But it was hard to watch. And I'd much rather talk about something else."

"Are you sure? I don't mind talking about him. Yes, I want to physically maim him, but I'm not going to do that unless you ask me to."

I bark out a laugh and lie back on the bed, getting comfortable for a long chat, because I could listen to his raspy voice all night. "So, as long as you don't tell me you're getting back with him, I'm here to listen."

Laughing again, I switch the phone to video call and wait for him to answer. When he does, my heart races at the sight of him. His thick hair is a mess on top of his head, and his eyes have that just woken up shine. He's naked, or at least he's shirtless, and has the most beautiful smile lighting up his face. A smile that has the corners of his eyes crinkling.

"You're so beautiful, Luce," he says, interrupting my gawking.

"Huh?"

I'm so distracted by *his* beauty, it barely registers that he's commenting on mine.

He laughs and the sound hits me within.

"I said you're beautiful, Lucy. Where's your head?"

A slight frown crosses his face as though he's worried about the answer, but it's gone in a flash.

"I'm lying there next to you," I whisper shyly and love when Wes's smile returns.

"I need that to happen again real soon," he says, running a hand down his face. And while I want that too, it's not that easy.

"It will," I promise. "It will just take time."

"I know, and like I said, you're worth the wait."

Chapter Thirty-Four
Wes

L ucy and I try to see each other as much as we can over the next week, but life is against us. I'm so desperate, I want to either pull her into a utility closet or ravage her in the lunchroom, but of course, I don't, because she wants to keep things on the down low. I get it; she's nervous about losing her job, especially now that she has the distant threat of Katie's dad hanging over her head. He may not have even mentioned custody to her, but I know it's always in the back of her mind.

The college season officially kicks off tomorrow, and just like Lucy said, I've grown to love these guys. Baby Bennett—or Mini B as I often refer to him—is killing it as quarterback, the team's back to full health, and they're actually gelling together. We might even have a shot at a championship this year. *If we keep it up.*

I've seen Katie a couple of times since we spent that day together, and she's well and truly wormed her way into my heart. I've found myself looking forward to our time together, something I never saw coming. So, with the first game being tomorrow, I invited her to sit as close to the action as possible. And I just might have become her favorite person. Watching her eyes light up brings me as much joy as spending time with her mother does, and I'm growing attached to them both. *How that happened, I have no idea.*

It's now been twenty-four hours since I last kissed Lucy, and I'm having withdrawals. While she's always on my mind, I'm not losing my focus like I usually do. This time around it feels like everything just fits, like she's always been here and I don't need time to adjust. It's a strange realization, but a good one.

With my nerves kicking in for tomorrow's game, I stay back in the office later than normal, even though I don't really have anything to do. I shouldn't be so worried; I've done this a million times before. I even have a pregame ritual. But that's for Wes the player. Wes the coach? I don't know what the fuck he does. But it's stressing me out, that's for sure. When I finally head out to my truck at around eight, I have jitters. I'm tense, and I keep clenching and unclenching my fists, bouncing my shoulders, cracking my neck, anything to get myself out of my head.

I played in a Super Bowl for God's sake. *Get yourself together!* Running my hands down my face, I groan out loud, then freeze when the most beautiful voice enters my head. When I open my eyes, my gaze locks on the exact thing I need. Or more specifically the exact person I need.

"Fuck, are you a sight for sore eyes," I say with zero chill.

Lucy laughs before biting down on her bottom lip, making my shorts instantly tighten. She's a devil in disguise. While she looks angelic in a simple white summer dress and flip-flops, it's the hint of a black lace bra underneath and the fire in her eyes that give her away. She's here to ruin me, and I'm ready to drop to my knees and let her.

"Are you here for me?" I ask, despite knowing the answer.

"Is this your truck?" she sasses back quickly, lifting her foot up to the running board.

"Does that mean I can kiss you?"

"I should hope so; I've been waiting a while."

I huff out a laugh as I shake my head. "What if someone sees us?"

"Do you care?"

"Hell no. I'm only doing that shit for you."

"Then get your ass over here, Johnson. I need those lips."

"Yes, ma'am."

She lifts up onto the running board and falls forward when I reach her, wrapping her arms and legs around me. I waste no time pressing her against my door, grinding into her.

"I want you so badly," I rush out as I take a breath between kisses. "But there are cameras everywhere." More kisses. "Your place?"

Lucy shakes her head as she rolls her hips.

"*God*, my place?" I groan out, struggling to talk.

She shakes her head again, and I almost cry out in frustration.

"Lucy." Kiss. "I need you." Lip nibble. "Right now." My length pulses as I pump into her, and she moans in response before ripping her mouth from mine.

"Let's go parking."

"What?" I stare at her in disbelief.

"Our places are too far away. Let's park somewhere."

My head tilts to the side as I study her with a puzzled expression. "Who are you?"

Lucy blushes. "Right now, I have no idea. But I need you too."

Good enough for me.

Walking around to the other side of the truck, I open the door and drop Lucy onto the seat before running back to the driver's side.

Since I'm not a sixteen-year-old kid anymore, I have no idea where to "go parking," so instead, I drive to the nearest deserted street, put the car in park, and slide my seat all the way back, before unbuckling Lucy and pulling her on top of me.

She laughs at my wordless motion, but it dies when I grip her hips and hold her still as I pump up into her, rubbing against her core.

We grind together for a few minutes until I'm so worked up I can't take much more. It's break time. Lifting her up, I reposition her with her weight on her knees instead of my lap, then without warning, drop the backrest and sink down until I'm almost to the floor with my face positioned perfectly between her legs.

"Now you can sit," I say, looking up at her from below.

Her chest rises, and I can just make out eyes widening in the dark. I'd bet my life savings that her skin is now a perfect shade of pink too, only I can't tell in the low light.

Despite her reaction making me certain she understands my meaning, she doesn't move.

"Sit, Lucy," I growl before reaching up and pulling her down onto my face, chuckling when she gasps in surprise.

As I suspected, she's wearing another thong, so my tongue easily slips underneath it, making her cry out in pleasure. "Fuck, Wes."

Moving the strip of fabric to the side, I lift up slightly to suck her into my mouth, but she's not making it easy on me. She's hesitant, refusing to rest her full weight against me, and that won't do; I need her closer.

I alternate between licking and sucking a few times until I feel her legs start to shake and I know I've found my moment. The next time I lick her, I use all my strength to pull her down and she buckles, sinking on top of me, smothering me with her heat. *Fuck yes!*

With my back now flat on the seat and easier access, I'm able to work her into a frenzy of gasps and high-pitched mewls, until she's a writhing mess on top of me. And fuck, is it a beautiful sight.

Squeezing her ass in my hands, I suck one more time, and she jolts before crying out my name and falling back against the steering wheel, giving me an even better view.

"Maybe I should have positioned you like that," I say with a chuckle that turns into a full laugh when she squeezes my head between her knees.

"That's enough out of you," she replies breathlessly seconds before she lifts up and moves back to her side of the truck. "I need a moment to get myself together."

I bite back a cocky grin. "Take your time. In fact, where's Katie right now?"

Lucy's eyes flash to mine, confused by my sudden mention of Katie, and I can't help but laugh.

"As in, do you have to pick her up?"

"No, she's at my place. Summer's staying there until I get home."

"Perfect, you rest. I'll drive us to my place and then drop you home before you turn back into a pumpkin."

Lucy laughs. "You know Cinderella didn't turn into a pumpkin, right?"

"I do, and I also know that I'm no Prince Charming."

She laughs again as I put the truck in drive and head to my place. It'll be the first time she's been there, and something tells me she's going to get a shock.

The second we pull up, Lucy opens her door and bounces out of her seat, her eyes raking over my modest three-bedroom house, with a small front yard and a white picket fence.

"You continue to surprise me, non Prince Charming. *Every day*," she says, beaming my way.

I grimace with a fake laugh. "Let's hope those surprises are good things."

"Trust me, they are."

With a small nod, I follow her to the front door and let us both into the house, switching on a light as we walk in.

"*Fuck*! Way to wake a guy up," Grayson's voice comes from the living area.

Lucy screams, and I curse under my breath as his head lifts off the couch and he shields his eyes from the light. "Can you turn it off?"

"Can you fuck off?" I counter.

"Nope."

"Same answer."

He groans but then reluctantly uncovers his eyes, smiling when they lock on Lucy.

"Fuck me. I didn't think I'd see you again."

Lucy's brows furrow and her gaze flits to mine. She either doesn't recognize him, or thinks that I'm keeping her a secret.

"He didn't think he'd see me again," she says with a raised brow. "I thought you were close?" The latter then.

Gray laughs as Lucy shakes her head.

"He knows about you. He's being a dick."

307

Grayson nods exaggeratedly. "It's true, I am. I thought he'd screw it up before we got a chance to meet again."

"Is that likely to happen?" she asks Grayson. Not me, *Grayson.*

"Not sure yet." He shrugs and I roll my eyes. "He's got a lot of baggage, but he's a good guy," he continues, digging himself a grave. "And—"

"Are you done?"

"I wasn't, but I can be...for now." He nods. *Fucker.*

Turning back to Lucy, he studies her face and then smiles. "You haven't changed one bit."

Lucy blushes shyly, probably because she thinks that she has, but recovers quickly and smiles. "Well, you've now got stubble," she observes, causing Grayson to crack up as he runs his hand over said stubble with a nod.

"That I do. I'm not the eighteen-year-old you once met."

"No, you most certainly aren't."

My eyes flash to hers because that sounded flirty, but when I note her expression, she's laughing silently at me. *Very funny, Lucy. Yes, I'm the jealous type.*

As if reading my thoughts, she laughs out loud before getting comfortable on the couch beside Gray, settling in for a long chat, while I make a note to change my locks.

Lucy yawns and I glance at my watch to see we've all been talking for an hour. I need to get her home.

"We better go, Luce. It's getting late."

She checks the time herself and gasps. "Shit. It is. I'm sorry. It was nice seeing you, Grayson. Hopefully we can catch up again."

"I'd love that."

After saying goodbyes, we head to my truck in silence, and once we're on the road, Lucy's hand flies to her mouth and her breath hitches. "I never returned the favor. Pull over."

I can't help but chuckle at the shocked look on her face as I lean over to pat her leg.

"As tempting and *romantic* as that sounds, I'm not keeping score here."

"You're not?" she asks seriously, and my humor fades. *The fuck?* Yet another red flag with regards to how Lucy's been treated in the past. Katie's father better hope we never cross paths. Sexual assault is obviously bad enough, but he was one hundred percent emotionally abusive too and that's fucked-up. It's hard to imagine how someone as confident and strong as Lucy could end up in a situation like that, but it's not inconceivable. Like I said to her, not all our scars are visible. Everything about the situation with her ex makes me want to do anything in my power to keep her safe, but at the same time, I know she wants to prove to herself that she can go it alone, and that scares the hell out of me.

I drop Lucy off with a chaste kiss to her lips and brows before heading home to deal with whatever happened to lead Grayson to my couch. But as it turns out, he was actually worried about me, and by the time I get into bed a couple of hours later, I crash hard, sleeping right through until my alarm goes off, not even once thinking about the game.

Looks like I've found my new ritual—Lucy.

Chapter Thirty-Five

Lucy

After surprising Wes at his truck last night, I completely forgot to actually wish him luck for today. The sole reason I was there. Okay, not the sole reason, but the main one. Okay, not that either but... *ugh!*

I knew he was nervous after seeing him in the lunchroom and hated not being able to do anything about it. Not that I calmed him down when actually given the chance. But he definitely had *me* forgetting all of life's problems. When Wes takes control like that, he completely owns me, and I can't get enough. But I probably should have—

"Can I have a sleepover, Mom?" Katie asks out of the blue, cutting off my inappropriate thoughts. She's playing beside me while I finish the breakfast dishes. *And daydream, apparently.*

"Ah, sure," I say, acting very interested in the plate I'm cleaning so she can't see my blush. "Shall we invite Aunty Summer again?"

"No. I want Wes," she quickly responds, not even looking up from the figurine she's playing with. The plate I'm holding drops in the sink, and I spin around, my hands covered in bubbles. "Wes?"

"Yep." *That's it. That's all she gives me.*

"Um, well, I guess I could ask him."

"Tell him we have popcorn and if we're really good we might get chocolate milk."

I have to bite back a smile before responding. "How could he possibly say no?"

When she finally looks up at me, her face shines with a confident smile as she replies, "Exactly," before going back to her toy.

Exactly. I mean, what more could you want?

"We've got your party this coming weekend too. How about I invite him to that and then we'll see."

"Okay."

Okay. It seems so easy; why am I nervous?

"Can Greg come?"

What?! "To the sleepover?" *That's not happening.*

"No, the party."

My chest tightens, but I put on a smile when I look her way and give a noncommittal answer. "I don't know, sweetie. You can invite Wes to the party after the game today. Greg might be busy. Now you better grab your bag because Delilah will be here soon to pick you up."

"Yes!" She runs off to her room, singing as she goes. Joel and Delilah are taking her to the game today while I work. Did I use that as a distraction just now, knowing Delilah was still thirty minutes away? Yes. But I needed to change the topic away from Greg. Even though I know the guilt will hit me and I'll end up inviting him.

Why does my life have to be so complicated?

I sneak down to the perimeter of the field a couple of times during the game, but most of my day is spent in my room. It's a close one, but when the whistle blows, we get the win, and I'm both thrilled *and relieved* for Wes.

I'm finishing up with one of the players when I hear Katie in the hall.

"Hold up, Katie. Your mom's door is closed so she might have someone in there," Del says, and I can picture Katie stopping right away, something that never happens when I ask.

"She should be almost done," Wes's deep voice follows, and it takes work on my part not to react. "I'll pop in and see how they're doing. How about you show Joel and Delilah my office?"

A knock comes seconds later before the door creaks open and Wes's gorgeous face peers through. "Are you decent?" he says with his eyes closed.

Jackson's mouth forms an O and he panics.

"Stop being an ass, Wes," I call out. "Of course we're decent."

He opens his eyes and walks deeper into the room, his shoulders lifting into a shrug. "You never know who's sneaking around in this place."

Jackson relaxes and even laughs. "You're not wrong. I saw—"

Raising his hand, Wes shakes his head. "I'm going to stop you right there. It's better if I don't know."

Jackson shuts his mouth and nods, once again looking nervous until Wes's next words calm him down.

"Good game today. We'll see you fit and healthy at practice on Monday."

"Thanks, Coach," Jackson says with a smile. A smile that grows when Wes pats him on the back as he walks out.

As soon as Jackson's gone, Wes turns his attention to me, a cocky grin in place. "So I got invited to a party *and* a sleepover earlier."

I grimace and cover my face in my hands. Katie was supposed to wait for me before asking about the latter. Wes laughs at my reaction and pulls me into a hug. "I told her I'd love to come. I'll even bring my favorite stuffed animal."

Gah! My ovaries.

"Thank you. That was lovely. I'm sure you'll be very comfortable on the floor under her fort," I joke. There's no way I'm letting him stay in my house and not sleep in my bed, after Katie's asleep of course.

"The floor sounds perfect to me." He winks. "Can I help with the party at all? It's not her birthday, right?"

"Her birthday was months ago, but she wanted to wait to have it at Dylan and Summer's new house, so we're only now celebrating. And as for help, thank you, but I think we have it covered. Just show up with a smile and I'll be happy. Oh, and I'm going to have to ask you to keep it there."

"Keep what there?"

"The smile. Katie wants to invite her dad. I think I'll just tell him it starts a few hours later than it does. That way he's not there the entire time. It's too risky."

"Why? Do you think I'm going to deck him?"

"I think there will be a line for that, yes."

Wes huffs out a laugh, mumbling "It would be deserved" under his breath.

"I know, just please behave."

He smiles at that. "For you, always." Then bows with a cocky grin.

Why does that not give me confidence?

On the day of the party, Wes arrives at Dylan's place an hour before it starts in his signature jeans and black tee. I've noticed a move toward black from his previous blue wardrobe and have to wonder when that happened. Something for another time. He's carrying a box on his shoulder, making his bicep bulge from the effort, and my God, it's hot. I quickly look away so I don't get busted staring but find I'm not the only one. Delilah and Summer aren't even trying to hide their appreciation of his form.

"I've said it before and I'll say it again," Joel announces as he wraps his arms around Delilah's waist. "He's smoking hot."

Summer and I burst out laughing as Delilah nods. "He's not kidding. He said it a few times last night. I think the term 'man pretty' was thrown around."

"Credit where credit's due," Joel says with a laugh and a shrug before walking over to help Dylan set up some chairs.

"Joel's right," Summer says. "He's even more dreamy than the last time we saw him and—did he just drop the box midjourney to hug Katie? My God!"

I laugh, but that's exactly what he did. Whatever's in the box was quickly discarded to say hello to my little girl, and my heart is thumping because of it.

Wes helps Dylan, Joel, and Logan continue setting up around the yard while I busy myself inside. I'm plating up some snacks when his strong arms wrap around me from behind and he sighs.

"Please tell me we don't have to be a secret here? You didn't invite any coworkers, did you?"

He reaches for a chocolate from the bowl in front of me but I slap his hand away.

"None other than Dani, so yes, we can show a little more PDA. But not too much. We've still got Katie to consider."

"Of course." He presses a kiss to my cheek and heads back outside, stealing two chocolates as he goes.

"No PDA for you," I call out and laugh when he waves over his head, his shoulders bouncing as he undoubtedly chuckles.

The afternoon goes by quickly and painlessly as I fly around playing host. With a beer in hand, Wes spends most of his time hanging out with the guys, and they appear to be getting along well. I'd know, because my eyes have pretty much been on him or Katie all day. And since Katie's all good—currently playing tag with Liam and Addie, Cory and Nate's little one—Wes is my focus right now.

"You've found yourself a good one there, sis," Dylan says, joining me at my side.

Wrapping an arm around his waist, I couldn't stop my beaming smile, even if I tried. It's been a long time coming, but I have. I've finally got myself a keeper.

"He's alright," I say, making Dylan laugh.

"I was watching him play with Katie earlier. They definitely seem more comfortable together than she and Greg do. At least from the two times I tagged along. Maybe the last one was different."

He shrugs while I sigh. "No, you're right. Greg's trying. I have to give him that credit, but they're not really connecting. She seems to have instantly bonded with Wes, and I don't know why."

Dylan's brows furrow as we both watch Katie run toward Wes and hide behind his legs. He plays along, jokingly pointing in the opposite direction when Liam comes looking for her.

My chest fills with a lightness I don't think I've ever felt. *Can I really have a guy and Katie in my life, and make it work?*

"Could it be something to do with how *you* feel about both guys?" Dylan says, interrupting my thoughts. "Maybe Katie's picking up on your vibes." He shrugs.

Shit! My eyes shoot to his and I frown. "Oh God. What if you're right? That's not fair to Greg."

"Bullshit, the guy deserves every negative thing coming his way."

"He's Katie's father."

"He's bad news, Lucy. Always has been. And if he ever steps out of line, he'll have a lot of people to answer to. And the first person on that list is currently showing your daughter *exactly* the kind of man she should have in her life."

My gaze follows to where Dylan's pointing at Katie up on Wes's shoulders, and I swallow a lump in my throat. Let's hope Greg never does anything to warrant that, because Dylan's right... I have no doubt Wes will be the first one to throw a punch.

Despite me begging them not to, Joel and Nate set up karaoke at Katie's request. Nate and Cory sing first while Katie watches with stars in her eyes. You'd think they were famous with the way she's staring at them.

When they finish, and Joel sets up for his song, Katie comes running over, her face full of excitement.

"Can you ask Wes if he'll sing with me? Please?"

I bark out a laugh and look over my shoulder, into the house, where Wes is restocking the drinks with the ones he brought. I'd love to see that, but I can't imagine he'll say yes.

Joel groans into the mic, drawing everyone's attention, and I start to laugh until I see why he's so pissed off. Greg's walking through the gate, almost exactly on time, with flowers in hand. His eyes scan the crowd, presumably for Katie, but she hasn't noticed him yet.

"Your dad just arrived. Didn't you want to sing karaoke with him?" I ask, pointing in his direction.

The words taste like poison on my tongue, but ever since Dylan mentioned my feelings affecting Katie's, I can't stop thinking about how I can fix that.

Katie shakes her head almost violently without even looking Greg's way. "Nope, I want to ask Wes!" She stamps her foot as though I'm stopping her, when in reality that's definitely my preferred option.

"Okay, go and ask him. He's inside the house."

Katie skips away, calling his name as she does, and I want to laugh but I can't. *This is going to be a train wreck. I can already see it.* Although, if I'm lucky, maybe it will break the tension of Greg's arrival.

When I step closer to Joel, he announces he's taking five and joins me by my side as Greg walks over. "Lucy, thank you for inviting me today."

Joel's shoulder subtly bumps mine, reassuring me that he's here, giving me the strength I need to pretend everything is good. "Thank you for coming. Katie's going to be thrilled. She's inside at the moment, but should be out shortly."

Greg smiles, his eyes scanning the yard.

"There's a present table over there." I point. "If you don't want to carry the flowers around, you can put them down. I'll get a vase."

"Thank you." He nods and then walks in the direction I just pointed.

I release a sigh as soon as he's out of earshot and immediately turn to Joel. "Am I doing the right thing?"

"You're doing the best you can, Lucy. I hate this for you. But I'm here, for whatever decision you make. I'll always have your back."

"I'm just so scared. What if he tries to take her away?"

Joel notices something over my shoulder and smiles. "I'm not going to lie and say he won't try that, but along with us, you've got someone else that I'm almost certain will fight to ensure that doesn't happen."

I don't have to look to know he's talking about Wes.

"Thank you, Joel. You're right. I need to be positive."

He wraps his arm around me and pulls me into a hug before kissing the top of my head. "I know you're holding something back, Luce. And I wish I knew what it was so I could better help in this situation. But from the information I do know, all I can say is that you're doing the right thing by both him and Katie. And it doesn't hurt that you've got your guard up. Trust your instincts, and if you're ever worried, call me day or night. Call any of us. We're all here for you."

Chapter Thirty-Six

Wes

"**P**lease. Pretty please," Katie begs, her tiny hands framed under her chin like she knows it'll make her look cuter. And she's right. It does. *Dammit!* I'm not sure I can say no to her, and that's not a good way to start a relationship with her mom, because I'm totally going to take Katie's side every time they're arguing. Eh, *not my problem right now.*

"Do you have a song in mind?"

Katie's face lights up and she squeals. If that means yes, God, please don't let it be Spice Girls. *Do kids even listen to them anymore?*

Grabbing my hand, she drags me into her room for a costume before we make our way outside ten minutes later. Thankfully, the costume is just for her, but it gives nothing away about her song choice.

As we near the stage set up, Joel's finishing up a rendition of "You Can Leave Your Hat On" by Joe Cocker—which has Delilah almost in tears of laughter. *Inside joke maybe?*

Katie leads me to the booklet that lists the songs and flips through it until she gets to the page she wants. *Has she been studying this list? Of course not, she's four.*

"Is this one okay?" she asks, pointing to a star on the page. That makes much more sense. Someone helped her find it. The fact that she's asking me if it's okay has me saying yes before I've even looked at the song she's pointing to. She cheers and wraps her arms around me like I single-handedly made her day, and my chest flutters with a feeling I don't recognize, but one that's not at all unwelcome.

Joel moves our way and hands over the mic with an encouraging pat on my back. "Go be a star, Katie. Good luck, Wes."

"Ha, thanks." *I'm going to need it.*

We step up to the screen, waiting for the song to come on, and as soon as the words appear, I bite back a groan and force a chuckle.

"Shake It Off," by Taylor Swift.

I was really hoping for rock, but what was I expecting with a preschooler?

"You sing the other part and I'll do the main bit," Katie rushes out as she lifts her mic to her mouth.

Does she mean chorus? And for me to sing the verse? The music starts and I'm not at all ready. *Fuck!* What do I do again?

Words fly across the screen, and I must miss my cue because Katie tries to whisper-yell, "It's your turn," but it comes out at full volume and everyone watching laughs.

I manage to catch up and sing along—badly—until the chorus hits and Katie takes over. She's so fucking adorable my heart melts, and when I see Lucy with tears in her eyes, I decide the embarrassment in this moment is worth it. At least Carter and Gray aren't here. That's a bonus.

The next verse begins, and while I sing more confidently, I still suck. I've never really been able to hold a tune, and today's no exception.

My gaze flashes between the words on the screen and the many faces smiling up at us, trying to ignore the ones that are laughing, but I can't. Dylan seems to find it utterly hilarious, while Summer hides her smile behind her hand. I'm shaking my head with a grin, laughing at the situation I have myself in, when my eyes lock on a new arrival at the party. He's staring directly at me with a menacing gaze. His fists are clenched at his side, and all I can think is...*What the actual fuck?*

I miss my cue again, and Katie lets me know it, pulling at the hem of my tee until I snap out of it and smile at her, checking the screen and singing my part.

As soon as the song finishes and everyone surrounds Katie in congratulations, I slip away, beelining straight for Greg with my hands clenched at my sides, matching his look from earlier.

"What are you doing here?" I bark out when I reach him, not wasting any time.

"Nice to see you too, big brother. It's been a while."

"I'm not your fucking brother. Why are you here?" *Surely he's not here for me? God, did he track me down?*

Greg laughs so hard that his head flies back. "Real... step... whatever. You haven't figured it out yet, have you? I thought you were just trying to ignore the fact that you're hooking up with my ex."

"Your ex?"

"Don't play dumb. Lucy and I dated for *years*. I was supposed to marry her. Maybe I still will."

What the fuck?

"She might be fighting it right now, but she always comes back. How does it feel to know that while you were together, she was pregnant with *my* baby?"

Greg is Katie's father? Greg...

Without thinking about the consequences, I slam my fist into his jaw before grabbing his shirt and shoving him against the wall. Blood pools at the corner of his lip, but I don't care.

"You raped her," I whisper through clenched teeth, as I slam him against the brick over and over. "You fucking raped her,"

I say again, with a bite to my tone. I'm conscious of others around; otherwise I'd be screaming it in his face.

"I didn't rape her." He pushes back, trying to break free. "Who the fuck said that? We were dating. It's not rape."

"It is if she says no."

"Fuck off. She wanted it. You're just pissed off because she came back to me after being with you."

The fuck I am. And that didn't happen. Wait. He knew about me back then? My fucking stepbrother. I feel sick. I feel murderous, and I need to walk away before I do something I regret. Stepping back, I release him from my tight hold, just as he sniggers and bounces his eyebrows.

"Felt good knowing she was choosing me. That it was me inside her when she could have had you."

What is he talking about? Rage takes over me, and I growl before throwing him to the ground and slamming my fist into his face over and over. I can vaguely hear someone screaming behind me, but I don't really process it because all I see is red.

"You're delusional and a piece of fucking shit. You don't deserve to be in their lives."

"And yet, I am."

Lifting him up, I slam him back down to the ground and cringe at the sound of his head hitting the concrete. I would feel worse if the fucker wasn't smirking at me the entire time.

"Stop!" someone yells a little closer this time, but it still doesn't register that it's me they're screaming at until arms lock around me and I'm hauled into the air.

Greg laughs despite the fact that he's lying in a pool of his own blood. "You've just made things so much easier for me."

"Let me go! I'm going to kill him." I thrash about but whoever has me is stronger.

"It's not worth it, man. Leave it be," he says in my ear, and I recognize the voice as Logan's.

Dylan and Joel move into my line of vision, lifting Greg off the ground, helping him stand, both with scowls on their faces.

"You need to leave," Dylan says, pointing toward the back gate. When Greg doesn't move, the two of them escort him, ignoring him when he argues.

Logan's grip loosens slightly, and it feels like he's just about to let go when Katie's scream overshadows everything. "Let him go!"

"Katie, no," someone calls behind her but it's not Lucy. Lucy is missing in action.

I turn to see Katie running from the back door in our direction, and I feel ever worse. I just beat the shit out of her dad. *Fuck!* What the hell is wrong with me?

I chance a look at Greg and see his smirk widen before his expression morphs into one of pain.

My head falls in shame. I can't watch this. She's going to hate me. Dropping to the ground with Logan still holding my shirt, I sigh as two little hands wrap around mine and begin yanking me away from his hold. "Let. Go. Loge," she says with each pull.

Logan lets me go instantly, and Katie wraps me in a hug, comforting me as though I'm the one that's injured.

I hear Greg curse and watch out of the corner of my eye as Joel shuts him up, pushing him through the gate.

When my full attention turns back to Katie, I squeeze her tightly in my arms, whispering "I'm sorry" into her hair as my heart thrashes in my chest.

Movement catches my eye, and I look up to see Lucy standing behind her, her arms folded over her chest and a frown locked in place.

"Come on, Katie. Inside. *Now.*"

"But, Mom."

"But, nothing. Inside!"

Katie reluctantly lets go and follows Lucy toward the door as I watch them walk away. From my position on the ground, a feeling of regret takes over me as my girls move farther into the distance. *What the fuck did I do?*

Please turn around, Luce. Please turn around.

Lucy disappears out of view without so much as a backward glance, and as soon as she's gone, Logan lifts me to my feet.

"Don't worry, she'll come around. Any guy would have done the same in your position."

I stare at him blankly, confused by his meaning. "What's my position?"

"Meeting the ex face-to-face, knowing he's hurt Lucy in the past."

Okay, so he didn't hear the stepbrother part. Did anyone? And is no one knowing a good or bad thing?

Chapter Thirty-Seven

Lucy

I pace the kitchen as Delilah takes Katie into the other room to play. I don't even think Katie noticed a bloodied Greg being dragged away. At least I hope she didn't. As far as I can tell she just saw Logan holding Wes and ran.

What the fuck was he thinking? Wes, I mean. If I'd had the strength to pull him off Greg myself, I'd have done the same as Logan. But Wes... We joked about him not hitting Greg. What changed?

Wes walks in at that moment with a dejected look on his face. My heart beats faster at the sight of him, but I can't let that stop me from saying my piece.

"What the hell were you thinking?" I repeat my earlier thought.

He winces at the obvious pain in my voice and reaches out to touch me, wincing again when I move away.

"No, no. Don't touch me. Do you even realize what you've done?"

"Yes," he rasps, barely above a whisper.

He's completely breaking me, but I can't stop because I'm so freaking mad.

"He's Katie's father, Wes! Whether we like it or not. And...and...and you shouldn't have done that."

Wes's entire body sags before he runs his hands down his clenched and broken face. I'm about to say more when the sight of one hand catches my eye. *Shit!*

"Wes, you're bleeding."

He doesn't even look before shaking his head and whispering, "It's not my blood."

"Like hell it's not. Look at it."

I race over and gently secure his hand in mine. It's an absolute mess. God, if his hand looks like this, I can't even imagine Greg's face. I didn't get a good look.

"He pounded the pavement at one point when Greg dodged his strike," Dylan says, joining us inside.

"I did?" Wes looks to the ceiling, lost in thought. He's not at all himself. In fact, he looks really spaced out. What's going on in that head of his?

"You didn't feel it?"

He shakes his head. "No."

I gently run the pad of my finger over his knuckles, not even caring about the blood, and he flinches as his eyes close. It's like he's only just now realizing he's hurt.

"Come on, let me fix you up."

Leading him into the bathroom, I make him sit on the edge of the bath before I grab the first aid kit. I can feel his eyes follow me around the room as I move, and when I turn back to face him, they lock with mine, and the sadness reflected there shatters my heart. Though it shouldn't.

He reaches out for me again, but changes his mind and pulls away at the last second. "I'm sorry," he rasps, still completely out of sorts.

I go about cleaning his cut, trying to appear calm, when in reality my heart's pounding in my chest and I feel sick. I'm worried about him. And I don't mean the cut. Thankfully that doesn't look deep enough for stitches, but the internal damage he's suffering... God knows what that will take to heal.

As I apply a bandage to his hand, Wes's gaze flits between his fist and my face, silently taking everything in. When I move to clean up the sink, he clasps my wrist and stops me, locking me in place.

"Did you know?" he whispers, raw emotion and uncertainty in his eyes.

"Know what?"

"That Greg..." He clears his throat. "That he's my stepbrother? Is that why you kissed me that first day?"

What?! That can't be right.

I stare down at him, completely speechless. I have no idea how to respond to that. The shock of it is too much to process. Greg and Wes? No. I would have known. Right? *Did I even know Greg had any stepsiblings?*

"I...wha...but...I've told you about him. You never made the connection?"

"You never said his name. Not once. I would have known."

Jesus.

My chin drops to my chest and I sigh. *Stepbrothers?* I can't even fathom that. *What does it even mean?*

We're both silent and still for a moment. So quiet that I can hear Wes's short shallow breaths. He's not at all coping with everything that's happened, and I understand it must be a shock, but this seems like more than that.

Stepping between his open legs, I run my hands through his messy hair and then down to his cheeks. He closes his eyes as his head falls back, a soft exhale leaving his mouth. His chest shakes as though he's fighting back tears, and it makes my own eyes glassy.

Taking a deep breath, he opens his eyes as his huge palms wrap around my waist, and when his gaze locks on mine, I see every emotion clear as day. He's breaking. The revelation that I dated his stepbrother is killing him. *But why?*

"I'm so sorry, Lucy," he whispers in a gravelly voice. "I didn't know. We don't talk. *Ever.* I'm sorry."

He drops to his knees in front of me, hugging my legs tightly, and it breaks me more than I already was. Tears silently fall as I pull free of his grasp and join him on the floor.

"It's okay, Wes. It's okay."

I curl myself into his body and welcome the feelings I get when he wraps his arms around me, gently rocking us from side to side.

We stay like that until Wes clears his throat and moves back, shaking himself off. "We better get back out there," he rasps. "I'm sure Katie's wondering where you are."

Before letting me respond, he jumps up and pulls me to my feet, rubbing his eyes a few times. I quickly wipe away my own tears and smooth out my clothes, a little shocked at this change in pace.

"Come on," he says, with a facade now in place, before linking our fingers to lead me back into the kitchen where the group is hovering, looking a little unsure. But when my phone rings on the counter the second we enter the room, it snaps them out of their weird mood.

"Whoever it is has called a few times," Dylan says, picking up my phone. "I was going to answer it, but I wasn't sure if you'd want me to." He shows me the screen, and I see it's an unknown number.

"Thanks, I've got it."

When he hands me the phone, I answer before it cuts off. "Hello."

"Is this Lucy?" a deep voice grates from the other end of the line. He sounds as though he's in his sixties or seventies, but I don't recognize who it could be.

"It is," I confirm, unsure if I should give more.

"This is Bryan Johnson, Greg's dad."

Fuck! What the hell? My eyes shoot to Wes's as he watches me with a furrowed brow, no doubt desperate to know who's on the line.

"Hi Bryan," I say, once again keeping things short, my eyes never leaving Wes's so I can see his reaction. His eyes widen, and within seconds he's by my side, confirming that I'm talking to *his* dad too. Though the last name gave it away.

"Greg asked me to call you because he's in a pretty bad way. They've got him at San Francisco General Hospital." I gasp as he continues to talk. "I think that's what he said it's called. Anyway, he'd like you to go and visit."

"What?"

"Greg's in the hospital, love. He wouldn't tell me what happened but says you're his girlfriend so he wanted you to know."

"The fuck?" Wes yells, his booming voice making me jump. It's the first time he's said anything above a whisper since he came inside.

I take a step away, so he can no longer hear Bryan's side of the conversation and apologize.

"Sorry, Bryan. Do you have any more details? A room number or floor?"

"As far as I know he's still in the emergency room. We don't live in the same state, so it would make us feel better knowing someone who cares about him is there."

"Of course. Thank you for letting me know."

Turning around, I find several sets of eyes locked on the phone in my hand. I expect Wes to start arguing, but it's not him who speaks first.

"Tell me you're not going?" Dylan says, pushing past others to get to me. He grabs my shoulders and looks me square in the eyes. "Lucy, you can't go. You need to think this through. I'm not condoning what Wes did, but I'm also not going to say he did the wrong thing. You owe Greg nothing. *Nothing.*"

I sink down onto the stool behind me and drop my face in my hands. *What do I do?*

"Mom?"

Katie's voice draws my attention, and I look up to see her and Delilah entering the room. Delilah mouths "I'm sorry." But I could use the distraction so I wave off her apology.

"Hi sweetie. Are you okay?"

Katie nods and runs to my side, pulling me down to whisper in my ear. "Is Wes okay?"

I turn his way as his eyes open in surprise before he digs his palms into them and sighs. Once again, Katie's attempt at a whisper failed.

"He's okay, but your—"

Joel clears his throat and shakes his head, causing me to stop talking immediately. *God, what was I thinking?* I don't need to offload that much weight on a four-year-old. I need to check on Greg before I mention anything to her. Right now, she needs this party to start again so she can forget any of this happened.

"I think it's time for cake!" I cheer, surprising more than just Katie, and despite everyone's obvious concern for me, they all play their part, acting like the party never stopped. The music starts up again, and the party hats come out. And while Katie's worries are thankfully forgotten, mine have only begun.

Chapter Thirty-Eight

Lucy

The party's dying down when Thomas's face lights up my phone, right on cue.

"Katie, Thomas is calling," I yell out and watch as she drops the book she's reading with Joel and comes screaming into the kitchen where I'm waiting for her.

I lift her into my arms and connect the call with both our faces on the screen.

"Hi, Thomas. How are you?"

"Much better now I'm seeing two of my favorite girls...plus you, of course, Summer," he yells at the last second in case she's listening.

"She's not in the room," I say with a smile, one I'm sure doesn't quite meet my eyes, but he doesn't notice.

"Ha, lucky. How are you, princess?" he says, turning his attention to Katie.

"Good. I got—"

"Before you start," I interrupt, "I'm just going to talk to your uncle, Katie. Can you hold my phone?"

Katie bounces up and down in my arms, reaching for the device. "Yes, we can talk about secret stuff," she says to Thomas, trying to wink.

I put her down on the floor, and she immediately launches into conversation while I head over to Dylan. I'm midway through another lecture from him when Katie yells "finished" and drops the phone to the floor before walking away.

"Go and grab your phone," Dylan says, ending his anti-hospital visit rant. "Chances are Thomas is still there and most likely still talking. Katie's always disappearing on me halfway through a call."

I bark out a laugh before jogging into the kitchen, and sure enough, Thomas's smiling face is staring up at me from the tiles.

"Hey, down there."

"I can see up your skirt," he jokes.

"I'm wearing pants."

"And they say these new camera phones are better."

My lips pull into a smirk and I roll my eyes at his poor attempt at a joke. "Oh, Thomas. I miss you."

I know we're not technically family—we're both just in-laws to each other's siblings, but he's always treated me like we are and I love him for it.

"I miss you too, Wifey," he jokes, and I chuckle at the nickname he gave me when I first took the Kelly name. College Lucy would have been swooning over that, but now he's more like a brother. *Brother*... That word now has me cringing as an image of Wes and Greg comes to mind.

"Your dad jokes are on point, Thomas," I say, needing to get out of my head. "And you're not even a father."

"No, but I'm soon to be an uncle again."

Like the rest of my friends, Thomas treats Katie like she's his niece. However, with Summer and Dylan's son soon to be born, he'll *officially* be an uncle.

"Speaking of being an uncle," Thomas continues, "Katie sounds like she had a great day."

"She did, thank you. And thanks for the gift you sent. You didn't have to do that."

Thomas laughs. "Of course I didn't have to. I wanted to. My namesake deserves the world."

My lips pull into a grin. "That she does."

"So what's going on with you and Dylan?"

The grin drops. "What?"

"I could see the two of you in a heated conversation in the background. Katie's not the best at keeping the phone focused on her face."

Shit! "It's nothing."

"Do I have to kick my brother-in-law's ass for you?"

How I have so many amazing people in my life I will never understand.

"Nope, he's actually looking out for me, just like you are."

I quickly explain what happened at the party and that Greg wants me to visit him in the hospital. By the time I'm finished, Dylan and Joel are standing behind me asking him to back them up.

"I'm sorry, guys, but I'm going to side with Lucy on this one."

What?! My heart jolts as I look between the guys beside me and Thomas on the phone. Dylan frowns while Joel has an amused smirk on his face.

"I know he's treated you like shit, Lucy, but from what you've told me, he's trying with Katie. Everyone deserves a second chance. Take it from someone who's lucky he got one with Summer."

Summer yells out, "Love you, Bro," as she walks into the room, eliciting a warm smile from Thomas. He's right. He and Summer went through hell together and she forgave him. While I may never forgive Greg, I need to give him a fighting chance with Katie and actually show her that I'm trying.

I don't love that he told his dad...stepdad, I was his girlfriend, but it may have something to do with giving me access to his room. I can't jump to conclusions before I see him.

"Thank you, Thomas. I'm going to go."

"Good. But Lucy, if he does anything else to hurt you, I'll be joining the guys in their quest to fuck him up."

"I know."

Katie crosses her arms over her chest as I try to leave. "I thought Wes and I were having a sleepover?" she announces, and the room falls quiet. *Ah shit.*

With all eyes on me, I want to hide away. *Thanks, Katie.* Joel and Logan both bite back smiles, while the girls are all heart eyes and swooning. *Yes, yes, he's amazing with Katie but he just beat the shit out of her dad.*

"Wes can't make it anymore," I lie. I've yet to tell him the sleepover is canceled but I'm going to assume that he knows. "And Summer practically begged me to let you stay here instead." Another lie.

"She's right, I did." Summer backs me up even though *I* begged *her.* By saying yes she has to deal with Dylan's wrath. Because if she'd said no, then maybe I wouldn't be going to the hospital. I'd hate to be her right now, but I love her for it.

When I make eye contact with Dylan, he's standing stiff as a post glaring my way, proving my theory. He's not happy. Katie, on the other hand, is fine.

It doesn't take much to sway her in Summer's direction, and before long I'm grabbing my keys to leave.

"This isn't a good idea," Dylan says again, like a broken record.

"God, you are making this so much bigger than it needs to be. He's not going to do *anything* to me while he's in the hospital. I'll be fine. Just focus on your night with Katie and leave me be."

I take a step toward Wes, ready to say goodbye when Dylan gets one last verbal jab in.

"This is bullshit. You need to stop her, Wes. Tell her she can't go."

My jaw falls open as someone or maybe multiple someones gasp.

"What—"

"Are you kidding me with that, Dylan?" Wes booms, moving to my side like we're a united front. "You want me to tell her she can't go?" he repeats, not even bothering to mask his shock. "I may not like what she's doing, but it's not my decision to make, and I certainly can't force her to do anything. Nor would I want to. Isn't that what you hated about Greg in the first place? The way he manipulated her? Or did none of you see that?" Dylan stiffens and I can tell he's about to argue back when Wes continues.

"Lucy wants to do this. It's *her* choice. And frankly, after my fuckup today, it's probably necessary. I'm with you, man. I don't like this at all, but Lucy's right...he's not going to hurt her. And if he did—"

"We know what you'll do," Logan interrupts with his hand on Wes's shoulder. "You ready to go?" he asks me.

My brows furrow as I give him a questioning look.

"You're not going alone, and I'm the one less likely to attack without cause," he says with a slight lift to his shoulder.

I huff out a laugh because he's probably right. Most of the others would—

"Hey! I take offense to that," Joel cries out, biting back a smile. "I'm not about to bust up my hand unless it's necessary."

"Yes, but you'd probably verbally attack him," Delilah adds from beside him, her lips pulled into a smirk.

Joel looks to the ceiling in thought before he nods. "She's got a point. As you were, Logan."

A small laugh comes from beside me, and I have to hold myself back from giving Joel a hug. He broke the tension, and he absolutely knew what he was doing.

"Okay, let's go." I grab Logan's hand before anyone else tries to argue and pull him toward my car.

"Lucy, wait," Wes calls as he jogs down the steps behind us.

Logan stops when I do, but I wave him off. "I'll meet you at the car."

When Wes reaches me, he stands a few feet away, giving me space. "I just wanted to apologize again."

"It's done. It's okay." I shrug, but it's not a lie.

"It's not okay, Luce. I fucked up and I'm sorry. I hate watching you leave to be with him, but I understand why you have to do it, and I know it's my fault."

"It's no—"

"It is. Just accept my damn apology and tell me we're going to be okay."

I recoil slightly until I see the suppressed smile on his face. "Yeah, we're okay," I say reluctantly, trying not to smile myself. "I'll call you when I'm done. And this time, I'll remember."

Wes leans forward and presses a chaste kiss to my brow before walking back inside, taking a piece of me with him. While I wish he hadn't *fucked up* as he put it, a little part of me loves his fierce protectiveness. And while I like to think that these days I can take care of myself, there's something about a man willing to risk it all to defend you. Because make no mistake, Wes was risking a lot with what he did.

"Am I doing the right thing?" I ask Logan when I'm settled in the car beside him. It's a question I keep asking because I'm still not sure of the answer.

"I think so." Logan nods, his eyes on everyone watching us from the porch. "Trust me, you don't want this to end in a custody battle. They hurt everyone involved, especially the kids." Finally turning my way, he cups my shoulder and smiles. "You're making the right decision *for Katie*," he says, almost repeating Joel's words. "So how could that ever be wrong?"

After putting the car in reverse, he backs us out of the driveway and smiles with his eyes on the road. "You've always been a badass in my mind, Luce. You can do this."

Greg's eyes light up when I pull back the curtains to enter his room. "You came," he says with a beaming smile, and I feel sick. His face is swollen and bruised, he can barely open one eye, and there's a bandage around his head. *God, Wes, what did you do?*

"I'm here. And you look like shit," I say honestly but cringe when the words leave my mouth.

Thankfully, Greg laughs. "Thanks. You always knew how to make me feel loved."

As hard as I try to stop it, my lips pull into a small smile and I shake my head. "I was too good to you."

"Yeah, you were." He sighs. "And I realize that now. Hopefully not too late."

337

So late, the ship has well and truly sailed.

"Why am I here, Greg?" I say, moving on.

"Because your boyfriend attacked me."

I cringe again, but he's right, only that wasn't my question.

"Why am I here?"

"Because your boyfriend attacked me," he repeats, "*and* I wanted you to see what kind of man he is."

My eyes narrow. While I'd love to believe that's his only motivation for asking me here, I'm skeptical.

"He is your boyfriend, right?"

Is he?

"Not sure yet, but I'm more interested in what he is to *you*."

"I barely know him."

I scoff. "But you knew he was your stepbrother? That wasn't something Wes sprang on you today, was it?"

Greg rolls his eyes. "Of course I knew."

"Wait... You knew when you sent me that article, didn't you? You must have." Holy shit, he's known the entire time.

"I found out you were dating him when I first read it."

My insides squirm and I grimace. *Why the hell wouldn't he have told me?*

Crossing my arms over my chest, I stare him down, trying hard to figure him out. "Did you provoke him?"

"Why the fuck would I provoke him? I'm trying to get onto your good side." With his eyes wide with shock, I almost want to believe him.

"Why?"

He drops his head back to the pillow and groans. "So I can spend time with Katie. So we can work things out between us."

I sigh, much louder than I mean to, shaking my head. "There is *no* us, Greg."

"Not right now there isn't."

I have to bite my tongue so I don't speak. Greg's in the hospital because my *boyfriend*, as he put it, beat him up. Pissing him off isn't a smart move.

"Plus, I could easily report Wes for assault. If I wanted to. But I won't."

And he just proved my thoughts. *Is that a threat?* God, I wish I knew, but I can't tell. His face gives nothing away. Possibly because it's so messed up. By Wes.

"Let's just focus on you getting out of here and getting to know Katie. She's a wonderful little girl, and I know she'd love to spend more time with you."

I swallow a lump in my throat. Having to say all of that wasn't easy.

Greg smiles knowingly, but I'm not sure what he thinks he knows.

"That sounds like a great plan, Luce."

I'm about to make an excuse to leave when a nurse comes around signaling the end of visiting hours, and I almost sigh in relief, I'm so happy to see her. Coming here wasn't a mistake, but I definitely don't need to stay any longer than necessary.

I depart with the promise to increase his visits with Katie, and almost fall apart when I meet Logan out in the hall. Having Wes and Greg in my life is going to be a challenge. *God, I hope it's worth it.*

Chapter Thirty-Nine
Wes

G reg only spent one night in the hospital before being released, but he milked it for all it's worth. I do feel bad that I pummeled him, but the fucker absolutely deserved it. *My fucking stepbrother.* I knew he was a piece of shit, but I never thought he was capable of rape. *Fuck*, it kills me to even think of that word. Not to mention the emotional abuse he's subjected Lucy to.

Seeing him at Katie's party and discovering their connection ignited a rage inside me that I never thought was possible. In that moment I could have killed him if Logan hadn't stopped me. Hell, I wanted to. I've never felt that out of control in my life. To think of what he did to Lucy, and that he's trying to be part of her and Katie's life *sickens* me. And to know I can't do anything to stop it makes it so much worse.

My only relief comes from knowing he's a deadbeat so doesn't have the means to fight Lucy in court—*oh fuck!*

I'm calling my father before the thought has fully formed in my mind. Please for the love of God let me be wrong. That it was actually his sister, Bridget, that needed the cash.

Dad answers the phone and I bark out my question before he's even said hello. "Who needed my money, *Dad*?"

"Hello, son."

"*Who*. Was. It?"

Dad sighs, and I hear the telltale sign of a beer can being opened, a sound I have memorized from before he left Mom and me.

"Greg told me everything. Well, at first he said Lucy was his girlfriend, but he's since cleared that up."

Fuck! Standing up, I pace my living room, running a hand through my already mussed hair. "Okay, then what's the money for?" I don't care what he has or hasn't told my father. I just need him to answer *one* question.

Dad's voice rises. "So he can provide for his child! What do you think it's for?"

"So he's not going to file for custody?"

"What?" Dad huffs out a laugh and takes a sip. "You really think so low of him, don't you. He's trying to do the right thing for a child he had no clue about, and co-parent with a woman who's dating his brother." *He's not my brother.* "It's not easy, but he's trying."

My entire body deflates. *God, I hope he's right.*

"Sorry. They just both mean so much to me."

He lets out a long sigh, and when he speaks, I can hear the smile coming through in his voice. "I can't wait to meet her. I'm a grandfather, Wes."

"You're going to love her. I just wish it was *me* that was introducing you."

The thought that it's not breaks my heart and my world stops. I wish Katie was *mine*. Actually, no. I don't wish that at all. Deep down, it already feels like she is. My mind whirs as I think about Katie and the need to protect her.

"It's a complicated situation, that's for sure," my father says, interrupting my thoughts. "But I promise, he wants to do right by both of them. Right now, he's taking Katie to the beach."

What? The hairs on the back of my neck spike as my body covers in goose bumps.

"She said she's not doing swimming lessons anymore, so Greg's going to start teaching her."

What?!

"Where are they?"

"Huh?"

"Where. Are. They?"

Dad huffs. "Fuck, I don't know. The beach near his house?"

"Send me his address and phone number. Now, Dad. I need to go."

"Ah Wes—"

"*Please*, Dad," I beg, my heart racing as I wait for him to answer.

"Okay." *Thank God.*

I don't know why I'm so worried, but the tightness in my chest tells me I need to run, because if something happens and I didn't go, I'll never forgive myself.

Greg's phone goes to voicemail with every attempt I make, and Lucy's phone does the same, though as I dial hers, I'm not sure what to say.

It's been a week since the party at Dylan's, and she's already letting Katie and Greg have time alone. I guarantee she's trying to make up for what I did, and it sickens me to think this is all my fault.

I drive through the streets in a panic, but thankfully there's only one small stretch of beach close to Greg's house, and it's fairly easy to find.

Parking my truck diagonally across two spots, I leap from the open door and take off in a run toward the water, my heart thundering in my chest. I hope I'm wrong. That this physical reaction I'm having is *wrong*, but I can't shake the feeling that something is going to happen.

When I get to the shoreline and scan the water, there's no sign of Katie or Greg. Running a hand down my face, I blow out a deep breath before dropping to the ground with the weight of the tension I'm holding becoming too much.

I've barely had a chance to pull my hands from my face when Greg's raised voice carries with the wind.

"Katie, stop! You're being ridiculous."

Jesus, fuck.

Pushing off the sand, I take off in the direction of his voice and see Greg trying to grab Katie's arm as she runs away from him.

I don't think or process what's happening before I yell, "Leave her alone," and pump my legs harder to get to her.

They both freeze at my voice, until Katie takes off running again, but this time it's in the opposite direction, straight into my open arms.

She crashes into me at full speed, almost bouncing back as though she's hit a brick wall. It would be comical if my heart wasn't lodged in my throat and I wasn't worried to the point of feeling nauseous.

My arms wrap around her on instinct as I press my cheek to her head. "I'm here, Katie. It's okay."

What the fuck happened?

Katie stays curled into my chest until Greg approaches, huffing and cursing under his breath.

"I don't want to. Don't make me," Katie rushes out, gripping my tee in her tiny hands.

My gaze flashes to Greg's before moving to Katie. It doesn't take much to guess what she's referring to, but why would he try to force her?

"You don't have to do anything, Katie. I'm sure Greg didn't know about your lesson."

"She said she's scared. All the more reason to get in."

Is he for real?

"She's *four.*"

"She needs to learn."

"That's fair, but is the ocean really the best place to do that?"

Greg grips the back of his head and scowls. "Come on, Katie, let's forget about swimming and get something to eat."

Katie shakes her head, gripping me tighter.

"How about I just take her home to Lucy?" I offer, thinking only of the scared little girl in my arms.

Greg's hands move to his sides and he stands tall. "She's *my* daughter."

I stiffen, but remain calm. "No one's disputing that. How about we ask Katie? Katie—"

"You, Wes," Katie blurts out, almost crawling into my lap to get closer. I'll repeat my earlier question... *What the fuck happened?*

Greg's body sags, and he nods until a cocky smile comes to his face. "You know you need a car seat, right?" *Dickhead.*

"Yup, I'm covered. Can you grab me Katie's things so we can head off?"

He reluctantly moves to collect her bag as I lift her into my arms and walk back toward my truck. Thank fuck I had a car seat installed last week. I'd hoped but didn't expect to need it this quickly.

Katie's silent for most of the trip, but when we're almost home, she finally opens up. "I didn't want to go in but he said I have to. Do I have to?"

Fuck!

I meet her eyes in the rearview mirror and smile. "I think it's a good idea for you to get back into the pool, but we can work up to it. Maybe we can play in a kiddie pool next weekend. You don't even have to put your head under." *Baby steps.* I hope I'm saying the right thing. *God, this parenting shit is hard.*

Katie's eyes light up and she nods before turning to look out the window for the remainder of the trip, singing the chorus to our duet over and over until we get home.

As suspected, Lucy is livid when I explain to her what happened, and while she mumbles to herself that it's her fault, I know a part of her still blames me. She probably wouldn't have given him alone time so soon if I hadn't messed up. But it's done now. We just have to figure out how to move forward.

Despite Katie wanting me to stay, after only a few minutes, I make an excuse and head home. Lucy may say we're fine, but it's not hard to miss the change in our relationship, so I want to give her time to forgive me.

A little time anyway. She can have another week. I don't think I'll last much longer than that.

I've barely been home for five minutes when there's a knock at the door. My pulse spikes as my first thought is Lucy, but I know that's unlikely. And when I open the door, my guest is the last person I want to see.

"How did you get my address?" I say with my arms folded across my chest, standing at my full height. I know I can be intimidating, and I usually hate it, but right now, that's the look I'm going for.

Greg rolls his eyes, seemingly unaffected. "Your dad was more than willing to hand it over when I told him I wanted to sort things out with my darling brother."

I roll my eyes in return, as I call bullshit. "Dad doesn't have my address."

"Okay, so I followed you one night; sue me." He shrugs.

What the fuck?

Up until now, I'd never thought of Greg as a threat, except for his ability to take Katie from Lucy. But in this moment, my spine's tingling and I'm a little on edge. *Has he been stalking me?*

"Why are you here, Greg?" I say without changing my stance, trying to appear unaffected.

A hint of a smirk lights up the asshole's face as he looks me square in the eye. "I thought it was time we had a little chat."

Fuck!

Chapter Forty

Wes

G reg's arms cross as he tries to mirror my stance, his eyebrow's raising as he waits for me to respond.

"Okay, I'll bite. Say what you've got to say. And fast. I'm kind of busy."

"With what?" He laughs. "Lucy doesn't want to see you and there's no football today. What else could you have going on?"

He's right, but I don't need to tell him that. Instead, I stare at him with a blank expression. "Just talk."

A hint of nerves flits across his face before he recovers. "I need more money and you're going to give it to me."

I roll my eyes and move to slam the door in his face. *What a joke.* Greg runs forward, stopping the door with his foot, seconds before it closes, ripping it open again. "You're going to want to hear me out."

"Five minutes," I grunt in frustration.

After taking a deep breath, he leans against the doorframe and speaks. "I need money so that I can give Katie the life that she deserves. You know I've got nothing. I want to make sure I've got a decent place to live, nice things for Katie—when she comes around—and enough left over so that I don't have to live paycheck to paycheck."

My jaw drops. He's delusional if he thinks Katie will be spending *any* time at his house after the shit he just pulled.

"Get a better job. Work for it. I've given you enough payouts."

Greg's features morph into something almost sadistic, and his eyes narrow. "No, I don't think you understand. This isn't a question. If you don't give me the money, I'll press charges against you. Maybe even get a restraining order. Anything I can do to make it impossible for you to see Lucy and Katie."

Fucker. I should have known this would happen. "How much do you want?" If it's another ten grand, I'll do it to shut him up. He can't do much damage with that.

"Five hundred."

What? "Fuck off." I try to slam the door again but he pushes through.

"I'm serious. I've done the math, and I need five hundred grand."

He's kidding himself if he thinks I believe for a second that he needs that money for Katie. He's been asking for payouts his whole life, and I'm the idiot that started giving them to him.

"And if I don't do this—"

"Katie suffers."

He's bullshitting. She's going to suffer either way. He won't spend a cent on her. *I'm calling his bluff.*

Shaking my head, I get in his face and sneer. "I'm not doing shit for you. You need to realize how amazing that little girl is, *before* it's too late. She deserves a father that understands money *can't buy happiness.* She just wants your love."

"Says the guy with millions of dollars. I'm just asking for enough to give her the life she wants."

"You don't even know her. How could you possibly know what she wants?"

Greg's lips pull into a smile and he huffs out a laugh. "Lucy's with you, so she's obviously attracted to money. It's not hard to think Katie would be too."

"You really have no clue."

"It doesn't matter anyway. Pay the money or lose them both." He shrugs like he's going to win either way, but his voice wavers. He's nervous. He's not going to report me. He's too gutless. Plus it will piss Lucy off and he doesn't want that.

"I'll take my chances, asshole. Now get off my property."

I step back again and slam the door in his face with more force than my previous attempts, watching as he moves out of the way just in time. Five hundred grand? The nerve of him. Money may mean so little to me, but I'm not about to hand it over to a piece of shit like Greg.

What a fucking day. After tossing and turning for an hour with no sign of sleep, I get up and start pacing the room.

I feel sick about Katie. What if I hadn't been there for her? What would Greg have done? I thought I was clueless when it came to kids, but Greg... I have no words. And then to ask for money? He's insane. He must be. And he's going to be in Lucy's life forever. *Fuck!*

Pulling out my phone, I text Lucy to check in. Katie would be well and truly asleep by now, and I have a feeling Lucy would have fallen apart the second she was down.

Wes: I'm so fucking sorry. I know I messed up, but you and Katie are my number one priority. I'm here for you if you ever need me. Any time. For any reason

It's going on eleven p.m. when I click send, so I don't expect a reply. However, thirty minutes later, I get one.

Lucy: Thank you for being there for Katie today. It means a lot to me. More than you'll ever know

It's not hard to read between the lines of that message, so I call her before she has a chance to leave her phone. When she doesn't answer on the first try, I call straight back, desperate to talk to her. On my third try she answers.

"Hello."

"Answering on the third call? Taking a page out of my book?" I joke, hoping to lighten the mood right off the bat.

"Huh? You do that?" Lucy asks, her tone flatter than usual.

I huff out a laugh anyway. "Only every time someone calls."

"You've never done it to me." *What?*

"Really?"

"Yes, really." She softly giggles and the sound brings me so much joy.

"Well, there you go. Sorry to call when we were texting, but I wanted to make sure you were okay."

Lucy sighs, but it's so quiet I wouldn't have noticed it if I wasn't looking for signs of her feelings.

"I'm okay. Just tired," she lies.

"Lucy..."

"What do you want me to say, Wes?"

She's trying hard to come across strong and unaffected, but the quiver in her voice gives her away.

"I want you to tell me the truth."

Her breath hitches and then she huffs. "What truth? That I messed up. That I made a stupid mistake that could have hurt Katie. Or worse?"

"It's not your fault. I—"

"I know it's not all mine, but I'm still partly to blame." *Ouch!*

My chest tightens thinking about my part in all this. She wouldn't have granted Greg any unsupervised access if I hadn't fucked up. And I hate that I'm the cause of her hurt.

"Can I come over? I need to see you. I hate this distance between us."

"I'm—"

"I get it, Lucy. I do. And I've been giving you space. But fuck, I miss you and I really want to hold you right now."

Lucy sniffs, providing me with even more proof that she's not okay. "I miss you too, and I do want to see you, but this week's pretty crazy. The weekend?"

I hold back a sigh; it's better than nothing. "The weekend sounds great. In the meantime, I'm here if you need me."

"Thanks, Wes."

"Bye, Lucy."

I only see Lucy once over the next couple of days and it kills me. Work goes by slowly, even though the season's started. And I just feel like shit in general.

I'm ready for a night on the couch when there's a knock on my door. *Too many people know where I live these days.*

"Hey! We were in the neighborhood, and my buddy here is a huge fan of yours," Greg blurts out as soon as I've opened up. "I had to show off my big bro..."

He keeps talking, but I only take in half of what he says because no matter what the rest was, I know the neighborhood part is a lie.

I try to hide my suspicious thoughts, but my brows furrow without permission. "Okay. Sure. Hi."

"I'm Tye."

"Hi Tye, it's always a pleasure to meet a fan. Are you excited for the coming season?"

"Absolutely! I think we've got a good shot this year."

"I agree."

"Especially since we secured Mathers. I can't believe *you're* Greg's brother," he says to me before turning to Greg. "And that *your* future brother-in-law is Mathers."

Huh? Fucker! He's lying again. I take a deep breath and smile, hoping it doesn't come across as fake as it is. After that comment, I'm done.

"I'm really sorry to cut this short, but I was actually just heading out," I say, quickly changing my couch plans to include leaving the house. I know Greg's got a reason for being here. I'm just not sure what it is.

"Sorry, yeah man. We won't keep you," Tye rushes out with a frown and moves to walk away.

Greg nods but doesn't move. "Of course. It was good seeing you, brother. Oh Tye, I was almost certain you'd ask him to help convince me to press charges." Greg laughs. "But too late now."

My chest tightens. *What?*

"I should have." He chuckles. "I've been trying to convince Greg to destroy the asshole that beat him up. I'm fully prepared to bury him, but Greg's not talking."

"How would you bury him?" I ask curiously.

"I'm a cop at San Francisco PD."

I internally cringe. "Right. That makes sense."

Fuck! Greg is not at all the spineless asshole I thought he was. Lucy said he manipulated her without her knowing it, and that's exactly what he's doing to Tye. I should have been more focused on what Lucy said about her ex, especially now I know it's Greg. But when I found out she was referring to my stepbrother, I spiraled and never really reconciled the two people as being one and the same.

"Whoever did it deserves everything coming to him," Tye continues, as I try not to appear unnerved. "So if you could help me convince Greg, that'd be great." He smiles like he's proud while I hold back vomit.

"I'll try my best," I say with another fake grin. *Motherfucker.*

"Okay, big bro, we'll leave you be. Have a good evening. I'll be seeing you." He smirks at me before walking away, and my insides squirm. *What the fuck was that?* Actually, I know the answer. That was my warning. Give Greg the money, or Tye gets what he so desperately wants. *I'm screwed.*

It's almost ten p.m. when I hear the knock I've been expecting since Greg and Tye drove away.

"Change your mind, big bro?" Greg asks when I answer the door.

"Nope. Your threats mean nothing to me."

"Okay, that's fair. But does this?"

He hands me a piece of paper, which on inspection is an official statement outlining what happened when I *allegedly* attacked him *unprovoked* and a request for a restraining order. All that's missing is the name of the accused...me. And a signature. *Jesus, this guy doesn't mess around.*

"Won't take much for me to file that. It's all ready to go. Tye helped me with the wording. Says he knows what to say to ensure it's taken more seriously."

My body stiffens and I close my eyes, trying to block out the need I have to kick his ass. When I open them again, Greg's glaring at me. Waiting for a response.

"The money's all for Katie?" I ask, calmer than I feel.

"Yep, all of it. Well, as I mentioned, a lot will go to a better house, but that's for her in the long run."

I sigh in resignation. I can't get him out of her life, but I can make sure he's got the means to make it better. "It'll be in your account by morning."

Greg shakes his head before pointing to my pocket. "Get out your phone. Transfer it now."

What? "Come on. I can't transfer that kind of money on an app."

"I'll come with you to the bank. I trust you about as far as I can throw you, and I'd be lucky to lift you up."

I roll my eyes. "It's ten fucking p.m., Greg. Banks aren't open. You'll get your money."

He stares at me for a moment—looking for some kind of answers—then nods. "I'll be back if I don't. You've got a lot riding on this. An arrest won't look good for your rep."

"I don't give a fuck about that. I'm doing this for Lucy and Katie."

"Keep telling yourself that." He smirks.

Ignoring him, I turn to close the door, moving quickly so I don't punch him again. "Goodbye, *brother.*"

"Pleasure doing business with you," he rushes out as the door shuts in his face.

Fuck you.

As promised, I call my bank the next morning to arrange the money transfer, and hate myself the entire time. In all of twenty minutes, I signed over more money than Greg's had in his lifetime, and I'm almost certain he's going to fuck up.

You wouldn't think it was that easy to hand over five hundred grand to someone else, but since I've made a transfer to him once before, it's a painless process. If you don't count the pain in my chest.

I expect that to be the end of the conversation. That when the money shows up in his account, we'll be done with it. But I'm wrong, and fuck I wish I wasn't.

Chapter Forty-One
Lucy

I t's almost a week after the fact, and I still feel sick over what happened with Greg and Katie. She hasn't mentioned it much since Monday, so I'm hopeful that means she's okay, and not that she's too traumatized to talk. I don't even really know what happened. I have both of their stories, but God only knows if Greg is being honest. All I have to go by is how angry Wes was when he dropped Katie home, and the way she clung to him like a lifeline.

If he hadn't been there...*no, I can't think that.*

I've got to bring myself out of this fog I'm in.

After Katie had fallen asleep that night, I slid down the wall opposite her room, dropped my head in my hands, and cried. Tears fell until I reached the point of hyperventilating, struggling to take in air as the severity of my mistake consumed me.

I can't continue to live like that, but it's not going away. I knew I was doing the wrong thing. I'd been on edge from the moment Katie left in Greg's car, but when she got home, with Wes, it took all of my strength to hold myself together until I was alone. *Why would I allow that? Why didn't I go with them?* Everything I've done, all my life, has been for Katie, and then I make that colossal mistake. I'll never forgive myself for it. I shouldn't have trusted in that message he sent. The one that convinced me to say yes. It was absolutely bullshit because he didn't protect her at all.

Greg: Thank you, Lucy. I promise I'll take care of her with my life. She means the world to me. I'm so grateful to you for letting me get to know her better

While the tears may have slowed down, they still come, every night, as soon as Katie's asleep, and maybe I deserve that. To forever feel like I failed my daughter. Like I failed as a mother. Because make no mistake. I absolutely did.

Even now while I'm in the ring, attempting to throw a few punches at my sparring partner, I can't get my mind to stop. I try to remain focused on my movement, my technique...hell, even my instructor...but nothing seems to be working and I'm off my game, which has never happened to me before. This is usually my outlet. The way I rid myself of negativity. But right now my practice partner, Gina, is totally kicking my ass.

How could I be so stupid? I'm supposed to be stronger. Katie is the most important person in my life, and I fucked up. Greg shouldn't have had alone time with her. I knew in my gut it was the wrong decision but as with the past, he managed to get his way, and this time it could have been fatal.

A fist connects with my shoulder, and I flinch with the pain. *Jesus.* I need to concentrate. Standing tall, I bounce on my toes a few times and assess my position before attempting a jab. I barely clip Gina's arm as she moves away, and I curse under my breath.

Dammit!

But how could Wes put me in such a difficult situation? While Greg didn't exactly threaten to press charges against him, he mentioned the fact that he *hadn't* enough to reiterate that he could. And if Greg presses charges against Wes, the media would be all over it. They'd drag Katie into it, and Dylan. None of it would bode well if there was ever a custody battle. I just—

Oof, fuck! Gina gut punches me, literally, and it's exactly what I deserve. In fact, I deserve a lot more than that. I'm not perfect, but I should have followed my instincts and kept Katie home, something I'll always regret.

God, get out of your head, Lucy.

Gina hits me three more times before the trainer calls time on our session. She packs a mean punch, and it's obvious I'm not coping. I'm surprised it lasted as long as it did.

After apologizing profusely for lack of competition, I head off for a cooldown on the treadmill, still needing to do something to release this tension. I'm covered in sweat and feeling a little achy—okay, a lot achy—when Joel walks in.

"What are you doing here?" I puff out, wiping the water from my brow.

"Been coming every day since our session a while back."

At that I smile. "Bullshit."

"Okay, you got me; the trainers are hot." He bounces his eyebrows and looks behind me. Since I know my trainer, Anika, just left, I burst out laughing before looking at the guys he's referring to. I mean...

"Tell me I'm wrong?"

"I can't. You're not wrong. But *why are you here*?"

Joel sighs. "I wanted to talk about Greg. I'm here for a workout too. It's just, whenever I come to your house, Katie's there...obviously. So we can never really discuss him."

I take a deep breath and stop my machine.

"Go ahead. What do you have to say on my least favorite topic?"

Joel drops down on a bench against the wall and pats the seat beside him, crinkling his nose when I sit.

"Shut up, you accosted me in a gym. I'm allowed to smell."

He nods with a crooked smile. "Fair call. Anyway, after Wes, umm…gave Greg a touch-up, we got to talking. Wes and I. He's under the impression that his brother is a low-life, brainless, piece of shit. They may have even been his exact words."

"Okay." *I'm not going to argue.*

"He's not brainless, Lucy. Not even a little." I suck in a breath as my eyes flash to his. "He kept you coming back *for years.* He knew exactly what he was doing to get his own way, while still keeping you in his life. You never even questioned him. I don't believe for a second that he didn't know about you and Wes. After all, he sent you that article with the photos of you two. He's calculated and manipulative and I'm worried about you."

"I…I…I don't know what to do, Joel. I can't cut him from our lives. I tried that. It didn't work."

"Just be careful, Luce. Question *everything.* I don't know his angle, but I don't like it, whatever it is."

I sag into the seat with a sigh. "Where were you *before* I gave him unsupervised time with Katie?"

"What the fuck?" Joel's eyes widen in disbelief. "That just proves my point. Calculating and manipulative."

Running my hands down my face, I shake my head as my heart aches.

"I know that's hard to hear, but remember you're not alone in this. You have a lot of people on your side."

"I know. But unfortunately, that may not help me."

Joel walks me to my car after we've finished talking, making me smile when he heads straight to his motorcycle instead of back inside. *Workout, huh?* Leave it to him to always know the right things to say and do in every situation.

When I'm settled behind the wheel, I check my phone before I start driving. Like I always do, just to make sure Katie's okay. This time I wish that I hadn't.

Greg: Can you meet me at Bailey's diner? We need to talk

That's the last thing I want to do, but there's nothing stopping him from turning up at my work or the house, so if he has something to say, it's probably best to be out in public.

After letting Summer and Dylan know I'm running late to pick up Katie, I shoot Greg a text before showering and heading straight there.

Since I left the stadium as soon as the game ended today, it's still early evening, so the diner's busy when I arrive.

I spot Greg in a corner booth with a stack of paper in front of him, and bile immediately rises in my throat. This is it. He's going to do it. He's going to file for custody.

I walk slowly toward the table, as though I'm walking to my death because it sure feels that way. I shouldn't be so worried about this but I am. Greg mentioned he has money, so he could probably hire good lawyers. And there's the fact that I kept Katie from him for years. That's not going to help in my favor. *How did I not see this coming?*

I'm silent as I sit down. I hate that he holds all the cards right now, and he's getting his way, just like Joel said he does. I could have refused to meet him here and changed the location, but this isn't a power play; this is about my daughter. I just want whatever this is over with.

Greg smiles, and it's somewhat genuine. *Fuck!* He's trying to do it again. To pull me back in.

"I'm going to get straight to the point," he says immediately and I almost thank him for it. "This is a contract giving me joint custody of Katie, split fifty/fifty."

I scoff and lean back in my chair, acting calm, while inside I feel like I'm being suffocated and unable to take in air. "Why would I *ever* sign that?"

"Because it's either this contract *or* I file a police report against Wes."

I laugh but it's a little mechanical. "So you're threatening me with reporting Wes?"

"Not exactly. Here's the deal. Wes promised me a large sum of money if I promised to look after Katie and destroy the police report. I don't trust him. So I had an idea...do *you* trust him? I need reassurance. A reason for Wes to hold up his end of the deal. Sign the contract, and I'll rip up the police report, and even sign this agreement"—he waves a second piece of paper in my face—"stating there will be no charges filed in relation to this assault, now or in the future. You'll have your own reassurance. Wes will be safe." He pauses as if he's letting that all sink in, so I nod. "*Don't* sign it and we have bigger issues than your lack of trust in someone you seem to care so much about."

I swallow a lump in my throat. This isn't just a question of trusting Wes. This is about what I want for my daughter, and while I love Wes—shit, I fucking love him—it's not enough.

I trust Wes, I do, but I don't trust Greg. Wes never once mentioned giving Greg money, and he hates lying, even by omission. If he was going to hand anything over, he would have told me. *Wouldn't he?*

This can't be real. None of this is real. "What kind of person plays with people's lives like this? You're discussing the future of a four-year-old like she's a possession. Isn't it enough that

I'm trying here? We've been working together to build a relationship between the two of you. This isn't how you want to start your life with her. And you told me you've got money? Why do you need more?"

"That's my business."

No, I can't do this. Joel's right. He's smart, but I'm smarter.

"I can't sign it," I whisper defiantly. "I won't."

I expect Greg to be pissed but he just shrugs.

"Are you sure about that?"

I stare between him and the paper he's holding, then nod. His confident demeanor never wavers as he places the first document in front of me.

"Not even after seeing this?"

Chapter Forty-Two

Wes

W hen I pull up in my driveway after the game late Saturday night, Greg's waiting for me on my porch steps. I
should have been home hours ago, so the thought that he could
have been waiting a while gives me a little pleasure.

He stands as I approach, making himself taller than I am on
the landing above me. Nodding in acknowledgment, I make a
mental note to call my realtor tomorrow. *Fuck, I need to move.*

"I got the money," he says, as though that's information I don't
have.

"I said I'd send it. What more do you want?" I raise an eyebrow. "I'm going to need you to sign something to say you won't
be asking for more. Continuously showing up here is not on."

Greg laughs. "That's not why I'm here."

"Then why the fuck are you back?" I say, raising my hands in
the air, my patience nonexistent.

The fucker gives me another one of his sadistic smiles, and I
know I'm in for a world of pain. "It's simple...I want you gone."

My eyes flash to Greg's, hoping to find even the smallest hint
of amusement. But there's nothing. It's not a joke. "*I want you
gone.*" What the actual fuck?

"I want you out of Lucy and Katie's life," he adds, as though I
didn't understand him the first time. *Heard you loud and clear.*

"Okay, why would I do that?" *He's definitely insane.*

"Because if you don't, I'll be using that money you gave me to file for full custody." *Motherfucker.*

"You actually gave me the idea. Well, Dad did, but he got it from you. I thought showing Lucy I was a good dad and that we could be a family would have been enough for her to forget about you, but she can't seem to break the habit. Which is a pity because all of this could have been avoided."

I feel physically sick. Again. My stomach twists in knots and I want to vomit. *I did this?*

He stares at me with no emotion. No regard for the fact he's messing with the life of a child. *His child.*

I huff out a laugh though this is absolutely not a laughing matter. "They have no reason to take Katie away from Lucy. She's a great mom."

Greg takes a step closer, trying—but failing—to be intimidating. "A mom who kept Katie's father away from her, a mom who lets an abusive man near her daughter, a mom who is soon to be out of a job, unable to support herself."

"The fuck?"

"I know about the policy at your work. Won't take much to prove you've been dating the entire time she's worked there. Isn't her boss kind of a stickler for the rules?"

As hard as I've tried not to react, I lose it at that and get in his face. "How the hell do you know all this?"

He smirks. "Lucy's my business. I make it a point to know."

Holy fucking shit. This guy is unhinged.

"I'm not leaving Lucy. It's just something you're going to have to get used to. Do the right thing and we won't have a problem."

He's bluffing. Surely he's bluffing.

Greg steps back, raising his hand to stop me from talking. "This isn't up for discussion, asshole. You break up with her, or I take Katie."

"Fuck off. There's no way they'd give you full custody. Not a chance," I scoff, shaking my head. "We'll fight it. You may have some of my money, but it's only change compared to my actual savings. I won't even notice it's gone. We'll fight you. Every step of the way."

"And how are you going to do that with a restraining order in place? Not to mention the fact that you tried to pay me so I wouldn't press charges. That doesn't look good on your part. Think of the media. Lucy and Katie will be dragged into the spotlight. So will Dylan. I wouldn't want that for my family, that's for sure."

I'm seconds away from beating the shit out of him again and that's exactly what he wants.

"If you wouldn't want that for your family then why make it happen?"

"Because they're not my family...yet."

"That's messed up. And no one will believe you. You're my stepbrother. I could easily explain away the money."

"Are you willing to risk that? You've never once mentioned us in the media. That fact alone is scandalous."

I reach out to grab him but pull back at the last second. "I don't give a fuck about the media coming after me."

"What about Katie and Lucy? Are you really that selfish?"

My fists clench at my sides as I physically shake. I want to punch him. I want to break his nose. But that's only going to work in his favor. He's got me on a leash and he knows it. *Basically, I'm fucked.*

"We'll fight it together. Letting Lucy go is not an option."

"Even if staying with her is causing her pain?"

"What?"

"She came to me today, offering me fifty percent custody if I dropped the charges against you. She was completely heart-

365

broken when she handed it over to me. But your actions are forcing her hand. Wouldn't she be better off without you?"

I internally flinch. "I don't believe you."

"I didn't think you would." Reaching into his pocket, Greg pulls out a piece of paper and hands it over to me. A joint custody agreement, signed by Lucy and dated today. *Jesus Christ. What am I doing to her?* All because Greg is my fucking *brother.*

"Fine."

"Fine?" he repeats. "That easy?"

Gripping his shirt, I spin him around and slam him against the brick of my house. "It's not fucking easy. But I would do anything for those girls, and if this is my only option, I'm not going to let them down."

Meanwhile, I will figure out a way around this.

Greg leans forward until our faces almost touch and smiles. "Good decision. Make it happen and all this goes away. I'll be the doting dad Katie deserves."

I tighten my grip on his shirt. "You know Lucy won't go for this, right?"

I need to talk to her. Surely that document is a fake.

Greg sneers. "She probably won't. You need to *make* her believe it," he says, finally trying to push me away.

Letting go, I step back and blow out a deep breath, speaking between clenched teeth. "I'll do what I need to do. But I need proof that you'll never go after Katie, that you'll never file for custody, and you'll do everything at Lucy's pace. She makes the decisions."

Greg nods. "Already ahead of you."

He hands me a signed contract from a local lawyer that states everything I asked for, proving he's definitely smarter than I thought. A mix of relief and agony swirls inside me, now that I have to go through with my end of the deal—but knowing Lucy gets to call the shots for them makes things a little easier.

Greg puts the agreement back in his pocket and smiles heartlessly. "End it, and the contract is yours. You can even come with me to have it notarized."

I nod before stepping closer and whispering in his ear. "If I *ever* find out you've treated either of them less than the royalty they are, I will *end you*. Consequences be damned."

"Noted," he says, moving away with a smirk. He knocks my shoulder as he walks down the driveway, just as Grayson pulls up across the street. It takes everything in my power not to chase after him and throw him to the ground. But instead, I watch him until he opens his car door, before I move toward the house, feeling utterly defeated. I've just reached the top step when he yells out.

"Oh and Wes...if you ever decide to change your mind, *remember this*...everything awful that's happened to Lucy is your fault. *Everything*."

Grayson gives me a "what the fuck" look as he walks across the road, hearing every word. Greg's not even trying to be discreet.

"Including the night we conceived Katie," he adds.

What?

"I knew she kissed you that day. I wanted to prove she was still mine, and she was. I slid inside her like..."

He keeps talking but I don't listen. A rage fills me as I run toward him at full speed. I'm so close, I'm already imagining his bloodied face.

"Stop, Wes."

Grayson slams into me with such force we almost fall, but as soon as I've gained my bearings, I push him aside to get to Greg. "Stay out of it, Grayson."

"Stop, he's not worth it," Grayson yells as he continues to get between us while Greg laughs behind him, jumping into his car and rolling down the window, out of harm's way. *Coward.*

He looks me square in the eye with a sinister smile on his face as Grayson holds me back. "I'm going to ruin you until you have exactly what I have—nothing."

And with that, he drives away.

I sink down to the carpet as soon as I get inside and drop my face into my hands. I feel nauseous, I'm tense, and sweat is already starting to pearl on my brow. I'm physically repulsed by what I'm going to do. But I can't change my mind.

Grayson hovers above me, and he's talking but I can't hear a word he's saying.

Greg raped Lucy *because of me.* Because he saw us together? I didn't even fucking know her back then. Fog fills my head and I can't think straight. I'm hurting her. Staying with her is hurting her. I wish there was something I could do, but he's never going to give up. He's actually right; I need to leave her life. I don't want to but it's for the best. I'll watch from the sidelines. I'll never let him hurt her again. But I have to end this. *Fuck, how can I end this?*

Tears prick my eyes as my breathing shallows. Pulling on the strands of my hair, I try to *feel something* but I'm numb.

I sit like that—for how long, I don't know—until I'm hit with a cup of freezing cold water, snapping me out of it.

"What the fuck, Gray?"

"*I'm* helping *you* for once. You were freaking me out. Get your shit together. He's gone."

As I shake off the water droplets running down my face, a moment of strength fills me. I can do it. I can end things. For Lucy. For Katie. I've been without them before; I can be without them again.

Pulling myself up off the floor, I stretch out my muscles and grab my phone from my pocket, sending Lucy a text.

Wes: I need to see you

And then I fall apart with Grayson picking up the pieces. *My, how the tables have turned.*

Chapter Forty-Three

Wes

I drive to Lucy's in a daze, pulling up as Katie gets into a car with Nate and Cory. She waves enthusiastically through the window and my heart aches. I'm not just leaving her mom. I'm leaving her too.

"We're taking Katie for a play date with Addie. We'll be back in a few hours. Enjoy your alone time." Cory winks and I have to force a smile. *Nothing about this is going to be enjoyable.*

"Thanks, Cory. Bye, Katie."

"Bye, Wes," Katie calls out, just loud enough for me to hear it through the glass.

My stomach heaves but I ignore it. I can't show any emotion or Lucy will see right through me. *Fuck, this is hard.*

Looking up toward the house, I find Lucy waiting in the doorway. She's smiling shyly, but it's a cover for the nerves she's trying to hide. They're written all over her face. I'm not sure why *she's* nervous though. All I said was that I needed to see her. I've given her no clues as to why.

The sound of Nate's car fades, and when it's barely a whistle in the distance, Lucy rushes toward me, clearly panicked. "I'm sorry, I couldn't sign it. I don't want him to press charges against you, Wes, but I can't just hand him Katie. No matter how much trust I have in you."

What?

"I'm sorry. You never told me about the money, so I had to wonder...what if Greg was lying? I just..." She fades off as I finally catch up with what she's saying. She didn't sign the custody agreement. It wasn't her?

I should feel relieved, but I don't. It changes nothing. Greg's going to continue to go after her if I don't do this. Contract or no contract, I can't see him giving up.

"It doesn't matter," I say, emotion stripped from my voice as I walk with her into the house.

"No, it does. I'm sorry. I didn't know about the money. I mean, did you give him money?"

"I did." I nod once. "It hit his account on Friday."

Lucy's eyes widen in shock, before they narrow again. "Friday? But I saw him yesterday, and he said—"

"It doesn't matter," I repeat sternly. "I'm not here about that."

"You're not?" Uncertainty flashes across Lucy's face while my insides fill with dread. These next words are going to kill me.

"I think we should stop seeing each other," I croak out and inwardly flinch at how unconvincing it sounds.

Lucy recoils. "You what?"

"I don't think—"

"I heard you. But—"

Digging deep, I find it in myself to make her see reason. "It's never going to work between us. Greg and I don't get along, and he's going to be in your life forever. It's a lot of drama that I don't need right now."

Jesus! That sounds so awful. What an asshole excuse. A lump clogs my throat, but I don't swallow it. I can't afford to give the game away.

Lucy's body stiffens and her fists clench. "You don't need the drama right now? That's what you're going with?"

"It's the truth." I shrug.

"Well fuck, Wes. I'm sorry my life isn't picture perfect enough for you. I'm sorry I have *drama*. And you know what? While we're at it I'm sorry you're an asshole." *Yep, just like I thought.* That hurts, but a part of me is happy to see her fight back. To see the strong version of Lucy. After all, her strength is one of the things I love about her.

"I'm sorry too. But I just can't..." I trail off, only making myself look more like a dick.

Lucy shakes her head in disbelief. "Because it got too hard? Jesus, Wes. I thought you were better than that."

I shrug again. "Guess you were wrong. I never claimed to be a good guy, Lucy. Not even once."

She scoffs, shaking her head. "Saying and doing are different things. You *showed* me you were a good guy. Are you trying to say it was all an act?"

I don't know what to say to that so I stay silent. A look of disgust crosses Lucy's face before she runs her hand over it, ending with just a frown. "What about Katie then? Is she too much *drama* for you? This will devastate her. She loves you."

My heart stops before starting up again with a low thud, my skin prickling with goose bumps. *Katie.* My eyes close briefly without permission. It's only for a second, but when I open them again, Lucy's staring at me wide-eyed.

"I knew it! What's going on? Why are you really ending things?"

Fuck!

"I told you why, Lucy. You just threw me by mentioning Katie," I rasp, my voice laced with anxiety.

"Did you only just realize how much you mean to her?"

Gripping the back of my neck, I sigh. "To be honest...yes. I mean, I knew she cared but..."

I trail off because she loves me? *Fuck.* Of course I know how much I mean to her; I feel the same. *In my head she's already like a daughter to me.* But love?

Lucy nods, holding back her emotions. *I need to leave.*

"I don't think it's a good idea for me to see Katie either. Not right now, anyway. I think a clean break is best. Plus, with Grayson, I already have someone to look after. I don't need *or want* someone else."

Lucy flinches and I hate what I'm doing to her. I once mentioned to her that Gray can sometimes be a burden. It was a shit thing to say, but it was the truth. Comparing Katie and Grayson now is like telling her that Katie would be a burden to me...something that will break her.

Lucy closes her eyes, her forehead creasing. "You're really ending this? Without giving me an explanation?"

"Isn't *not wanting* to be in a relationship with you reason enough?"

Her eyes fly open as my voice rises slightly. I'm panicked. Why won't she fucking believe me? I can't keep doing this.

Another wave of nausea takes over me. Allowing these lies to exit my mouth is making me physically ill as it goes against everything... My mind wanders as an idea hits me.

"You know how I feel about lying, Lucy. So believe me when I say, *I'm done.*"

Lucy stares at me with tears welling in her eyes, and my chest aches. I knew that would work, and yet it fucking hurts to see her reaction.

"I believe that you're done. But I don't believe your excuse," she whispers. "Why are you doing this?"

"Lucy..." *Please, please let this go. I'm begging you. Let us go.*

"Why, Wes?!" she yells. "Why? Cut the crap and tell me the truth. Why? Why?" She won't let up, asking me over and over while I try to focus on why I'm doing this...why I need her to believe me. But that backfires when I yell back. "Because he'll take Katie if I don't!"

Lucy freezes. "What?"

"I'm going to go."

She doesn't respond or even process that I've spoken, so I slip out the door in a rush. Tears prick the back of my eyes, but I bite my cheek to stave them off. I can't let her see me like this. I shouldn't have said what I said.

I make it five steps down her driveway when she chases after me, screaming my name.

"Wes, stop! Dammit, stop!"

I do as asked but don't turn around. I can't. It won't help either of us.

Lucy doesn't stop moving until she's standing in front of me, her face full of anger. "Are you fucking kidding me, Wes," she yells, shoving me back toward the house with a force I'm not ready for.

"You think it's that easy?" she continues, switching from shoving to pounding my chest. "That you can just walk away, again?"

Left, right, left, right. Her speed increases and I take it all. Letting her get it all out.

"Fuck, no. You don't get to leave. You don't get to make that decision for us. We fight together, asshole. Fight *with* me!"

She screams the last part as her fists crash against me in quick succession and the tears in her eyes start to fall. "Why would you walk away? Do we mean that little to you?"

Her fight goes, and it's not long before she's barely even connecting with me. She's utterly destroying me, but I don't know what to say. I can't risk her losing Katie. I'm not worth it; *nobody* is.

"Are you really going to just stand there and say nothing?" she whispers with a scratchy voice.

I nod. "Do your worst."

"Fuck you."

She slaps me across the face and walks away while I'm frozen in place, unable to move until a car driving past snaps me from my inner madness.

"Lucy, wait!"

She's standing still when I turn to face her, her eyes boring into me. "Have you changed your mind?"

Shaking my head, I take a tentative step closer but stop when she steps back.

"He hurt you because of *me*, Luce. He raped you to prove he could still have you after *we* kissed. I can't..." I trail off, unable to get the words out with emotion clogging my throat.

Lucy's tears start up again and she frantically wipes them away.

"Please let me do this," I beg, my gaze never leaving hers. "I need to know I've done *everything* I can to keep you and Katie safe."

"But you're leaving us. How is that keeping us safe?"

"Because he won't come after Katie, and you never have to give him any unsupervised access. And you'll never be alone. We may not be together, but I'll never let anything happen to you."

She huffs out an ironic laugh. "He still wins. If you do this *he* wins."

I'm already shaking my head before she's finished speaking because she's wrong. So wrong. "No, Lucy, he doesn't. He'll *never* win because he fucked up. He fucked up the best thing to ever happen to him, and if he doesn't have you and Katie, he loses."

"But he will have Katie."

"No, he'll get to *see* Katie. On your terms. There's a difference." I take another step forward, and this time Lucy lets me.

"I hate this," she whispers. "And I hate *you* for doing it, but I understand it, and I think I hate that even more."

My face falls. I hate it too. "I'm so sorry, Luce." *More than you'll ever understand.*

"I know," she whispers again. "But sorry doesn't change things. Stay away from me at work, okay? I can't do this if you're constantly around."

I inwardly flinch, but on the outside I'm stone. "Okay, Luce. Okay."

With that, she rushes off toward the house, slamming the door as she goes.

I don't know how I get home. I don't remember driving, and yet I must have, because I'm now lying face first on my couch with tears in my eyes. Of all the shit things I've done in my life, that would have to be the worst, and I will never forgive myself for the hurt I caused, or forget the look of absolute loathing on Lucy's face. I deserved the slap, and yet I didn't even feel it. I feel nothing. I'm still numb. And maybe that's for the best.

Two days later, I still haven't left my house, and my voice messages are piling up. I know I'm letting the team down, but I can't focus on that long enough to care. I hurt the one person I promised never to hurt again, so I deserve whatever life throws my way. *Give it all to me! Make me suffer.*

Banging starts on my door, and while it's deafening, it's easy to ignore. At least until the door slams open a second later and a booming voice enters the room.

"Get the fuck up. People are worried about you."

Did I leave the door unlocked?

"Did you hear me?" Carter yells again. "What the fuck is going on?"

I wish I knew. The world is so fucked-up right now.

"Wes!" *Grayson. I'm taking his key back.*

"What?" I groan, not even bothering to move.

"Why aren't you answering your phone?" Carter says, continuing to attack me. "And why do I have one of my teammates all up in my grill because you broke his sister's heart and then disappeared?"

Fuck!

Finally lifting my head, I look up at the two men that are supposed to be my closest friends and roll my eyes.

"I broke up with Lucy." *Obviously.*

"Yep, we got that part. But why?"

"Because Greg threatened to take Katie if I didn't."

Carter laughs until he sees I'm serious. "That was a joke, right? What's he going to do? Pay someone in stolen goods? That guy doesn't have a cent to his name." *That gets my attention.*

"You know about Greg?"

"*Fuck.*" Carter sighs as an apologetic look crosses his face. "Not at first, but when I saw him at your work, he looked so familiar and I couldn't shake the feeling that I knew him. I only just figured out he was your stepbrother. I mean, it's not like I really saw him that often—you hated the guy—but when Grayson told me his name was Greg, I put two and two together. If I'd figured it out sooner..."

Motherfucker! I want to kick his ass only I can't deal with that right now. But Grayson can and he does; he slaps him across the back of his head and calls him a dickwad. Good enough for now.

Running my hands up and down my face, I shake my head and groan.

"Is that why you're so messed up? Because he's your brother?"

"He's *not* my brother, and fuck no. It's all for Lucy. I feel sick, Carter. I've barely slept. I can't eat. I don't even have it in me to drink myself into oblivion. I'm just empty." I pause before groaning again. "I think I'm in love with her and I just broke her heart." *Both our hearts.*

Carter's eyes just about bulge out of his head. "No shit, Wes. You've been in love with her for years. You should've never let her go. Then or now. What were you thinking?"

"What was I thinking? Are you fucking kidding me?" Sitting up, I hold my clenched fist by my side to physically stop myself from hitting him. "He's going to take *everything* from her, and I gave him the means to do it."

"What do you mean?"

"I gave him money!"

"What the fuck, Wes," Grayson finally joins the conversation.

"So rather than running away, why not help her?" Carter adds.

Sucking in a breath, I stand up and get in Carter's face. "What do you think I'm doing, asshole? He said if I stepped back he'd leave her be."

"The fuck? All this is about you? Why?"

Why? Don't punch him. Don't fucking punch him.

"He's unhinged, Carter. He's hated me for most of his life. That's why."

Carter's brows furrow as he frowns. "Nope, I'm not buying it."

I take a step back, giving us some much-needed distance because if I can reach him, I'm going to knock him out.

"You're not buying it? Which goddamn part?" I yell and immediately hate myself for it. *I never used to be this angry.* But I'm not wrong; those were his exact words—"I'm going to ruin you until you have exactly what I have...nothing." *Wait!*

"I've got to go," I blurt out, taking off in a run toward the front door, grabbing my keys from the stand before I'm gone. I don't even give a shit if they lock the door behind them. This needs to end. I need to end it. *Now!*

Chapter Forty-Four

Lucy

After calling in sick to work for the next few days, I spend my alone time staring at a blank wall, alternating between being angry and hurt. Aaron calls me several times, but I don't tell him a thing. "Just a stomach bug," I repeat over and over, hoping it sounds believable. And I guess it's somewhat true. I'm nauseous all the time and my heartbeat's out of sync. I definitely don't feel like myself, and facing work *and* Wes is the last thing I want to do. The only person getting any real smiles from me is Katie. She's my reason for being, and no matter how broken I am inside, she can pull me out of it. In *that* moment, anyway.

By Friday, however, I know I'm going to have to sort myself out, so I make a conscious effort to do that. Dylan's playing at home again this weekend, so I have no doubt he'll be breaking down my door any second since I've ignored all his calls today. I told him I needed the week to myself, so really, I should have until Sunday. But, I guarantee he thinks five days is sufficient and is on his way over.

The roar of his truck filters through an open window barely five minutes later, and I have to laugh at how well I know him. Katie abandons her blocks and leaps up, racing down the hall toward the front door, like she always does when any of our friends or family arrive. *Even Wes.*

"Summer came, Mom," she yells as I finish tidying up the kitchen counter, waiting for them to come in.

Dylan drops a box of my favorite cookies in front of me and presses a kiss to my temple. "Have you heard from the f... from him?" he asks, cutting off his words just in time. Summer shakes her head as she pulls me into a hug and then joins Katie on the floor with her adorable baby bump now getting in the way.

"Have I heard from which f'er?" I ask, although the answer is the same.

"Either, but I meant Wes."

"Is Wes coming over?" Katie calls out, excitement in her tone. I cringe as though I'm shocked she mentioned Wes, despite knowing she's always listening.

Dylan nods toward the bedrooms, and I follow him down the hall, slipping into my room so we're out of earshot.

"So?" he asks.

I take a deep breath as my heart thuds in my chest. "It's been radio silence. From both."

Scrunching up his nose, Dylan curses. "Assholes, both of them. I'm so sorry this is happening, Luce."

I huff out a sigh. "Thank you. Me too."

"I take it since you're home right now it means you haven't been back to work? I called Mom to see if Katie was there first."

"And she didn't spill the details?"

Dylan's lips pull into the smallest of grins before it fades. "Not this time, so she must really be worried. Have you been back at all?"

Covering my face in my hands, I shake my head and mumble, "No."

"Lucy..."

"Don't fucking scold me. I'm doing the best I can. I went to the doctor and got a note. They're not going to fire me."

"And your boss is okay with that?"

"He's fine. He believes me. Or if he didn't, I'm sure his wife would tell him to back off. We're friends, and she knows a little about my past with Greg, so she's constantly on his back to look out for me."

"Does she know more than I do? Because you said he hurt you but you never gave me any more details."

Shit! I think about what Wes said and briefly close my eyes. This is going to kill Dylan.

"I've kind of been in denial for a long time, but Greg forced himself on me...when we conceived Katie."

"What?! Fuck, Lucy. Fuck." He drops to the bed as his face sinks in his hand. "God, Lucy, how are you okay? *Fuck*, I wasn't there to help. You never told me."

Sitting down beside him, I squeeze his leg and take a deep breath. "I never told anyone," I say, with my voice void of emotion. "Because until Wes pointed it out, I never considered it."

Dylan looks my way with a furrowed brow, his hand raised to scratch his head. "What do you mean?"

"I let him do it. I just..." I trail off. He doesn't need the details. "I just let him do it. I spent the entire time in my head, thinking about my kiss with Wes earlier that day."

"It was the same day?"

"Yeah. It was."

"*Jesus*. I'm so sorry, Lucy. I wish you'd told me back then. I thought we were close."

"We are, but I didn't think I had a right to be upset about it. He and I had slept together hundreds of times, Dylan. And I didn't fight him. I let it happen." Dylan begins to talk but I cut him off. I can't cry about this again. "Plus, isn't it in the Mathers' blood to keep things bottled up. You kept your secret for *years*. At least you thought you did."

"That's true." He sighs with resignation. "I still wish I'd known."

I grip his hand and pull him toward me, securing him in a side hug. "I know. But trust me, I've always felt like you were there for me, even if you didn't know you were doing anything to help."

After dinner, Dylan and Katie head outside, while Summer and I chat in the living room. As much as I try to avoid the topic of Wes, of course she brings it up. "How are you really doing? You're allowed to show your emotions, Lucy. You've been through a lot."

I flop back onto the coach and stare out the window, watching Dylan and Katie play catch in the yard. "I hate what he did. But I kind of get it. And I miss—"

A strange car pulls up in the driveway, making me lose my train of thought. An older man in a business suit and polished black shoes gets out, his eyes flashing straight to Katie. My heart lodges in my throat as I rush outside, midconversation.

"Miss Kelly?" the man asks, as he moves toward me. I nervously nod while Dylan eyes us both curiously. He must see something written on my face because he takes Katie into the house without a word.

"Can I help you?" I ask, taking small steps toward him, not really sure I want to get too close. The door opens again behind me, and I feel a presence on the porch instantly calming me. I should have known Dylan wouldn't leave me out here alone.

"Miss Kelly, I'm here to request your presence at a family court hearing to discuss the parental rights for Katie Kelly, on…"

He keeps talking, but nothing enters my consciousness as my world stops, and I struggle to take in air. Greg wasn't supposed to do this. Wes left me. Wes did as he asked. *How is this happening?*

I fall to a heap on the grass and feel Dylan's arms immediately around me. He holds on tight as I completely fall to pieces. And while I love him for it, I wish it was Wes. I want Wes here comforting me, helping me through.

"Lucy, you need to listen." Dylan shakes me a few times but I ignore him, trying to brush him off. I feel the first tear fall just as a car door slams shut and *his* voice enters my mind.

"Lucy? What happened?"

I feel a loss of warmth as Dylan moves away, muttering as he goes. "If you ever hurt her again, Johnson—"

"I won't."

I don't even care that he broke my heart; when Wes kneels in front of me, I throw myself into his arms.

"It didn't work, Wes. He's taking her. It didn't work."

Wes leans back and frames my face in his hands, his eyes boring into mine.

"No, Lucy. It's over."

"What?"

"It's over. You need to go to court because Greg's relinquishing his rights as a parent. He'll be out of your life, Luce. It's over."

I collapse into his chest and burst into tears, soaking his crisp white shirt as he presses kisses to my hair. He holds me while I cry, never once asking me to calm down or stop, something

Greg would have done in a heartbeat. *Greg... is this real? Is it really possible?*

Shaking myself off, I pull away and wipe the tears from my face. "How?" I rasp, looking between Wes and the uncomfortable looking man behind him.

"It doesn't matter right now," Wes answers. "What matters is that Katie's going to be okay. *You're* going to be okay, and you'll never have to worry about Greg again."

I shake my head frantically. "No, it can't be that easy. I don't believe you."

Wes touches his forehead to mine as his hands cup my neck. "I know I fucked up, but if you only ever trust me *once*, let it be *now*."

I nod against his head as fresh tears fall, and he gently rocks me back and forth, quietly humming "Truly Madly Deeply," by Savage Garden as he does. A memory of him humming once before enters my mind, and my insides warm at how right this feels. I'm ready to stay like this for hours until a throat clears and a voice interrupts me.

"Ma'am, I just need you to sign—"

"One minute," Wes says, cutting him off. "Take your time, Lucy. There's no rush."

I feel bad for the poor man and jump up right away, prepared to do what I need to do, thanking God that the hearing is set for only a few weeks from now. I don't think I could cope if this dragged out.

As soon as he's gone, everything finally sinks in, a frown forming as I turn to Wes. "I appreciate you being here when I needed you just now, but what about the last few days? You're right; you fucked up and you've just used up your *one moment of trust*. How can I be sure you won't run again if times get tough?"

Wes takes a step toward me and reaches out, linking our fingers. "Lucy, I'm not going to lie. I'd do it all again if the result was the same. All I ever wanted was for you to feel safe, for you to never have to worry about Katie. But I know I hurt you, and I'm going to work my ass off to prove to you that I'll never let you go again. Properly this time."

My brows furrow in confusion and Wes laughs.

"Be prepared for superior groveling. I've learned a thing or two since last time."

I bark out a short laugh, even though I'm still mad at him. "Well, you can't get any worse." I shrug just as Dylan walks back outside.

I'm about to ask Wes if he wants to come in, when he presses a kiss to my cheek and steps back. "I mean it, Lucy. I'm sorry. I promise to make it up to you."

He takes a few steps backward until he reaches my drive and then turns to walk away. Without saying another word, I let him leave, knowing it's for the best. I'm not sure I'm completely over what he did yet.

He definitely had something to do with Greg's sudden change of heart and for the fact that someone personally delivered the news, but he still hurt me and I need assurance that won't happen again.

Dylan circles his arms around me the second I'm through the door, lifting me into the air. "I'm so happy for you, Luce. And relieved. So fucking relieved."

I wriggle myself free and drop to the ground. "Me too, but what do you think Wes did?"

A smile pulls at his lips while his gaze moves to where Wes is getting in his truck. "I have a theory. But you should probably talk to him about it."

"Ugh." I shove him away. "You suck."

"Little brother duties," he says as he walks down the hall.

"Asshole," I call out and then cringe when Katie comes running down the hall, positive she would have heard me but too happy to care.

My beautiful girl is safe, and the weight I've been carrying for almost five years is close to being lifted. I bite my cheek to stop myself from crying again as Katie jumps into my open arms.

"I love you, baby girl."

"Love you too, Mom."

Chapter Forty-Five

Lucy

E very waking second of my weekend is spent with Katie, keeping her much closer than she needs to be. You'd think I'd been summoned to court because Greg was trying to *gain* custody of Katie, *not* relinquish his rights, but I just can't bear to be away from her.

We spend our time dancing around the house, playing dress-up, or baking. Katie practices her throw and I poorly catch, we cheer Dylan on in his game–which they win—and even go out to dinner to celebrate. All the while, my eyes never leave Katie.

Wes texts a few times, sometimes to check in, other times to say hi, but always short and sweet, so I don't have to reply. And yet, I always do, because I always want to. He's never far from my mind.

Back at work, first thing Monday morning, I find myself wandering past his office even though I have no reason for walking that way. But instead of Wes, I find our athletic director sitting at his desk with a scowl on his face, making me hastily keep moving. I don't need a scolding on my first day back.

When I round the corner, I hear Wes's deep voice coming from the offensive team offices. I don't stop as I walk past, but curiosity gets the best of me and I glance through the open door on my way. He's sitting behind one of the desks, playbook open in front of him as he chats with the offensive coordinator. My stupid heart does a little flutter when my eyes lock on his, and I choose to pretend it's got more to do with the strange scene I'm witnessing, rather than my feelings. Wes almost always makes people meet him in his office, and yet, he looks like he's made himself at home. I shrug it off and continue on my path, finding one of our linebackers waiting for me when I reach my room.

From then on, I have a revolving door of appointments, barely even stopping for lunch, except to quickly run to the kitchen to shove something into my mouth. My heart skips while thinking about the possibility of running into Wes, but on this occasion I don't. Aaron checks in at one point to ask about my stomach bug, but other than that, I don't see any other staff.

I'm leaning against my table at the end of the day, with my foot in my hand, massaging my aching joints. After hitting the right spot, I let out a soft moan then internally curse when Wes chooses that moment to knock on my door and wander in.

After taking one look at my pained expression, he silently glances toward my foot before he strides over to meet me, taking over my effort. Using his thick fingers to knead my arch, he gently moves my ankle around, as my eyes roll into the back of my head and another moan escapes me. It feels so amazing that I get lost in the moment. That is, until I realize what he's doing and snap out of it, hopping around as I try to pull my foot free.

"Ew, Wes, no. I've been on my feet all day. You shouldn't be touching them." I feel my chest heat as embarrassment takes over.

He laughs but doesn't let go, making it really awkward for me.

"Lucy, if I cared about that at all, I wouldn't have grabbed your foot. Plus you touch sweaty guys all the time; does it bother you?"

Did he just compare my foot to a player after a game?

"Shit! Let go!"

Wes's laughter grows louder as he finally lets go, causing me to stumble a little when I'm not quite prepared for the release. He reaches out and steadies me before I fall, quickly righting me to a standing position.

"It doesn't stink. You're worrying for nothing," he whines.

"And you're back to sucking in the groveling department," I counter, slipping my shoe back on and taking a step back.

"I just massaged a part of you some people wouldn't even touch. I'd say that's A-plus material right there."

"It's definitely not if you have to point it out."

I sound like a brat, but he threw me off and I need to get my shit together. Crossing my arms over my chest, I tap my wrist where a watch would go before motioning to the door.

"I've got to go. I promised Katie I'd be home on time tonight."

"Of course. I just popped in to apologize again. Please tell her I said hi."

He moves to the door but pauses when he reaches the threshold. "It's nice seeing you smile again. I've missed it." *Huh? When did I smile?*

Wes chuckles at the confusion that I can only imagine is written all over my face.

"I caught it when you were on your way to get lunch today. If you can call that protein bar lunch," he mumbles the last bit and I huff out a laugh. That is what I called lunch, and I think that was the only time I smiled all day. I know exactly when he's referring to.

"You must have been thinking about something pretty amazing. My money's on Katie," Wes says and then disappears down the hall.

My second smile for the day tugs at my lips as I watch him leave, shaking my head as he goes. *Nope. It was you, Wes. I was thinking of you.*

I only see Wes intermittently throughout the next week, but he always makes sure he's on my mind. Lunch arrives in my office on a busy day. Little notes somehow appear right when I need them. Some telling me to smile, others reminding me that everything's going to be okay, and one that made me cry—a note telling me that Katie loves me no matter what, even when we're apart. That one appeared on my chair when I was at a low point after a late-night meeting.

We may have only been together for the shortest time, but he *knows* me. Almost better than I know myself. He sees me. He understands things about me that I didn't even think I'd explained. And he's definitely winning me over.

On Saturday morning, Wes stops by my office with Aaron, a sight that has me doing a double take. "My buddy Aaron wants to give you the afternoon off so you can enjoy the game with some friends," he says, patting Aaron on the back in a condescending way, but strangely, Aaron just laughs it off.

"Wes is right. We've got tickets for you, Katie, Logan, and Liam, along with something a little special."

My eyes narrow as I look between Aaron and Wes. Aaron seems okay with this. He doesn't look angry about giving me the time off on our busiest day. But Wes does have a mischie-vous look on his face, so I can't be too sure.

"Ahhh…"

"It's fine, Lucy. Please, it's all arranged," Aaron reassures me. "Wes isn't forcing my hand."

I huff out a laugh as Wes shrugs. "I mean, I would have if I had to, but Aaron went along with my plan willingly."

"Okay, so what time do I finish?"

"Now, Luce. You need to go *now*."

Wes hands me the tickets and practically pushes me toward the door until I remember I need my car keys and my bag. Aaron walks out ahead of me so when I follow, Wes smacks me on the ass on the way past, earning himself a dirty look. "We're not there yet," I scold.

"Worth a try." He lifts a shoulder as his lips pull into a line. "Enjoy the game, Luce."

We've only been sitting down for five minutes when one of the security guards gets my attention from the end of our row. I squeeze past a few people to chat with him so I don't have to yell over everyone.

"Noel, how are you?"

He smiles shyly at the use of his name before pointing over his shoulder toward the exit. "I've been asked to grab you and Katie for a surprise."

My eyes widen and I laugh. "What surprise?"

"Now, I can't tell you that, ma'am."

"Good surprise, though, right?"

He smiles again. "Yes, ma'am. A very good surprise."

Katie's already watching me curiously, and when I wave her toward me, she runs, forcing the other fans to stand and let her through, all while she thanks each of them as she goes.

I lift a shoulder in response to Logan's raised eyebrow as Noel chuckles beside me.

With Katie's hand in mine, he leads us to the back end of the tunnel, and my heart flutters. Baby Bennett, a.k.a. Ryan, is standing with Wes, both with big smiles on their faces. Ryan bends down to Katie's height. "Ready to run out onto the field with me, Katie? I hear you're a big fan of the game."

Katie squeals as my hand flies to my mouth. *Dammit, Wes, you're making it really hard to stay mad at you.*

Katie starts walking down the tunnel without any instruction until I call her back, suddenly nervous about her going out alone.

"Wait for your mom, Katie," Wes calls out at the same time. "She and Ryan are coming with you."

We race to catch up to her, just as the rest of the team arrive behind us, slowing their pace so that their quarterback and Katie are the first onto the field.

Katie's eyes bounce around the stadium as mine stay firmly locked on hers, and there's no doubt in my mind that she'll never forget this day.

With the excitement of the game, and Katie's energy after her moment, I don't really get time to process everything until I get home. Katie and Liam run off to her playroom while Logan calls Dani.

Staring out the kitchen window, I pull out my phone to call Wes, but pause to think about what to say, wondering how to express how grateful I am for what he did for Katie today. But I can't find the right words. After realizing nothing I say will ever be enough, I send him a simple text.

Lucy: Thank you

He writes back instantly, and I can picture his genuine smile.

Wes: Anytime

When I arrive at the gym the next day for an extra boxing session, Wes is waiting by the entrance, geared up in his work-out clothes, with a water bottle in his hand. "Any chance I can earn some extra credit by letting you beat me up?" he asks and I bark out a laugh, shaking my head.

"No, but if you give me a real workout by being a worthy opponent, I'll consider it."

He smirks as he opens the door for us both, pressing his palm to the small of my back as I go. "Done."

I try not to react as I move through ahead of him, but stop when his hand grips my waist and he leans in close to whisper. "Oh, and Lucy, I've been practicing."

My pulse spikes and my legs clench as I remember the last time we sparred and what happened after it, but I push the thought from my mind. *Nope, Lucy. Head in the game. He's not done groveling. He wants to do this.*

Chapter Forty-Six

Lucy

I'm a sweaty mess on the floor by the time Wes and I have finished our session, and as I stare up at the ceiling, his large frame fills my vision from above.

"How are you doing down there?" he asks with a big smile on his face.

"I'm...fine," I huff out between breaths, my chest still rising and falling in rapid succession.

Wes laughs and sits down beside me, resting his elbows on his knees. "Once again you blew my mind with your power, Luce. Your strength...in *and* out of the ring...you're incredible."

My face heats as I blush. I've never been good at taking compliments, but coming from Wes, it seems even harder. "Thank you," I say shyly, closing my eyes as I do.

We stay silent after that until I'm finally able to breathe properly, and I sit up to mirror Wes's posture. "You really have been practicing. You had some nice moves, Johnson."

His face lights up and he smirks. "Well, they do say 'couples that sweat together, stay together.'"

I can't stop my laugh and am about to ask him if that's really true when he continues.

"It's something that's important to you, Lucy. I wanted to know all about it."

I swallow a lump in my throat as I fight to keep my emotions at bay. In all my relationships, I've been the one fitting in with my man. It was always about his interests. I either learned to love them, or he enjoyed them on his own. But there was never any discussion about what I wanted. With Wes, I've never once felt that way. He always lifts me up, even at times I thought I was already standing. I'm not at all used to this attention. But I think it's time I learned to love myself and believe that I can be loved for who I am as an individual, not just because I happen to make my partner happy. *How the hell didn't I see anything was wrong for all those years?* Why did it take someone finally treating me right to make me realize how wrong it had always been?

Yes, I knew things weren't working with Greg and broke it off a few times, but even then I hadn't realized just how bad it was.

Wes eyes me curiously as I wipe under my eyes and stand up, dusting myself off. "I'm going to shower. Thanks for the workout."

"Lucy?" he calls as I leave, but I ignore him, needing to hide away before tears prick my eyes.

When I'm finished in the shower, having somehow managed not to cry, Wes is waiting for me. He walks me to my car, pressing a soft kiss to my hand like I'm delicate, despite just saying that I'm not. I want to roll my eyes, but I can't, because it's so freaking sweet that butterflies take over my middle and I feel giddy. He's trying. Really trying. But unless we get everything out in the open, it's never going to work. With a deep breath, I finally take the next step we need if we're ever going to move on.

"Are you planning to tell me what you did anytime soon?" I ask when he releases my hand.

His eyes flash to mine, and his shoulders tense slightly. "Does it matter?"

"Of course it matters. You don't owe Greg for life or anything like that, do you?"

Wes laughs—which bugs me a little because this isn't a funny conversation—then shakes his head. "No, nothing like that. I wanted him out of our lives, not forever a part of it."

I sigh when he continues to give me nothing, then step back, opening my car door before moving behind it, creating some distance between us.

"Saying everything is fine but not telling me why is like lying by omission, something you hate. Either tell me the truth or don't bother groveling anymore. It won't work." *How my mood went from giddy to angry, I don't know. But here we are.*

Wes raises an eyebrow and huffs out a breath as he runs a hand through his hair. "Okay. But it's done. I need you to remember that. No one can change it now."

My gaze flashes to his as my eyes widen with worry. *Why would I want to change it?*

After running his hands down his face, Wes gives me a sheepish smile. "I gave Greg some money and stepped back from my role as head coach."

What? How didn't I know that? There's way too much to unpack there. First...

"How much is *some*?"

Wes winces at the raised pitch of my voice, and I find myself looking around to make sure we're alone.

"A lot..." he says with a shrug. "I gave him everything I—"

"What? No!" My eyes snap to his as I step out from my comfortable position and move closer. "I will *not* let you do that. You can't," I whisper-yell, as a wave of guilt runs through me, making me feel ill. "No way. It's not happening."

"It's already done," Wes says, unapologetically. "And Lucy, none of this is your fault. *None.*"

He tries to reach for me but I hold out my hand to stop him. "Wes..."

Blowing out a breath, he grips the back of his neck before sagging back against the hood of the truck parked next to my car. "None of it's your fault," he repeats, his eyes begging me to believe him. "It's mine."

What?

"It may have taken me a while to figure it out, but I realized it was never about you and Katie. None of it. Turns out he's known about Katie since the day she was born. He only came back into the picture because I did."

"What?" I say again, out loud this time as my body tenses and my teeth clench. "Are you fucking kidding me?" I'm absolutely livid. There's no chance of me whispering now. *What the hell is wrong with that man?*

"He wanted everything that I had," Wes continues. "Well, the money more than anything else. He wanted me to have nothing."

Holy shit! My anger subsides, making a place for nausea. "So you, what? Just handed it *all* over?"

"Not exactly. I gave him everything he knew about."

"Motherfucker."

Wes laughs. "My thoughts exactly."

"Okay, so what didn't he know about?"

"While he'll definitely be sitting pretty for the rest of his life, he's not as smart as we thought he was. I have investments and other accounts. So, yes, we may not be able to buy a celebrity-sized mansion or a yacht, but we'll have enough to live comfortably, and Katie will never want for anything."

My heart flutters, but I hide my reaction to his words. Instead, I bite back a smile. "'We'? You sound pretty confident that I'll take you back."

Wes's lips curl into a smirk. It's not cocky, but it's not innocent either.

"I'm hopeful, *not* confident. But Katie will want for nothing
regardless. She's kind of grown on me." He winks as his phone
alarm goes off, thankfully not noticing as I just about melt into
a puddle on the ground. *The way to this girl's heart is definitely
through her daughter.*

"I've gotta go," he says, interrupting my thoughts. "But I'll see
you tomorrow, and I'll be at the hearing Tuesday. Okay, Luce?"

All I do is nod as he kisses my cheek and walks away, earning
yet another gold star in my eyes.

The day after the hearing, I'm still on cloud nine but also a little
in shock.

As promised, Wes was there, distracting me with how well he
can pull off a suit, while also bringing me instant calm. And if
the hearing proved nothing else, it definitely highlighted how
amazing my friends are. Only two people were allowed in the
room with us, and yet all of them came to support Katie and
me, waiting in the hallways for it to be over. Even Thomas flew
in early, conveniently here for his football game against Dylan
on the weekend.

While I trusted Wes completely when he said it was over,
there's been a niggling in the back of my mind, always wondering... *what if it's not?* I needed the support, regardless of
the outcome.

But now it's over; it's really freaking over, and I can't keep the
smile from my face as I move behind my desk and kick off my
heels.

I finally have a break in my schedule, now that I'm back at work, and it's a welcome one. I've been run off my feet playing catch-up for missing yesterday, and I need to sit and relax for a second.

Connecting my phone to the speaker I have in my office, I play chilled music and lean back in my chair, closing my eyes. "Hotel California" by The Eagles plays first, and a relaxed state takes over me.

Taking deep breaths, my head moves slowly to the beat and my thoughts wander while song after song plays. I almost drift off to sleep when "Truly Madly Deeply" comes on, and I smile. This song will forever remind me of Wes now. Listening to him hum it to me the day I was summoned to court made me feel at ease, and hearing it now makes me realize I really should have thanked him for that, instead of just letting him walk away after everything he did for me. *What are the chances this song would play now, when I almost never hear it?*

"Please Forgive Me," by Bryan Adams comes on next, and I huff out a laugh but mouth along as more images of Wes play through my mind. God, I miss him, and I do forgive him, mostly...I think. I'm just so nervous about taking the next step and being hurt again. I want this to be *it* for me, but how can I be sure he feels the same?

The music stops abruptly midway through the song and my eyes fly open. "Kiss From A Rose" by Seal comes on as Wes's hand appears in my face, offering for me to take it. I jump at the sight of him as my own hand flies to my chest, my heart beating rapidly. I'm about to read him the riot act when I see my phone clenched between his fingers and it all clicks. *The songs weren't a coincidence.*

Raising an eyebrow, Wes waves his outstretched hand, prompting me to take it. My gaze moves between his hand and

TRULY MADLY DEEPLY MINE

his face, hesitantly waiting until he smiles shyly. That tiny gesture has my heart skipping and brings a flutter to my stomach.

Without a word, I clasp his palm and allow him to pull me to my feet. I expect him to hug me, maybe even press his lips to mine. What I don't expect is for him to start swaying me slowly, dancing with me, barefoot in my office, as he softly hums to the music.

It's not an overly romantic song, but I understand his meaning, and I blink away the tears that rise to the surface.

I'm his rose.

We dance until the song ends and then Wes steps back, keeping our fingers connected. "Lucy..."

"Turns out you're not as bad at groveling as we first thought," I say, cutting him off before I suck my lips into my mouth to hide my smile.

Wes laughs. "I told you I'd be giving it my all, and I plan to keep going until you realize how sorry I am. I've only ever wanted to do right by you. And that's never going to change. I won't be stopping until you know that. It's amazing what one can do when they're in love."

In love? I release a gasp as my heart stops and my smile breaks through.

My chest fills with something new, something all-consuming, and it suddenly occurs to me that while I've said I love you many times before, I've never actually felt it romantically...until now.

Chapter Forty-Seven

Wes

Lucy stares at me with a shocked expression mixed with something like awe. Why she's shocked that I love her is beyond me. I thought that was clear, but maybe I needed to spell it out sooner.

She opens her mouth to speak but then closes it again, and I'll put every last dollar I have—which is a lot less these days—on her wanting to ask if I meant what I said.

"You love me?" she finally questions, and I almost laugh, but that would be detrimental to helping her believe that I do.

Lifting her fingers to my lips, I gently kiss her knuckles as she smiles up at me.

"I love you, Lucy. I'm *in* love with you. You are the one for me. You're it. My end game. My ride or die... Help me here—are there any other ways to say it?"

She giggles and the sound is my undoing. *She's* my undoing. Thank fuck we never had to go along with my stupid breakup plan, because I honestly don't know how long I could have kept it up. She's my everything, and it's about time she knew that.

"Lucy, I want a life with you and Katie. I want to experience all the ups and downs, teach Katie to swim, teach you how to catch—you really should be better considering who your brother is."

Lucy swats at my head with her spare hand, but I duck in time and she misses. "I knew that practice would come in handy." I wink. "Joking aside, I—"

"But what about everything that happened?" she says, cutting me off. "Aren't you annoyed that you had to give up so much for me? Isn't there a little part of you that resents me for that?"

"Not even my smallest cell. It wasn't about you. Is there a part of you that resents me for Greg coming back into your life?"

"No, of course not, but—"

"There's no *but*. I don't blame you. And that's not something that will ever change. Plus, Greg fucked up. He wanted me to have nothing, and yet he'd already succeeded when he took away the two things I wanted most in the world. But he traded them back for possessions and money. He can take everything that I own and I'll still be happy. Because Lucy, if you let me back into your life, I will always have what I need. *Everything* I'll *ever* need. *You and Katie.* I'll always have *you.*"

Lucy's eyes shine with unshed tears, and she nods.

I'm hoping the nod is a good sign but have to ask. "Does that mean—"

"Yes!" She throws her arms around me and burrows her face into my chest before looking up at me through hooded eyes. "Yes, I want us to be together. You'll always have me."

Framing her face with my hands, I press a kiss to her forehead, then her nose before gently brushing her lips with mine. She sighs, rising to her toes to increase the pressure as my hands move into her hair, securing her in place. Our lips open at the same time, allowing our tongues to explore, and I groan at the feel of finally having Lucy back where she should always be—in my arms.

Our kiss remains soft and unhurried yet it feels like a deeper connection, and when I finally pull back with a lazy smile on my face, Lucy looks up at me with a sassy grin. "So, 'Truly Madly Deeply,' huh?"

I huff out a chuckle at the change in direction and shrug, like it's no big deal, and yet... "It's kinda our song. At least it is for me."

Her brows furrow as though she doesn't believe me, and I laugh out loud, running a hand through my hair. "Okay, you got me. The first time I hummed it was because I'd heard it early that day and I couldn't get it out of my fucking head. But when you smiled, even though I thought you were sleeping, it kind of became a song that reminded me of you over the years. So of course, I really fucking hated it when we were apart. But now it's not so bad."

"So romantic." She rolls her eyes and bites back a smile, nibbling on her bottom lip. Pulling her back into my arms, I squeeze my eyes shut and try to focus on anything but her lips, knowing that if I do, she'll never get back to work.

"How many more players do you have on your schedule for today?"

"Just the one, in..." Lucy looks at the clock on her wall. "Shit, right now. You need to get out. We still have to talk through our work situation. Should I resign? I mean—"

"What? Why would you resign?"

"Because of the policy?"

"Don't worry about that. I'll sort it out. There are always ways around these things. And if there weren't, it wouldn't be *you* resigning. Don't even think about it. I'll have it all worked out before you've finished for the day."

Lucy nods as one of our running backs knocks on her door, freezing when I open it. "Ahh shit. I can come back."

I smile and shake my head. "No need, I was just leaving. I'll see you tonight, okay?" I say, turning back to Lucy.

"Okay," she mouths as she moves about the room.

It takes all of two seconds for me to get written approval for our relationship. Turns out, we weren't hiding from anyone, and Aaron submitted the application weeks ago. Maybe he's not as bad as I thought.

After supervising a workout session with some of the team, I jog back to the office to meet Lucy before she finishes for the day.

"It's taken care of. We are officially on the approved couple list with HR," I say as soon as she steps out of her room.

Her brows furrow in confusion. "There's an approved couple list?"

"No idea, but either way, we're good. We don't have to hide it. And it wasn't even my doing. Aaron handled it."

Lucy barks out a laugh before covering her mouth. "Sorry, how did that make you feel?" she whispers knowingly.

"Cheated!" I grunt and I'm not lying. "I feel cheated. I wanted to be your hero," I half joke, laughing until Lucy's expression turns serious.

"You already *were* my hero," she says, taking a step toward me. "From the moment I met you."

My heart pounds in my chest as I grip Lucy's forearms and walk her backward into her office, slamming the door shut behind us with my foot. The second we're locked inside, I lift her onto her PT table and push open her legs, stepping between them.

"You're *my* hero, Lucy. Fuck, I love you."

Cupping her neck, I slam my lips to hers, groaning at the feel of her touch, as she moans into my mouth, frantically clawing at my polo shirt. My hand travels down to squeeze her breast, and from then on, I can't get enough of her.

"God, Lucy. I need you. Right now."

Reaching for the hem of her dress, I give it a tug as Lucy gasps. Without a word, she lifts her ass off the table, allowing me to bunch the material at her waist, leaving her deep purple panties on full display. I drop to my knees in front of her, desperate to taste her again and I've just run my hands up her legs when she calls out "no."

I freeze, my fingers at the apex of her thighs, as she stares at me with a panicked expression. *Fuck!* "Shit, Lucy. I'm sorry—"

"No, that's not...I mean, I don't want to stop. I just..." She buries her face in her hands. "I never said I love you back."

Chuckling as I stand up, I pull her hands away and lean my forehead to hers before turning serious. "You don't have to say it at all. You've shown me. Several times. But if it will make you feel better..."

"It will." She nods. "Wes Johnson, I love you. Then, now, and always. You are it for me too."

I blow out a raspberry and joke, "It's about time," with a wide smirk, as Lucy playfully shoves me back with her palms on my chest.

Stepping closer again, I run my knuckle down her cheek while she grabs my shirt in her fist.

"I will never tire of hearing that."

Lucy blushes, her eyes blinking up at me, looking so beautiful, I can't wait any longer. "So...where were we?" I ask.

With a raised eyebrow, Lucy bites her lip, only releasing it to speak. "I believe you were about to ravage me."

"I was? Okay."

I drop to my knees again but Lucy stops me, pulling me back up.

"I need you here," she says, pointing to her mouth before dragging a finger down her lips. A deep groan rips from within me as I grab her arms to steady her, crashing my mouth to hers while grinding against her core.

Moving one hand down her body, I cup her heat, while sliding the other up to her neck and wrapping it around her jaw before tilting her head higher to deepen the kiss. Lucy's mouth drops open as she moans, allowing me to sneak my tongue inside, pumping my hips at the same time.

After sliding her panties to the side, I run a finger through her slick heat before pressing it inside her, watching her head fall back as she rolls her body in time with my movements, crying out when I add a second finger. "God, Wes. Yes."

I hear voices in the hall, so I slow my pace, expecting Lucy to pull away any second. But she doesn't. She grabs my forearms, digging her fingers into the flesh, trying to pull me closer. "Don't stop, please."

"Wouldn't dream of it."

My fingers pump in and out as my thumb runs circles across her sweet spot, causing her to pant and writhe around uncontrollably.

Moving my hand from her jaw into her hair, I hold tight as her eyes squeeze shut and she screams silently. "Oh god," she whispers, her hand mimicking mine, pulling at the curled strands near the base of my neck, her moves frantic and sloppy.

When I feel her walls tighten around me, I prepare for her climax when she pushes me away, sliding her free hand into my pants. "I need this, *now*."

Jesus! I dutifully comply, freeing myself from the painful constraints of my briefs and watching as Lucy runs her thumbs across the tip. *Fuuuck!*

"Wait, Luce. Let me get something." Grabbing a condom from my wallet, I quickly sheath myself before gripping my length and pumping it a few times as Lucy watches on.

Covering my hand with her own, she bites her lips as she joins in, assisting with my pleasure while I move closer, running the head through her heat. "God. That feels amazing."

I repeat the movement a few more times until I'm so worked up I could explode any second, and that's not how I want to finish. Gripping her waist, I take my time pushing inside her until she bucks her hips, forcing me to slam into her, sinking to the hilt.

"Yes, Luce, fuck. Can I move?"

"Please, yes."

I pump into her, slowly at first before increasing the speed and intensity. She meets me thrust for thrust, her hands frantically roaming my body, her forehead pressed to mine.

"I'm... I can't..." she breathes out.

"Let go, Luce. I got you." Leaning forward, I push Lucy's legs wider and slam into her one last time before she covers her mouth with her hand and cries out in ecstasy.

My length pulses as she tightens around me, and when she reaches between us and gives me a squeeze as I pump into her, I grunt out through gritted teeth as the added pressure sends me flying over the edge.

"Jesus Christ!"

I collapse on the table as we both catch our breath, my eyes locked on Lucy's.

"Yep, it's good to have you back," I huff out with a smirk, knowing Lucy would have expected me to say something romantic.

She giggles and she lazily backhands my chest, her eyes full of love. "It's good to be back."

As we walk out to the parking lot a little while later, a thought occurs to me and I laugh. "Fun fact you didn't know, but if I ever had a daughter, I'd always planned to call her Katie."

"What?" Lucy comes to a halt, her eyes wide in surprise and maybe even disbelief.

I bop her on the nose and keep walking, waiting for her to catch up before I continue. "Do you remember me telling you about my gran? The one that took care of me after my mom died."

Lucy's eyes widen to an almost comical level as she chokes out, "I do."

"Her name was Katie, and she—"

"She lived in the hotel with you, right?"

"Yeah, right across the hall. You probably saw her around. Here..."

Pulling my phone from my pocket, I flip through my images until I find the last photo we took together, handing it over to Lucy. When her eyes lock on the screen, she bursts into tears. *What the hell?*

"Shit, Lucy. Are you okay? What did I do?"

"That's Katie? Your gran?"

"Yeah..."

"Well, you may not have a daughter named after her," she says with a sniffle, wiping her eyes. "But you do know someone that is."

Holy shit! "Mom *named me after a lovely lady with a big heart.*" My mind flashes back to a conversation with a little girl in this very parking lot. *Katie.* Holy. Fucking. Shit!

"Katie's named after my gran? How?"

"When I was at my lowest, she picked me up and helped me through, without even knowing my name." *Sounds just like her.*

"When? When did you meet her?"

"The day I found out about Katie. My entire world had just flipped upside down. I discovered I was pregnant by a guy who'd forced himself on me. I lost you. I was terrified to tell my family because I was going to have to raise my child alone, and I felt completely helpless and unsure. But after talking to your gran, I felt better. And after she was gone, I realized that no matter how bad things got, I knew one thing for certain. If I had a daughter, her name would be Katie. And that made it feel real. And once it was real, I knew I'd fight like hell to give my little one the life they deserved."

I swallow a lump in my throat and stare at the incredibly strong, beautiful woman standing before me. How I managed to find someone so perfect, I'll never know. But one thing is for sure. I will never take her for granted. I will never make her feel anything less than she is, and I will always love her with all my heart. I had a strong feeling this girl was special, and now I know... Lucy's my soul mate. And Katie was always meant to be mine.

"So, what you're telling me is that I got what I always wanted... I have a daughter named Katie?"

Lucy's eyes water again as she launches herself at me, slamming her lips to mine. I catch her before we stumble back into my truck, gripping her under the legs, my fingers digging into her ass.

"Take me home, Wes," she says between kisses.

And that's just what I do. Not even questioning where home is, because it's not a place; it's exactly where Lucy and Katie are.

Epilogue One
Lucy – Three months later

Oomph. That caught me off guard.

"Okay, I'll give you that one, Johnson. But I'm not holding back anymore," I joke as I pretend to wince from the "hit" I just took. Wes and I have been sparring now for the past few months, and he's really holding his own these days. Not that I'm a boxing pro or anything, but I always had technique on my side. He's catching up.

"Alright, Mathers...show me what you've got." Wes raises his gloves to his face and bounces on his toes. It looks more like a dance move than a boxing one and he knows it gets a rise out of me. Every. Single. Time. It's why he still does it.

I try hard to bite back my smile, but when he starts comically shadowboxing, I'm done for.

"You need to stop," I huff out between laughs, shaking my head. "You don't fight fair."

"I'm always fair when it comes to you, Luce. You know I only do it because I love seeing that smile."

Ugh. Then he says stuff like that and I'm swooning. It always puts me completely off my game and allows him to—

Jesus! Got me again.

"Nice hook, Wes," Summer calls out, and I shoot her a glare before my annoyance turns back to Wes.

"I thought you were always fair."

"I am, mostly. But I'm also one to seize every opportunity." He shrugs as though he's unfazed by my reaction, but I know deep down he's waiting for my smile, so I give him one.

"And all is right in the world again," Summer jokes, and I can't help but laugh.

She's been having withdrawals, she claims, but I actually think she's nervous about the impending arrival of her little one, and wants to be around friends. While Cory had a fairly straightforward childbirth, mine was anything but, and Summer was my support person. I may have traumatized her. Though, as always, she's acting like she's fine.

"Want to tag in, Summer? Wes will go easy on you. Or at least he'll say that's what he's doing. But really it's his lack of—"

Oomph again. Only this time I'm thrown over his shoulder in a move so fast, I never saw it coming.

"I think training is over for the day," Wes announces. "I'm taking you home."

Summer laughs as he carries me toward the ropes, only letting my feet drop again when we're there.

Surprisingly, getting in the ring with Wes has done wonders for my self-confidence. He's a strong guy, and unlike when we first boxed together, he no longer holds back—within the bounds of boxing—meaning I get to test my skills on someone who could easily overpower me. While he never actually forcefully connects, it's been really helpful and it's extremely therapeutic. Not to mention the fact that it's a fun way to keep fit. As he once said, "couples that sweat together stay together," and I think he's spot on. It's our time. Almost like a date night, and we both love it.

It may have only been three months since we officially got together, but our relationship already feels different to the others I've had in the past. It's more solid. More grown-up.

Maybe it's because we've got Katie to think about, so the stakes are higher. There's no time for messing around and Wes knows that. He knows Katie and I are a package deal, and he's completely embracing it. He went from a grumpy bachelor to having an instant family overnight, and it seems to have settled him. He's no longer an asshole to everyone at work, he's enjoying his job and the team, he juggles multiple balls at once… He's taking everything life throws at him and just rolling with it.

Which is kind of how you have to be as a parent. And make no mistake—Wes is a parent. He took on that responsibility the second I let him and there's never been anything but smiles.

"What time's Katie due back?" he asks as we reach Summer, with Katie never far from his thoughts.

"Dylan just called to say he's on his way home, so he'll pick her up from your mom's," Summer answers for me. "Want us to keep her for a while?" she adds, bouncing her eyebrows.

I'm about to say yes when Wes beats me to the punch. "Nah, I miss the little bug. I didn't see her much yesterday because of the game."

And there goes my heart again. This man.

"You, Wes Johnson, are a keeper. Dylan would definitely have said yes to alone time," Summer says with a smile on her face.

"Don't be so sure about that," I say with a raised eyebrow. "We'll see what happens when my nephew enters the world."

Summer's smile widens as she lovingly rubs her huge tummy. "I can't wait."

After stopping for takeout, we pull into the driveaway at the same time Dylan does.

I jump out with a big smile, ready to greet them both until I see him practically throwing Katie from his truck, albeit in a gentle way.

"What's going on?" I ask, taking in his obvious panic.

"Summer's in labor," he rushes out. "I have to go!" He lifts Katie with one arm and grabs her bag with the other before running to my side. All while I stand shocked.

"What?" I breathe out, confused. That can't be right. "We were just with her. It's been less than an hour."

That pulls him to a stop. "You were? Yes, you were! But she messaged to say she needs me at home asap and there were lots of exclamations and—"

Wes starts laughing as a small smile plays on my lips.

"What's so funny?"

"Do you really think she'd text you to tell you she was in labor?"

Dylan's face falls. "Ahh...nope."

"Then is it possible she needs you for *something else*?" I ask, emphasizing the last two words as Wes adds, "Like the very thing that made the baby in the first place."

Oh Jesus! I was trying to avoid saying that.

"What made the baby?" Katie asks, tugging on Wes's tee, and I have to hold back my glare.

"We'll talk about it soon, honey," I say, taking her from Dylan. "We just need to help Uncle Dyl. Let me take that," I say, reaching for Katie's bag. "You go home. For whatever Summer needs."

Wes grabs the bag from Dylan's hand before I've had the chance and pats him on the back. "Have fun with that emergency." He winks.

"Thanks, I plan to." Dylan chuckles before saying goodbye.

Katie runs ahead to the front door when Dylan's gone, and I take the opportunity to smack Wes in the stomach. Thankfully, he at least has the decency to look regretful.

"I'm still learning?" he says as an excuse and I love him for it, because he is learning, but aren't we all.

"It's fine." I smile. "I'll handle Katie's talk, but you have the next one."

What?! I jolt as soon as the words are out of my mouth and pick up my walking speed, hopeful he didn't get my meaning. *Shit.* It's only been three months. We haven't spoken about kids yet, and—

"Deal," he says, matching my speed, before jogging ahead and unlocking the front door.

"Who's ready for pasta?" he asks as though we didn't just decide we were going to have a child together one day. *Another child.* I never thought I'd want that, but now I do. I want that for Katie, for us.

Like always, Wes holds the door open for me as I approach, and when I step through the threshold, he pulls me close, his breath on my ear as he whispers, "I'm ready when you are."

My eyes flash back to his to find him shrugging exaggeratedly, while my heart beats erratically in my chest. *No big deal. Right?*

When we've finished dinner and chatted about our days, Wes takes Katie off to run through her bedtime routine, while I settle on the couch. He doesn't stay over every night, but when he does, it's like a break for me, which is something I'm not at all used to. On top of putting Katie to bed, he gets up with her at the crack of dawn and makes her breakfast, allowing me time to wake up naturally.

This is what I've been missing. A teammate. Someone to share the load. My family and friends have always been amazing. But this is something else.

Wes drops onto the couch beside me, wrapping his arm around my shoulder just as my phone rings.

I almost laugh when I see it's Dylan until a thought hits me and I stop. "Shit, it's Dylan," I say, waving the phone in the air.

"So, answer it," Wes states matter-of-factly, like it's the most obvious thing in the world. *Oh wait...*

"Dylan," I rush out instead of a proper answer.

"Yeah, so you were right earlier, but now it's go time. They're just getting a room ready for us."

My heart stops for a second before picking up speed. "Dylan! I'm so excited. I can't wait to meet him. What do you need me to do?"

"Um..." He pauses, and I can picture him gripping the back of his neck. "Can you call Thomas and then head to the hospital? We'd both feel better if you were here."

My chest tightens at the nerves in my baby brother's voice, but I put on a smile and tell him I'm on the way.

Twelve hours later, Dylan's pacing the halls while Summer has a moment to herself. There's a commotion down the hall, and seconds later, Thomas comes screaming around the corner. "What'd I miss? Where is he?"

Dylan pauses his movement but doesn't answer, so I take the lead.

"Your nephew is still coming. You haven't missed anything. In fact, I don't think Summer expects you at all."

"She doesn't, but I wasn't going to miss this. Or any part of her life. I've already missed too much."

My heart breaks for Thomas, and even Dylan's face softens. Thomas vowed to be there for Summer when they reconnected a while back, and he absolutely has been. Though none of us expected him to come for the birth. He's still playing football in Seattle. Luckily he played today. Or yesterday... God, I've been here for so long.

My phone dings with a text, and I have no doubt it's Wes with another update. Bless him, it's his first night with Katie on his own, and even though she's been asleep for most of it, they'd both be up by now.

When I open the text, it's a photo of the two of them covered in flour, both with ridiculously happy smiles on their faces. Of course, tears prick my eyes.

It's moments like these that highlight just how lucky I am to have found Wes. We may have had a rough start, but I wouldn't change a thing, because I truly believe that wasn't our time. This is our time. And God, am I loving it.

"Earth to Lucy, everything okay?" Thomas asks, pulling my focus.

I spin around to find both guys staring at me.

"What?"

"You look a little teary."

I turn the image around without an explanation and watch as both their faces light up.

Dylan silently walks over and pulls me into a hug. "I'm so happy he's Katie's dad."

"He's—"

"He's perfect with her," he continues, cutting me off. Something I'm happy about, because despite the fact I was about to say that he's not her dad, he one hundred percent is, and one day I hope we make it official. One day.

Dylan heads back inside not long after my emotional moment, so Thomas and I get the chance to catch up. When Wes and I first got together, Wes insisted on meeting the guy whose last name I'd "borrowed," expecting to dislike him. But of course, to no one's surprise, they get along really well and have actually become good friends.

"Did Dylan tell you San Francisco is in the market for a quarterback?" Thomas says midway through our talk. And since our conversations regularly focus on football, I think nothing of the change in direction.

"No, but Carter mentioned it to Wes, and... Oh my God, have they approached you?"

Thomas bites back a smile. "Nope."

"Ah, man. What a way to get my hopes up—"

"I approached them. Or my agent did. We're in talks."

What? My eyes flash to his but I try to hold back my excitement. "You're coming home?"

"That's the plan. If it all works out." He shrugs, obviously still a little nervous about it all.

"Have you told Summer?"

"Not yet. It all happened so quickly, and I don't want to get her hopes up if it doesn't go through."

"Well, I'm so excited for you."

"Don't get too excited yet, we—"

"It's a boy!" Dylan yells from the doorway, making Thomas and me burst out laughing as we run over to congratulate him. Neither of us correct him on the fact that we already knew that little piece of information, with the pure love and awe on his face suggesting he's in his own bubble.

"Do we get a peek or are they resting?" I ask, knowing how overwhelming those first minutes can be.

"I'll find out."

He disappears just as fast as he came, and when he returns, his goofy smile is still in place. "Summer said to come in, but asked if you could call Katie first. She'd love for her to meet her new cousin, Joshua Dean Mathers."

With tears already in my eyes, hearing my nephew's name makes the first drop fall. "You named him after Dad?"

"We did. Sort of."

I can't help myself; I pull him into a bone-crushing hug until he shoves me away, which is surprisingly not as fast as it usually would be. "I'll call Wes and then come in," I say between sniffs as Dylan's own eyes water.

The call connects on the first ring, and it's Katie that answers.

"Can I come inside? Has Summer had my baby?"

"*Whoa* there. What do you mean can you come inside?" I hear Wes chuckling in the background. Probably laughing about the fact that she said *my* baby. Dylan and Summer have no idea Katie's coming for them.

"Ummm," she draws out and I know instantly they're here.

"Wes?"

"Katie kind of begged me to take her to the hospital. Just in case. So, yeah. We're in the garden."

I laugh at the fact that Katie has Wes wrapped around her little finger but also silently curse. They're going to gang up on me for sure.

"Then yes, Katie. Come inside. Summer and Joshua are waiting to see you."

"Eeek!" Katie squeals so loudly that the nurse walking past gives me a nasty glare.

"You'll need to be a lot quieter than that if you come."

"I will be, Mom," she whispers, then hangs up before I've given them any details.

After texting Wes the directions to labor and delivery, I wait, not so patiently, for them to arrive, but thankfully, it's only a few minutes before Katie's running down the hall toward me with her arms out for a hug. She leaps at me and squeals into my chest. Much quieter than before.

"Can I see him now?"

"We sure can."

The next few minutes are so surreal and contain moments in time that I will never forget. My baby bro has a baby of his own, along with a beautiful wife. Life is good.

"You did amazing, little sis," I say to Summer with a full heart as she cradles her precious little boy.

"Isn't he perfect?" she says, and I've never seen her so at peace.

When it comes time for me to hold my nephew, Wes stands close beside me, staring down into his eyes. And my heart jumps. I want this. I have this. I finally have a little family of my own and now, I can't wait for it to grow.

It's finally my time.

Epilogue Two

Wes – One year later

K atie stumbles into the living room with a box entirely too
heavy for her and drops it at my feet.

"A little help, maybe?" she sasses as she crosses her arms in
front of her.

I try hard to bite back my smile, but she's cute when she
pretends to play "grumpy" Katie, and within seconds my face
lights up.

"Stop," she says, trying not to smile herself. "That's not fair;
you always make me laugh."

"You still nailed it, kid," I say, scruffing up her hair.

Her eyes narrow as she stares at me before finally saying,
"Kids these days, no respect."

I burst out laughing and pull her into my arms as she laughs
along with me. God, I love this girl.

Katie and I have our own special thing. It started the day I
told her that Gran was the "lovely lady" she was named after.
Ever since then she's asked me to regale her with stories or
asked what my gran would do in certain situations. And right
now, she's playing her part. Pretending to say things she thinks
Gran would say in this very moment. The moment we all move
into our first home together. *Our own home.*

It still blows my mind to think that this is my life now. I have
a partner, a little girl, a life away from the spotlight where I can
be me, rather than the man everyone expected me to be.

There's only two things that could make it even more perfect, and I'm working on them right now.

"Katie? I told you not to bother Wes. He's trying to put together the... Oh, you finished it?"

Lucy joins us in the living room and looks between our new TV unit and me with a look of pure disbelief.

"What does that mean? 'Oh, *you finished it?*' You didn't think I was capable?"

"No, I just...I didn't hear any cursing, or things being thrown around."

A knot forms in my stomach at her completely straight face. Did she seriously expect that? My mind flashes back to the way she was previously treated by the exes and I sigh. "Lucy—"

She bursts out laughing as she pats me on the back. "I'm totally messing with you. Now hurry up; we have to be at Dylan and Summer's in an hour and you're still in your sweats."

"You love my sweats."

A hint of pink spreads across her face as she pokes her tongue out and walks away. *Yeah, she loves my sweats.*

"Sweats should never be worn outside the house," Katie says in her fake Gran voice, and I burst out laughing again. If Katie hadn't already been born when my Gran died, I would have sworn she was a reincarnation. It's scary sometimes.

Two hours later, the Friendsgiving party is in full swing. Just over a year ago, I barely knew these people and now they're like my family. No, they *are* my family. Seeing the way they all look out for Katie and Lucy made it impossible not to like them, and those feelings have only strengthened over the past year. Carter and Grayson are also here today, making it even better.

"Can I stay the night here? With Joshie?" Katie asks, as she half carries, half drags Josh to where Lucy and I are standing with Joel and Delilah. As though we wouldn't know who she was talking about if he wasn't with her.

The way she's bonded with Josh is incredible to see. I can't wait to give her a sibling. It's been on my mind ever since the day Josh was born, when Lucy accidentally mentioned us having kids. We've spoken about it a few times since, but never made any plans for it. First things first, and I'm taking that step tonight.

Lucy's eyes flash toward Summer as she answers Katie. "I'm not sure, sweetie. It's going to be a long day. Dylan and Summer might need a—"

"It's fine with us," Dylan says, interrupting her out of nowhere. She grimaces like she's annoyed, and I can't help but chuckle. I'd already called ahead and made plans for Katie to stay here. Not that Lucy knows that.

"Okay, great. *Great.* Thank you," she says slowly as Dylan walks away like it's no big deal. Don't get me wrong, Dylan and Summer are always happy to help, but they've got enough on their plate with a one-year-old.

As always, after a few drinks, the karaoke comes out—only this time, it's part of my plan. I sing a duet with Katie early on, something about building a snowman, and then let the others take over for a while, until it's my time to shine. *Before* Grayson. I'm not stupid enough to follow him.

"I'm up next for karaoke; are you going to come and watch?" I ask Lucy when I'm able to get her attention.

She bursts out laughing, like she does any time I mention singing. "Babe, it's sweet that you love doing this with Katie, but didn't the two of you just sing? We might lose the crowd." *The crowd. Meaning our family and friends. She thinks that low of my singing?*

I can't help but roll my eyes. "Shut it. Katie is a beautiful singer," I joke with a smile, knowing very well she was referring to me.

"It's not Katie I'm talking about," she mumbles, hiding her face behind the bowl she's holding so I can't see her smirk.

"Sorry, I'm no Dylan or Joel or *Grayson*, but would you get your ass out here?" I say, grabbing her waist and pulling her in the direction of the door.

"Ooh...I love when grumpy Wes returns."

"I'll show you grumpy Wes," I say, bouncing my eyebrows as I place her bowl on the counter and throw her over my shoulder in a fireman's hold, chuckling as she squeals between laughter. "Put me down, you big caveman."

"Nope, not until you listen to me sing...and love it."

A few of the guys cheer as I carry Luce outside, and I recognize Thomas's voice as I drop her feet to the ground.

"Don't let her move," I say to Thomas, giving him a knowing grin.

He nods, just as Lucy's eyes narrow in our direction. "What are you two up to?"

Thomas and I became close after Lucy and I officially got together, but now that he plays for San Francisco it's even better. Although, along with Carter, he's currently trying to convince me to throw my hat in the ring for the receiver coaching position they have going. But I'm finally happy. I'm not sure I want to risk losing that. So, while I'm sure I'd love to be around my old team and friends, I think I'll probably stay put. Plus, working for the Heartwood U Lions has one thing that the pros will never have…Lucy. Being in the same building definitely has its benefits.

With Thomas knowing what I'm about to do, he pulls his lips into his mouth and ignores Lucy's question, until she punches him in his arm.

I huff out a laugh and shake my head as I move toward the makeshift stage. "Just stay there. *Please*," I beg, only smiling when Lucy nods.

After picking up the mic, I wait for Katie to join her mother's side and then smile at my girls. My life. Those two are everything to me, and I'll forever be grateful for that day on the beach.

Katie gives me a nod as though she's in on my plan, making my smile widen. *She's got no idea.*

Taking a deep breath, I hit the button to begin and raise the mic.

The intro for "Your Song," by Elton John plays and my eyes find my family again, determined to block everything else out. I still hate singing—despite doing it for Katie whenever she asks me to—and today's even more nerve-racking.

When the chorus comes, I press pause and take another deep breath.

"Before I continue embarrassing myself—"

"We love you, Wes," Joel interrupts with a cheer, and I wave nervously.

"Thanks, man. Before I continue, I'd like to invite a special someone to join me up here. Over the past year and a half she's become my world, and I have a question to ask her."

My heart slams in my chest as my eyes lock with Katie, trying hard not to focus on Lucy.

"Katie Kelly, will you come up on stage?"

Katie's eyes widen and she squeals before turning to Lucy. I make the mistake of following her gaze, and the moment my eyes meet with Lucy's, my heart falters, seeing her tears. Dammit. I can't get emotional yet.

Biting the inside of my cheek, I wait as Katie runs toward me, and when she joins my side, I clasp our fingers together, dropping down to one knee. "Katie, this song is for you."

She smiles brightly and dances along as I sing, sometimes mouthing the words along with me. The second the song's finished, my heart rate picks up as my eyes briefly flash to Lucy's before settling back on the wonderful little girl in front of me.

"Katie, my Katie. You and your mother are my world. I'm the luckiest guy alive to have you both in my life. But I want more. Will you do me the honor of becoming my daughter and letting me marry your mom?"

Everyone's silent, so I hear Lucy gasp as Katie goes quiet for a beat, which is very unlike her. But after a second, she leans in close and wraps her arms around my neck.

"Yes, but I already am your daughter. I love you, Daddy."

Holy fucking fuck! There goes *any* strength I had left to keep my shit together. Tears prick my eyes as I squeeze her tightly before pulling her back to look in her eyes.

"Katie, you're right," I rasp, choking back my emotions. "You are definitely my daughter. But I want to make it official. So what do you say...do you want to become Katie Johnson?"

"Yes!" She cheers before turning around to find Lucy. "Mom!"

When I spot Lucy, she's already walking toward us with tears streaming down her face.

"So, I got permission..." I shrug, making Lucy chuckle. "While I'm down here, I was also wondering... would you do me the honor of becoming my wife?"

"Yes." Lucy nods between tears. "Yes, I would love to."

She leans over and wraps her arms around us both, almost pulling us off the stage, while our friends and family clap. And my heart fills with pride knowing this is the best decision I've ever made.

When we arrive home an hour later, I lift Lucy into my arms and carry her over the threshold like we're newlyweds, all while she tries to wriggle free. The more she moves, the tighter I hold, marching us straight to the bedroom.

"You just agreed to be my wife. I need inside of you *now*," I say, throwing her on the bed before proceeding to undress her. *Off come the pants.*

"I see you're being a caveman, *again*. But I want to talk to you about something first."

"Nope, no time."

"But...Wes." She grips my tee and gives it a firm tug as she sits up, stopping me instantly.

"Shit, sorry. Of course."

I once made it clear that Lucy would always be in control of what happens between us, and I'm not about to fail now, no matter how desperate I am to have her.

Lucy's face softens and she smiles. "Has anyone ever told you how amazing you are?"

I huff out a laugh. "Not nearly as often as I'd like."

After playfully shoving my chest, she turns serious again. "I want us to try for a baby," she whispers, moving her attention to the sheets, suddenly interested in the thread count or something, while my heart thuds in my chest.

"I—"

"I mean," she cuts me off without looking up. "Obviously if that's not what you want, or you're not ready then we need to talk about it, but I—"

Biting back a smile at how adorable she is, I interrupt her right there, needing to ease her mind. "I want it, Lucy. For me, for you, for Katie. I've been ready for a while."

Her eyes flash to mine as she visibly exhales. "You have? You do?"

"I really fucking do. In fact, how about we start right now?" I push her back down to the bed as she giggles.

"I'm still on birth control."

"Then lose it. That's it. We're officially trying for a baby. And this is practice number one. Better give it our best shot."

Before I've even finished talking, I have my hand inside her panties and my fingers running through her core. She bucks up into me as the word *yes* breathlessly leaves her mouth.

"I love you, Wes. I can't wait to give you a child."

"Lucy, Lucy, Lucy," I playfully scold her as my lips meet her ear. "You already did that. This is about us giving our daughter a sibling."

Lucy's breath hitches and she pulls me in tight.

"And Luce," I whisper again. "I love you too. Truly, madly, deeply. You're mine."

Thank you for reading Wes and Lucy's story. Want more from the Heartstrings characters? THE SERIES IS NOW COMPLETE.

If you haven't started the series, Dylan and Summer's story - When Nothing Else Matters, Joel and Delilah's story – Still Here Without You, Logan and Dani's story - It Had To Be Us, Thomas and Lainey's story A Sky Full Of Stars and Nate and Cory's novella - Ain't No Sunshine are all available on Amazon and kindleunlimited.

And the fun doesn't end there. Luke is getting his own book as part of my new pro football series – San Francisco End Game. Beautiful Storm is now available for pre order.

Keep reading for a special sneak peek of A Sky Full Of Stars.

A Sky Full Of Stars Sneak Peek

P eople *suck*. I mean, yes, there are a few decent people in the world, but most of them suck. And I don't say this lightly. It's not something I'm simply throwing out there. I've spent the last few days thinking this through, analyzing the things people say—their actions. I even have a list. And after careful thought and consideration, that's the only conclusion I can come to...people suck.

God, that makes me sound bitter, or a brat, and maybe I'm both of them, but for the past few months, almost everyone in my life has started comparing me to everyone else. Pointing out my faults, providing advice on how I could better my-self—*unsolicited advice*—and I've had enough.

"*Luke finds the time to practice football, keep fit, and maintain his studying. All while still having a social life. Maybe you just can't handle the balance.*" My dad's response when I mentioned I was too tired to practice after being kept awake by one of Luke's parties.

"*Did you know they've reduced the intake for Jaiton next year? Maybe we should up your rehearsal hours. I don't think you're ready.*" My mom, in response to me asking what's for dinner.

"*I heard that Mike's taking Piper to junior prom because she puts out. I bet he'd choose you if you offered him something.*" A so-called friend.

And my favorite this week...

432

"*You better keep dancing. That tight figure is the* only *reason guys are interested in you.*" That one was from a fellow dancer in my class. A guy. Out of nowhere. I'd literally just sat down.

The thing is... I didn't know any guys were interested in me because the only one I want *isn't.*

So, yeah, people suck. With the exception of Luke and—

Tap. Tap. Tap. *Thomas.*

My heart races as I jump up from my bed. I wasn't expecting him today. *Not that I expect him any day.* But I don't usually get a visit during the daylight.

Running my hand over my crinkled school uniform, I try to smooth it out and cringe. God, I wish I'd changed when I got home. Thomas doesn't need the reminder that I'm still in high school.

I hesitate with my hand on the curtain, wondering if I should pretend I'm not home. But when he knocks again, my need to see him wins out.

Taking a deep breath, I peek through the material to find his easy smile, instantly relaxing me. And when he holds up two grocery bags, mouthing the words "hurry up," I can't help but laugh.

"About time," he jokes, when I open the window. "I had a killer practice session today, and I don't think my legs could handle having to outrun your dad if he finds me here." He fakes a grimace, his eyes scanning the yard.

"Shut up," I say, pulling him inside. "You could easily outrun him on his best day," I joke back, playfully rolling my eyes, acting as though there's no chance of that happening, when in reality, my dad would probably attack without question—he's a lot like Luke that way. Thankfully, he's not home. "You should be more worried about Luke," I add. But when Thomas's back is turned,

I can't help checking for myself, making sure that no one saw him, before sliding the window closed and shutting the drapes.

"I've told you before I'm not worried about Luke; I can take him." He turns back to face me as he speaks, catching me in the act. "You just checked, didn't you," he asks with a suppressed smirk before making himself comfortable on my bed, grabbing some cookies from one of his bags. My *favorite* cookies.

"No. You worry too much," I lie, biting back a grin while ignoring the way my heart flutters.

Thomas chuckles, and like always, the sound hits me in the chest. This damn crush is going to destroy me one day. I can sense it.

"Alright. I brought donuts, cookies, and candy. What kind of day is it?" he asks, moving on and making it even harder to keep my feelings platonic. *He's Luke's friend. He's my friend. But he's also* Luke's *friend.* No matter how many times I tell myself that, it doesn't sink in.

When I don't answer right away, Thomas waves the bag in front of my face as he laughs again, and I can't stop the responding smile from spreading across my face.

"It's a donut *and* candy day," I say with a wince, though I know he won't judge me.

"Sheesh." He winces back. "That bad?"

"You be the judge. I was told my tight figure is the *only* reason a guy would ever be interested in me." I laugh as I jokingly run my hands over my body, trying to play it down. "So..." I shrug, finally looking up to find Thomas with his hand hovering in mid-air, his eyes locked on my waist. I hold my breath under his intense gaze as butterflies fill me. He blinks a few times before shaking his head, perhaps clearing his thoughts, and chuckling along with me.

"He's obviously never seen you rap, because that's *damn* impressive."

I shove at his chest before crawling up onto the bed beside him and crossing my legs to get comfortable, while Thomas lies back into the pillows. "You were never supposed to see that."

"Maybe not, but I'm lucky I did. That's something I'll never forget."

Like always, we lose track of time talking, and it's not until I start yawning that Thomas moves to leave. The part I always hate, never knowing when he's going to come back.

He's just opened the window when a banging starts up from the other side of the room. "Lainey! Can I come in? You'll never guess who I just saw," Luke yells, making Thomas drop to the floor in a panic.

I cover my mouth to stifle my giggles and send out a thanks that Luke's respectful of my privacy. "One minute!" I yell back before crouching down to Thomas's level. "Are you still going to pretend you're not scared of my brother?" I ask, sucking my lips into my mouth.

Thomas's eyes flash to my tight-lipped grin before he shakes his head and stands.

"You know he can get a little crazy, right?" he whispers, his eyes now firmly locked on my bedroom door. If he wasn't worried, he'd have already told Luke about our friendship, and so would I. We're both secretly nervous.

"That I do. You better go before my minute's up." I smile, pushing him outside as I glance over my shoulder.

"You don't have to tell me twice." He laughs quietly before checking the coast is clear and jumping the railing, only stopping to wave when he reaches the shadows at the edge of the yard.

My heart sinks when he disappears, but I don't get time to dwell on it with only three seconds before Luke's invasion, and maybe that's a good thing. Because while Thomas's visits always lift me up, every time he leaves, I fall even further.

A Sky Full of Stars is now available on Amazon.

Also by Katherine Jay

SAN FRANCISCO END GAME

Beautiful Storm (Luke and Amelia)

HEARTSTRINGS SERIES

When Nothing Else Matters (Dylan and Summer)
Still Here Without You (Joel and Delilah)
It Had To Be Us (Logan and Dani)
Truly Madly Deeply Mine (Wes and Lucy)
A Sky Full Of Stars (Thomas and Lainey)
Ain't No Sunshine Novella (Nate and Cory)

SYMPHONY OF SOUND DUET

The Sound Of Silence (Jesse and WIllow)
The Sound Of Forever (Jesse and Willow)

AVAILABLE NOW ON AMAZON AND KINDLE UNLIMITED

For more information, visit
http://www.katherinejayauthor.com

And if you want to stay up to date with all things Katherine Jay, come and join my Facebook Reader Group for fun, exclusive content and sneak peeks. Or sign up to my newsletter via my website.

Are you following me on social media? If not, you can find me on Instagram, Facebook and TikTok.

Acknowledgments

Thank you for reading Wes and Lucy's story. This book will always have a special place in my heart. I started writing it long before I had any of the other Heartstrings characters in mind, but then shelved it when I realized it had to come later in the Heartstrings series. And now it's here! I have so many people to thank for helping to get this book out in the world, but first...

My readers... thank you for the ongoing support. Whether this is your first or fifth book of mine, I am grateful for each and every one of you. I have so many stories rolling around in my head and because of you, I plan to keep writing until they're all out in the world. Thank you for supporting this dream of mine.

Sarah, Sarah, Sarah – I could write a book on how grateful I am for you... for the support, the love, for calling me out on a regular basis... and for standing firm when I push back. For keeping me on track. For demanding chapters. For loving Lucy and Wes from the very first line. For being a shoulder to cry on... But mostly, for your friendship. This book is for you.

To my hype girl and friend, Sara. I don't think I have the words for how in awe I am of you and all that you do. You are an indie author's angel. And I'm lucky enough to get to call you my friend. Thank you from the bottom of my heart.

Keelan – Thank you for once again being there for me. For the chats, the guidance and the friendship.

Adi and Inka – Never leave me! That is all... no seriously, I can't thank you enough for all that you do. None of my books would be the same without your input and I am so incredibly lucky to have found you both and to be able to call you my friends.

Nikki – Thank you for signing on to beta read for me and for reading Wes and Lucy's story after my slight panic. I hope you know you're stuck with me for life now.

Felix - you are a wealth of knowledge and I'm so thankful for your help.

To the BEST STREET TEAM EVER! How did I get so lucky? Seriously... how? You are all freaking amazing and I'm so grateful for all the love you show me and my stories.

My cover designer Megan... Another masterpiece. Thank you.

To Madison – I will forever be a fan of yours. Your photos are perfection.

To Ann and Ann, my editors – Have I ever told you that you are AMAZING? Because you are. I could not do this without you. Thank you for all that you do.

And to my family, your continued support means the world to me.

Thank you all for supporting indie authors. If you enjoyed this book, please shout it from the rooftops and leave a review on Amazon or Goodreads.

About Author

Katherine lives in Australia with her hubby, two kids and a mind full of characters. She spends her days partaking in role play, building fortes and dancing. While her nights are spent reading and writing.

Her debut series, Heartstrings, is an emotional and angsty romance with love that's worth fighting for and characters full of heart.